UNTIL WE MEET

UNTIL WE MEET

Camille Di Maio

FOREVER

New York   Boston

Copyright © 2022 by Hachette Book Group, Inc.
Reading group guide copyright © 2022 by Hachette Book Group, Inc.

Cover design by Daniela Medina
Cover image © Myron Davis/The LIFE Picture Collection/Shutterstock
Cover copyright © 2022 by Hachette Book Group, Inc.

Forever
Hachette Book Group
1290 Avenue of the Americas, New York, NY 10104
read-forever.com
twitter.com/readforeverpub

First Edition: March 2022

Forever is an imprint of Grand Central Publishing. The Forever name and logo are trademarks of Hachette Book Group, Inc.

The publisher is not responsible for websites (or their content) that are not owned by the publisher.

The Hachette Speakers Bureau provides a wide range of authors for speaking events. To find out more, go to www.hachettespeakersbureau.com or call (866) 376-6591.

Library of Congress Cataloging-in-Publication Data
Names: Di Maio, Camille, author.
Title: Until we meet / Camille Di Maio.
Description: First edition. | New York : Forever, 2022.
Identifiers: LCCN 2021041411 | ISBN 9781538738047 (trade paperback) | ISBN 9781538738023 (ebook)
Subjects: LCGFT: Novels.
Classification: LCC PS3604.I1157 U58 2022 | DDC 813/.6—dc23
LC record available at https://lccn.loc.gov/2021041411

ISBN: 9781538738047 (trade paperback), 9781538738023 (ebook)

Printed in the United States of America

LSC-C

Printing 1, 2021

To the group of ladies whose Zoom visits uplifted every moment of a wacky year with their spirit and prayers: Kathryn Haydn, Lori Helms, Anita Hertford, Catherine Liberto, Mary Clare Sabol, Karen Tompkins, and Regina Yitbarek

And to my aunt Melissa Wittman, who, from book one, has told everyone she's ever met that her niece is an author. That kind of love and support is a treasure, as is she.

ACKNOWLEDGMENTS

I wrote this book from the small house we'd bought as not-too-far-off empty nesters, only to have coffee shops and libraries close down with the rest of the world. My adult children came home for the duration, and solitude became an endangered species.

So first, I am thankful to my family for allowing me the space and grace to sometimes be an impersonable writer as I cranked out word counts and met deadlines. I know you're rejoicing as much as I am that my usual hangouts have reopened.

Thank you to my agent, Jill Marsal, who first visited with me about this story and for being an unparalleled guide in my writing.

I so appreciate my editor, Madeleine Colavita, whose collaboration and visits were essential in the creation of this story. Someday we will meet in person and swap embroidery-nerd stories. For now, photos.

To the ladies of Megunticook Market, especially Rachel Green and Jaci Russ, who sustained me through several writing pushes with their creations. And to the ladies of Buttery

Baking House in Virginia, who pivoted and persevered in trying times and kept me well-stocked in pastries. My waistline does not thank you, but I do.

Thank you to Valerie Arthur, Susan Schlimme, Elise Metzger, and Joyce Hoggard, whose sidewalk happy hours and other socially distanced get-togethers were such sustaining highlights to me.

To Ashley Peebles. An instant forever friend. Thank you for your garage and most especially for your dependably positive outlook. Someday I'm going to write a Southern book and dedicate it to you.

Thank you to my aunt Cheryl Remmert, who gave me a place of respite for a generous amount of time this year. It was bliss.

Thank you to Rochelle Weinstein, who embodies every dear quality that a beloved friend should have. Becoming a writer was worth it just to have you brought into my life. Together with Lisa Barr, we are Dots, Duds, and Goober.

I cannot possibly thank all of the amazing Bookstagrammers and book world friends who show their love and support all the time. But to name a very few—the women of My Book Friends (join us on Facebook!)—Andrea Katz, Suzy Leopold, Marisa Gothie, Terry Pearson, Jen Sherman, Travel With a Book, Bookapotamus, Ann Marie Nieves, Wonder Woman Bookish, Zibby Owens, Dell Gray, Joy Jordan Lake, Eileen Moskowitz Palma, and Ken and Judy Rodriguez.

Finally—bookstores have had a tough couple of years and yet they are irreplaceable supporters of authors. I hope to give back just a little here by encouraging readers to shop brick and mortar and I want to give a shout-out to a few of my favorites: Owl and Turtle (Camden, Maine), Sundog Books (Seaside, Florida), Fountain Bookstore (Richmond, Virginia), Tattered Cover (Denver, Colorado), The Last Bookstore (Los Angeles, California), Bookish (Malakoff, Texas), The Twig (San Antonio, Texas), Shakespeare and Company (New York City), Book People (Austin, Texas), Parnassus (Nashville, Tennessee), Page 158 Books (Wake Forest, North Carolina), Politics and Prose (Washington, DC), Blue Willow Bookshop (Houston, Texas), and Battery Park Books (Asheville, North Carolina).

CHAPTER ONE

September 1943

$\mathcal{M}$argaret Beck closed the door of her family's narrow Brooklyn row house and rested her head against the wood. The black paint had peeled enough to reveal the whorl-like curves of its grain, and its faded color matched her mood. She slipped her hand into her coat pocket and pulled out the key, inserting it into the lock and turning it until it made the robust *thunk* that assured her that the safety lock had engaged. The sun had not yet appeared over the chimneyed rooftops, and her parents would not wake for another half hour.

She was on the early shift at the Navy Yard today and she hadn't gotten any sleep since last night. Worry was a poor bed companion.

What had begun as a normal evening had taken a turn that left a pit in her stomach.

Margaret had just sprinkled the dregs of their last box of Dreft powder into the water, watching as it fizzed into foam when she swished her hand around in it. There were no more to buy on scant grocers' shelves, purchases limited to two boxes per household since the company's equipment had been recommissioned for Uncle Sam's use and others were following suit. From now on, her mother would be making a paste of lye flakes and vinegar, and Margaret could already imagine the havoc it would wreak on their hands.

Dottie had come in from the back entrance and Margaret knew from the slam of the screened door and frenetic pace of her movements that something was wrong. Her friend picked up a towel and started drying the dishes with such force that the enamel was in danger of rubbing off.

Margaret knew better than to ask what was wrong. Dottie would say so as soon as she was ready.

The sound of the radio blared from the overhead bedroom and the girls could hear Margaret's parents laughing to *The Great Gildersleeve.*

It was good to hear them laugh. There had been too little of it lately. But the merriment it gave her wasn't reflected in Dottie's face, as it normally would be.

"Margaret," Dottie said, glancing up, as if to make sure they couldn't be heard. She took a deep breath and exhaled in a nervous stutter. "I'm . . . I'm just going to say this."

Margaret set down the jadeite bowl she was holding. Dottie had been looking uncommonly tired lately and Margaret feared that her friend wasn't getting enough to eat. Much like the rest of them. Dinner tonight had been watered-down tomato sauce over rice, hardly enough to keep anyone full overnight. They saved their chicken cards for Sundays.

"Say what?"

Dottie lowered her voice to a whisper. "I'm receiving a visit from the stork."

Blood rushed from her head to her toes.

She immediately pictured the implications, much like how people's lives were said to flash before their eyes before they died. This was not the joyous news it would have been in a different circumstance. Dottie's devout parents would surely be livid and turn her out. She'd be let go from her position at the Navy Yard.

She'd be destitute.

Because John had been drafted before the wedding could take place.

Margaret grabbed Dottie's hands, suds forming a bubbling cuff, and squeezed them to keep them from trembling. Though she couldn't tell who was shaking harder. "Are you sure? Did you go to the doctor?"

Dottie shook her head, and her long, dark curls bounced from side to side. "Of course not. The rabbit test would be too expensive, and I'd be devastated for one to die on my behalf. But it explains my nausea. And my exhaustion. And why...why my monthly didn't come."

"The rabbit test?" Margaret asked. Dottie had been a nanny for an Upper East Side family last summer when the mother had become *in the family way* for a third time. So of course she would know the latest things like that.

"Yes. They make you"—she lowered her voice even more, looking around as if someone might come in—"*go* into a cup. And then they inject it into a female rabbit and cut it open to see if its ovaries reacted."

Margaret was appalled, and the image of it distracted her for a moment from the weight of the news. "They really *do* that?"

Dottie nodded and her curls fell over the right side of her face at their part. "Well, I guess the doctors for rich women do."

"That might be the only thing that makes me grateful I'm not rich."

A thin smile spread across Dottie's face. "Me too."

"How do you know that's even true?"

"The woman I nannied for was a showgirl before she became the second wife of a banker on Wall Street. The things she talked about would curl your hair."

Margaret laughed. "Is that how you got this mop?" She ran a finger down a lock of Dottie's hair and it bounced right back into position.

Dottie smiled, bigger this time. "We've been friends for more than half of my life. You know I come by these honestly."

"Honestly with a little help from pomade." But all joking aside, this was serious news. Margaret drew Dottie into a hug and could feel both of their heartbeats racing. Dottie's slender frame was rigid at first, but at last she rested her head on Margaret's shoulder, heaving staccato breaths as tears surfaced.

Margaret pulled away after some time and handed Dottie a handkerchief. She led her to the kitchen table and set a newly washed cushion on the wooden chair. Then she joined her on the other side. The tension of the situation was enough to steal the air they breathed.

"What are we going to do about it?" she whispered.

Dottie raised the handkerchief to her nose, reddened, perhaps, by the chill in the air. But more than likely, she'd shed some tears before even coming here. "What do you mean, *we*? This is my problem."

"Dottie." Margaret lifted her friend's chin up with her hand and mustered a firm look that she hoped was more convincing than she felt inside. "This is *our* problem. And let's not even call it a problem. That's my little niece or nephew in there. Do you realize that? That's *John's child*! John's going to come home and he's going to marry you because he loves you and has loved you for as long as I can remember."

"But my parents..."

"...are not going to find out until we figure out a plan."

Dottie ran her hand along her waistband. "We'd better figure out something soon. I don't know how long it will be before it will be obvious to everyone."

"How far along are you? John left for basic training six weeks ago."

Dottie nodded. "That long."

Margaret bit her lip as she was thinking. Maybe Dottie could come live here and stay in John's bedroom. She was sure her parents would rather do that than see Dottie turned out. Although, if word spread that they were harboring an unwed woman who'd gotten herself into trouble, people might take their business elsewhere and their shoe shop might suffer more than it already was.

But then—a solution. Or at least the fledgling hope of one.

"I know what we'll do," she said. "We'll talk to Gladys."

It had been impossible to get any rest after that. Dottie had stayed until *The Great Gildersleeve* gave way to *Dreft Star Playhouse* on NBC and it had occurred to Margaret that its host, Marvin Miller, had the unenviable task of promoting a product that was no longer available. Even the loss of something as otherwise insignificant as dish detergent was like another knife in her already worried heart. Each one took her by surprise—there was no solace to be found in everyday routines because they, too, had been altered.

Regular reminders that nothing was what it should be.

At last the radio turned silent as Margaret's parents went to sleep. Dottie looked at her watch and apologized for the late hour and hurried home with Margaret's promise that they would get through this together.

It was a night saturated with concern. For John. For Dottie. For the world. When Margaret's alarm clock sounded in the dark early hours, she swung leaded feet onto the floor and pulled herself up by her bedpost, exhaustion weighing heavily on every bone in her body.

Margaret stood now, head to door, eyes closed and listening to the sounds of the morning as it mustered the energy to turn into day. Birds perched on electrical wires, the baker's ovens hummed, car horns blared as drivers maneuvered their way down streets that fell into worse disrepair as each day passed. Resources were needed elsewhere.

She felt *unraveled*. It was the Word of the Day in yesterday's *New York Times* and she thought it an ideal term for the circumstance. Like spiraled heaps of yarn laying waste after discovering a flaw in a knitting project.

Dreams were like that too. You imagined what your life

would be like and it didn't turn out to be so. She remembered sitting under red-and-white umbrellas at the shore the first summer she met Dottie and all the ones after that. Little girls with big plans who never could have imagined what a world at war might look like.

What having a baby under these circumstances would mean.

Indeed, Dottie's news had left Margaret feeling tangled up inside. That her dearest friend was pregnant should have been something to celebrate. Their childhood full of dolls and dress-up and playing house was about to blossom into something real and wriggling.

It was all they'd ever wanted.

But one paramount step in the long-ago playacting had been bypassed: the wedding.

It's not that Margaret held any religious opinions on the order in which things had happened. The joy she felt at the revelation was genuine—in seven months or so, a little niece or nephew would make an entrance into the world. Margaret's brother, John, was the father and she had always known that he would make such a very, very good one.

It was the need for secrecy that unsettled her.

The worry over what Dottie's family would do when they found out.

And the fear that John might never make it home.

That part, she couldn't share with Dottie. Not in her condition. But every day, the local newspaper posted the names of the dead and missing from Brooklyn. How could they presume that their family would be spared the great tragedy that had befallen so many others? At least for now, John was safe, training in England, parachuting from the airplanes he loved so much. Out of danger as far as they could tell. But how long would it be before his unit was called up to the front and the real peril began?

War draped every breath in a cloak of uncertainty, and Margaret ached to tether herself to something dependable. The need to keep quiet about Dottie's pregnancy only added to the many shadows that had been cast upon their lives.

She pulled herself away from the row house door, one beleaguered step at a time until she made it to the bus stop and the short journey passed by in a haze.

Twenty minutes later, they rolled up to the entrance of the Brooklyn Navy Yard, and Margaret's spirits were raised by the pride that arose every time she saw the masts of the three unfinished ships through the dusty glass panes. The handiwork of tens of thousands of men. And more recently, a handful of women like herself. A flag stood outside the entrance, billowing in the morning breeze. Forty-eight stars reminding her that her troubles were mere droplets in the vast sea of sacrifices being made here and around the world.

Just two weeks ago, she'd stood in this spot along with thousands of civilians watching thousands of troops board the *Samaria*, bound for Liverpool. Once a grand passenger ship in the Cunard Line, it had been requisitioned by the Royal Navy for troop transport. Including her brother. He'd gone to basic training in Georgia and then jump school in North Carolina, and by some unexpected twist, his company in the 101st Airborne was departing from right here in Brooklyn. Right here in the Navy Yard, just a few miles from where he'd been born. She'd hoped to see him, but the soldiers had been given no leave time for visiting families since few of them were from this area. Instead, she and Dottie and her parents had stood in the bleachers hoping to catch a glimpse of that one face they loved so much.

It was to no avail, but John knew they'd be there in that crowd and she hoped that was enough to bolster him as the shores of his homeland disappeared from view. They'd watched with handkerchiefs pressed against their faces as the uniformed young men sailed off, about to learn that war was more than the playacting they'd done in their youth.

The memory brought tears to her eyes once again, a salty concoction of pride and fear, but she wiped them away as soon as they formed, leaving only their tannic burn behind. She had to stay strong. For John. For Dottie. For her parents. For all of them.

She wished she had someone who could be strong for her.

Margaret pulled her identification card from her bag and strung it around her neck before stepping off the bus, avoiding puddles from an overnight rain. The fumes from the exhaust and the fishy stench of the East River made for a nauseating combination, but seeing Gladys Sievers's bright red hat near the fence brought a smile to her face.

"There you are, doll," Gladys shouted through a haze of cigarette smoke. She smoked the unfiltered kind, preferring the gravelly, husky contour it gave to her voice. "Maybe if I sound more like a man, I'll be treated as well as one," she'd say with some sarcasm.

She dropped the butt onto the sidewalk and ground it down with her stiletto heel.

Entirely unsuitable footwear for this weather and this place—they had to walk over steel grates to get to their workroom—but she insisted it was all part of the picture she liked to paint about rights for women. "Men know deep down they couldn't take two steps in these babies, though I'd like to see them try. Ha! That would show them what we're made of."

Every breath Gladys took was tinged with the burden of a father who'd left and a mother who had quite literally worked herself to death before the preponderance of unions and workers' rights. So she never missed an opportunity to advance the causes that combated such injustices, in all ways large and small.

She didn't have any more money than the rest of them, but Gladys was a whiz at embellishing old pieces and making them look snazzy. As Margaret approached, she could see that today's heels were red with gold embroidery. She recognized the shoes as one of Gladys's thrift-store purchases. One had a coffee stain on the toe, if she remembered correctly. But the way Gladys had used gold thread to create a flower pattern on them had made them look brand-new.

"Where's your sidekick, sick again? Dare we hope she's loosened up at last and given herself over to a night of debauchery?" Her thick gardenia perfume nearly masked the cigarette smell and it put a tickle in Margaret's nose.

Margaret checked her wristwatch, relieved that she'd be able to clock in on time. She smiled at her friend. There were some things the war could never change. Gladys would always be a force unto herself, her words and ideas and sarcasms a perfect storm of originality that had earned her the nickname of *Hurricane*, at least between Margaret and Dottie.

"Yes—well, at least to your first question. She must have

eaten something rancid. She hasn't been able to keep anything down."

Margaret winced at the untruth, but Dottie had begged her not to tell anyone about the baby yet. Not even Gladys, whom she wanted to tell in her own time. Not until she could think things through. If her mother got wind of her pregnancy before they made a plan, she'd be sent away to a home for unwed girls, where the child would be taken away as soon as it was born.

It had happened to Dottie's older sister, and the poor girl had never been the same from the grief of it. She walked as if she were broken inside, and Margaret would give her life to prevent that for her best friend.

Gladys offered her usual advice. "Nothing a cup of brandy wouldn't fix, but Dottie isn't one to imbibe, is she?"

"She's never had a liking for it."

"Too bad. Brandy for Belly Aches. Vodka for Viruses. Whiskey for Woman Troubles. Dr. Gladys's prescription for a long life."

Margaret grinned and held up an imaginary cocktail glass. "Here's to that."

"Cheers, doll."

They joined the long line of women who were reporting for the first shift at the Navy Yard. They were bright-eyed and chatty, incongruous given the early hour. But they were used to being awake before the light of the morning blanketed the city, and Margaret wondered if she would ever consider the soft-lit dawn as routine.

This shift paid an extra dollar per week, though, and Margaret was glad to have the opportunity to contribute to the family coffers in exchange for a few hours of sleep. She was hoping for a promotion out of the flag-sewing wing and was counting on her punctuality and her ability to adapt to be among her assets when an opening in the new mechanic section became available. The other would be her vocabulary. They accepted only the smartest girls—replacing the engineers and hard-hat workers who had been sent overseas—and though she'd been an average student, she read the Word of the Day every morning and maneuvered it into conversations to help her stand out.

Gladys had already made it into the ranks that most of the women just dreamed about and relished the chance to show the men that she was every bit as capable as they were.

So far, nothing had materialized for Margaret, but the foreman over there promised to put in a good word for her. George was John's best friend and would do anything for the Beck family. And a promotion like that would mean an additional *two* dollars per week.

That would leave some leftover money to buy herself a few of the posher cosmetics at the Macy's counter rather than the ordinary ones from Woolworth's. Like a Pink Perfection lipstick from Elizabeth Arden. She'd once seen it in an advertisement in a library copy of *Vogue* and had thought of it ever since.

It would also mean that her father could work a few less hours in their cobbler shop and give his arthritic hands a rest. Though other girls in their early twenties had fathers about double their age, hers had been a good bit older than her mother when they married and was frequently mistaken for Margaret's grandfather when they were out together.

George Preston was exactly the kind of Brooklyn man her parents would love to see her settle down with. Dependable. Hardworking. Well-mannered. He was as good a guy as they came. But there had never been the kind of spark between them that romance novels promised. She'd not yet felt more than a passing flutter for a boy. Nothing she could call love— nothing that resembled the possibility of longevity she so admired in her parents. Or John and Dottie.

Margaret believed it was better to love vicariously through the printed word in books than to pursue a fleeting feeling built on quicksand, and she was determined to either hold out for the real thing or not have it at all. She'd seen too many marriages among her parents' friends turn rancid in the wake of the difficulties the world put forth.

Better to be alone than saddled in misery to someone chosen in a bout of head-in-the-cloud youthfulness.

In this regard, she admired how Gladys stuck to her guns.

John and Dottie's story had started years ago when the Beck and Troutwine families had rented small cottages next to each other on Brighton Beach. Margaret had been excited when she saw a girl her age sitting shoeless on the front porch, sand baked onto her feet. When their parents discovered that they lived only one subway stop apart, the girls became inseparable.

But as soon as her brother was old enough to consider girls as something more than a nuisance, it became forevermore Dottie and John, John and Dottie. As if one name couldn't be spoken without the corresponding *other*. And Margaret didn't mind. The two people she loved most in the world loved each other. It didn't get any better than that.

Their wedding had been planned for October. But John was drafted and sent out to basic training in July.

War was a particular kind of thief that stole not only the lives of the boys who went overseas, but also the plans and aspirations of the families at home.

Among Margaret's friends, doubt had seeped into the traditions they'd been raised with as life and loss permeated their conversations in ways they'd never had to consider before. Instead of trifles such as how to make the perfect gravy or what ice cream cone flavor to choose at the pharmacy counter, they worried: *What if the men don't make it back? What if the Germans come here across the Atlantic?* And the corollary response: *Do what you want to because this all might end.*

(*Corollary* had been a recent Word of the Day, and Margaret had already used it three times in conversation. And once in her thoughts: The *corollary* to John shipping off unexpectedly was that he and Dottie had the wedding night before the wedding.)

Gladys changed into a pair of flat leather boots just after they passed through the iron gate at the security check. The twin carcasses of the USS *Maine* and the USS *New Hampshire* towered above them, sparks flying from welders' blowtorches as they disassembled the battleships piece by piece. Margaret watched in fascination, never tiring of seeing the power of fire against metal.

Five such ship orders had been canceled here and in Philadelphia and Norfolk, their superior firepower capabilities falling into less favor than the new class of ship that could serve as a sea base for air operations. *Aircraft carriers.*

Ships built like runways so that airplanes could land and refuel in the middle of the ocean.

The war, at least, produced marvels that might otherwise have been relegated to futuristic fiction.

Margaret regretted the years of toil that Brooklyn workers had poured into the battleships, only to have to erase their own efforts. Thankfully, their shipyard had been chosen to build the vessels that introduced a cause for hope.

It was like a death. A death that also brought new life. Sorrow and joy could only be known because of the existence of the other.

She paused as they passed the third one—the USS *Missouri*. The last of this class of battleships. Too far into production to cancel. The one that connected the past to the future.

Much like Dottie and John's baby.

The work siren blew, echoing through the foggy air and shaking Margaret from her wistful thoughts. This was not the time to be defeated by worries and musings. The future of this little child would be secured only by taking action. Not just here at work, but in the hours between.

John's most recent letter had arrived yesterday and it had given her an idea.

"What are you doing tomorrow night?" she asked as she slipped her yellow card into the punch clock.

Gladys grinned and Margaret watched her sort through some of the more scandalous answers that she would have characteristically given. But she restrained herself, perhaps as eager to get the workday started—and finished—as Margaret was.

"Nothing I can't back out of. What do you have in mind?"

"Something you won't want to miss out on. Meet me at my pop's shop at seven. I'll tell you then."

CHAPTER TWO

The air was brisk, the newness of fall descending on Gladys and Margaret as they stood outside of the cobbler shop.

"Darling, if this is your idea of an *exciting* Saturday night, I am going to pen an obituary and etch a tombstone for you right now, because you're already dead and buried."

Margaret grinned. "And would you have come if I told you that we were going to be knitting?"

Gladys shook her head, her curls bouncing with newly set perfection. Unlike Dottie's natural ones—assisted by only the tiniest bit of gel—Gladys's spirals were the result of painful nights spent in foam rollers. Her hair was fiery—something Margaret always thought was a fitting crown for her personality. Between them, they made a complete set. Dottie with her ebony locks, Gladys the redhead, and Margaret with the shiny straight hair that her grandmother used to call "spun gold."

And these were exactly the girls with whom she wanted to grow gray someday.

How she missed the days when how you styled your hair was the worst thing you had to worry about.

Gladys shivered and pulled a flask from her purse. "Hot chocolate," she insisted before Margaret could comment. "I'm not a total lush despite reports to the contrary."

"I wasn't going to ask."

"Sure you weren't. Look—I can prove it." She pulled a small envelope from her coat pocket and opened it. Margaret could smell the rich aroma of the chocolate powder, even though she could scarcely make it out in the dim light. The blackout hour was nearly upon them and shopkeepers in the neighborhood had begun the process of shuttering their windows for the night.

"Did you get that at Rockwood?" Margaret asked, referring to the factory that sat near the Navy Yard. In the right wind, the scent of cocoa teased the workers, and more than once, Margaret had found her mouth watering as she sewed stars on a flag.

Gladys closed the lid and returned it to her pocket. "Not on your life. All of their stuff is going to the boys overseas. Getting chocolate out of them would be harder than breaking into Fort Knox. Nah, this here is from Ebinger's."

"Ebinger's! Mama said she's going to treat me to one of their Brooklyn Blackout cakes for my next birthday. Have you had one yet?"

"Sure I have. What's the use of having a sweetheart working in a sweetshop if you don't get a little sweetness on the side?"

"Gladys!"

"I'm pulling your leg, doll. You know I'm not seeing anyone, but gosh, I love your lack of guile. I saved some pennies and bought it with my own money since I don't have a husband to make me account for every little whim. How long have you known me?"

Margaret sighed. "Until the day I die, Gladys, I'm not sure I'll ever know when you're kidding."

"Keep 'em on their toes. That's my motto."

"You have a lot of those."

"Have a lot of mottos. That's my motto."

Margaret rolled her eyes but knew that Gladys wouldn't see that in the dark. "You're *incorrigible*."

"Is that another one of your fancy words?"

"Yes. From two weeks ago. I just haven't had the right opportunity to use it. Until now."

Gladys chuckled. "I know big words, too, you know. You don't have the corner on the market. You'll be *jubilant* to learn that I brought enough chocolate packets to share with you and Dottie."

Margaret's cheeks warmed at the image of the rare treat.

"Thank you, Gladys," she said, mollified.

"You're welcome. You've got a hot plate in there?"

"Yeah. Pops likes fresh coffee while he's working."

"And milk?"

"Nope. Mom uses all the milk rations for baking bread. So it's black coffee for us until the end of the war."

Gladys frowned. "And watery hot chocolate. Ah, what can you do? Just one more loss to lay at the feet of Hitler."

"I think there are a few worse things attributed to him than that. Read the paper."

"No doubt, doll. I pray every night that the bastard gets a bullet right in the heart. And by American hands, if possible."

She folded her arms. "But tonight I can also resent him for ruining the full Ebinger's experience."

"Of course you can."

"Well, we'll make do. We always have."

"Hi, girls!"

They turned to see a silhouette of Dottie sidestepping something on the pavement.

"Oh my," she said as she approached. "They need to repair that hole. Someone could get hurt." She brushed the front of her skirt with her hands. "Anyway, I brought some yarn like you asked, Margaret."

"Whatever would I do without you?"

"May you never have to find out." Margaret knew Dottie was grinning as she said it. It was a familiar exchange between them, an echo of their barefoot days playing on the Brighton Beach boardwalk. Margaret had once splintered her heel running after a stray kite. Dottie, with saintlike patience, had worked with the tweezers, plucking it out in triumph. The first of many incidents in which the banter was apropos.

It was no wonder that Dottie was the first of them to be getting married and having a baby. She'd been a little adult ever since she was half the size of one.

Gladys took a swig of her hot chocolate. "My bones were not made for freezing, ladies, and my head wasn't made for nostalgia. Shall we move this party inside?"

Margaret inserted a rusty key into the lock, marveling at how old it was. Her father inherited this shoe-making business from his father, and the key was an original. Her family lived just a block from the store, which made for an easy commute and saved on the expense of bus tokens.

She ushered the girls inside and closed the door behind them. Pops had already shuttered the store for the evening, and the curtains had been drawn to keep any errant light from slipping through the metal sheets that covered the windows. This new routine had quickly become habit ever since a few tankers had been sunk in New York Harbor by German U-boats using the Manhattan skyline as an unintended flash-light. Now, all of Brooklyn had to live in "dim-out" conditions once the sun set. Even motor cars drove without headlights. Times Square and Coney Island were likewise darkened.

New York became a ghost town at night.

Once the door was closed behind them, Margaret flipped on the switch and the overhead lights—hanging by their wires—flickered until they cast a yellow glow across the room. The Becks' bread and butter money came from the rugged boots popular in workman's Brooklyn. The shop served those at the Navy Yard, along with laborers at the nearby sugar refineries, dockyards, and glue factories.

They used to sell women's shoes as well, embellished with buckles and embroidered flowers. Black patent leather. Flapper shoes designed for endless hours of dancing. Her mother, quot-ing Abigail Adams, had implored her husband to *remember the ladies*, and the side offerings had brought in a modest profit.

Now, everything was utilitarian in construct. Unimagina-tive, and a poor waste of her father's talent for the trade. Instead of the needlepoint Margaret had once assisted with, her off-hours were often spent slicing through leather hides and fitting them around wooden lasts shaped like toeless feet.

She'd once had a nightmare about those lasts—people were dancing, but their feet were bare, made only of the smooth, featureless wood. She'd been just five years old, but the rows of them that her father had hanging on the wall still gave her the heebie-jeebies.

And yet she loved working with her hands. Creating something both useful and beautiful. Sometimes she envisioned joining John in carrying the family business into a third generation.

"We can set up in the workshop," she said, pointing to a back room. Gladys and Dottie followed.

The tanned smell of the leather was so familiar that Margaret no longer noticed it. It was the scent of her childhood as a cobbler's daughter. Even Dottie was unaffected, having spent much time here while John fashioned the grommets for shoe-lace holes. This was not Gladys's everyday scene, however, and Margaret watched as her nose wrinkled.

"Let's get this business done and maybe we can catch a few hours with the rest of the young New Yorkers who are out having a *good* time."

"Is anyone having a good time during the blackout?" Margaret asked. Of late, she'd spent the hours after dinner reading by candlelight, as if it was the era of pioneers in caravans heading west.

"There are places that are still lively after the sun goes down. Windowless basements where music and cigarettes and homemade alcohol flow in abundance. You know, the Stage Door Canteen is hopping all night. Admission costs a bag of sugar or something else they can use to fill their pantry. And you can dance the night away with a handsome soldier or two. It's downright patriotic, if you ask me. Almost un-American if you don't go."

"Is this really so bad, Gladys?" Dottie's voice, always sweet and considerate, sounded ruffled.

"Not if you want to live your life in a humdrum. I worked next to a girl at the canteen couple of weeks ago who is going places. She was on the cover of *Harper's Bazaar* back in March. The one featuring the American Red Cross. You remember that one."

Dottie nodded. "I do. I donated some blood after they ran that article."

"Yeah, that was her. The girl in the white hat smack on the front of it. And there she was next to me, elbow to elbow, making five hundred ham sandwiches together on a Monday night. You know what? *She's* not sticking around here. She's going to Hollywood. Just got cast in a Bogart flick and is heading out next month. Her name is Lauren Bacall. I'll bet you now—we're going to see her name in lights."

"So you want to be like this Lauren girl?" asked Margaret. "You've never had the acting bug."

Dottie giggled. "Though you *do* have a knack for theatrics."

Gladys ignored her. "Nah. Not the acting bug *per se*. It's just that she set her sights on bigger things. And me, I want to do something bigger too. Not"—she shrugged—"knit socks like an old granny on a weekend."

Margaret gave her a light punch on the arm. "Well, when my brother's feet freeze in the cold English winter, it will bring me great comfort to know that you were hobnobbing with movie stars."

Gladys slumped into her chair. "See? You're an old granny. Already adept at guilt as thick as molasses."

Dottie settled in next to her and opened the bag so the girls could examine the bounty. The skeins were leftovers in various states of use, remnants of other projects, but entirely suitable for tonight's purpose. Margaret's fingers tingled with possibility, just like they did when she entered a fabric shop or walked by a window display with art supplies.

The skills she'd learned from her mother were not being put to their best use at the Navy Yard, where she spent hour upon hour sewing the straight red and white stripes of the American flag. And sometimes the stars. Easy enough work for a beginner, let alone someone who had practically been born with a needle in her hand. It would be little to go on when she interviewed to be a mechanic, but at least she could count on the precision and quality of her work as a recommendation.

Margaret dusted wood shavings off the seat of her father's fraying tweed chair and scooted it over to where Gladys and Dottie were sitting. She looked at Dottie, confident that years of friendship would convey in an expression what they didn't say in words.

When are you going to tell Gladys about the baby? she asked by raising her eyebrows and nodding ever so slightly at Dottie's belly.

Dottie shook her head, nearly unperceptively. *Not yet*, she seemed to say.

Margaret worried that Dottie would keep a lid on this secret for too long, and until it was too late. For all one could say about Gladys, she was resourceful. Margaret was certain that she would know what to do.

Gladys shivered and pulled her sweater tighter around her

shoulders. "It's either an icebox in here or a ghost just walked through me."

Margaret grinned. "No ghost would dare haunt you."

Gladys sat up straight even as Dottie ignored them and started sorting the skeins on the table between them. "Whyever not?"

"Because you'd tell them to wrap up whatever business was keeping them on this planet and go along their merry way."

"Damn right I would."

Dottie's head jerked up. "Gladys! You can't talk like that when—"

Margaret's heart stopped. She knew what Dottie had been about to say. But maybe it was for the best.

Gladys didn't miss a beat. "When what?"

Margaret could see the defeat in Dottie's eyes. And then the beginning of tears.

"What did I say? Have you never heard a woman say *damn* before?" Gladys leaned forward in her chair, hands on the arms, looking like she was about to spring up. "You're more of an innocent than I thought."

"No. It's not that. It's not you." Dottie shook her head and pulled a handkerchief from her pocket. "I was going to say, you can't use words like that when...when the baby comes."

Margaret breathed an inward sigh of relief. They couldn't do the work of taking care of this until Gladys knew. But Margaret would never have been the one to tell. Not behind Dottie's back.

Gladys was speechless. For about ten seconds, which might have been some kind of record.

"A baby," she whispered in reverential tones. "You do beat all, Dorothy Troutwine. You do beat all. So much for being an innocent. You've gone and gotten randy on us!"

Dottie's cheeks reddened. She and Margaret waited for Gladys to speak again and were rewarded by one of her classic retorts.

"I suppose our boy Johnny will be safe during this war. Because apparently he can hit a target." She grinned.

"Gladys!" Margaret and Dottie shouted her name at the same time. Margaret flushed with embarrassment, but she was both relieved and surprised by what happened next: Dottie broke into a fit of giggles.

She hadn't heard Dottie laugh like that in many months, and it was as delightful as the twinkling lights that were put around town at Christmastime. The corners of her own lips widened until Margaret, too, started laughing. Gladys had already contributed to the harmony, and Margaret had to admit that it had been far too long since they'd given themselves over to such joviality.

When they'd settled down—and after Gladys had dribbled some hot chocolate onto her white blouse—Dottie repeated all that she'd told Margaret the night before, including her concerns about what her parents might do. Just one more Troutwine girl who would disappoint and scandalize the parishioners of St. Charles Borromeo if they didn't intervene.

Gladys scooted up until her knees were touching Dottie's. She took Dottie's hands in her own. "Dottie. First of all, what is it *you* want? Do you want to keep this baby? There are places..."

Dottie pulled her hands back and sent Margaret a horrified look that needed no interpretation.

"Of course I want this baby. This is John's *child*. It's... it's just all happening earlier than I would have wanted, but I couldn't go through life as Mrs. John Beck knowing that I'd... done that."

Gladys leaned in farther. "No, that's not what I meant, honey. Don't you think I know you at all? Goodness, I've already sent a letter to the Vatican asking them to open a case for canonization. Though I have to say, this predicament doesn't help your cause."

She grinned at her own humor. "Anyway, I was going to ask if you wanted to give the baby up for adoption. And if not, there are places that can help women in your situation—unmarried—get what they need to get through it. Lodging, food, diapers. Leave it to me. I'll see what I can find out."

Dottie leapt from her chair and wrapped her arms around Gladys's shoulders, dropping the skeins on her lap to the floor. Margaret knelt to pick them up and picked off the leather shavings that had embedded themselves into the yarn. She smiled at the large figure that her friends made, huddled as they were together in an unlikely embrace. Gladys was not known for her affection and Dottie couldn't pass a dog on the street without petting it. So Margaret was pleased to witness the soft side of Gladys that cared more than she usually let on.

It was Dottie who pulled away first, wiping her eyes with the sleeves of her coat, which she had not yet removed.

"You are both the best. Just the best. Gosh, this is the first time I've felt some hope. I'm going to get through this. I'm going to do this for John, and our future. Which is why we're here tonight."

Margaret was surprised to find a stash of powdered milk in her father's cabinet next to his ground coffee tin. It wasn't as tasty as the fresh stuff but was more preferable than water. And she knew he wouldn't mind if they used it. After she'd warmed it for their hot chocolate, she cleaned the residue out of the little pot so that there wouldn't be any dried flakes in it when her father came down in the morning. For all the good things she could say about her brother, he was not proficient with the small details of life. It was always a particular gripe of her father's when John was not thorough about wiping down the hot plate or making sure that the milk pot was fully cleaned.

In the meantime, Dottie was telling Gladys about Margaret's idea to knit socks for John's unit. A decidedly un-Gladys thing to do. But these were different times that called upon them all to stretch the boundaries of what they'd done in the past.

"I know it doesn't sound like much. But John wrote both of us and said they're going to need good footwear heading into the winter. They're expecting to march so much that their socks will thin out within days. Sure, we could go to Woolworth's and buy some, but it's about the morale. Just think about what it will mean to them if we take the time to create these by hand. Something that reminds them that they are worth our time. Something that reminds them what they are fighting for in the first place."

She said this in a single breath and Margaret could only

imagine what her friend must be feeling. It was suffocating to be so uncertain about what tomorrow might bring, and Margaret understood that these little efforts were as much about rescuing themselves as it was helping the men. Any little thing they could grasp on to when everything else was in disarray brought a brief sense of peace.

Gladys looked convinced, though not enthusiastic.

"I'm in. On one condition," she said.

Margaret looked at Dottie, who shrugged.

"Name it."

Gladys folded her arms and grinned. "Next time, I pick the joyride. Even preggers here can come along."

Margaret inhaled sharply. She could only imagine what mischief Gladys would get them into. But she'd promised to help Dottie, so she would say yes to anything.

"You're on."

Dottie suggested that they continue their makeshift conclave. She pulled yarn from her bag. Gray for Margaret, blue for Gladys, and brown for herself.

"We're going to start with a simple pattern. I've got supplies for both of you."

She pulled out a package of long, slender knitting needles and unfolded a tattered piece of paper.

"These are called Wonder Socks," explained Dottie. "The design you see here in the heel and toe is supposed to save on yarn by letting you take out those pieces and replace them when they wear. So we'll also knit some extra heels and toes and send them along as well. Other than that though, it's a pretty straightforward pattern. I picked wool yarn since it's the warmest and holds up the best."

Gladys held up one of the needles and wielded it like a sword, challenging Margaret to a silent duel.

The needles made a *clinking* noise as they tapped against each other, and after a minute of playful fencing, Dottie called it a draw.

"Well," Margaret said, pleased at how the evening was turning out. "These will be *our* weapons, then. A woolen battlefront to make the soldiers' feet comfortable as they fight in Europe."

Dottie smiled, but it was wan. Margaret understood. The gravity of what they were doing was not forgotten even among their cheer. They were both worried about John. She didn't want to lose a brother. And Dottie didn't want to lose a husband before she even became a wife.

Gladys walked over to the Emerson radio that sat on a nearby workbench. She set aside the leather strips that laid across it and turned the dial until "In the Mood" by Glenn Miller came on, nearly at the beginning. The spirits in the room were immediately lifted and the girls got to work.

After Dottie showed them how to cast on and make the base row, they got the hang of the pattern—knit, purl, knit, purl. The difficult part was learning how to maneuver three needles instead of the two that Margaret was used to, but even that became routine as they cast stitch after stitch. It gave her a small thrill to see it come together as a kind of a tube and she could envision how it would turn into a sock.

Margaret noticed that she was stitching along to the beat. Distracted by the music—Bing Crosby, Duke Ellington, Tommy Dorsey—and the twittering of their conversation, she was surprised that an hour later, she had produced the base of a sock that, while not storefront-perfect, was something to be proud of. Despite her adeptness with a sewing needle, she'd always felt inferior with a knitting one in comparison to Dottie.

Perhaps her flaw was the meticulous scrutiny she gave her projects. Worrying over every blemish to the point that nothing felt good enough. Another of her mother's favorite quotes came to mind, this one from Voltaire: *Don't make the perfect the enemy of the good.*

John and the boys on the front had enough enemies. She didn't need to let her insecurities add to them. They would surely love these socks, mistakes and all.

And to be honest, they were not likely to notice.

Margaret looked up and saw that Gladys was about as far along as she was while Dottie was well on her way to finishing the matched sock that would complete the pair. At this rate, they could clothe the whole army in a short time.

Dottie leaned in and showed them how to change the pattern in order to create the ribbed part that would hug the shin. Knit two, purl two.

As she continued, Margaret thought about the boys who would wear them and about a special request that John had asked of her.

Could you write a note to my buddy William? He hasn't received any letters yet, and I don't know why. But I think it would mean an awful lot to him. Something cheery. You're just the girl to do it.

She paused to glide a finger along her nearly done piece and thought about who this William was. Would he put the pair on right away? Or would he stash it in his rucksack for later? But most important, would he smile at the thought that some girl in Brooklyn had spent a Saturday evening making this for him?

She was grateful her brother had enlisted her help. It gave her the kind of purpose that she felt working at the Navy Yard. That in some little way, she was contributing to the war effort.

"Margaret, watch out!"

Dottie was pointing to the pocket of the red sweater that Margaret's grandmother had made for her many Christmases ago. It had seen better days—Margaret wore it frequently to the Navy Yard, and it had caught on her work more times than she cared to count. She missed her grandmother, having lost her two years ago to pneumonia, and the sweater was a warm reminder of the woman she'd loved. Margaret still felt the void at the dinner table every night as her grandmother's seat remained empty. And now John's.

She saw the problem that Dottie was pointing to. A piece of the yarn had come loose and had wound its way around the gray wool skein. The last row of Margaret's stitching had the beginnings of an unintentional red border.

"Looks kind of nice, if you ask me," offered Gladys.

Dottie stood up to inspect the work. "I think she's right, Mags. It dresses it up a little bit. Makes it stand out." She dug through her bag. "I don't have a red skein, but I have a yellow one if you want to make a border on purpose." She held it up.

Margaret took it from her hand but wasn't convinced as

she put it next to the sock. There was something dull about it. Yellow on gray. Whereas the red reminded her of some of the flashiest dancing shoes her parents used to make.

She shook her head and gave the yellow back to Dottie. Then she tugged on her sweater, loosening the yarn even more.

"I'm going to stick with the red. For all the socks I make. It will be like having my signature on it."

"Oh, Margaret!" exclaimed Dottie. "What do you mean? That's your favorite sweater!"

Margaret's heart beat faster as she doubted herself, but she knew deep down that this was something she had to do. "That's why. It's *because* it's my favorite. What if this little sacrifice means something? Like the amount of our effort somehow elevates theirs?"

Gladys set her project down on her lap. "Like it's in the stars. The more good you put out there, the more comes down to them."

"Or"—Dottie seemed enthusiastic about the idea now— "it's like sending them a bit of your grandmother's goodwill. Letting her be their guardian angel too."

Margaret smiled. "Yes. Exactly like that."

"I like it. And so would John."

Margaret stifled a yawn. It was only nine o'clock, but she still felt tired from the sleep she'd missed from the early shift yesterday. This work was too important, though, and this evening with her friends was too dear to wrap up early. Another Glenn Miller song came on—"Knit One, Purl Two." The girls fell into another fit of giggles. The song had dominated radio stations last year, and its appearance at this moment felt like it was all meant to be.

"You know what?" said Gladys. "I think I'd like to do this every Saturday night after all."

Margaret smiled at Gladys's response to the silent wish of her heart. She whispered a prayer for the boys who would receive the socks and went back to work.

Tomorrow, she would write a letter to William and slip it into the box before shipping it out.

CHAPTER THREE

*F*rom the shelter of the rotund folly, Tom Powell could almost believe that there was not a war going on beyond its columns. In almost every direction, he beheld the gentle slope of hills in a palette of green hues. And closer to the estate house—which looked miniature from this perch—lay perfectly manicured hedges shaped into precise geometric patterns. The kind in which a child might delight in a round of hide-and-seek.

He'd been dispatched to Littlecote House to deliver a message to Colonel Sink, and his luck at borrowing a bicycle to take on his way from Chilton Foliat had saved a few minutes over walking. When he'd arrived at the estate, it had looked nearly deserted. So he was reveling in this extra time by sitting under the shade of the white pavilion before heading to the large manor and completing his assignment.

It was a far cry from just weeks ago when they'd been packed—five thousand men in a vessel built for one thousand—in the *Samaria*. Fresh from training in the debilitating heat of Camp Toccoa, Georgia, and more schooling in North

Carolina. (Still hot, but fewer bugs to contend with.) Even as their stomachs lurched from seasickness, his friend John Beck had told him his secret for staying hopeful among the intensity of the training and the fear of what was to come. Stop when you can. Close your eyes. Smell the air. Listen for the birds. Imagine that it was a vacation that brought you over the Atlantic.

A seeming impossibility considering the few hours of sleep they were afforded. But now Tom wanted to try it, especially in a place as beautiful as this.

John was right. Even on the ride over, Tom paid special attention to his surroundings and already, his spirits were lifted. The warm aroma of yeast had wafted from a bakery window. Children's voices had echoed from a nearby alley, their British words and accents still a novelty that surprised him every time. The River Kennet had glistened as he traveled along its gravel path.

He could imagine easily enough that he was back home in Virginia with a front porch view of the Chickahominy River and that his mother had peach pie warming in the oven. Always a treat after an afternoon of picking the fruit in their orchard. The best ones were reserved for the market, and the bruised ones were held back for baking. His father would be sitting at his desk reading the newspaper, an armchair commentator on every decision President Roosevelt made. Opinions informed, at least, by his own military experience.

His father had been so eager for Tom to enlist, following family tradition. And Tom had never questioned that he would do otherwise. Photographs of Powell ancestors from as far back as the Civil War crowded the mantel of the redbrick fireplace at their home, and stories dating back to the Jamestown settlement taunted Tom to be among the next generation of heroes.

"A career in the military is the only path for a man," his father was famous for saying. The patriarchal enthusiasm was tempered only by his mother, who insisted that Tom go to college before joining up. A tactic that Tom knew was merely the desperate wish of a mother's heart to delay her son buttoning up a uniform.

But a master's degree in history was not likely to do much good when rifle met rifle. The time to step out from behind a desk had come and Tom was ready.

Like his classmates, he'd grown up playing cops and robbers at recess and painting diecast soldiers, reenacting stories they heard at their dinner tables and read in their textbooks. But when the Japanese bombed Pearl Harbor nearly two years ago, the recreational aspect of exploring one's fledgling manhood was put to the test. And the all-too-real prospect of going to war became a silent terror concealed by outward bravado.

Would his father be happier if he made it home safely or if he died gloriously on the battlefield?

As to his own feelings about it, they were drowned in the brackish waters of his parents' conflicting expectations, laid out since the day the doctor had declared, "It's a boy!"

He'd done his best to please them ever since.

He'd not yet seen combat, but the training had been fierce and had carved a camaraderie between those in his unit. Especially among himself, William Farlane, and John. William had two sisters back at home and John had one. Tom lacked any siblings at all. So they became each other's brothers. Tom was enriched by John's ability to remain calm in surrounding storms and by William's entertaining stories of home in Arlington as the son of a congressman.

Tom glanced at his watch and was disappointed that this little respite was over. He mounted the rickety bicycle and approached Littlecote House, which emerged from the landscape like something from a movie. He recalled seeing *Rebecca* a few years ago—when Laurence Olivier drove up to Manderley and his young bride marveled at the expansive brick and stone manse covered in ivy.

It was just like that.

From this view alone, he could count seventeen redbrick chimneys.

Who needed *seventeen chimneys*?

Tom never dreamed he'd see such a place for himself, and it was easy enough to take John's advice and be convinced— even for a moment—that he was here as a tourist.

The feeling was short-lived. The sound of a Willys Jeep rolled down a distant road and soon enough, he saw the open-aired vehicle kick up dirt as it sped toward the house. The passenger was likely one of the many high-ranking brass who came and went from the grounds. It had been requisitioned for the regimental staff of the 101st Airborne. The Screaming Eagles.

The rank and file like himself were scattered around private homes in Ramsbury, Chilton Foliat, Froxfield, and Aldbourne. He, William, and John were bunking together in a farmhouse with an elderly couple who'd turned down the compensation offered from the government to house American troops, insisting that at their ages and with no children of their own, it was the least they could do for the war effort. Completing the makeshift family was the Browns' blind sheepdog named Victoria, whom they doted upon as much as any parent would a child.

William had originally been assigned to stay alone in a carriage house on an estate near Aldbourne, but gladly gave up those swanky digs when the Browns told John and Tom that they could accommodate one more.

It was a five-mile walk—or as it was measured here, eight kilometers—from the farmhouse to their training ground in Aldbourne. On days where there was no vehicle with which to hitch a ride, they convinced themselves that it was a lucky opportunity to become even more fit. But on most days, Mr. Brown was kind enough to give them a ride in his hay wagon, at least one of the ways.

What a luxury it would be to have a Willys Jeep like that one!

The Jeep was his cue to keep going. As he approached the house, he wondered which of the many doors he was supposed to enter through. One was quite a bit grander than the others, so he leaned the bicycle against the wall next to it and pulled a rope. The sound of a bell rang on the other side, echoing through what sounded like a vast chamber.

He half expected a tuxedoed butler to answer, if the movies were to be believed. Ideally with a tray of sweet tea. But he'd discovered that the Brits liked their tea hot with cream, not iced with sugar. He probably missed that more than anything.

Sweet tea coursed through the veins of every Virginian.

Instead, a middle-aged woman appeared, dressed in an olive-green dress that downplayed her likely connection to this fine estate.

"Yes, sir?" she said. She squinted against the sun that was setting behind Tom, and he shifted to the right to block it for her.

"I'm Private First Class Thomas Powell. I've brought a message for Colonel Sink."

She nodded and opened the door wider, motioning for him to come in.

If the outside was impressive, the inside was beyond description. And indeed, it was as vast as he'd imagined.

Everywhere he looked, the opulence of history dripped down Tudor-style walls. Though it occurred to Tom that they were likely *original* Tudor. Not replicas. Dark panels were adorned with portraits of men dead for centuries, their eyes seeming to leer at him as he followed the woman down the hall.

The closest thing he'd seen to this was in Richmond, forty miles from his home. Fifteen years ago, two businessmen had purchased a fifteenth-century manor called Agecroft Hall, dismantled it piece by piece, and shipped it across the Atlantic to be rebuilt on the eastern banks of the James River. He'd seen the pictures in the newspaper and his mother read the story to him as they both marveled at the feat. But forty miles might as well have been four thousand, too far away to go without one of the new automobiles that were coming to market. And though they'd eventually purchased one, it was not until last year when some ladies at church chartered a bus to make a day trip that he and his mother finally got to see it for themselves. A festival full of period reenactors immersed them in the bygone time and whetted both of their appetites to see England for themselves one day.

Now, to be in the halls of an even more vast estate, sitting on its original land, was an experience that left him awestruck. His mother would be beside herself.

He hoped in a peaceful world, she could come here too.

Tom followed the woman as she continued through the manor. Their footsteps echoed just as the bell had, despite lavish tapestries hanging from the tallest ceilings he'd ever seen.

"Wait here. I believe the colonel is in a meeting. Would you like some tea?"

"Yes, thank you."

"With ice?" She grinned. Clearly, she'd grown accustomed to being around Americans.

"Yes, please."

When in Rome, William had said, taking a liking to the British presentation. But John and Tom had not yet discovered an affinity for it.

Tom sank into the proffered chair. Who might have sat here before him? Kings? Queens? And now, Thomas Robert Powell of Charles City County, Virginia. It sent a shiver through him. Some of the very people who had walked these halls might well be the ones his ancestors had fought in the revolution. And now he would fight alongside their descendants against a new aggressor. Enemies turned allies.

The woman returned and smiled at his awkward position-ing on the chair. Even his tall frame was no match for the enormity of the furniture.

"You'd think they were made for giants," she said. "But in fact, the original family to own this house was quite diminutive, like most people of their day."

"Then why all of this?" Tom waved his hand around the room.

"It's for show. It was expensive to make furniture in this scale. And especially to have it upholstered. The larger it was, the more it showcased your wealth."

They exchanged a look that Tom understood to be an agreement that such things were insignificant now, especially in light of the reason they were all gathered here. *Extravagance* was an unknown word in this age.

"Here's your tea," she said, handing him a gilded tray. He smiled at the jingle of ice cubes in the glass. The first time he'd had such a treat since he'd landed in England. "And a pack of cigarettes. The current owner of the house is my cousin, Sir Ernest Wills of Imperial Tobacco. I think he's on a mission to convert the entire American army to his brand. We've been instructed to hand them out like candy."

"Thank you," said Tom. Though it was fashionable to do so, he hadn't taken up smoking. The one time he'd tried it, it had prompted a harrowing fit of coughing. Friends told him that he would get used to it, but what was the point of acquiring a taste for something he didn't care for in the first place and cost money he didn't need to spend? He put the pack in the pocket of his coat. John and William could arm wrestle for them. They had an ongoing contest with occasional prizes for the most recent winner. So far, John was ahead with an impressive tally of victories and therefore worthy of this bounty. But Tom knew that John would share with William without question.

The woman departed and he watched her walk through a door that opened to yet another cavernous room, adorned, he could see, with swords and antlers arranged in decorative patterns.

His father, being a hunter, would have liked it. And his mother would have gushed over the gilded tea tray. Tom wished he could explore the manor further, though it would probably take him a week to see every space. He'd have to include details in a letter to home.

He heard deep voices coming closer to a nearby door and then it opened to reveal several uniformed men emerging from their meeting. From where Tom was sitting, he was hidden from their view. He was just about to stand up and salute when he heard something that made him stop.

"General Alexander doesn't believe that the guerrillas in Italy are going to be effective in fighting off the Nazis, so he's postponing his participation."

"What does Roosevelt say to that?"

"He wants to wait and see what the CLN does. In the meantime, there are rumors that Churchill and Roosevelt are trying to broker a meeting with Stalin, maybe as early as next month."

"Can Stalin be trusted?"

"Right now, he's Hitler's enemy. And you know what they say."

"The enemy of my enemy is my friend."

"Exactly. But God help us all if we get into bed with the Russians."

Tom cleared his throat and stood up. He recognized Colonel Sink and Major General Lee, having seen them walk by during many drill inspections. Their chests were laden with pounds of medals, the kings of the army looking right at home in these palace-like environs.

Give him Dick Winters any day. A first lieutenant who knew how to get into the thick of things and who preferred the austerity of a bunk to posh surrounds like this.

"Yes, PFC Powell?" Major General Lee didn't know Tom from Adam, but the precision of a military uniform revealed his name on the brass tag and patch on his arm.

"A message for you from First Lieutenant Winters." Tom handed him the sealed envelope.

"Not another missive about Sobel, I hope. That bastard whipped Easy Company into shape like nobody's business, but dammit, I've never gotten as many complaints about someone either."

Tom stood at attention, as he'd been taught. As if there was a metal rod holding up his spine. He had his opinions about Sobel but knew he wouldn't be asked to share them.

"I wouldn't know, sir."

"Of course you wouldn't. Did he want a response?"

"I don't believe so, sir."

"You don't *believe* so? That's a yes or no question, son."

Tom curled his toes in his boots. Though he was inches taller than Lee, the man had a terrifying countenance. He reminded him of his father.

"No, sir," he decided. Surely Winters would have told him if anything more than the delivery was expected. But he hoped that it was another plea to send Sobel elsewhere—he had demoralized Easy Company with his draconian expectations and had a history of inventing infractions back in Georgia just for kicks. The men felt more loyalty to Dick Winters as the head of their platoon than they did to Sobel as the company commander.

But Lee didn't open it in front of him, so Tom had no hope of finding out if Captain Sobel's days were, at last, numbered.

"Dismissed."

Tom saluted and turned, exiting the elaborate front door without ceremony and stepping back into the crisp evening air. He exhaled a breath he didn't even realize he'd been holding.

He hopped on the bike, not looking back at Littlecote House. Not looking back on what he'd heard.

The United States. Britain. Italy. Germany. Russia. Just a few of the countries mentioned in the brief conversation he'd overhead. Not to mention all the news coming out of the Pacific.

This was, indeed, a world war.

Tom hoped he and his friends would survive it.

The little cottage in Chilton Foliat might as well have been in a different world from where he'd just ridden in from. Owned by their hosts, Mr. and Mrs. Brown, it was as unpretentious as their surname. But it was tidy, and Mrs. Brown kept timber in the fireplace all day so the boys could play cards and read from their small collection of books in the scant spare time they were afforded. Mrs. Brown made an unbeatable Yorkshire pudding and always had a batch ready when they returned from drill, hungry and tired.

Tom had written to his mother to let her know how much she would love the place and to assure her that her son was in good hands.

He returned to the attic bedroom the three men shared. William was stoking the embers in the stone fireplace as they mellowed into a dull orange glow. Heat gave way to the chill of the evening. John was crouched next to the hearth, rubbing his hands together.

"Where've you been? Necking with a local girl?" William looked up and grinned. His ribbing was good-humored, though Tom had come to suspect that his joviality was a mask for troubles he kept to himself. William's sleep was restless, night after night.

Tom shrugged. William knew that Tom had ridden up to the estate. Unlike some of the boys in the 101st, Tom thought it unseemly to take up a romance with a local girl when today, tomorrow, and the next were so uncertain. Such things would happen for him once he was well settled into army life, a swath of medals and stripes adorning his shoulder.

And such distractions wouldn't serve them well in the field.

"Well, we all know Johnny Boy was behaving himself. Here." William tossed a twine-wrapped package to John, who had just walked in from a jump.

"For me?" he asked, catching it with ease.

"You're the only sorry soul who gets presents around here. I haven't even heard from my mom yet."

William grinned, but the sadness in his eyes told a different story.

Why had he not yet received letters from home?

"That reminds me." Tom pulled the pack of cigarettes from his pocket and placed them on the table by the fire. "Johnny Boy's on top on the scoreboard, but I know you'll play nice and split these."

"Jolly nice of you, ol' chap," William said, wobbling over on an imaginary cane and adjusting a phantom monocle. He took one from the box, tapped it on the table, and put a match to it.

Tom rolled his eyes. "Don't tell me you're taking on the affectations of the English. *Jolly nice?*"

William exhaled slowly, letting some of the smoke escape through his nose. "Affectations? Do you inhale dictionaries since you don't inhale tobacco?"

"Cut it out, you two," John said as he pulled out his army knife to slit the box open. Inside were some of the things he'd asked for. Raisins, soap, chewing gum, and peppermints. He sifted through the letters, and Tom watched him slip one from Dottie under his pillow for reading later. They were all familiar with Dottie's large, loopy handwriting. Unless there was something of a private nature, the boys all passed around their letters as if a note written to one was intended for all.

He pulled out a brown paper bag and handed it to Tom. Likewise, goodies sent were meant to be shared. Tom opened it to find six pairs of homemade wool socks and laid them out on the table next to the cigarettes.

"I'll take a set," said William, "unless twelve feet have suddenly bloomed from your skinny legs."

"Which one?" Tom stood and held them up one at a time, swinging his hips as if he were some pin-up girl modeling them.

William let out a catcall and John's shoulders shook with laughter.

"The gray ones. With the red border."

Tom balled one up and threw it at William. It struck him in the forehead. Right on target.

William took off his own pair, full of holes. Tom's and John's were in the same ratty condition. Their toes poked out of the frayed ends. Army supplies were made for cost, not for constancy.

John grinned. "Hold your nose, Tom. We could send William and his feet to Hitler and get him to surrender."

It wasn't true. Tom was learning that this was the way guys talked, a novelty to him, having been raised without siblings. And a father who ruled like the general he imagined himself to be.

"Ahhh...that's the stuff. Warm and cozy, as my mom would say." William slipped on the first sock, and then the second. His face wrinkled in confusion.

"Wait—what's this?" He slipped his finger down the tube of it and pulled out a piece of paper. He unfolded it, grinning as he read.

"What do you know? A letter. A letter from a girl."

CHAPTER FOUR

October 1943

$\mathcal{M}$argaret paused over her sewing machine halfway through stitching a star on the flag. The corners were tricky even for someone with experience. Some girls slid by with shoddy work knowing that their stars and stripes would be flying high up on ship masts where no one could scrutinize the details. And though Margaret didn't care to pass judgment, she was determined to set herself apart and be considered for that promotion.

Inferior work would not be tolerated in the mechanic's wing, where precision was vital to safety. Even the tiniest miscalculated measurement could result in a leak. Or a torpedo sent off course.

The flags were symbols of a nation's pride and prowess. But the engineering of such mighty battleships was a matter of national security. Small details made big differences.

She looked up from her handiwork in time to see Dottie rubbing her lower back. Her friend sat kitty-corner to her, one row ahead and one over.

Four rows of seven stations filled the vast space, flags in

varying stages of completion draping over their fronts. The room was lined on three sides with floor-to-ceiling cabinets that held their supplies as well as the half-done handiwork they'd store at the end of their shifts. Margaret was one of the lucky ones who was assigned to a table closest to the wall of windows, an administrative miracle that allowed her to squint less than others did as light shone in.

Though when winter came, she suspected that it would also be the coldest spot, as the single-paned glass was a poor insulator.

"Dot," she called over the humming all around them. "Dot—are you feeling all right?"

Dottie turned around and Margaret was alarmed to see the pale tones of her skin.

"I'm fine, Margaret. It's probably just from sitting for hours and hours. I'm going to take a walk on my break."

"I'm coming with you, then."

"I'd be glad for the company."

Margaret could hear the fatigue in her voice, and it worried her. These early shifts were hard enough, but Margaret couldn't imagine doing them while trying to grow an entire baby. She wished she could persuade Dottie to cut her hours back or quit altogether, but Dottie would never hear of it. And with her future uncertain, she needed every cent she could earn.

They worked for another half hour, chitchat stymied by the volume of whirring machines and the watchful eye of the shift supervisor. Margaret stood up and walked around her table to Dottie's. Dottie had completed her fourteenth star for the morning, compared to Margaret's eleven, all of them finished to the kind of perfection that looked effortless.

If anyone was to outshine her own abilities, she was glad it was her best friend.

"Ready to go?" Margaret asked.

Dottie got up and put her sweater around her shoulders and followed Margaret out the door.

The wind nipped at their cheeks as they stepped outside and Margaret doubted they could stay here for even the fifteen minutes they had free. But for the moment it was a welcome change from the stuffiness of their workspace. They went from one cacophony to another, though. The chatter and machines and radio music in the sewing room competed with the sharp sounds of welders and drillers that echoed across the East River.

There was an otherworldly feeling to the outside, not from the weather, but from the smoke that poured in from the towering brick stacks of the Navy Yard. On a cold day like this, it had nowhere to rise, and its cloud hovered like an eerie industrial phantom.

They'd walked all of a hundred feet when a figure started running toward them from far down the walkway. At first, he was concealed by the shadow of the USS *Missouri*, but as he got closer, Margaret smiled.

"Hi, George!" she called when he was near enough to hear them.

"Margaret, Dorothy," he sputtered, out of breath. His face was beet red, a symptom of the brisk temperature. But even on the warmest days, George turned pink when he was in Dottie's presence. Margaret had never drawn attention to it, and she was certain that Dottie remained unaware. Yet George's affection for her friend could have been discovered by even the most innocent child playing junior detective at recess.

He leaned against the iron railing, and Margaret worried that he'd hurried over to them as he had.

George was what Gladys called "a fine specimen of a man." Every girl who knew him called him "Blue Eyes" behind his back, though the comparison to Sinatra stopped there, as he couldn't carry a tune to save his life. With a medium build and an admirable physique, he could have been a poster boy for a soldier. But Margaret knew that sometimes a person's ills were not of the visible kind and George had been devastated to discover that a heart condition rendered him unsuitable for the army's needs. He'd begged to be given a desk job—anything to help the cause—but they refused, citing their concern that he wouldn't make it through the rigorous basic training.

He had received several white feathers when out and about, quite undeservedly. A popular symbol of shame in Britain, the practice had gained a steady and unfortunate foothold on this side of the pond as well. Well-meaning women handed them out to seemingly able-bodied men of drafting age, making the assumption that they had somehow wiled their way out of military service.

And yet, despite what the doctors said, George had the strongest heart of anyone Margaret knew, metaphorically speaking. (That was a Word of the Day in September, but one that she already knew.) Upon his rejection from the army, he had immediately applied for work in the Navy Yard. George had little need for money—his family owned one of the country's largest appliance companies, and John had affectionately dubbed him the Refrigerator King. But his zeal for helping with the

war effort led him to the modest work here in Brooklyn that
fulfilled him more than selling state-of-the-art machines that
could wash your dishes to Upper East Side matrons.

His college degree had quickly catapulted him to the position of foreman of the engraving section.

Margaret bit her tongue and held back an admonishment.
She was worried that he would collapse one day if he didn't
take things easier, but she knew it was hopeless to ask him to
do anything halfway.

She'd always thought he would have been an ideal match
for Dottie if John had not already won her heart.

"I have good news for you," George said, his voice steadying.
"I couldn't wait to tell you. Your promotions came through
and I'm happy to announce that you both can start in the
engraving section, second shift, as soon as next week."

Margaret's cold cheeks warmed at the news. She and Dottie
exchanged looks, and it was the first smile she'd seen on
Dottie's face all day.

"So soon?" she asked. "Who did you have to pay off to
make that happen?"

George laughed. "You think too little of yourself, Margaret.
I've seen the work that you and Dottie do. And I've known
you both since John and I met at Scouts. Now, I know that
it's not in the mechanic's section like you'd hoped for, but I
promise that it is an advancement, with an extra dollar per
week. If you prove yourself there, you'll be a shoo-in when
something even higher up becomes available."

"Shoes are something I know well," Margaret joked.

Dottie rolled her eyes and exchanged a bemused glance
with George. "The early shift turns her into a cornball."

"My brother's not here with his usual levity, so I consider it my duty to step in."

"He has more years of practice," George added, though she could tell he appreciated the attempt.

Dottie rescued her by changing the subject. "Please tell us more about what kind of work we will be doing in the engraving department." Her voice was quiet and songlike, and Margaret could barely hear her in the wind tunnel created between the brick building and the massive ship to their right.

But George heard easily enough. Attuned, perhaps, to the inflections of the woman he loved in secret. "You'll be working with machinery that engraves the ordnance."

"The ordnance!" Margaret exclaimed. "I didn't know we might be working with weapons. Will it be safe?"

Her assignment in the sewing department had only confirmed how much she liked working with her hands, but she shuddered at the element of danger that this suggested.

"Yes, very safe," George assured her. "Nothing you'll be handling will be loaded. That comes later after they send it to munitions. You'll engrave casings, cannon shells, guns."

Margaret felt relieved, but goose bumps gathered on her arms at the gravity of a job like this. Although the flags were important, the ordnance played an essential role in the war. That meant that Margaret and Dottie would be playing an essential role.

One more small thing to help John.

Dottie put a hand on George's arm. "We can't thank you enough for putting in a good word for us."

Margaret felt bad for having jumped into the details without even acknowledging the gratitude he deserved. And of course, Dottie would have the consideration to do so. George beamed at her touch.

"Think nothing of it. You know I would do anything for you," he said, looking at Dottie. And then he caught himself. "For both of you," he hurried to add.

Margaret sensed his embarrassment and filled the awkward interlude to spare him. "We are in your debt, George. Now and always. You have come through for us at every turn." And it was true. Not only had he vouched for them to get this promotion, but he'd also shared his sugar and coffee rations with them since the dawn of those measures, insisting that he didn't care for them. Even though before the war, Margaret knew him to be a three-cups-a-day coffee drinker with heaping spoons of sugar. He'd also given Dottie his bicycle last month when the bus broke down. Not lent—given. And he'd brought over a chicken and string bean casserole a few years back when Margaret and John's grandmother died.

How could they ever repay him?

Dottie shuffled over to Margaret and leaned against her as if she needed the support. It was nearly imperceptible; no doubt she didn't want to alarm George and invite questions she wouldn't want to answer. Margaret put her arm around Dottie's waist and was grateful that such gestures were commonplace among her and her friends. Her hands lay against Dottie's thin back, separated only by her cotton blouse. It worried Margaret. Dottie should be gaining weight. But she felt alarmingly skinny.

Margaret made excuses for their hasty goodbye. "Thanks again, George. You're one in a million. We have to get back to work."

He put his hands in his coat pockets and rocked on his heels. "I'll see you both on Monday."

"Bye, George," added Dottie. Though Margaret could tell that it took effort for her to push the words out.

When George had walked far enough away so as not to overhear them, she turned to Dottie.

"We need to get you out of here. You look terrible."

Dottie smiled wanly. "You sure know how to make a girl's heart flutter."

Margaret wrinkled her brows. "I mean it. I don't have any experience with this, but I don't think you're supposed to look like death warmed over. Aren't pregnant women supposed to have some kind of glow about them?"

They started walking back, Dottie clinging to Margaret.

"I think it's a myth. I don't know who profits from it, but there is absolutely nothing glamorous about spending the morning losing everything you forced yourself to eat for breakfast."

"Oh, Dot. Is it really as bad as that?" Margaret felt distinctly helpless.

Dottie nodded. "It's amazing that something the size of a pea can upend your entire body."

Margaret paused and pulled Dottie in for a hug. "Well, I'll bet that sweet pea is going to be worth every second. She's going to have your eyes and your disposition and John's chin and his good sense of humor."

Dottie pulled her head back. "What makes you so sure that it's a girl?"

Margaret grinned. "She has to be. Back when we used to play with dolls, they were *girl* dolls. You can have as many boys as you want with my brother. Just give me one little niece to dote on first. Ribbons and lace and frills. The works."

"Ugh, I can't imagine ever going through this again."

"Oh, dear. Is there nothing I can do to make this easier?"

"Just be my friend, Margaret. Like you always are. I'm not going to be able to do this without you."

They both welcomed the warmth of the stuffy sewing room when they returned. Margaret stayed by Dottie's side until she was sitting at her station. Perhaps too solicitously, but her worries hadn't abated.

She was glad that their sewing tables were positioned as they were. She could easily keep an eye on Dottie from where she was sitting.

The end of their shift was a bittersweet one. Word of their promotion had spread in that mysterious way that it does and the girls they'd sat near for months congratulated them. Promises to keep in touch and meet for lunch passed between them. And even though Margaret acknowledged the words with polite yeses, the reality was that they would have little chance for interaction. Different shifts and different sides of the Navy Yard might as well have had them living on different planets. The Navy Yard employed well over ten thousand people and was a small city in and of itself. It was uncommon to run into people you knew if you didn't already work together.

Margaret took slow steps on the way to the bus stop to match Dottie's labored strides. "Are you sure you don't need to go to a doctor?"

Dottie shook her head and her curls swung back and forth. "I'm told this is normal. Don't fuss over me."

"Hey, ladies! What's cookin'?" Gladys called from behind them, and it took her no time to catch up.

"Dottie isn't feeling well."

Gladys lifted Dottie's chin with her hands. "Good God, Dorothy. She's not kidding. Let's get you home. I'll ride all the way with you and I can walk back to my apartment later."

Thankfully, Dottie didn't protest, and Margaret was glad she'd have the extra help if anything were to happen.

They boarded the bus that would take them to East Williamsburg. They were only two stops away from their respective town houses when Dottie slumped onto Margaret's lap.

Margaret shook Dottie's shoulders, but there was no response.

"Stop the bus!" she cried. "My friend has fainted."

The bus came to a stop and Margaret looked out the window. There was the Polish bodega on the corner. That meant they were only one block from Gladys's apartment.

Gladys sprang up from several rows away and hurried over to them. "Let's take her to my place. I'll call a doctor from the hall line."

A young man stood up in the back row and came toward them. "Can I be of service?" His deep British voice was a surprise, but Margaret had too little time to think about it.

"Yes. Please. Could you help us carry her to my friend's apartment? It's just one block away."

"Of course. In fact, let me see if the driver will bring you right to the door."

Gladys followed and relayed her address to the driver, who pulled up just shy of her building, blocked from going farther by a garbage truck lingering in the middle of the street.

The man picked Dottie up in his arms with little effort and followed Gladys and Margaret down the stairs of the bus. They garnered a good number of curious looks and people instinctively parted on the sidewalk like the Red Sea. With so many of the young men of Brooklyn off at war, the neighborhood was full of old women and elderly men, children and their weary mothers, none of whom would have been of much help, and Margaret was grateful again for the man's assistance.

For the first time, Margaret was glad that Gladys lived in the basement unit of a brownstone. The man didn't have to take too many steps to carry Dottie inside.

Gladys ran ahead, opened the door, and cleared her sofa of all the books and magazines that were always lying around in various stages of being read and annotated.

Virginia Woolf, Isak Dinesen, Pearl Buck. Gladys read only female authors.

There was also a blue sock, half-knit, that Gladys had begun working on during their most recent Saturday night get-together. They'd knit twenty pairs over the past few weeks and would ask John in their next box to share them with more men in his company. At this rate, they might have the entire battalion covered by Christmas.

They hoped it did as much good for the boys as it did for them.

"Set her there. I'm going to call for a doctor. And, Margaret, go down two doors to the right. Apartment 3B. A friend of mine lives there. A midwife. She might know what to do in the meantime and I know she'll come quickly if she's home."

Margaret hurried as Gladys had directed and her racing heart rejoiced when Gladys's friend opened the door. She explained their emergency, and the woman readily agreed to help.

"I'm Catherine, by the way," she said as she grabbed a black leather bag and put a sweater around her shoulders.

"And I'm Margaret."

"Margaret. Yes—Gladys has told me about you. And your friend Dorothy. I'm sorry—I didn't know that Dorothy was with child. Gladys hadn't mentioned that."

"We've only just told her. And it's not exactly news that Dottie is shouting from the rooftop."

Catherine nodded. "I understand. We've seen many such cases since the boys have gone off to war. The results of an overly romantic goodbye?"

Margaret hung her head as if she were the one in the troubling situation. "Yes. Exactly."

Catherine shrugged. "Not that I wish I was over there fighting, but we women have our own battles as well, don't we?"

Margaret nodded, holding back tears. Even during the nighttime hours in her bedroom, she tried to be strong, convinced that the best way to be a home-front soldier was to resist anything that resembled weakness. If John could do it, so could she. It was the only way she knew how to be there for her parents and for Dottie. But with so few words, this woman understood.

Catherine stepped forward and rubbed her hand along Margaret's arm, her quiet reassurance softening the hard edges that Margaret's worries had sharpened. She let out a breath, one that seemed to come from the farthest recesses of her lungs, and was surprised that such a small gesture could be so invigorating.

For all that seemed nice about having a boyfriend, Margaret didn't think it was a substitute for the friendship of women.

Margaret thought about Catherine's words as they walked down the steps and into the windy afternoon. In the brevity of the moment, Catherine had showed her that gentleness was its own kind of strength.

It was something she wanted to put into practice as well. To resurrect the Margaret she'd been before she had let herself become shrouded with worry. To rediscover who she was instead of who she'd let outside forces shape her into.

When they arrived at Gladys's apartment, Catherine sent them all outside so that she could examine Dottie in privacy.

Gladys leaned against the railing of her building and pulled out a cigarette. She offered one to the man who'd helped them, knowing that Margaret would decline.

"Mags, this is Oliver. Our hero of the hour. He hails from Eeeengland," she said, drawing out the name.

Margaret noted Gladys's casual way of introducing him. Just his first name. A quick familiarity that refrained from all formalities.

"We owe you quite a debt, Oliver. One we can never repay."

"It's my honor. Please think nothing of it."

Oh, that accent! It's what she imagined the heroes of the books she loved to read sound like. Mr. Rochester. Mr. Darcy. Heathcliff. And what she'd heard in the movies. But she couldn't recall ever having encountered it in person.

Despite the delight of that, Oliver was not the sort that she ever imagined herself falling for. His nails were too clean. His coat too tailored. His manners too perfect.

If pressed, Margaret would have said she preferred a man

with a more rugged nature. Maybe it was a consequence of growing up in working-class Brooklyn, where sweat and toil and labor were the currency of respectability. There was a distinction to her between a man and a *gentle*man. Which was not to say that Oliver was delicate in any way. He'd carried Dottie all the way over here. But there was a genteelness to him that was just a little too polished for Margaret's taste.

But one glance at Gladys told her that her friend held a distinctly different opinion. There was something surprising about the way she was looking at him.

Besotted. A recent Word of the Day. That was it. It was a revelation of sorts. Gladys—the most self-sufficient, grounded woman she'd ever known—seemed to be floating. At least to one who knew her so well.

"What brings you here to the States?" Margaret asked him.

"He's a correspondent for the *London Times*," Gladys answered on his behalf. "Sending news about the Yankees back home."

"The baseball team?" She wasn't surprised. The World Series had just begun, and already the Yankees were tied one to one with the St. Louis Cardinals. The third game would be played tonight just half an hour away at Yankee Stadium, and all of New York—even Brooklyn Dodgers fans like herself—were wild with excitement. It was the best kind of diversion from a world steeped in tragedy.

Gladys laughed. "No, doll. Not *the* Yankees. I just mean us. Americans."

Margaret wanted to roll her eyes. She was sure no one living south of the Mason-Dixon Line would take kindly to being lumped in with Northerners like herself. But that might be too nuanced for a foreigner.

All this time, Oliver was silent, folding his arms and watching Gladys with a look of bemusement on his face.

Margaret nodded and turned toward Oliver. "You'll have to excuse my gaffe. The World Series is big news around here right now."

He smiled. "I practically grew up on a polo field. But I have to admit, I've been quite swept up in the enthusiasm for the American pastime. In fact, I've acquired tickets for the game tonight. Something a little different to send to the office back at home. If either of you . . ." But he was looking at Gladys.

Gladys's eyes widened, and though Margaret was delighted by the unexpected dynamic between the two of them, she desperately hoped that her friend wouldn't accept. She was nervous about taking care of Dottie by herself. At least not until they knew what was wrong.

But Gladys came through, and Margaret should have had more faith in her. "Thank you, but I'm sorry. Sick friend beats lonely Brit. Another time, though?"

Margaret breathed a sigh of relief.

"Of course," he answered. "I believe the following games are in St. Louis, but perhaps you would accept dinner as a substitute."

Before Gladys could answer, a stout, gray-haired figure walked toward them, carrying a larger black bag than the one Catherine had brought over. He was a good head shorter than both women, and Oliver's significant height over him would have been comical in any other circumstance.

"I'm Dr. Feingold. Is this where I can find the pregnant woman?"

No euphemisms for this man. Why add flowery language when he saw the grit of human illness every day?

Gladys pulled her attention away from Oliver and stood up straight. "Yes. Right through that door there. A midwife is in there with her. I can show you the way."

"That won't be necessary. The fewer people, the better."

Margaret hoped that his skills were more profound than his demeanor. Then again, he must be particularly busy with such cases right now. According to Catherine, Dottie's predicament was not an uncommon one.

It didn't matter, as long as he took good care of Dottie.

The doctor departed, closing the door behind him, and the next fifteen minutes were nerve-racking for Margaret. Gladys and Oliver continued their conversation with palpable ease, as if there was not a sick woman just feet away from the other side of the brick façade. Margaret was distracted with worry and heard little of what they were saying, though it seemed that Gladys said she would *consider* meeting up next weekend at a restaurant that Oliver was keen on. Margaret decided to walk around the block to clear her head and circled the route four times before an update seemed forthcoming.

Her heart clenched when Catherine came back outside.

Please let it be good news.

CHAPTER FIVE

The Browns' house in Chilton Foliat backed up to a finger-like branch of the River Kennet. At that point, it was not much more than a stream, but it still attracted some of the rainbow trout that the river was known for. Open-windowed mornings at the kitchen table invited the sound of the gentle babble of its movement over the stones in its bed. Tom found peace listening to it, accompanied only by some distant noises from nearby Leverton Lane.

Autumn trees had begun to boast a spectrum of colors, and it made Tom miss his favorite season back in Virginia.

He liked being near the water because it was easier to pretend that he was back at home. Though in the Chicka-hominy, the bounty was different—often yellow perch and black crappie and his favorite—largemouth bass. When he closed his eyes, he could taste the bass with lemon, garlic, and pepper—a Friday night staple at his house, and later the dish his mother always made when he returned home on the first night of a semester break.

So he was delighted to discover that Mrs. Brown prepared

the trout in much the same manner. A reminder of simpler days, quelling the ache of being so far away.

It was one of the few things about England that reminded him of home. Because otherwise, there were reminders all around him that he was far from it. The accents. The automobiles driving on the opposite side of the road. The village of Chilton Foliat was peculiar to him as an American with its thatched roofs and stone fences. In fact, he wasn't even sure if the word *village* was correct. He'd also heard *parish*, *estate*, and *hamlet*. They seemed interchangeable to him, but the locals understood the minutiae of difference in all of them and he had not yet cracked that code.

Only two streets ran through the village, perpendicular to each other and lined with sagging redbrick houses. St. Mary's Church sat at the westernmost point and was a common gathering spot for the community. It was surrounded by farmland—wheat, barley, and root vegetables—and nearly every household sat on a small plot of land on which they sowed and harvested. The Browns were partial to parsnips, along with the trout, and Tom, William, and John had been treated to all sorts of variations of the humble root.

They didn't know why the Browns hadn't had children, but they appreciated how the elderly couple doted on them.

Mr. Brown was bald save for scattered patches of thin white hair, and he was perpetually bent over at a twenty-degree angle. Mrs. Brown was the healthy kind of plump, with a wide face and fewer wrinkles than Tom might have expected for her age.

Though "the boys"—as the couple called the trio—offered on many occasions to help with the cooking, cleaning, and parsnip picking, the Browns were adamant in their refusal.

"You boys have to keep your strength up for fighting Hitler," they would say in the perfect unison of two people who'd spent decade upon decade in each other's company. Tom knew that they were getting off lucky—others in their platoon were made to feel that the lodging was provided for the purpose of having extra hands to help with farm chores. Never mind that the Browns had a point—the majority of their days in the 101st Airborne Division were spent training, parachuting, shooting, and marching, with few daylight hours to spare.

Tom looked out at the river from the upstairs bedroom that he shared with William and John, and ran his hands through the hair that he'd kept a bit longer than the buzz cuts that his friends preferred.

John's snoring was keeping him awake and it drowned out most of the sounds of crickets that populated the nighttime hours. Would John's fiancée mind this particular disruption after they'd married? By all accounts, Dottie was an angel, and she would probably put up with it.

The intimacies of marriage both fascinated and frightened Tom. Not the most obvious aspect of it. That part was no longer a mystery to him, thanks to a brief encounter years ago with a college girl from William & Mary. She was doing some historical research at a plantation near his family's orchard over one weekend and made a very persuasive case to then-eighteen-year-old Tom to spend some time with her in the barn. He'd thought he was in love after that, this creature who swept into his life and seemed so unlike the few girls he

knew in the surrounding area. But wh
father's truck and driven to Williamsbur
laughed at the wild daffodils he'd picked f
that she preferred the company of academic

He didn't bother to tell her that he'd just
the University of Virginia. If she could laugh a
should he offer her his future?

After that, he was reluctant to take up with a g
though some of the co-eds in Charlottesville presented n
than enough opportunities. He knew his mission—join the
military after graduation. Or after his master's degree, if his
mother's influence prevailed. Love and family would come
much further down the line, and he didn't care to playact
them casually in the meantime.

But John and Dottie—though he knew her only through
John's descriptions—seemed ideally suited, and Tom's faith in
love was restored through the ardor with which his friend
talked about her. It resembled the flame that Tom wanted to
feel in his heart for a girl.

Next time, though, he would be more discerning. Love
was not instant. He would take his time to really get to know
her. Cherish her for what she said and not what else came
with a romance.

Whomever and wherever she was.

"You can't sleep, either, with the freight train in that bed
over there?" Tom asked. The room was lit with a streak
of moonlight and Tom could see William as he sat up in
his cot.

William didn't sleep well most nights, and Tom had been in
on John's idea to have his sister write letters to him. It seemed

worked—Margaret Beck had written William a letter, John had asked. And though it was no substitute for the he'd hoped to receive from his family, it had bolstered a bit.

He had yet to write her back, but Tom planned to encourage him to remedy that.

"It's not that. Well, in part, it is. I guess my thoughts keep me up," William admitted. "That and this damn hand."

William had fallen on his right hand on their last jump, and though he mustered up the ability to shoot on the rifle range, he didn't hide his pain back at the cottage. He'd turned down John and Tom's pleas for him to see a medic because he was afraid they would sideline him.

"Care keeps his watch in every old man's eyes. And where care lodges, sleep will never lie," Tom mused.

"What's that, Professor?"

"Shakespeare."

"Of course it is." William threw a pillow at him. "You college boys love to show off."

"Hey," Tom defended. "We're sitting in the *land* of Shakespeare. Cut me some slack."

"I know, I know." Tom could see William grin in the dim light and he was relieved for it to make an appearance. William continued. "Have you taken a good look at a map? My pops would be happy to know how close we are to Oxford. He was a Rhodes scholar. A fact he inserted into every stump speech on the campaign trail."

"I know what you mean. You would think from hearing him talk that my dad's Bronze Star was the flippin' Congressional Medal of Honor."

William's mouth twisted and he lowered his voice. "You know, son, I walked six miles uphill both ways to school and I expect you to shine my shoes with your tears of gratitude."

Tom laughed. "Yeah. Something like that."

"Really, though, my pops once gave me a ten-dollar bill for my birthday. And on the envelope, he wrote 'Here is milk from the cow that got no respect.'"

"Ouch."

"Maybe that's why he hasn't written. He's waiting for me to do something worth writing a speech about."

William's words hung thick in the silence. There was no response for what Tom, too, felt so deeply, words betraying him. He could only return to what they'd begun talking about.

"You know, Stratford-upon-Avon would be less than an hour from here if I could only wrangle a Willys Jeep for a bit. What I wouldn't do to send my mom a postcard from there."

Tom thought about all the places he'd only read about that were so very close. London. Oxford. Cambridge. And Paris, across the English Channel, still quite a distance and under siege by the Germans. But the French roots on his mother's side had always felt alive in him, and he wanted to see the place where his ancestors had walked.

If only a war weren't going on and they could go exploring. And yet, without the war, they wouldn't be here in the first place.

"If I see an opportunity, I'll find us a Willys and we'll go. Maybe Dick Winters will need me to head that way on an errand," offered Tom.

"Not likely. It's to Littlecote and back for you. But thanks, anyway."

They were quiet again, only the sound of John's heavy breathing between them. A melancholy had sunk into Tom ever since this morning when he'd walked past a cottage with an open window, through which he'd heard a small child playing a labored version of "Greensleeves." Her mother sat with her and they talked about the girl's part in the upcoming pageant at St. Mary's Church in December.

The rigors of their march today had suppressed his thoughts of the upcoming holidays, but now the stillness of the nighttime had brought them back to the forefront.

"William?"

"Yeah, Tom?"

"Do you realize that next month will be Thanksgiving? And then Christmas."

William sighed, and his voice sounded flat, the way Tom felt. "Don't think about it. Anything can happen between now and then."

"Sure. But there's no chance that we'll be home. Whether we're here in the English countryside or out on the battlefront by then, the point is that we won't be with our families. I guess that finally just sank in."

William paused. "Thanksgiving. It's my favorite."

"Yeah." Tom's father would shoot a turkey. And his mother would prep it. Removing the feathers, boiling the innards, and dressing it in a bath of spices and vinegar to sit in overnight. The highlight of the day, for Tom, at least, was not the meal itself, but what his mom did on the afternoon of Thanksgiving. She pulled out a large cast-iron pot that was used just this one time every year, a Cousances that had been owned by her great-grandmother and brought over two generations ago from France. She simmered the carcass for hours and then added the meat, the vegetables from earlier, and some barley, and it turned into what they called Leftover Soup. They'd store it in the refrigerator and eat it for the next three days, letting the glow of the original holiday dinner extend just a little longer.

Earlier in the week, if the weather allowed, he and his father would take canoes to the James River and make their way up to the banks of the Berkeley Plantation, which argued that it, and not Plymouth, was the site of the first Thanksgiving. Preceding the more well-known location by a year and a half.

This is the first time he'd be missing it.

"It will definitely be different this year," William lamented. "Thanksgiving. Christmas. New Year's Eve. My mother will cry. Maybe my sisters. Not my dad. He'll pretend to be strong."

"Mine too," Tom added. "I'm their only child. I don't envy my mom having to be alone with my dad. He's . . . he's got a very strong personality."

"So it seems. He doesn't hit her, does he?" Tom could see the alarm on William's face as moonlight streamed over his bed.

"No. Nothing like that. Never. But when he's around, it's like he sucks up all the air in the room and no one else has the chance to breathe." He looked down and shook his head. "That probably doesn't make any sense."

"It makes perfect sense."

"I just hope someday when I get married, I don't turn into that. The kind of girl I'd like is one who smiles all the time.

And I would never want to be the reason to take that away from her."

William grinned. "You know, Tom, that there are some very specific and time-honored ways of keeping a perpetual smile on your girl's face."

Tom tossed his last pillow at William's head. "That's not what I meant and you know it."

"You're so easy, Powell. You walk right into these things. No guile at all." William laughed quietly, though they'd learned that the Browns were hard of hearing at their age and if John's snoring didn't keep them up, surely William's laughter wouldn't.

And it was so good to finally hear it.

"I just mean that I'd like to have a wife who finds delight in things. Who comes to the dinner table with stories about her day and has an interest in mine. Give and take. I don't want to rob her of all that makes her what I fell in love with in the first place."

William tipped an imaginary hat on his head. "Ladies and gentlemen, I give you a Thoroughly Modern Man."

Tom shrugged. "Right shouldn't be modern. It's just... right." He couldn't find a better word for it.

"It shouldn't. But all too often, it is."

"What about you?" Tom was eager to turn the tables. "I saw the smile on your face when you found that note in your sock from John's sister. Maybe there's something there. If you play your cards right, he could be your brother-in-law someday."

William shook his head, and his voice took on a tone that Tom didn't quite understand. "It's not like that. First of all, you can't fall in love through letters."

Tom paused to consider this and wasn't sure he agreed. His weekend with that girl long ago had shown him that although being with a girl physically had its delights, what he craved was a connection of the heart. Wouldn't that make the physical part even better? And what more ideal way was there to make sure that you were really getting to know a girl than through a letter? Where the distraction of her beauty didn't take away from the words you were sharing.

But he didn't say that to William. Despite having a few years on them, John and William liked to tease him for his simplistic views about such things.

"What is the second thing?" he asked instead.

"What second thing?" said William.

"You said, 'First of all, you can't fall in love through letters.'"

He didn't speak for what felt like a long time. If William hadn't been sitting up, Tom might have thought he'd fallen asleep. And maybe he had. His shoulders were hunched over. Tom was about to ask again, when he heard William exhale a long breath.

"It's not like that for me."

"What do you mean? You don't like letters?"

William paused again. "Not letters. Girls."

It took Tom a minute to think about that. Did that mean what he thought it might? He'd heard about men like that, but he'd never met one in person.

He might have misunderstood. But if he hadn't, he didn't want to worry William that it made any difference in their friendship. It was his turn to say something.

"You don't *like* . . . girls?"

William's shoulders were still hunched, but he shook his head.

"Not in the way you'd expect."

Tom felt a pit in his stomach. Not so much at the revelation. William was William. Loyal. Smart. And a heck of a paratrooper. It didn't change all that. But he couldn't imagine the difficulty William must have to encounter at every turn. What a secret to carry. Tom had so many questions, but William looked fragile in the moonlight, a shell of the robust man that Tom knew him to be. Maybe the best approach for now was to act like he always did.

Tom cleared his throat and forced his voice to sound light. "Dibs on your sock girl, then. Looks like she's wasted on you."

William turned his head to him, and his smile told Tom that he'd said just the right thing.

"In your dreams, Professor. She's probably a dish. She'd be wasted on your ugly mug too."

"You don't know that."

William shrugged. "She wrote a pretty good letter, though. Most girls—if they wrote at all—would have stuck to the kind of basics that you exchange on a first meeting. Not Margaret Beck. Heart and soul, that one. Hard to believe she's related to that blockhead over there sawing logs. You'd think he was a lumberjack."

Tom pointed to the box by the foot of John's bed. He'd received another package today and had promised to open it after dinner, but training had been especially difficult. Four jumps and long walks back through fields, followed by endless training on the makeshift shooting range. He'd fallen asleep as soon as they got upstairs. His boots sat untied on his feet.

"You think there's more socks in there from the girls?"

"If there is, I'm claiming the one with the red border again. Maybe there's another letter in it."

"You're not going to share?"

"Every man for himself. Get your own pen pal. But I will let you read anything she sends."

"Whatever you say. Maybe I'll start writing one of *your* sisters."

"Too late. They're both engaged. Mom's over the moon. Double wedding planned for after the new year. You missed your chance, buddy. Though I'd trade you any day for the drip my oldest sister is going to marry."

The moon had shifted since they first started talking, and its light rested now on the package as the rest of the room sat in silhouette.

"Are you thinking what I'm thinking?" asked William.

Tom shook his head. "We can't. It has John's name on it."

"What, are you getting lawyerly on me now? You know we share all the goods anyway. John won't mind. Besides, we have an early day. There won't be time to properly appreciate it if we wait."

William was right. He knew John would encourage them to open it. But it still felt funny. And yet, after William's revelation, this was just the kind of distraction he probably needed.

William picked his army knife off the bureau next to him and leaned over to slice open the top of the box.

"Oh, look at that! My knife slipped. Right through the twine."

Tom laughed and shook his head in disbelief. "I guess we don't really have a choice now."

"I guess we don't."

William finished cutting it open in perfect, clean lines. When he removed the top piece, he smiled at what he saw.

Nestled on top of everything else the box contained sat a pair of gray socks with a red border. And in it, another note from Margaret.

William looked it over and then handed it to Tom.

Dear William, she'd written.

I've been thinking about how the sun rises for you five hours before it does for us.

And by the time you see the moon, your day has been spent while ours has yet to fully play out.

I have spent much time lately looking at the sky. Its constancy is an anchor when I don't know what the news of tomorrow will bring. The one gift that the dimout presents to us is that we can see the stars from our windows. Something previously unknowable in a Brooklyn lit at all hours of the day and night by streetlights and headlights and factories that never close.

But even the patient and sharp-eyed observer will learn that the stars change too. The ancients saw pictures in them and turned them into gods. The navigators of old set their courses by their placement.

Tom felt a shiver go through him. William was right. This was no ordinary girl.

William smiled, no doubt appreciating her philosophical

musings as much as Tom did. "What a dolt I am. I waited too long to write her back. And now I can't. That kind of letter deserves a response."

He held up his hand, the bruising on it looking worse by the hour. Tom continued to be concerned that he wouldn't get help for it, but since William was being stubborn on that point, Tom wanted to assist in any way he could think of.

"Don't worry about that. I'll write her for you."

Tom pulled out some paper and tried three pens before finding one that worked.

"What do you want to say?"

William shrugged. "How every letter starts, I guess."

"Dear Margaret."

CHAPTER SIX

The midwife approached Margaret, Gladys, and Oliver, stepping carefully over a large crack in the sidewalk that sprouted small shoots of weeds. The disrepair of it felt like metaphor.

"How is she?" Margaret asked. The worried look on Catherine's face unnerved her.

Catherine took Margaret's hands in her own but looked up at Oliver before speaking.

He seemed to understand what she was inferring.

"I'm going to go pick up some things at the market over there. I'll be right back."

Margaret was relieved at his discretion. Though she was grateful that he'd come to their aid, and amused by Gladys's unexpected interest in him, there were some things that seemed too delicate to discuss in front of a man. She watched him walk away, long paces that weren't long enough, her heart racing with impatience.

When he was beyond earshot, she turned back to Catherine. "Tell us everything."

Gladys looped her arm through Margaret's and pulled her close.

"The baby is fine," began Catherine. "Your friend had what we call 'spotting.' It's normal at this stage of the pregnancy, though it can seem frightening."

Margaret let out a huge sigh with breath that had begun to make her lungs ache.

"And Dottie?" asked Gladys. Margaret noticed the quiver in her voice, a departure from the always-confident woman she knew. In a strange way, it was a relief to not be alone in her concern.

Catherine continued with reassurance. "Dottie will be fine as well. But she's very weak. She has all the signs of being anemic—fatigue, cold extremities, pale skin. If that is not remedied soon, I believe these fainting spells will become more frequent."

"What can we do to take care of her?" Margaret felt the surge of powerful instinct to protect Dottie and the baby. She suddenly understood how a mother would think nothing of standing between a charging bull and her own child. Or how men like her brother John could go into battle.

Because if Margaret could trade places with Dottie right now, she would.

The midwife finally smiled. "She will greatly benefit from iron-rich foods. As much as she can handle. Which is difficult, I understand, in the early weeks when it's hard to keep anything down at all. But maybe with support from her friends, she'll be able to do it. Spinach. Beans. Red meat. Fish. Chocolate."

Gladys's chest puffed out at that last word. "We'll have

no problem getting chocolate for her. I have some squirreled away."

Margaret nodded. "And I'm sure we can trade some ration coupons for the other items. Certainly we could find someone willing to trade coffee coupons for spinach."

George came to mind. He would do anything for Dottie. But Margaret wouldn't want to take advantage of his generosity that way. How would he even take the news that Dottie was with child? Though he would never interfere with her engagement to John, certainly the discovery would have a finality to it that made Margaret sad for him. If John weren't her brother, if he and Dottie weren't so in love, she would have been happy to see her and George together.

Gladys pulled her arm from Margaret's.

"She's going to stay with me," she declared.

Margaret looked at her, surprised. Though she lived alone—the only girl they knew who did—Gladys's basement room was barely large enough for one. It housed her small bed, a couch she'd rescued from a sidewalk, a table, and a cabinet whose doors were missing. By some miracle, though, she had her own shower and toilet and didn't have to share that with anyone else in the brownstone. Which made it all worth it.

Despite the limitations, she'd turned her place into something that felt surprisingly homey. Her flair for embellishment came not only from her mouth but also from her hands. Still, Margaret couldn't imagine how another person could fit.

"But you said there were places she could get help," said Margaret.

"There are. And I've visited some of them. They're all right when there are no other options and they mean very well.

But now that I'm picturing her in one of them, I'm not sure I can stomach it. I'd rather be squeezed than to feel guilty when I could have done something."

"Where would she sleep?" asked Margaret.

"On the bed. I'll take the couch."

"I'd thought about this before, but she could come to our house. And stay in John's room. That would seem fitting."

"And you can somehow promise her that your parents won't tell her parents that she is expecting a baby?"

Gladys was right. That was a wrinkle. There would be no disguising the fact that something was amiss with Dottie, and though Margaret's parents would welcome the news despite the circumstances, they would not feel right about keeping it from the Troutwines. At least in this case, Dottie could just say that she was rooming with Gladys for a while. That alone would scandalize them—moving out before being married— but it was better than the near certainty that she would otherwise be sent away and forced to put her child up for adoption. This gave Dottie, Margaret, and Gladys some time to consider contingencies and make plans.

And it might make their Saturday evening knitting nights easier. Her father was reluctant to let them keep using the shop, given the dimout rules.

Catherine looked at her watch. "I'm so glad you came for me and that I was able to help. But I have another appointment to go to. Dr. Feingold will leave his office address and phone number with Dorothy. Please encourage her to call him if she needs to. Day or night. And even to come in for regular visits. A baby has the best chance if the mother is seen by a doctor throughout her confinement."

Gladys didn't have a telephone of her own, but there was a party line in the hallway of her building. Even if someone was using it, surely they would relinquish it in the case of an emergency.

Margaret and Gladys thanked Catherine and she refused when they offered to pay her. Yet another time today when the kindness of a stranger had dispelled the gloom of war, reminding Margaret that there was more goodness in the world than not. Out of the corner of her eye, she could see Oliver lingering outside the door of the market, seeming to wait for the right time to rejoin their group.

And when he did, he'd brought four oranges, one for each of them.

Margaret was grateful that the new position in the engraving department began on Monday. She'd sent word to the head of the sewing wing that she and Dottie would be unable to finish out the week, confident that they had already heard the news and were counting on them leaving anyway. She cringed at the loss of a few days' wages, but nothing was more important than taking care of Dottie and the baby. And she'd make it up in time with the money from the promotion. She came in the early hours while Gladys was at work and then spent the afternoons shopping for things she could make for their dinners.

It was no small task, and one that was beholden to the old trial-and-error method. Dottie's baby let its aversions be known, which included nearly everything that was supposed to be good for it. Dottie couldn't hold down the beans, no matter how Margaret cooked them. And the mere smell of red meat had Dottie rushing for the toilet. They hit the jackpot, though, at the discovery that she could, in fact, withstand the two things they thought would have been the worst offenders: spinach and fish.

Fresh spinach was nearly impossible to come by at this time of year, or so they thought, until, near the end of the week, a paper bag with two ribbon-wrapped bunches of it appeared at Gladys's front door with a note attached.

> *Gladys—You deserve roses, but I think you might appreciate this instead. A friend of mine has a victory garden growing in his rooftop greenhouse. I talked him out of a few bunches for now and will use my very persuasive powers to finagle more. Similarly, I'm hoping to use them to talk you into going to dinner again with me on Friday night. I'll come by at seven o'clock with high hopes.*
>
> *—Oliver*

Dottie was glad for the gift. Gladys feigned nonchalance, though her friends knew better. And Margaret was happy to look up a word that had not yet appeared in the *New York Times*—finagle.

"Come on. Hand it over. There are no secrets in the Sock 'Em Club."

"The Sock 'Em Club?" Margaret slid William's letter deeper into her coat pocket as she asked the question of Gladys. Instead, she picked up her latest project, blue socks in a new pattern that Dottie had shown her. With the red border, of course.

"Yeah. If we're going to be spending our time here knitting socks like old ladies, I figured we needed to call it something. It has two meanings. By sending socks to the boys, we're sockin' it to Hitler."

"Are we ten years old again?"

"Humor me, doll. You and Dots have known each other since you were kids. Let me in on some of the fun."

Margaret smiled. "I like it. But you're the last person I would have thought would want to revert to childhood things. I thought you sprung out of the womb all grown up, heels, cigarettes, and all."

Gladys plumped her curls and spiraled one around her finger until it bounced back into place. Despite work and knitting nights and taking care of Dottie, Gladys made no revision to her nighttime routines.

"Don't be deceived by appearances," she scolded. "If we're honest, we all wish we lived back in a time when we had no worries and other people took care of things for us."

"Ah, yes. But then you wouldn't have this den of iniquity all to yourself."

Gladys scoffed. "Hardly to myself. My friend got knocked up and took over my bed. Put a real cramp in my love life."

Margaret held back a smile. Despite all of Gladys's posturing, Margaret knew that neither of them had spent a night with a man. As for Margaret, she rather liked the romantic notion of waiting until she was married. And Gladys's opinions about the superiority of womankind set a standard that only the most remarkable of men would be able to meet. So far, none had. Though Oliver held some promise.

Dottie walked out of the tiny bathroom and seemed to have heard everything they were saying.

"Don't let her fool you, Margaret. Gladys is a mother hen deep down, and I don't know what I'd do without her."

"I know it," Margaret acknowledged. "She's just such fun to tease."

Gladys sank into the little couch and patted the cushion next for her, inviting Margaret to sit. Dottie crossed the room and sat back on the bed that had become her own.

"Now," said Gladys in a firm tone. "Cough it up. I want to see that letter."

"What letter?" asked Margaret. She really didn't mind them seeing it, but it was fun to antagonize Gladys.

"Don't play dumb with me. It's from the boy in John's unit, right?"

Margaret knew that if she didn't turn it over, Gladys would have no compunctions about grabbing it by force, even if Margaret had put it down the front of her blouse.

"I'll give it to you if you tell us whether or not you're going out with Oliver again."

Gladys folded her arms and sank back into the tweedy fabric. "Well, as I haven't made up my mind yet, there's not much to tell."

Dottie spoke up. "I'm declaring Rule Number One. There are no secrets in the Sock 'Em Club, Gladys. You've read and reread Oliver's little note more times than I can count.

And last time you went to dinner with him, you came home blushing like a freshly picked apple."

"Elizabeth Arden, darling. It's the rouge I put on my cheeks."

Margaret pulled William's letter from her pocket and handed it to Gladys. "Here. In good faith. And in the hopes that you say yes to Friday night. Don't get too excited, though. William's a boy who is overseas and at war for the first time. He says all the things you might expect from one in that circumstance."

Gladys snatched it from her fingers with more force than was required, as Margaret was readily giving it up.

Dear Margaret, she read out loud.

Thank you for sending another letter. And more socks. I am under no illusions that you writing to me was mere happenstance. When I pressed, Tom admitted that your brother had asked specifically for you to do so, as I have yet to receive letters from home. But don't write to me out of pity. I am bunked with the two best guys in the world and I am good. Still, receiving your notes has been a delightful surprise.

I hope you'll continue sending them.

I know John has written to you all about me and our buddy Tom. So I won't bore you with the kinds of trivialities that read like a resume. Tom said that girls like to hear about what we're feeling and there's plenty of that to share.

So here you go. A slice from the life of a soldier far from his own shores.

Have you ever given thought to what lies outside of that which you were born into? I'm from Arlington, you're from Brooklyn, so we're both children of the cities. And I never believed I'd be anything else. In other areas of my life, I've had to give great consideration as to where I fit in. But not in regard to geography.

Until now. Last night, we woke up to a clatter behind the house. A fox had broken through the fence and was preying on the chickens in the coop. I had no idea what to do, so I opened the window and started yelling. Which did absolutely nothing to deter it.

Then, a rooster flew out of the coop. It is not made for significant flight, but he managed to elevate himself above the fox's head and spread his wings and scare it away. It's a sight that I'd never imagined, let alone expected to see, but it is just one of the many things that are enlightening to me about country life.

Chilton Foliat is about as far from a big city that one can imagine. Teasel flowers instead of traffic. Crickets instead of car horns. I can feel the charm of the village casting its spell on me.

John encourages both of us to stop and quite literally smell the flowers. I think Tom picked up the habit right away. I am a late bloomer to the notion, if you'll excuse the pun.

John and Tom. I've always had my family. But now I have friends. Brothers. I don't know what I'd do without them.

Training takes up nearly all our waking hours, and we come back to the Browns' house in the evening, where Mrs. Brown has dinner and a pudding ready for us. (Did you know that the British call just about anything sweet a 'pudding'? Hers is more like flaky bread.) John and Tom are as exhausted as I am, and we have some cigarettes and whiskey and go to bed to do it all over again.

We've been plucked from all that is familiar and placed in this foreign land where certain horrors lie in wait in the months ahead. I try not to think about it, though it's what we train for every day. But we're doing it together. My words for that feeling are inadequate, but it is something akin to "whole."

Likewise, the packages that you and your friends send are more welcome than you know. It may seem like a trifling thing—knitting socks for soldiers you've never met. But, speaking for myself, it means everything. I'm glad you told me that the red border you put in yours comes from your grandmother's sweater. And the stories you shared about what she means to you. It's something to anticipate. Something that makes me feel like I matter to somebody.

Tell your friend Dorothy that John is doing well. He keeps her picture pinned to his pillow, which has merited endless razzing from myself and Tom. Some of the soldiers are like cats on the prowl and some of the English girls are all too willing to make their acquaintance. But John is as loyal a fiancé as Dorothy could hope to have. Tom is a country boy who must have had too many fairy tales read to him as a child, because he says he's holding out for true love. And me—well, I'd rather spend a free evening with those two knuckleheads than in a pub chasing skirts.

Thanksgiving is upon us. Which of course, they don't celebrate here. But I can imagine that my mother is already selecting the perfect cranberries for her sauce. I hope that yours is a good one and that you have many things to be grateful for. As for me, I'm grateful for you.

All the best,
William

P.S. Tom just protested that he never said the words "true love" and that I made that up to make him sound like a juvenile. Full confession—I did. But it's still my observation of him. Tom's going to find himself a nice girl someday and she can be relieved to know that she's getting one of the good ones.

P.P.S. Congratulations on the Yankees win! Four to one. Pretty impressive. Nice of Joltin' Joe DiMaggio to enlist, but I hear they're keeping him stateside. Couldn't have a star baseball player getting a scratch on him, right?

At the bottom of the page lay a sketch of a purple flower that looked like a thistle. *A teasel flower*, it said next to it. *In case you didn't know what it looks like.*

"My, my, my," Gladys pronounced as she set the letter down. "Aren't you the little vixen, Margaret Beck? You and your soldier boy sound like you're getting pretty cozy with each other."

Dottie rolled her eyes and tossed a pillow at Gladys. "There is not one word in there that suggests that Margaret and William are anything more than friends."

Gladys held the letter close to her face and reread one line with dramatic inflection. "*I feel like I matter to somebody.*"

"I found that rather sweet," Dottie responded. "But nothing more than that. I know Margaret. We'll realize that the right man has come her way when she gets a particular kind of smile on her face."

Margaret turned her head toward Dottie. "What do you mean?"

Dottie set down the sock she'd been knitting and looked up in the air before deciding what to say. "I've only seen it a few times, but when you *really* like something, you get a crooked smile. The right side of your mouth stretches all the way to your cheekbone. And the left side is almost its mirror—but you hold just a bit of it back. As if whatever it is might be too good to be true."

Margaret wrinkled her eyebrows and couldn't imagine what Dottie was describing. Wasn't a smile just a smile?

"Oh yes! I know what you're talking about," said Gladys as she clapped her hands. "I've seen it maybe three times. Once when there was a spectacular sunset a few years back after that storm that took out some houses in Long Island. When you tasted cotton candy for the first time at Coney Island. And whenever Cary Grant came on the screen in *Penny Serenade*. Or any other movie that he's in."

It surprised Margaret that they knew her so well. Better than she knew herself. "That's silly," she protested, though. "Anyone would smile over those things."

"Cary Grant is no thing, doll. He's a tall, dark, and handsome drink of water."

"But he's not real. I mean, to people like us. And a sunset or cotton candy. They're as ordinary as they come."

"That's your charm, though, Margaret," added Dottie. "You're not moved by the extraordinary. It's the everyday things that put that particular smile on your face."

"Did it happen when I read William's letter?" Margaret didn't feel like his words evoked anything more than the warmth of camaraderie, but it was also difficult to judge oneself with accuracy.

"No," Gladys conceded. "You did smile. But it's not your special one."

Dottie returned to her original conversation. "And there you have it, Gladys. Just because your head is in the clouds over Oliver doesn't mean that every friendship between a man and a woman has to be anything more than that."

"My head is *not* in the clouds over Oliver, no matter what you two girls have been dreaming up. I'm just saying that this boy clearly, let's say, holds Margaret in high regard."

"As he should," Dottie confirmed. "And he seems to think the same of his friends too. How nice for the three of them to have been assigned together. From what John tells me in his letters, he thinks he's bunking with the best two guys in the 101st Airborne."

"Still," Gladys continued, waving the paper in the air. "It's not inconceivable that a romance could bloom on these flimsy little pages. Am I wrong?" She held them up to the light, and indeed, they were quite translucent. "Wow," she said. "Let's hope this friendship—or whatever you're calling it—is built on something stronger than these. I couldn't blow my nose on paper like this."

"Don't be crass, Gladys," Dottie admonished. "You know that they have to be light because of the cost of air mail."

Margaret shifted in her seat, eager to deflect the direction of the conversation. "I, for one, think Gladys is stalling from answering the more important question."

"Which is?" Gladys raised her eyebrows.

"Are you or are you not going out with Oliver on Friday?"

"For a woman in a weakened condition, you sure are unrelenting."

"I learned from the best."

Gladys folded the letter and gave it back to Margaret. "Margaret, tell our friend that I'm not the sort to have a man lead the dance."

Margaret grinned. "If the right one comes along, you just might."

Dottie threw her hands in the air. "Hot off the presses! The Sock 'Em Club to welcome Oliver on Friday night! Check out the evening edition for details."

CHAPTER SEVEN

$\mathcal{T}$he weather was too foggy for a jump, so some company commanders let their men have the day off to explore the town of Swindon. Others ordered their men to perform maintenance on Littlecote. But not Easy Company. Sobel saw it as a matter of pride that his troops worked longer, harder hours than anyone else.

So despite not being able to see two feet in front of them, William, John, Tom, and the rest of the company endured a ten-mile march through Hungerford. Full gear. One canteen to last for the day.

"Because water is for weenies," John said halfway in, paraphrasing various forms of misery that Sobel seemed to enjoy putting them through.

"I'm *hunger ford* a sirloin steak right now," William joked.

Tom rolled his eyes. "Is it too late to exchange roommates?"

"If you do, we're keeping the Browns. I'm not giving up her puddings just because you can't handle a pun." John patted him on the shoulder.

"Nah, I'm not giving them up either. I guess I'm stuck with you two."

"Hey, save your breath," huffed William. "If Sobel hears us talking, he'll double the hike."

"Sobel can—" John started.

"Don't say it. You're better than that." Though Tom conjured several words that could have easily followed that sentence.

They kept walking. Tom felt the sharp pain of a pebble in his boot, but he knew better than to remove it. If he stopped, Sobel would make them all pay by adding miles, and he couldn't do that to his fellow soldiers.

At last they came to the end, finishing up at Aldbourne, exhausted and feeling chilled as their sweat mingled with the crisp air. Tom hoped they'd be able to spare a Willys Jeep to take them back to Chilton Foliat.

"Easy Company," Sobel barked. "Now that you have finished the hike, a hike you did in record poor time, I might add, we are going to test your skills on the range. We will split up into two teams. The team with the highest combined accuracy will be able to join the other lazy companies in Swindon for the remainder of the day. The losers will be on latrine duty at Littlecote. I asked them to save that job especially for Easy."

Groans could be heard throughout the company.

"Any complaints will automatically put you with the losing party."

Tom swung his rifle around and sighed. There was no use arguing, as much as he wanted to. He looked at First Lieutenant Dick Winters, hoping for a flicker of dissent. All the men agreed that Winters would make a far better leader, and Tom wondered what had been said when Winters had gone up the chain of command to complain on their behalf. But, excellent soldier that he was, he would never publicly disagree with an order.

The three of them were put on the same team along with Malarky, Muck, and several others who were good marksmen, so Tom felt confident that they would earn the night off. He'd not yet been to Swindon, but he'd heard that it had some good dance clubs, and he could use a beer.

"William, what about your hand?" It had not yet healed and, in fact, had swelled into something worrisome. The long hike surely hadn't helped.

He held it up and shrugged. It was red and puffy, and the strain on William's face showed that he was in a lot of pain.

"You can't shoot like that. You really need to see a medic."

"And let the team down and have Sobel revoke the leave for everyone? Not on your life."

"It could be *your* life if you're not careful."

William walked past him and took his position at the range. He balanced his rifle on his bad arm and used his left hand to pull the trigger.

He was off, hitting the outer rim of the target.

John stepped in. "Tom is right. You need to go see a medic. Today. Now."

He ignored them and switched hands. He pulled the trigger with his bad one.

Almost a bull's-eye. Even with a bum hand, William was a decent shot.

Malarky was about to take his place on the line when

William suddenly fell back in pain. The recoil had been the last straw. He curled up, holding his hand to his chest.

"Easy Company, back to your places," Sobel barked.

Dick Winters ran over.

"He needs to see a doctor," Tom offered. "I can drive him."

Winters patted him on the shoulder. "You do that. There's a Willys to the right of the range. Take that."

"I can go with you," said John.

"You know Sobel's not going to let both of us go. Shoot your best. Go to Swindon. And have a pint for me."

The medic's station in Aldbourne was a brown bricked building, one story tall with a steep roof. It looked like all of the other structures nearby and it could only be identified by the small white sign with black letters indicating what it was. The military was not known for its creativity nor for its architecture. Uniformity and cost were its values. Tom wondered what the British do with these when the war was over. They certainly held none of the charm of the surrounding towns.

He pulled the brake on the Willys Jeep and hopped out, coming around to the other side to help William down. The fog had lifted in the afternoon sun and it had been an easy drive over.

"It's my hand, not my legs," William complained. "I can get there on my own."

"Suit yourself."

Tom walked closely behind him, though, as they approached the door.

Once in, he saw that it was an orderly space. Few patients were waiting to be seen as Airborne had not yet been in combat and were only experiencing training scrapes. From what he observed, William was in the worst shape, a conclusion agreed upon by the register nurse.

"Private Farlane," the doctor said after examining him. "You have yourself a broken hand. When did this happen?"

"A few weeks ago."

The doctor pursed his lips. "I suspect that when you first injured it, there was just a fracture. The bulk of your problem is that you let it go and kept working through it."

Tom withheld an *I told you so.*

"Just soldiering on, sir," William replied. He winced in pain as the doctor began wrapping it.

"There's soldiering on and there's stupid, son. I admire your effort to stay in the game. But you'll be no good to anyone if you let things like this go in the future."

"Yes, sir. It's not something you'll send me home for, is it?"

At the beginning of training, Tom knew that most boys would have gladly taken an injury that was just bad enough to send them home and just good enough to have no long-term consequences. He'd originally had that impression of William. But the Airborne weeded out the boys from the men, and by the time they'd arrived on the shores of England, they were a band of brothers, toughened and determined to stay in the fight. He was proud of William for how much he'd grown.

The doctor grinned. "I like your spirit, Private. Don't worry. You can resume some duties with the cast—not jumping, of course—but if you treat it properly, you should be doing much better in a few weeks and you'll be good as new in a few months."

Tom watched a mix of emotions wash over William's face. *Months* seemed like a long prognosis, but the good news was that William could stay. Sobel might try to send him elsewhere, but Tom was confident that Dick Winters would stand up for him and find work in some capacity. William had trained hard and by the time they were called up, he'd be ready.

If he took care of himself. Which Tom and John would insist upon.

The doctor left them, saying a nurse would be in to complete the cast.

The sun was growing low through the window, and Tom hoped that their team had made it to Swindon.

"Well, looks like I'm going to need a little help." William sighed, lying back on the cot.

"Just as long as you can shower and piss by yourself. But anything beyond that, yeah, I'll help."

"Ha-ha, Tom. Very funny. I mean writing to Margaret."

Tom nodded. For the couple of letters William had written to the girl in Brooklyn, he had dictated and Tom had volunteered his handwriting. He'd also drawn the teasel flower on the first letter and a primrose on the second. Now he seemed to have established a pattern—one she might be looking forward to—and he wondered what he might find to sketch today.

"What day is it?" asked William.

"Friday."

"That means there's a mail plane leaving tonight. Can you help a chap out and write again so that I don't have to wait another week to send a letter off to Margaret?"

"Chap?" Tom smiled. "Sure, ol' pal. I'll ask the register nurse for some paper."

Tom stood up, but William grabbed his arm with his good hand.

"Tom? Promise me no matter what that Margaret always gets letters. She's a nice girl and she deserves it."

"I promise."

The register nurse didn't have the sort of paper needed for international mail, so Tom walked to several of the offices until he found one that could oblige. By the time he got back, William's cast had been set, but his friend was sleeping soundly.

He put the paper aside, but then reconsidered. William had been adamant that the letter go out tonight rather than waiting a week. And, knowing what letters from home meant to the soldiers, he imagined that Margaret might also be eagerly awaiting the next one. He and William lived the same details of the same days. Surely he could conjure up what his friend might want to say.

Dear Margaret, he began.

Though he'd written the words several times before, a liberating sensation came over him. The chance for this to be his own, as if he were writing in a diary. Which he might as well have been. Margaret was just a name on paper—faceless to him. Anonymous, save for her brother's stories and her compelling observations in the few letters that William had received. Tom felt like he could say anything to her.

It was not as if they would ever meet. It was not as if his name would be signed at the bottom.

I didn't know until coming to England that fog has an ever-changing personality. It can be thick as oatmeal, nearly suffocating you when you step into its opaque mist. It can be translucent, distorting your vision of reality. It can be dangerous—our planes were grounded today. And yet, in the right circumstance, I can see how it has crafted for itself a permanent place as a character in old-time British novels.

I've learned that you can't light a fireplace in such weather—the heaviness of the fog acts as a closed flue, sending smoke into a home.

I imagine that war is a similar entity. Difficult days surely lie ahead of us. And yet, it has also bred friendships unlike those I have never known before. The men I'm serving with— I would die for them. And they for me.

Today's weather has lifted at last and the sun has set so low that all that remains is a purple glow through which the small buildings surrounding me look like silhouetted dots. Fickle thing that fog is, tomorrow morning is expected to be clear and sunny and excellent for flying.

That is how I have to think of the future. As a sunrise, full of promise.

Tom laid the pen down and reread the words, surprised that there was an almost poetic tone to them. He'd earned high grades in his literature classes at University of Virginia, but not until now did he realize how the lyrical writings of the classic books he loved could permeate a man's thoughts when they were bent toward such musings.

He thought again that there was such freedom in this exercise. The favor to William was a gift to Tom as well, and he was almost envious that his friend had this outlet of writing to the girl in Brooklyn. Maybe Tom would find a pen pal of his own as soon as William had recovered enough to resume his correspondence.

Tom looked at the large clock on the wall. Ten till seven and the mail plane left at seven-thirty. He scribbled *Your friend, William* at the bottom, disappointed that there was no time to ask her how she was doing. Surprised that he would really like to know.

He thought about the garden around the Browns' house and sketched a quick water violet at the bottom. They were nearly all white, so he could make it beautiful without the benefit of the colored pencils he had back at the house.

He addressed the envelope, having memorized Margaret's address from the previous letters.

Satisfied that it was the best he could do for William, he hurried out of the medic's office and dropped the letter in one of the mailbags just as they were being loaded onto the propellered plane.

CHAPTER EIGHT

November 1943

*M*argaret had been working in the engraving department for several weeks when a new letter from William arrived at her house.

Her mother had begun to notice the air mail letters that arrived with frequency. And that they put a smile on Margaret's face. Although not *the* smile, as her friends had pointed out. In fact, the discussion at Gladys's apartment had caused her to scrutinize her facial reactions ever since. To their credit, she became aware that the movement of muscles was a symphony unto itself. And that indeed, the very word *smile* was a rather generic term for something that had endless variations.

It made her wonder—would she ever meet a man who garnered that reaction? Now that she was aware of it, it was apparent that Dottie had a special look when talking about John. And Gladys—though she would deny it—had a particular expression when talking about Oliver.

Until then, she had her friendship with William. Which was really all she wanted at the moment. New opportunities for women were opening up every day, and she felt she was standing at the dawn of a new age that she dearly wanted to be a part of.

Gladys was poised to place herself in this new world full-force, rectifying the wrongs that had been done to her mother, be it through political means or bringing issues to light in the public sphere. Dottie was going to be a mother herself soon enough and would certainly follow the path of so many women generations before her. Staying home and raising her children.

Margaret saw the beauty in both. This was her time to discover what it was she wanted.

"Are you sure you're not sweet on this boy?" her mother asked one afternoon. She'd just taken the wooden spoon out of her pot of vegetable soup and tasted it. She sprinkled some salt and returned to stirring.

"He's just a friend," Margaret had answered, tiring of the question. Why was romance the assumed motivation behind any interaction with the opposite gender? "You know how much John likes to hear from us. William likes letters too. I'm sure they all do."

"Is he the one you knit the socks for?"

"Yes. But I send some to John and their other roommate, Tom, as well."

"They must have the warmest feet in all of England!"

Margaret grinned. "I certainly hope so. And we're well on our way to making enough for their whole company. If it takes cozy toes to defeat Hitler, then you can be damn sure I'll knit until my fingers fall off."

"Margaret Jane Beck!" her mother scolded. "Did you pick up that kind of language at the Navy Yard?"

She would be scandalized to know that *damn* was the least of what Margaret heard the men at the Navy Yard say. And some of the women.

"Sorry, Mom. It just slipped out."

Margaret climbed the narrow steps until she got to her bedroom, enjoying the scent of the simmering soup and already thinking about dinnertime. She shut the door and ran some scissors along the top of the envelope.

The familiar handwriting was such a source of peace for her. It was very neat, as if William was well practiced in the art of it. Though given the beautiful flower sketches he'd been including at the end of every letter, it made sense that he would be elegant with a pen.

John's handwriting looked like chicken scratch in comparison.

The Browns surprised us with an American-style Thanksgiving, William wrote.

> *Remarkably, they'd saved and traded ration coupons for weeks in order to do so. They kept the secret well! John said that Mrs. Brown made apple pie even better than your mom does (though don't tell her he said so), and Tom and I had to agree that she'd bested our mothers as well. She'd never made it before, she insisted, and I don't know her secret, but we're hoping that she'll bake another even though the holiday is over. Maybe we'll look ahead to Christmas.*

She read the rest of the letter—a tome on Tom's surprising talent for playing cards, with gin rummy being his favorite—and a few new words for her to ponder. She pulled out a fresh sheet of paper. It took no effort to think about what to say to William. The words flowed as if they were having a conversation over a pot of coffee. Or tea, as it would be if they were visiting in England.

Thank you for the additions to my word list, she penned. *I wouldn't have known how different our two English languages could be. "Jumper" where we'd say "sweater." "Lift" where we'd say "elevator."*

She'd paused when his list included the word *nappie* for diaper. Dottie had begged her not to tell John about the baby, lest he be worried and distracted as they headed into war. Margaret disagreed. She knew that her brother would be exhilarated by the news that he was going to have a son or daughter and that the knowledge of it would make him even more determined to come home safely. But Dottie's role as fiancée bested Margaret's as sister and so far, Margaret had respected her wishes.

Keeping the news quiet was even more difficult on the home front. Dottie had rebounded from the anemia better than they could have hoped and had bolstered herself enough to make it to the first day of their new work at the Navy Yard. The nausea and frequent morning trips to the toilet had initially kept her figure slim, but her appetite was finally beginning to keep pace with her condition, and she had started to let out the waists of her dresses. It would not be much longer before she'd have to make new clothes altogether.

When it was announced that Dottie was moving in with Gladys, Mrs. Troutwine entered a crying spell, accusing her daughter of being a *modern woman* as if that were pejorative. Mrs. Troutwine was still reeling, perhaps, over her first daughter's untimely pregnancy some years back, and it set her on a course of additional rigidity with Dottie. But all the wrath Dottie had incurred from that decision was nothing in comparison to the fear of being sent away if her mother found out the truth too early.

So Dottie's concerns were legitimate. But Margaret didn't see where the harm was in telling her brother.

She looked down at what she'd written so far. After several rounds of back-and-forth, the letters between her and William had grown well beyond introductory exchanges, and she discovered that they shared a mutual sense that the war was going to change everything they'd come to expect for their lives.

She found it a bit like writing in a diary, save for the kinds of intimacies one would keep for their own eyes. William might have been flesh and blood, but he was thousands of miles away and really only took shape in the curves and strokes of the ink with which he wrote. John had asked her to send a picture so he could show the boys what his sister looked like, and she'd included one in a recent box. Though she didn't reveal that she'd had one specially done rather than find one that was already lying around. Gladys had done her hair and makeup for it. Restrained, at Margaret's request, so that she looked natural but *enhanced*. She'd even embroidered a little design on her collar to freshen up its plain look.

She still didn't know what he looked like, though. And contrary to Gladys's ribbing or her mother's inquiries, there was nothing on the pages that suggested a budding romance between them. But that didn't mean that she didn't want to have his image pinned to her wall. She could say good night to her friend and give shape to her prayers for his safety with more ease if she knew the particulars of his face.

I'm glad you liked the photograph, she continued.

I'll send another once we've put our Christmas tree up. Did John ever tell you that he likes to take pictures? Before the war, he worked in our father's cobbler shop, but he got up extra early to deliver the Brooklyn Daily Eagle *because he wanted to buy a camera and have money left over to develop the film. How I wish he'd become a war correspondent instead of a paratrooper, but you know my brother as well as anyone at this point. He's not going to be talked out of anything he sets his mind to.*

And I guess he wouldn't have met you and Tom then. Still, his interest was our gain. We have more photographs of our family than most since we're one of the few to have a camera of our own, thanks to John's hard work. Now that I'm working in the engraving department, I enjoy a little extra jingle in my pocket as well and will take some photographs of our Christmas tree to send to John. I'll be sure to tell him to share them with you and Tom.

Margaret glanced at her watch. It was almost time to catch the bus, and she wanted to get the letter out before the mailman arrived. She and William had determined that it took about a week to get a letter from one to the other. This was aided by her location in New York and his in a training area in England. Both were well-traveled mail routes compared to those closer to the front lines. Or deeper west into the United

States. They knew once he headed into combat that delivery would likely be more sporadic.

Sometimes she included the letters in the boxes she and Dottie and Gladys sent. They'd knit about sixty pairs of socks over the Saturday nights, and more men in the company were asking for them. By the time William received this letter—being sent on its own—it would be just a few weeks until Christmas. She would have to think of something special to send for the holiday. Not only for William but also for her brother. And she couldn't leave Tom out. The third Musketeer, to reference the name they'd given themselves. Unoriginal, but meaningful just the same.

She folded the letter and licked the envelope but paused before sealing it up. She turned it over to the part where she'd signed her name and added a postscript.

There is something I must tell you about Dottie. Please don't tell John. But I want one of you to know in case it ever becomes opportune that he should know. A baby is coming . . .

Margaret wrote a few more details and hoped that John wouldn't discover the letter. But instinct formed a knot in her stomach, and it compelled her to share what Dottie didn't yet want to have known. She trusted William to keep it a secret.

She sealed the envelope before she could change her mind and hurried downstairs to slip it into the mailbox on her way to the bus stop.

Engraving ordnance was not unlike embroidering. Instead of needle and thread, her tools were hammers and chisels and gravers. It was not difficult per se, though it did require precision, much like any other kind of handiwork. Currently, they were outfitting the USS *Missouri* with artillery shells for their sixteen-inch guns. When George first told her that this was the kind of ordnance she would be working with, she pictured something akin to pistols that were sixteen inches in length. But before their first shift, George had taken Dottie and Margaret for the closest look at the *Missouri* that they'd ever gotten.

"No," he explained in his kind way that held no trace of condescension. "That measurement refers to the width of the opening of the gun. They're going to be massive, ladies. Bigger than anything we've ever done. Capable of launching rounds as far as twenty miles away and destroying enemy ships with one hit."

He arched his arm against the sky as if envisioning what that might even look like.

Twenty miles. That was like going from Brooklyn to Yonkers.

Though she'd thought herself prepared for it after his description, Margaret was astonished as the first shell casings lay in front of her. They were enormous. Brass behemoths that would be slipped into guns that were sixty-six feet long and weighed nearly four hundred thousand pounds! The USS *Missouri* would be capable of carrying nine of them.

She couldn't imagine that any ship would be able to withstand one of these falling atop of them.

Holding the casings evoked conflicting emotions—that of pride in the might of the United States military. And regret that mankind felt the need to fight one another with them.

George was a patient teacher, so much so that Margaret thought he may have missed his calling. He showed them how to first write on the metal with a pencil what needed to be engraved. Currently, the words were USS MISSOURI, 406MM, BROOKLYN.

After that, they would take their graver—a chisel-like tool with a diamond-shaped head—and trace the block letters from the pencil marking with a light touch that scratched the surface of the shell. Once they were confident in that step, they would retrace it and go deeper until the work was complete.

By the end of the first day, small piles of metal shavings lay around their feet. They were instructed to collect them and put them in a bin at the end of the room. They would then be taken to the ordnance center to be melted down and remolded into more shells.

Nothing was wasted.

The Brooklyn Navy Yard had only a small ordnance department. Around the country, eighty-five thousand women were putting themselves in danger's way by constructing the munitions that would be placed in battle. The two most significant being at Springfield and Harper's Ferry. But Brooklyn boasted its own little version, tucked away at the farthest corner of the Yard in case of explosion.

In that section, George explained, not a speck of dust could be tolerated, as it could set off the gunpowder. Women had to wear uniform shoes that contained no metal, nor could jewelry be worn lest it set off an electric spark. The few married women who refused to take off their rings bound them in tape so as not to expose them to their work.

Margaret couldn't imagine thinking that a ring was important enough to put yourself in such danger. But she wouldn't have to consider either for some time—both the marriage part and the work in the munitions wing. For now, she was glad to work in the safety of the engraving department. One step further in her advancement and something that felt a bit more useful to the war effort than sewing. But her priority now was Dottie and the baby. So she would remain in the safety of this department for as long as possible.

She confided as much to William in their next exchange of letters.

I'm glad you're staying safe, he wrote back.

My sisters have begun their training as nurses and are both hoping for positions overseas. Though I know they won't see front lines, it is still dangerous work. I applaud the doors that the war is opening for women. It's my humble opinion that they are the most capable of our species. But we are inching closer to the day that we will see battle and it does us no good to worry about the women in our lives. My sisters cause me a great deal of sleeplessness as I think of it. So it is a comfort to know that my dear friend Margaret, at least, is protected from the clutches of the worst of this.

You were right to tell me about Dottie and the baby, he continued.

Someone here should know. I've shared this with Tom—the boy is a vault, I promise—and we've already decided to spend

the next few months secretly procuring a supply of cigars so
that when the news of the baby's arrival comes—at which
point we assume that she will have told John—we will have
a proper celebration on our end to welcome the little Beck.

Margaret would include her next reply in a box that she, Dottie, and Gladys were putting together for the boys. This time, it would include Christmas presents. Socks woven in red and green. Scarves and mittens to match. And an assortment of sugared treats she'd bought at Economy Candy in the Lower East Side.

Occasionally, Oliver dropped by with treats for them. As he was an ocean away from his own family, his mother enjoyed sending him packages full of goodies from England. Hard butterscotch candies and bins of loose Earl Grey tea were among Margaret's favorites.

Gladys had refused that Friday night dinner invitation a few weeks ago, leaving a note for him that she was unavailable. But she said that he could come by the following evening if he liked. Margaret knew it was bunk—Gladys had no plans, as they'd called knitting night off so Margaret could take her parents to dinner to celebrate their anniversary. But she liked the idea of keeping him on his toes. Much like having a new puppy, Oliver was hers to train. Dottie found it unseemly, but Margaret knew better. Any man who hoped to capture Hurricane Gladys's attention for more than a few days had to let her set the pace. She was not a filly to be wrangled and any projection of docility would have been unfair to a man seeking tradition in a woman.

It was a test of sorts. And so far, Oliver had passed.

"I know you love writing your beau," Gladys said as the knitting evening convened. Tonight, they'd moved it to the Becks' house, as Gladys's apartment building had suffered a roach infestation and the landlord had ordered everyone out for a few nights.

Margaret rolled her eyes at the misguided statement, but otherwise ignored it. "So I've learned about something new you might want to try. It's called Victory Mail."

"What is it?" asked Dottie. She'd been writing letters twice a week to John and lived for the postman's arrival at Gladys's apartment. Thankfully, John had accepted her explanation that she'd left her own home in order to have the adventure of having a roommate before they got married. Letters were nice like that—it slowed the back-and-forth that conversation would have prompted and it made difficult things easier to gloss over.

"The good news," continued Gladys, "is that we're certainly doing our part keeping up morale over there. So much so that the volume of letters going from one end of the Atlantic to the other is taking up valuable cargo space. So here you go— I've picked up some Victory Mail paper for each of you."

Margaret took the sheet and looked it over. It was thicker than the usual air mail paper, but smaller in size.

Gladys continued. "You write your letter on this paper and they photograph it and put it on microfilm. Then they send the microfilm overseas—much less bulk than thousands of letters— and print them up on the other end in miniature."

Margaret gasped. "That's amazing!"

"Exactly." Gladys took her place on the Becks' afghan-covered sofa and picked up her knitting needles. She'd volunteered at the

Stage Door Canteen last night, so she was game for a mellow evening in with the girls. "I think the letters are about one-quarter size. Eventually, the actual letters make their way over—perfume and lipstick stained—but only as room is available."

Dottie was already five rows in, compared to Margaret's two, amazingly unencumbered by the pillow she'd set across her lap to hide her gently expanding waist. "But won't that be easy for people to read? It seems like your letters would be quite visible that way."

Gladys grinned. "That's why you save all the lovey-dovey mush for the regular letters. But if you have to say something faster, give the Victory Mail a try."

"You sound like an advertisement for them," said Dottie.

"Is that the kind of thanks I get for good information like that?"

Margaret was grateful to have the sheets. They provided a lot less space to write on, but for shorter letters she could definitely send these to William. Another tiny way to do her part. Posters plastered all over New York reminded her that every little bit helped. Some of them were quite clever. Such as *Knock the "Heil" out of Hitler!* And *Let's catch him with his "Panzers" down!*

When the war was over, would they return to the kind of regular life that took small things for granted, or would they forevermore use every piece of a chicken, save every bit of scrap metal, and make a cup of coffee by counting out the exact number of beans that would make the stash last a week?

She hoped not. And yet, it did bring about a sense of appreciation for things that had previously gone unnoticed.

Gladys turned the radio on in time to hear Perry Como croon out the popular songs of the day. Christmas tunes abounded, and though they were mere days past Thanksgiving, it was a cheery thing in these trying times to usher in the favorite holiday as early as possible. Wreaths and boughs were already adorning the front doors of Brooklyn, to Margaret's delight. That the radio hosts were also in on the sentiment was a welcome surprise.

The girls sang out the familiar words of "Joy to the World" and "O Tannenbaum." Gladys had a sparkling voice that could have found a place onstage if she cared to make a career out of it, but as yet she'd declined the chance to entertain the troops at the Canteen. Margaret and Dottie could keep a tune, but with less pizzazz. However, the merriment ended when the radio announcer began a live address across the country:

"What would this season be without a new Bing Crosby hit? Last year, 'White Christmas' became an instant smash and sent children to their windows pleading with Santa Claus to bring snow along with their presents. It's too soon to tell if New York will be blanketed in a winter wonderland, but one thing that we can all agree on is that we miss our boys and girls, whose absence will leave an empty chair or two around our family's table. And with that sentiment, here is Bing with his new one, 'I'll Be Home for Christmas.'"

Margaret adjusted herself on the sofa next to Gladys, basking in the glow of the candles they'd lit and the hot chocolate treat that Gladys had procured. She'd even gotten some milk, though Margaret suspected that was something Oliver had found for her.

Oh, making it with real milk was such a creamy comfort.

I'll be home for Christmas, you can plan on me.

She closed her eyes and pictured a holiday meal where John had returned and he and Dottie were married and their son or daughter sat in a high chair tasting their mother's homemade applesauce. Presents sat under the tree, bestowed with more meaning than in previous years because they'd all come to appreciate the preciousness and fragility of life.

It had been difficult to see his seat remain empty as their mother set the turkey on the table, his favorite sweet potato casserole still made even though he was the only one who liked it.

Margaret hoped this would be the only holiday season they'd have to be without him.

Please have snow and mistletoe and presents under the tree.

Perhaps another year in the future might have her standing beneath the doorframe of the house as winter's flakes began to fall. A man—tall, dark hair, but a face in shadows—pointed to the mistletoe and swept her into his arms as they kissed.

*I'll be home for Christmas, where the love
    light gleams.*

She looked at the faces of Gladys and Dottie, whose expressions mirrored her own dreamy one. Bathed in love light, not merely from the men who cherished them, but also from the friendship they shared with each other. This was the bliss that made the struggles worth it.

I'll be home for Christmas, if only in my dreams.

The last lyric jolted Margaret from her wistful state. John's absence was felt with bitter intensity. He would not be home for Christmas. He would be in another country, across the Atlantic, away from all who loved him. The song had lulled her into the pleasantness of holiday spirit only to pull it from her so heartlessly. Delivered in the false security of Bing Crosby's smooth voice.

The song repeated itself verse by verse, but by this time, she saw that Gladys and Dottie, too, had been similarly affected.

"Well," huffed Gladys. "That's a bubble burst if I ever heard one. Thanks a lot, Bing."

Dottie tugged at one of her stitches. "He didn't write it. He just sings what's given to him."

"And makes a lot of dough doing it, to be sure. Lure me with touching sentiments and then—pow!—remind me of how miserable it will be this Christmas as we're scattered around the globe."

Margaret shrugged. "That just means that next year, we'll

look back on this time and be even more grateful when our families are together again."

Gladys rolled her eyes. "Cut the Pollyanna act. Even if John comes home, how many people do you know whose tables will be forever empty?"

The doorbell rang and Margaret never had a chance to answer.

CHAPTER NINE

Tom was jolted from a deep sleep when John snuck up behind him and started blowing kissing sounds in his ear. The morning sun sent bright streaks of light through their attic bedroom and he shielded his eyes from its brightness.

"Get off me, man," he said. Though it was all in fun. The brotherhood of John, William, and Tom grew every day. And along with it, the teasing.

Tom relished it.

He was the latest target. When William's pen pal, Margaret, had sent her picture a few weeks ago, Tom felt something lurch inside him in a way he'd never felt before. She had long blond hair that appeared white in the photograph. Her eyes, too, were light—probably blue in person like her brother's—and her cosmetics perfectly enhanced her already beautiful features. Though she didn't seem like she'd need them. She was that girl-next-door type that populated his part of rural Virginia, but she had a spark in her eyes that said this was no farm girl.

And that smile. He would love to be the reason a girl smiled like that someday.

William had shared all of her letters with Tom, and through them, he'd come to know this girl whose spirit and heart displayed themselves in black ink on thin paper. He was delighted to discover that she looked as friendly as she sounded in her correspondences.

Tom still wrote the letters back to her, as William's cast remained in place for the time being. So although they were William's dictations, Tom felt an affinity for Margaret Beck as well, his soul pouring its way to the page through the ink almost as if it were all his own. And indeed, he'd embellished here and there with a word she might enjoy learning or a turn of phrase he thought might delight her.

He'd also continued to sketch flowers at the end.

William had insisted that they bring her into the light on that point. He thought Margaret should know that Tom was the artist. And so, in the letter they were about to send out, Tom included a postscript, the third-person nature of it being something he grew ever more used to.

> P.S. Our buddy Tom has a knack for art, so I told him it was time to come clean and tell you that the flowers are from him.

He hoped she enjoyed those little additions.

John continued with the kissing noises.

Sometime in the night, one of them had taken Margaret's picture and pinned it to Tom's pillow. Just like John had Dottie's.

Tom woke up to the little image of the pretty girl from Brooklyn and wondered what it might be like to wake up next to her for real.

And so, the teasing ensued. John did not seem very

protective of his little sister where William and Tom were concerned. Perhaps it was a testament to the trust they had for each other. There was no better way to bond than jumping out of airplanes together. Each time a risk.

Each time, a readiness to die for a brother and for a cause.

Or perhaps distance made the whole thing a dream—and therefore John had nothing to worry about from his buddies where Margaret was concerned.

"Tom Powell is sweet on William's girl," John sang in an off-key melody of his own creation.

"She's not my girl," William piped up. "She my friend. And your sister could do a lot worse than Tom here."

"She could do a lot better."

"Thanks, meathead," Tom said. "Just for that, you have to take my next latrine duty."

"Fair enough. But are you thinking about writing her too?" John asked with sincerity as he sat on Tom's bed. The springs groaned under the added weight.

"Nah. I'll leave that to William. Though it's kind of her to remember me in the packages. William told her that my favorite color is blue, and the next package had a pair of socks in a bag with my name. Blue with a red border."

"I've known her for all of her twenty-two years, Tom. I've heard the chatter between her and Dottie back when they were schoolgirls. And taken them to the movies. Margaret's eyes get a special glisten to them when Cary Grant and his ilk are on the screen."

Tom shrugged. "What's your point?"

He stood up and started unbuttoning his pajama top. Sobel wanted them on the runway at seven o'clock sharp.

"I'm saying that I think you'd be my sister's *type*. Tall. Dark. And, William—is our boy handsome? You're the better judge of that."

William grinned. He'd shared his secret with John shortly after he'd told Tom. Tom and John both assured him that it made no difference. He laced up his bootstraps and jumped from airplanes just like the rest of them and that's all that mattered to them.

Such things were of no consequence when one had pledged to give his life for yours if the situation called for it.

"Definitely handsome," William assessed as he stroked an imaginary beard. "There is a fine symmetry to his face, a slight divot in his chin, and his jaw looks as if it was chiseled in marble by Michelangelo himself."

Tom rolled his eyes and walked over to the washbasin. He looked in the mirror above it. He wouldn't scare any crows from the field any time soon, nor did he think himself to look like a matinee idol. It was difficult to consider oneself honestly. "You two are full of it, you know?" He picked up the bar of lye soap and scrubbed his hands.

Tom knew that all of this was theatrics more than anything. The circumstances of the war made this whole scenario squarely hypothetical and easy fodder for the joking that was common among the men.

John pulled his uniform out of the wardrobe and picked a piece of lint off it. "Okay. Well, that might be an exaggeration on our parts. But you're no slouch, Tom. I think my sister would rather like that mug of yours. And I can't think of any guy I'd rather her go out with."

Tom felt his cheeks warm at the praise and at the very

notion that John would seem so sincere with his approval. It was a welcome thought, although it would amount to nothing in the end. Tom's plan was to stay in the military long after the war was over. He had no idea how a woman would fit into that picture.

"Well, you'll be waiting a long time," he told John. "She's over three thousand miles west of here and as far as I can tell, we're going to be old men by the time we get back home. Besides. She lives in Brooklyn and even when I return to the States, I don't think I'll ever get the country out of my blood."

"Don't be so sure. Love conquers geography."

"Well, the current geography is enough to make this entire conversation pointless."

He checked his watch. They needed to move faster.

They each began to get dressed. William had become adept with doing the task one-handed and would continue his role as radio support on the ground until he could get up in the air again.

Tom worried that today's jumps would be especially precarious given the winds howling outside their bedroom window. Not so much that the glider flights had been canceled, but they would have to take extra care to maneuver their parachutes into the targeted landing zone. Winters believed that unless it was inherently dangerous, every jump would go on as scheduled. Hitler didn't slow his advances based on the weather forecast and neither should they. At least here in England there were no enemies waiting to shoot them down. That was coming, no doubt about it. But for now, their mission was to perfect their skills, no matter what conditions the day brought, so that they'd be ready as soon as Uncle Sam activated them.

Tom could see the wistful look on John's face as he tied his boots and knew he was thinking about Dottie. "It's all well and good to be here with the two of you. But I, for one, can't wait for all this to be over so I can go back to my girl. Dottie and I—we were going to get married and then I got called up. But maybe it worked out better. Now you boys can come to the wedding."

Tom and William exchanged a look. As with all of Margaret's letters, William had showed him the one where Margaret revealed the news about Dottie and the baby. He'd agreed to keep it from John for now, but he didn't like having that kind of news sitting between them, unspoken. The three of them had held back nothing in the dark hours in the English countryside. Except this.

William spoke up. "I'm curious, John. Why didn't you marry her before you shipped out? Lots of boys did. That way they get to, well, you know, *be* with her before leaving if they haven't already. And on a more practical front, as a war widow, she'd have a pension if you bite the dust."

John shrugged. "I asked her. For that very reason. Well, the second one. And she refused."

Tom looked up from buttoning his jacket. "She said she wouldn't marry you?"

"We're definitely getting married. We already had the date planned and the church booked. But it was the other part. The pension. She said that moving the wedding up just to account for something horrible happening made it feel like she was signing my death warrant. Her very words."

"Is she superstitious?" asked William.

"I've never known her to be. But I think war does certain things to people. And she just got it in her head that planning for my death would be, well, *expecting* it, I suppose. Or bringing it about."

"And the other part?" William winked, and Tom blushed at the implication.

"I don't kiss and tell," said John. "But I will say, our goodbye was a special one."

More special than he realizes.

William looked at his watch. "Get the lead out, boys. We're going to be late. And you know how Sobel gets if we're not at the airstrip on the nose."

Training at Camp Toccoa had been unlike anything Tom had ever encountered in rural Virginia. He'd never even been up in an airplane let alone imagined jumping from one. His mother asked him why he'd chosen the Airborne and he gave her some bit about wanting an adventure. But in the quiet moments of the night when he asked himself the same thing, he came up with only this answer: that it was something none of the men in his family before him had ever done.

And therefore, there would be no one to whom he could be compared.

His father, his grandfather, his great-grandfather. They had such illustrious military achievements to their names. All medaled marksmen who could handle rifles with speed and deftness and accuracy. Family photos lined the mantel and certificates of merit hung in expensive frames around their fireplace. Taunting Tom, tempting him since before he could even walk, with the glory of a soldier.

An uncle who'd died in the Battle of Cantigny had his own shrine in the dining room.

It was a history to be proud of. But he'd known them long after the boys they'd been in those days. When they'd been whittled away, no longer the robust and muscular carvings of men who'd seen battle but old men who clung to the glory days and smoked cigars while they told stories of those they'd served with.

Tom was still untested. Patriotism mingled with unspoken fears. Could he do what they'd done? He wasn't sure. But it was expected of him all the same.

Paratrooping offered a unique solution. It was a brand-new division of the army. Neither his father, nor his grandfather, nor his great-grandfather had done it. Nor any of his uncles. And so, they could not worthily comment on his success or his failure at it. Because it would be an experience that was all his.

And what he'd told his mother had turned out to be true. It was an adventure, and he'd begun to understand why the men in his family reminisced with such regularity. His years at college and grad school paled in comparison to the exhilaration of jumping out of an airplane. The utter freedom of it. Even if he spent his career doing it, he knew he would miss the thrill of it once age forced retirement. Not to mention the camaraderie between the men, unlike anything he'd experienced at the university. A mutual pledge of shed blood if war demanded it was a hearty exchange that no study group could replicate.

He'd passed the requirements and medical exams and set off for training. The sticky summer—one of the hottest on record—found him in the swamps of Georgia. Sweating on grids of wood constructed many stories high as they conditioned their bodies into lean perfection. Marched endless miles in the large leather boots specially constructed to strengthen ankles as they landed. They jumped from ten feet, a hundred feet, two hundred feet in succession as they became accustomed to the kind of bounce unique to jumping out of an airplane. They entered wind tunnels designed to blow against their parachutes so they could learn how to maneuver with them on the ground.

They bore the monotony of being instructed on how to fold their parachutes. Bit by bit. With meticulous precision. All the while being told that "on your parachute hangs your life." It felt like a threat, though they knew it to be a warning. They coiled the cords until their vision turned dizzy from spiral upon spiral. Even in their sleep, they folded, coiled, jumped. Repeat.

The first time Tom jumped from an airplane, William and John were right behind him. On that occasion, they'd agreed that among the three of them, the one who landed farthest from the target had to buy the others a round of beer later that night. Or whenever the next opportunity presented itself. The precursor to their competitive arm wrestling.

Men, Tom discovered, were at their best when they had something to prove. Even in the company of friends.

The whir of the plane's propellers made it nearly impossible to hear each other talk, but Tom knew there were no finer two men than the ones on the line behind him.

He jumped. At first, the fall through the wind sounded like thunder. The skin of his cheeks flapped with the fluidity of a flag, and the scant contents of his stomach threatened to resurrect themselves. But at the right altitude, he pulled the cord of his parachute—desperately praying that it would work. And in a second, he was being pulled up higher and higher into the sky before the parachute found its place and he began the gentle glide to the ground.

From the air, he could see green farmland. Jagged ridges of scattered hills. The people waiting below who looked like colonies of ants. And as he descended, all of it grew closer to their proper proportions. He yanked the cords to manipulate his position in the air and landed—*thunk*—within the wide circle of the landing target. The velocity of the action tried to pull him off his feet, but he'd done well in the rehearsals and managed to steady himself.

He gathered the vast white canvas in his arms and looked up. John had jumped behind him and was nearing the landing zone as well.

Bull's-eye! He'd hit the center as if he'd done this a thousand times. William was not far behind him and landed on the outer edge of the chalk circle.

William bought them a round of beers that night, as Dick Winters had given them the evening off for a job well done. He also managed to keep Sobel busy so that he didn't realize that the men had slipped out.

Tom, having come in second place, offered a second round.

A competition between the three had begun.

Tom had stopped counting how many jumps they'd racked up since then, though the number was likely in the hundreds. Every time, he felt the rush of adrenaline as he stepped into nothingness, but the sensation had taken on a comfortable familiarity. It was drilled into them to never become complacent.

"Keep on your toes today, soldiers," said Winters as they lined up in formation on the airfield. "The wind is going to kiss you like my great-aunt Helga with the mole on her cheek."

"Tom is going to kiss her right back!" offered John. He nudged Tom in the rib cage, but he could barely feel it with all of the layers that padded their uniforms.

"You heard it, First Lieutenant Winters!" Tom was better at playing along than coming up with the barbs in the first place. "She's all mine."

They lined up as usual and took their places on the perimeter of the plane. Sixteen of them would be jumping today. It seemed, sometimes, like a waste of precious army resources to practice and practice and practice as they were, waiting for the inevitable day when they would be called into action. But First Lieutenant Winters assured them that perfection now was perfection in battle.

Winters's face was stoic, but Tom knew that Sobel had brought him up on exaggerated charges and Winters had requested that a court martial review it. After Major Strayer looked it over and dismissed it, Sobel charged Winters again the following day. And yet, despite the strain their first lieutenant must be feeling, his sole focus was on his men and the jump. He inspired confidence in the troops, many of whom saw him as a surrogate father, despite the closeness of their ages.

Today's roster listed Tom jumping first, then several more before John took the rear. They sat accordingly.

"Hey, Powell," said William as he helped them with flight prep. "All kidding aside, if you want to write Margaret a letter, too, I'm A-okay with that. I'm not territorial about my friends."

Tom shifted in his seat and clasped his hands together. It was silly that a girl's letters and photograph could elicit such nervousness in him, especially when he was not the intended recipient of either. He shrugged. "Nah, man. I'll find some English Rose to quell my lonely heart after all."

"Oh, gawd, you are maudlin, Tom Powell."

"There's a word she'd like."

William smiled. "See? You're always thinking of her. Whether it's a bonnie Brooklynite or an enthusiastic English dame, you have a bright future ahead of you. I'm going to enjoy watching your thick skull succumb to the fairer sex."

"Who sounds like a professor now?"

"I've learned from the best."

Tom rolled his eyes and got into position. The wind was vicious, and he was surprised they'd been given a go to fly.

William must have noticed his unease. "Hey, I'll be sure we radio the pilot if the weather gets worse while you're up there."

Tom nodded and William hopped off just as the door closed behind him.

The plane lurched and Tom slammed into Malarky, creating a domino effect down their row. The pilot steadied the aircraft and they pressed onward.

"Time!" shouted First Lieutenant Winters.

Tom stood and inched closer to the front of the plane, holding the line above their heads. The wind howled outside like the banshees he'd read about in one of Mr. Brown's books. The plane bounced and he almost fell out of the open door, but he gripped the sides, waiting for the word.

"And—go!" came the order.

Tom jumped and the same feeling of exhilaration came over him. For the few minutes of descent, no one needed anything from him. No one asked him to pick peaches or clean a latrine or march ten miles. Not even girls existed. This moment was entirely his to enjoy.

He fumbled with the release on his parachute and for a few panicked seconds, he kept missing it as the wind lashed at him and pushed his hands away. But at last, he gave it a good tug and waited for the comforting pull up before he glided down. He missed the bull's-eye of the target by only a foot, but today's practice was about how quickly you could release yourself from the shackles of the parachute coils and hit the ground running with your rifle.

With textbook precision, Tom did just that and hurried over to the waiting area where Sergeant Bethune congratulated him.

"Fine maneuvering, Powell. Fine maneuvering. Keep this up and I might have to recommend you for the new Arctic training."

"Will we be fighting the war all the way up there?"

"Not unless Santa Claus wants to take up arms with Adolf Hitler. But this war could go on long enough that you'll see winter terrain. We're forming a unit that will learn to jump with skis on and hit the slopes the second they land."

"Thank you, sir. I'm here to serve however the army sees fit."

"Atta boy. You'll have a long career here if you want it. Now. Let's watch and see how the rest of those clowns fare up there."

William ran up and joined them. He rubbed his hands together to keep them warm. "Hey, Powell. Did Great-Aunt Helga give you any trouble up there?"

Tom nodded. "I almost felt like she was pushing my hands away from my parachute release."

"Yeah. It looks like it was a doozy."

"I'd rather them all be boring."

"Yeah. You don't want to be the medical case where the doctor says, 'Isn't that interesting?' You also don't want to have memorable jumps."

They stood close to each other, clenching their bodies tight to keep warm as they watched one paratrooper after another land in or near the circle, release their chutes, and take up their rifles. The sky resembled a polka-dot canvas with its gray background and the white spots decorating its landscape.

"Hey, look!" shouted one of the youngest privates. "Something's wrong up there!"

Tom's and William's heads whipped up to where he was pointing. And indeed, as the plane hurried off, one parachute after another engaged and the jumpers floated down. Except one.

"He's coming down too fast!"

"Open it! Open it!"

The chorus of worried voices shouted commands that could not be heard by the jumper. And not that he would have needed it. Whomever was up there was well aware of his predicament.

He fell, faster and faster, past the men whose chutes had opened as needed and they watched with horror.

"It's Beck!" someone yelled. "He was the last one."

Tom didn't want to believe it. Not John Beck. He was the best jumper in their company. It had to be someone else.

But he knew it wasn't. John was the last one on the roster to jump. And it was the last man who was speeding nearer and nearer to the ground.

William and Tom and the whole company ran out to where he'd disappeared behind the trees, hoping against hope for a miracle.

CHAPTER TEN

November 1943

When the doorbell rang, Margaret laid the pair of socks she was knitting on top of her workbasket. Several skeins of yarn hid a half-finished baby's blanket that she labored over during free evenings, its delicate strands an indulgence that she was happy to pay for from her own hard-earned money. She'd nearly forgotten to hide it before Dottie and Gladys came over tonight. She didn't want Dottie to see it—not only because it was a surprise, but also because crochet was a new medium for her. She'd gone to the Harrison Street branch of the Brooklyn Library and checked out a book that explained patterns.

There were so many to choose from—mesh, moss, single, double—but she'd landed on a simple shell stitch. Its scalloped look evoked a sense of gentleness to her and she thought it would be such a sweet keepsake for the baby. Not one for pastels, she'd chosen an emerald green yarn—John's favorite color.

She opened the door before a second ring, not wanting to disturb her parents, who had spent the day reviewing the year's scant financial receipts for the cobbler shop and were now preparing for bed.

One look at the man in uniform turned her stomach sour. She slipped out the door and closed it behind her.

No, no, no, no, no.

Because there were only two reasons for such a visit, neither of them good.

"Telegram," he said, handing an envelope out. He stood at attention on the stoop and looked as if he'd prefer to be anywhere but here.

"Thank you," she whispered. Her voice caught in her throat, and she held her hand out, her actions moving slower than her racing mind.

She stuffed the paper into her pocket, opened the door, and stepped back into the house, watching him through the glass as he got back into his car.

Her heart beat rapidly and the heat of her worried breaths created a fog on the pane.

She rested her head against it and wondered how she'd muster the strength to face what seemed inevitable.

She turned around. Dottie was no longer in the living room—probably upstairs, citing lately that her bladder was the size of a thimble. Gladys was concentrating on a stitch that seemed to be giving her a problem.

So Margaret walked into the kitchen, needing a moment alone before sharing this with her friends.

She gripped the wood counter until her knuckles matched the flour still scattered over the surface from when she had made bread earlier in the evening. One loaf had just come out of the oven and its warm aroma still overtook the kitchen.

John loved that scent.

She let go and sliced the fresh bread into three thick pieces and spread some butter from the crock over its divots, watching detachedly as it melted into nothingness.

Despair washed over her and she hung her head. She took deep breaths, telling herself that nothing was wrong.

Nothing was wrong.

Nothing was wrong.

Dash it—her eyes welled up with tears and she wiped them away with a tea towel.

She placed the bread on a plate and walked back into the living room, taking a deep breath as she did.

"Margaret?" asked Dottie as she made her way downstairs. "Who was that?"

"T-t-telegram," whispered Margaret. She wanted to pull herself together for Dottie's sake, but found that it was taking all of her concentration just to move her feet and hands and mouth. She set the plate down and pulled the envelope from her pocket.

Gladys stood up and set her knitting on the table. "Let me have that, you ninnies," she said. "No need for long faces until you actually read what it has to say."

She hadn't seen that the man had been in uniform.

Margaret turned toward Gladys and felt like she was looking through a veil of water. Life, distorted. Because if this news was what she was fearing, she didn't know how things could ever be the same.

She pulled the telegram from her pocket with trembling hands and gave it to Gladys without saying anything.

Gladys stuck her red-glossed thumbnail underneath the seal and ripped the thing open.

"Probably just a solicitation for the volunteer fire department. They're always collecting this time of year."

Then her eyes grew wide.

"The 101st Airborne and the Department of the Army deeply regret to inform you—" she began, her voice wavering.

"No!" screamed Dottie. She collapsed onto the couch and Margaret snatched the telegram back from Gladys's fingers.

"The 101st Airborne and the Department of the Army deeply regret to inform you," she began again. "That your son, Private First Class John Francis Beck, died in performance of his duties and in service to his country on November 30, 1943, in a parachuting accident in Aldbourne, England. The department extends to you its sincerest sympathies in your great loss."

November 30. Today. John must have died just hours before they were luxuriating in the glow of the Christmas carols.

John was *already* gone even as Margaret had been imagining future holidays with his wife and children around the Beck table. As she'd been knitting a scarf for his Christmas box.

"Margaret?" Mrs. Beck spoke from the top of the stairs. Her hair was in pink foam curlers and she was tying the sash of her robe around her waist. "Is everything all right? Was that Dottie I heard just now?"

Gladys zipped over to Margaret's side and held her hand.

"Mama," Margaret said, infusing her voice with a steadiness she did not feel. "Please bring Pops down. I need to tell you both something."

Four days passed in the house as four years might have. It took all Margaret's willpower to accomplish even the smallest of things like brushing her teeth and buttoning her pajamas.

In any other family death, that span of time would have included a funeral and a burial. But there was no body to be buried. At least not here. Their John had died a world away from the people who'd loved him all his life.

Oliver and Gladys were unexpected saviors, cooking together and delivering meals that might have been delicious if the world had not turned tasteless.

Brooklyn was all too experienced with the process of mourning, and Margaret was aware that their acute pain was one shared by too many.

She suspected it was the same all over the country. The army had delivered a flag, and her mother had promptly hung it in the window. Red border, white background, one gold star.

It announced to passersby that they had lost someone. Marked their house as one well-acquainted with lamentation.

They wished they had more details than simply a telegram saying that John had died in a parachuting accident. And that his body would remain in England. Had he suffered? Had it been quick? Had anyone else been hurt?

It was an entirely new wound, a sense of emptiness that their family would never be complete again. Not only with him missing at their table but from his home shores altogether.

Dottie had spent the nights since then at the Becks' house, sharing a bed with Margaret, more tears shed than words spoken. The girls were careful to cover her up with baggy sweaters and blankets so that her growing belly did not show. It was thankfully still early enough that such precautions were successful and the weather was cold enough to make the costume believable.

They'd mustered the energy to make it to the Navy Yard, silently losing themselves in the monotony of engraving, grateful for the solace it provided.

And it was not as if there was a choice. Since she hadn't been a spouse, Dottie did not qualify for any bereavement leave.

In fact, if her condition was discovered, she'd be fired.

She needed to make all the money she could while she was able.

When William's letter arrived four days after the telegram's awful news, Margaret tore it open, gouging her thumb with a deep paper cut. Little droplets of blood stained the white envelope. She pressed her hand into a fist and began to read.

William offered the only answers they'd received, and it rescued Margaret through the dreary week.

My dearest Margaret, he wrote.

I don't know when this will find its way to you, but I am writing it only hours after we have lost our beloved John and I'm hurrying to have it be carried out on the next helicopter leaving Chilton Foliat. I know those army telegrams don't tell the families what their hearts most want to know, and I would hope that should the jaws of death ever take my life that someone would do the same for my parents and sisters.

And so, I am sending this out to you at the earliest opportunity.

William wrote at length about how much John had come to mean to both him and Tom ever since they'd trained together in Georgia. Only a third of the men who'd enlisted as paratroopers actually made it past boot camp into the Airborne in North Carolina, so they trusted each other's abilities, having proven themselves time and time again.

He'd become the brother that neither of them had. John taught them how to play "Yankee Doodle" on a harmonica, and as southern boys, William and Tom had pressed upon him the need to learn something with a different flavor. John had been kind to everyone they met and insisted on helping old Mr. Brown with chores around the cottage even though he, himself, was entirely spent after days of training. William wrote that for as long as he lived, John's example would be a guiding light to him.

And now, he continued,

a bit on what I know you've been wanting to hear about. John was one of our best paratroopers and Tom and I are certain that he was mere days away from a promotion to Specialist. It is too early to say what made his parachute fail. The smallest error in coiling it could have dire consequences. But more than likely, the culprit was the infernal wind that plagued us today. All the men had difficulties releasing their parachutes as the wind did its worst against us. Our first lieutenant is stone-faced, as his role requires him to be, but we've come to know him well. And I can tell that underneath his staunch military demeanor, he is as bereft as the rest of us. Maybe more than most, as losing a man you are charged with sending home safely must leave a feeling of profound failure.

This will be hard to hear, and so I give you fair warning that you may want to place this letter down. But I believe, Margaret, that you are as strong a girl as John always described. If that is the case, then you should know the details. John's fall was broken by a low-lying tree, and it likely kept him from dying on impact. You might believe that would have been a more merciful end, and in one respect, you would be right. But in the few minutes he lived, Tom and I were able to rush to his side.

We found him just feet above our hands, and Tom and I scrambled up a maze of branches to get to eye level with him. His body had been pierced with a particularly sharp limb, and it had cut clean through his abdomen. Tom took off his jacket and pressed it against him, hoping to stop the blood, but I knew that even the most skilled surgeon would not be able to repair what the fall had done to him.

But his last moments are sentiments that I think will give some peace to your heart. Please tell Dottie that his first words—in case they'd be his only ones—were for her. "Tell Dottie I'll love her forever," he whispered through labored breaths. "And Mom and Pop. And tell Margaret that I want her to find the happiness that I found with Dottie."

Margaret's heart clenched as if a vise had wrapped itself around her. John had always wanted for her the idyllic love he'd found with his beloved Dottie. And Margaret had told him that it was not a lack of wishing for it but a sense that she would know when it happened. It was not something she could rush just because many of her friends were settling down.

Leave it to him to give her such consideration even as he spent his last breaths.

And one more thing, added William.

Which I will leave to you to tell Dottie or not, as you see fit. But we told John about the baby. If that was wrong of us, please find it in yourself to forgive us. Tom and I looked at each other after John had struggled with the litany of his loved ones. And we nodded, understanding that he deserved to know. "There's something else," I said. And I spoke the words quickly, fearing that he had no more than a few seconds left. "Dottie is carrying your child. And I and Tom and your family will all be sure that your son or daughter will be loved and cared for." At this, Margaret, a sight I wish I could give justice to—he smiled a brilliant smile and it seemed in that moment that no amount pain could overcome his joy. "I'm a father," he said.

Those were his final words.

Margaret, by the end of this war, I fear that John's will be only the first of many deaths that we will have to witness, and I will admit that it terrifies me. No man, no matter how tough he proports to be, is prepared for the unnaturalness of a passing that is far too early and far too tragic. But John's bravery has bolstered me—and Tom too—and I believe that because of him, we will be able to withstand whatever lies ahead. And if I am grateful for one other thing, it is that

John escaped the ugliness I know we are about to encounter.
Perhaps, in the end, he is the luckier of us.

At the bottom, Tom had drawn an exquisite lily.

The days at the engraving department continued to roll into one another, anesthetized by sadness. Two weeks passed before Dottie moved back in with Gladys. She'd told Margaret that she had trouble breathing in a place whose air and walls and memories were so saturated in grief. Every time she walked by John's bedroom, her heart clenched at the thought of what might have been. Mr. Beck had barely spoken since the telegram arrived, and Mrs. Beck had become a ghost of herself. Her cooking lacked salt and she sat by the radio out of habit, but without any reaction to its output.

And though she herself would never get over John's death, Dottie knew she wasn't going to be able to begin to adjust unless she got out of there.

If Margaret had only herself to worry about, she might have let it all consume her as well. She might have buried herself in the quilts on John's bed and never left. But there was Dottie and John's baby to consider above all else. Margaret needed to rally from the grief to be the support that Dottie needed at this time.

Margaret knew that her parents' immediate gloom of the news would mellow into an acceptance of something one should never have to accept. But it was still too early. They'd lost their only son. And though she'd lost her only brother, she knew something they did not—that he lived on in the child that Dottie was carrying.

She hoped Dottie would be ready to tell them soon.

As it was, she showed William's letter to Dottie, revealing that she'd told him about the baby.

The discovery that John knew and was happy gave Dottie a peace she might not have arrived at otherwise.

On the first night of their return to the Sock 'Em Club—as Gladys continued to call their knitting klatch—Oliver had stopped by with flowers and chocolates for them all, and then left just as quickly as he'd arrived. Margaret had to hand it to him—with his gentlemanly manners came an extraordinary consideration not only for Gladys but for her and Dottie as well. This time, Gladys had even rewarded him with a voluntary peck on the cheek.

The following evening, they'd already made their way through half of the box, declaring the caramels to be their collective favorite.

"I, for one, think that the baby will be the best medicine for everyone," suggested Gladys as they began to talk again about the future. Death had a way of burying the living in the past. Gladys knew it well enough, having lost her mother so tragically. So she was just the one to pull her friends out of their grief.

Dottie nodded, her eyes still reddened by the burn of tears. "You're right. There haven't been a lot of reasons for hope lately. But this"—she rubbed her stomach with a flattened palm—"this is all the reason I need."

The women grew pensive with their own thoughts, and for a moment, all that could be heard were the staccato clicks of their knitting needles. Metal on metal.

"That would be a nice name for a girl," offered Margaret. "Hope."

"Hope Beck," Dottie tried. "I like that. It's simple. I'll add it to the list."

Gladys squirmed, and Margaret asked her what was wrong.

"It's nothing."

"Gladys, I have never known you to keep something to yourself."

Gladys pursed her lips but continued. "I like the name too. And I hate to be the one to throw water on that, but will the baby be a Beck?"

Margaret and Dottie looked at each other and realized the truth of her words. Without a marriage, the baby would be born a Troutwine.

The color drained from Dottie's face, and she put her hands to her forehead. "Oh my goodness, she's right."

It struck Margaret that Dottie had never lamented the loss of the army stipend that she would have received if she'd been John's widow. But the withholding of the legitimacy of his last name seemed to crush her.

"And the baby can't be a Troutwine either. My father would never agree to a bas—"

"Don't say it, Dottie," interrupted Gladys with a force that took Margaret and Dottie by surprise. "Don't even *think* that word."

Margaret nodded. "What you mean to say is that your father would not agree to a child born out of wedlock sharing his name."

Dottie's cheeks colored. "Thank you. That's exactly what I meant to say."

They turned upon hearing a knock at the door.

"That will be Oliver," said Gladys. "And don't you two get any ideas about what that means. I told him we'd be here tonight, and he wanted to stop by and check on you, Dottie."

Margaret held back a smile. Gladys could pretend all she wanted.

But it was not Oliver at the door. It was George.

CHAPTER ELEVEN

$\mathcal{T}$om set his pencils down on the desk near the fireplace in the Browns' house. He was testing out a sketch of a corncockle and wanted to get it just right before adding it to the bottom of the next letter. Its tips were a vibrant pink, which was difficult to accomplish with the limited colors in the box he'd bought at the newsstand. But at last he was satisfied and began to fade it into a white at the flower's base.

"Are you sure?" he asked William.

"I'm sure."

"But your cast is finally off and you've healed up well. You could start writing these letters yourself."

"Nah. Your handwriting is better than mine anyway. Probably from all those papers you wrote in college, Professor."

Tom shrugged. He wasn't going to put up any more of a fight. He'd come to anticipate writing to Margaret as much as anything he'd ever enjoyed. William continued to dictate, though he gave Tom carte blanche to fill in words of his own to make it sound better.

"Besides," William continued. "The girl has lost her brother. She needs constancy right now. No need to give her a jolt with my scribble when she's probably come to love receiving the envelopes you've written."

They both fell silent. John's absence weighed on them heavily and the mention of his name always brought a fresh sadness. Though he'd had the most comfortable bed in the attic, they left it vacant because something just didn't feel right about taking his spot.

Tom would give anything to be kept awake by his friend's snoring.

Tom nodded at William's suggestion. It made sense. No need to rock the boat for Margaret just yet. Surely she felt the loss even more acutely.

Victoria lifted her shaggy head, pulling them out of their thoughts. Her hearing was attuned to the particular sound of Mr. Brown's bicycle as he rode down the path that led to his house. She was always several seconds ahead of any human ears.

Mrs. Brown came downstairs, as was her habit, when this played out, and stood in front of the mirror by the door fluffing her thinning gray hair.

Tom smiled. What a delight to witness a couple married so long yet still preparing to greet the other with the care that one might with a new love.

If he ever married, he would like for it to look like this.

As predicted, Tom saw Mr. Brown set the bicycle against the side of the house and come around to the front door. William jumped up and opened it for him. He had a large parcel under his arm, which he handed to William.

"I ran into your Winters fellow while I was picking up flour near Littlecote," he said. "He asked if I could bring this to you."

"What is it?" William asked as he pulled a Swiss Army Knife from his pocket and started to cut the twine.

"Letters. A couple dozen of them, your Winters said. Looks like your family had the wrong address this whole time. They were sending them to that house in Aldbourne that you were originally assigned to. Since no one was at the carriage house, they'd just been collecting. The owners never noticed until they were given a new soldier to use the space. They drove them over to Littlecote hoping someone would know where you were."

It was the longest string of sentences Tom had ever heard Mr. Brown say and he was charmed by the joy in the old man's eyes at delivering something that had troubled William for the past few months.

William opened the parcel fully and looked at each one as if it were a Christmas gift.

"They've all written," he said. "Even my father." He held them all to his chest. "If you'll excuse me, I'm going to go read them upstairs."

February 1944

My dearest Margaret,

William's latest letter began the same way they always did, but it had a ring of sincerity each time.

Tom found a new word to share with you—"bespoke." So you can add that to your list, though if you use it in Brooklyn, people might look at you funny. It's the British word for "handmade." As in, "The scarves you made for Tom and me over Christmas were bespoke." I tried to find words to rhyme with it, and though Tom initially teased me, his competitive side—silent but deadly—came out and he made some woefully inaccurate attempts. But, after putting our heads together and setting the ground rule that the most authentic rhyme would be dual syllabic, we arrived at a few: "awoke, provoke, revoke." We challenge you to try all of those in a sentence!

Enclosed, you will find a birthday gift. "But you don't know when my birthday is," you will protest. And the lady doth be right. However, I looked at my calendar and I realized that we've been exchanging these letters for nearly half a year. Half a year—can you believe it? Anyway, I have either missed your birthday entirely, in which I apologize and sent this belatedly, or I am impressively early. I'll hope for the latter.

It's a photograph taken of John, Tom, and myself about two weeks before we lost John. Mrs. Brown borrowed a camera from the schoolteacher in Chilton Foliat, who had one as a matter of hobby. When she'd discovered John's love for it, she asked him to take a picture of her and Mr. Brown for their fortieth wedding anniversary, as they'd never had one done together. Then she turned the camera on the three of us.

Not having the opportunity in this small town to develop the film, we were at the mercy of the schoolteacher to have them printed once he'd finished the roll, and we've only just now received them back.

This is my only copy, and to be honest, I was half tempted to keep it for myself. But not only is it in safer hands with you—because who knows what the next few months will bring for our sorry souls. Take good care of it for me. I have every intention of surviving this war and snatching it back from you when, at last, I get to return to home's soil and meet you in person.

Margaret unwrapped the photograph from its brown paper packaging. She closed her eyes before looking at it. As excited as she was to see a new image of John, a myriad of them adorned every bit of her house, as if it had become a shrine. It was William's visage (a delightful new word she'd learned and would have to share with him) that she was most eager to see. In these six months, his friendship had sustained her more than almost anything else. A letter in the mail with her name on it, inked in the careful and familiar handwriting of a soldier who described what newsreels and papers never could, was even more of a delight than the chocolates from Ebinger's that had become Oliver's habit to buy for them.

Hello, William, she thought as she held the photograph, wrong side up. *It's nice to finally meet you.*

She opened her eyes and smiled at the picture of the

three young men standing just beyond the cover of a thatched cottage roof. There was John, the top button of his shirt loosened, surely the first thing he did at the end of any training day. He'd never liked for his neck to feel encased. His grin was achingly familiar, the kind saved for their sibling antics, and it pleased her to know that William and Tom could elicit it. She held the picture to her heart and bent her head down. Despite all of the photographs in the house, this was, indeed, something to cherish. How thoughtful of William to have anticipated that.

To his left were the two other men. She walked over to the window and sat on the sofa where the waning sunlight of the afternoon cast its beam across the cushions. She flipped the photograph over, expecting some kind of mention of who was who, but it was blank. Could he really have forgotten to tell her?

With no hints, she looked at the picture more closely. The soldier right next to John was about the same height as her brother. His hair was shorn close to his head, hinting at its likely brown color. His forehead held the creases of someone who worried too much. She couldn't tell if he was twenty, thirty, or forty. His face was ageless. Timeless. He was smiling, though not as widely as John. As if the camera had captured him one second behind the peak of a laugh.

The other soldier made her breathing stop. He was several inches taller than the other two and seemed to be wearing his dark hair as long as the army would allow. The picture was clearly taken just before evening, and the boy's face wore the telltale sign of the long day with the shadow of a beard that would surely be shaved the next morning when they again reported for duty. But until then, it gave him a rugged, earthy look. Like the others, he was smiling at whatever had delighted them.

His eyes, however, had an enigmatic look to them. If the stage of joviality had not been set by everything around him, his eyes might equally suggest that he was deep in thought. If this was William, perhaps he was thinking of his next letter to her.

Something about this one stirred her in a way that was entirely new.

Is this what John and Dottie had felt for each other?

It couldn't be. He was not Cyrano and she was not Roxane and it was not love through the proxy of ink and words because those things just happened in fiction. And yet... and yet, she had never known a man to whom she could pour out her heart, worry over, and await his return home.

She was working on a project for him. Something she'd give him at the end of the war. She'd raided her mother's box of embroidery floss and stitched out the beginnings of a bouquet on a canvas. Eighteen holes per square inch for maximum detail. For every flower Tom drew for her, she created it with a needle and thread, carefully placing each one so that their individual beauty was displayed while arranging them so that their particular colors looked complementary next to its neighboring one.

It would be a piece of both of his friends that William could have forever.

❧

March 1944

My dearest William,

I awoke hoping that the newest bespoke piece I am knitting does not provoke you to drastic despair, as I had to revoke my use of the red yarn since I am quickly running out of it, but I instead will create the next one in yellow so as to evoke the sunshine that I know you love.

Oh, my friends, your challenge was hardly one at all. And to prove it, I added a rhyme of my own. The two of you will have to try much harder next time.

But I do thank you both for the brief diversion.

How I wish such frivolities were the stuff that occupied the hours of our days. Instead, each new, terrifying headline in the newspapers fills my mind with dread for your safety and for Tom's. I had every hope that my brother would survive the war. And to lose him before his part in it truly even began has made me keenly aware of the dangers you both face every day. I know now that nothing can be taken for granted. And the understanding that you and Tom could meet a similar fate is one that eclipses my girlish heart with that of a woman. Isn't it ironic that when we're young, we want to be all grown up? But when we finally arrive at that promised land, we want nothing more than to go back to the days of toy trains and baby dolls?

A year ago this time, I was poring through bridal advertisements with Dottie as we dreamed about her walking down the aisle of St. Charles Borromeo with John. And a year before that, I was planting flowers in our rooftop garden instead of the cucumbers I breed now. And a year before that—months before any of us had ever heard the words "Pearl Harbor," let alone could locate it on a map—I was embroidering flowers onto dancing shoes, eager for an upcoming springtime formal.

So which is preferable? Innocence or that which whittles it down into a keen awareness of the realities of the world?

My answer is different every day.

In other, vastly more important news, our Dottie is hopelessly, obviously, pregnant. (I know that "pregnant" is such a crude word to use, but honestly, "in the family way" is saccharinely euphemistic, though perhaps it's a step above some of its competitors. An old one being "wearing the bustle wrong," whose meaning should be obvious. And one that I've discovered only recently through Dottie—"the rabbit died." I will leave you to your own detective work to learn its meaning because I, frankly, can't think about it without getting a bit sad.)

Any way you say it, there was no way to keep it hidden any longer, and Gladys and I went with her to break the news to her parents. There were tears and accusations from them both, and words exchanged that I dare not share even with a hardened soldier. In fact, their ire even turned toward me, with implications that as John's sister, I represented a morally corrupt family.

I'll spare you the ugly details, but needless to say, we were relieved that Gladys had already made a spot for Dottie in her apartment because they threw her out officially when she refused to go upstate for a few months. No euphemism there—she would have been expected to deliver the baby and turn him over for adoption before even holding her. (Or him, as it may be.)

There is some light in this darkness.

George, a friend of ours who serves as a foreman at the Navy Yard, has been particularly solicitous of our Dottie these past few months. At first, his company was a comfort to her after the loss of John, and when she told him about the baby—though he had certainly guessed since explanations of overeating in light of grief are fruitless given how terribly thin we all are from the rationing—he began to dote on her so that she wanted for nothing. Bringing books and treats that she would like. Winter flowers. And taking her for drives into the countryside for fresh air. He even insists on driving her to the Navy Yard—whether their shift is the same or not— so that she doesn't have to take the bus and "breathe in all that exhaust."

On days where our hours are the same, Gladys and I are the grateful co-recipients of his generosity.

It's never been a secret to Gladys and myself that he is in love with her, though I don't think Dottie has yet clued up on it. But George's attentions—which come with no strings and are offered merely out of the goodness of his dear heart— have been a boon.

He has assisted in our subterfuge in the engraving depart- ment, which entails an almost comical choreography of walking next to her, giving her light bags to carry to conceal her shape, and dark corners in which to work, all for the purpose of hiding her predicament for as long as possible. When it's discovered that she "has a bun in the oven" (really, that's no better than "in the family way") she will be summarily fired. And we all know that she's going to need every penny she earns once this baby is born.

*In other news, Oliver still comes around calling for Gladys.
He has joined her in rallies for the rights of women, protests
for the poor, and campaigns for all her causes. I can't figure
out if his heart is as activistic as her own or if he's just covering
stories for his newspaper back in England, but I'm guessing
that the Brits have far less interest in the living conditions of
children in the Bowery when there is a war in their own back-
yard. So I suspect it's infatuation. Or deference. Whomever
deigns to capture the heart of my beloved Hurricane Gladys
will have to possess a touch of both.*

William handed Margaret's latest letter to Tom as soon as he'd
read it, as was their habit.

Tom buttoned his pajamas and climbed into his bed. It had
been a long day—an eighteen-mile march with full gear, just
as the weather was beginning to warm. Word came that they
would be activated soon, so *Captain* Dick Winters—who had,
at long last, replaced Sobel after a revolt among the troops
that had garnered some demotions for those involved—had
ramped up the drills. Tom's legs and back ached decades
before their time, and a cut in his left arm from crawling
under barbed wire was worrying him. He'd seen a medic
and taken penicillin for infection, but it was red and burned
like the dickens. Still, he took Margaret's letter from William
and squinted as he perched on his side and held it up to the
bedside light.

A smile spread across his face as she talked of Dottie and
George and Gladys and Oliver. She'd written six pages and

affixed extra postage stamps for the weight—but he was grateful for her loquaciousness (a word he'd learned and would slip into the next letter) because she brought color to her descriptions of her friends and made him feel like he was reading a radio drama script.

He felt his cheeks grow warm and hoped that it didn't show. But William missed nothing.

"You're hot under the collar for Margaret Beck, aren't you?" asked William all of a sudden.

Tom jerked his head around.

"I am not. What a notion."

"Are too. I can see you blushing even in this light."

"I'm making an appointment for you to go to the eye doctor. Go to sleep."

The crickets outside chirped and Tom listened to them before William spoke again.

"Want to know something? I sent her your picture."

Tom sat up straight, his heart quickening. "You did what?"

"All right, all right," said William, waving his hands in surrender. "Not just *your* picture. The one that the Browns took of the three of us. You, me, and John."

Tom could no longer feel the pain in his arm. All of his attention had been pulled into this new turn in the conversation. He'd tried to bury any such thoughts that had arisen, convincing himself that it was the novelty of her letters that he liked. But he knew better than that—if he lived in the same town as Margaret Beck, he would want to take her out dancing. To see that smile in the photograph come alive as he held her in his arms. But these were not luxuries he could dwell on if he intended to further his career in the military.

William was spot-on with his observation.

"I almost told her that I was you and you were me, but in the end, I just left it blank. Do you want to know why?"

Tom was silent.

"Because you're the good-looking one," William answered anyway. "If she thinks the tall and handsome guy is the one who writes her letters, she might fall just in love with you."

"But you're the one the letters are from," Tom pointed out.

"Sort of. For now."

"For now?"

William leaned over the side of the bed in a conspiratorial stance.

"Look. I know what you and John were up to when he asked her to write to me. You both felt sorry that I hadn't received any letters. You were real pals for thinking of it. And she was a sport to go along with it. But now I'm getting more letters from home than I have time to keep up with. So why don't you just take over writing the letters to Margaret?"

A little thrill of possibility shot through him at the thought.

"And sign them as *Tom*?"

William shrugged. "If you want." Then he shot his arm up in the air. "Or better yet, no. Keep writing them as William."

Tom's brows furrowed. "Why would I do that?"

William settled back and propped himself up on his elbows. "Look. I have sisters. And once upon a time, I used to be a little imp and sneak into their rooms to read their diaries."

Tom's eyes widened.

"Yeah. I'm not proud of it," William admitted. "But I learned a little something. Now, I don't know if this applies to all girls, but it does to my sisters. They could lose their heads over a boy just because of a passing word he'd say and they'd pick apart meaning where there was none."

"What does that have to do with Margaret?"

"It's like this. You're Mr. Military. Despite that romantic heart of yours, it may be a long time before you're in a position to settle down. If you write as me, it keeps your head in the friendly arena. No temptation to get all mushy like you might do if I left you to your own devices. Really, I'm protecting you both."

"That sounds a lot more complicated than it needs to be."

William lay back and pulled a *Life* magazine from under the cot and opened it above his head. "You don't have to listen to me. Maybe Margaret Beck is the one girl in a million who won't fall for your charms. But I doubt it. You've got matinee-idol looks, my friend. And if you go and get all *Tom*-like in those letters, you're going to break that girl's heart someday. I guarantee it."

Tom popped a hard butterscotch candy into his mouth and ruminated.

William's idea made some sense. If he wrote as William, it might help to keep Margaret relegated to a two-dimensional pen pal in his mind. A place to put his thoughts. A distraction through what lay ahead.

As Tom, he might be inclined to let his thoughts go where they shouldn't. Not if he planned to stay on after the war and make a career of it.

William knew him well.

As it was, when he read Margaret's letters, he found himself spending hours composing responses in his head. Responses that never made it to paper. He wanted to tell her about

Virginia and the peach pies he made with his mother and about the way the rain smelled when it drizzled onto the Chickahominy River. He wanted to share with her new words and admit that he'd taken up studying them because of her and tell her about the English countryside he'd come to love on his walks from Chilton Foliat to Aldbourne. He wanted to describe the peppermint tea that Mrs. Brown steeped in the evenings and the lightness of her Yorkshire pudding. He wanted to confess that he'd kept her picture where William had pinned it on his pillow and that waking up to it every morning made him want to survive this war.

Yes, he'd thought about it plenty.

He had a lot to consider. But one thing was for sure— if William was too busy to write Margaret back, Tom would make sure that she got a reply.

CHAPTER TWELVE

April 1944

*T*he engraving room was unusually silent, as the lunch break had taken some of the other girls outdoors into the glorious spring weather that had befallen the city. Margaret would join them after she finished the last letters of her project.

She could almost taste the pastrami sandwich she'd packed from a trip into Manhattan to go to Russ & Daughters. She'd read that it was the first business in the country to add *& Daughters* to its title, so she and Gladys had taken the subway to East Houston Street yesterday to give them their patronage. Gladys said they needed to support women's businesses as much as possible in order to encourage more of them. She and Margaret had been saving their extra pay for little splurges that reminded them of what normalcy felt like.

While there, they walked the two blocks down Ludlow Street and went to Economy Candy to buy some Red Hots for Dottie. She'd been craving spicy foods, a vast departure from her normal palate. Margaret was continually amazed at how such a tiny being could bring about such drastic changes.

They'd been worried about leaving Dottie alone as her

due date was just a couple of weeks away, but she dismissed their concern.

"I don't need a babysitter," Dottie had insisted when Gladys and Margaret had first discussed the outing. "You both treat me like I'm some delicate piece of porcelain. And I'm not."

Gladys ignored her. "I know!" she'd said. "Let's ask George if he can sit with her for a while."

Dottie's mouth opened in protest, but she closed it before she'd uttered a sound. Margaret noticed the flush of her cheeks. Dottie's face revealed what her words wouldn't—she enjoyed his company very much.

Margaret wanted to tell her that she didn't mind. That John would want her to be happy. That five months since the terrible news and four more since they'd last seen him was a very long time. Dottie was young and beautiful and vibrant, and she had a wonderful man who cherished her as she deserved. How could Margaret stand in the way of that?

Now, back at work, she wondered if she should tell Dottie that she would have her blessing.

"Margaret!"

Dottie's scream pierced through the quiet engraving room and startled Margaret out of her thoughts.

She left her sandwich, pickle slices spilling onto the work counter, and hurried over to Dottie.

"What's the matter?"

Dottie wrapped her arms around her belly and rocked back and forth on her chair. "I think it's happening."

"The baby? Today?"

"Yes—today! Now!"

"But first babies are always late. That's what I read!"

"Well, this baby didn't read that book and I'm telling you, Margaret. This. Is. It!"

"Are you sure these are real contractions? I read that your body practices for the real thing before the big day."

"*Dammit*, Margaret! I've already had plenty of those! I feel like there's a watermelon that wants to get out of me *this very minute*!"

Dottie *never* cursed. This was serious. Margaret took a breath and collected herself, wiping away the sweat forming on her temples. "Right. Right. Right. Okay. George. Let's go find George. And Gladys."

"Owwwww! Hurry!"

Margaret started running for the door and looked back to see Dottie doubled over in the pain of the contraction.

"I'm hurrying! I'm hurrying!"

Margaret pushed open the heavy door of the engraving room and came upon the promenade, which was lit with the intensity of the noonday sun. Her pupils throbbed after languishing in the dim workroom for so many hours, and she shaded her eyes before taking another step.

It was the kind of day that might have otherwise tempted her and Dottie to play hooky in order to escape to the beach and pretend, even for a brief time, that the troubles of the world didn't exist.

But the troubles were all too real. If not across the ocean, then right here in Brooklyn. Where Dottie was about to have her baby.

In the engraving room, if they didn't act fast.

"George!" Margaret shouted with little hope of him hearing her. George walked the promenade at this time every day, but it was too long to see the end of either side. If she ran one way, he might very well be on the other side. So she stood here in the middle. At some point, he would be within earshot.

"George!" she shouted again.

It took four attempts, but before too long, she saw a figure coming toward her from far down on the right, silhouetted like an eclipse. He had the right gait for George, and as he approached, she saw with relief that it was him. She ran so fast toward him that he had to put his arms out to stop her.

"Margaret? Is everything okay with Dottie?"

She stopped and laughed incongruously. And that made her laugh even more. How charming that Dottie was always his first concern.

"Yes! No. I mean—"

"Margaret—is Dottie okay?" he asked again, with the first strain of impatience she'd ever seen in him.

"The baby is coming!"

His eyes widened. "Why didn't you say so? I'll go get my car!"

George ran ahead, and then looked back. "See if she can manage to walk to the parking lot. I'll drive up as close as I can. And tell her—"

"What?"

"Tell her that everything will be all right."

Dottie squealed in pain as she sat in the back of George's car with her legs slung over Margaret's lap.

"Can't you go any faster?" Margaret asked.

"It's not the car," George said, stretching his head up to see better and adjusting his glasses as if that might help. "It's the traffic."

"We could walk there with as long as this is taking!"

"Of course we could, but I don't think between you and me, we could carry a woman in her condition."

Margaret slunk back, feeling helpless.

"It's never like this on Navy Street. Can we cut over to St. Edward?"

George looked to his left, but in every direction, cars were stopped, either trying to find alternate routes or stuck behind whatever was keeping things from moving.

Margaret rolled the window down and stuck her head out. She pushed herself up until she could see beyond everything. She'd never encountered a backup like this and wouldn't have thought there were this many people in all of Brooklyn. But up ahead, she saw that four cars had collided. She squinted her eyes and shaded them from the sun. None of the emergency vehicles had pulled out gurneys as far as she could tell. Surely that would indicate the seriousness of it.

On the other hand, they had an emergency of their own right here.

She sat back down and looked at where Dottie was sprawled across the seat.

"How are you?" she asked in a voice laced with the sympathy and desperation of one who cannot help as she'd like. She rubbed Dottie's arm, eager to do something to ease her discomfort.

Dottie's face and hair were drenched with sweat, but she forced a smile anyway. "I'm in between contractions. Ask me in two minutes and I might have a different answer."

Indeed, two minutes brought a new round of wailing from Dottie, her screams filling the entirety of the vehicle to the point of hurting Margaret's ears. But it was nothing compared to what Dottie was going through, and they had at last crawled a few feet closer to their turn.

Margaret looked over at George, whose hands gripped the steering wheel until they were white, and back at Dottie, whose breathing was starting to relax again.

Margaret closed her eyes, needing to think of something good to distract her.

And then, something brought a smile to her face. Just a few nights ago, Gladys had been out at a voter registration drive for women. Margaret had planned to go but decided at the last minute to stay with Dottie, worried about something happening while they were gone. Dottie had protested, but Margaret insisted on staying in the tiny apartment to finish up some socks for their next shipment.

A knock on the door, and Margaret opened it up to see George. He had flowers and ice cream with him.

"Margaret!" he'd said, looking down at his feet. And it was then that she realized that she wasn't supposed to be here. That George and Dottie had arranged an evening together and she was an interloper.

She'd looked back at Dottie, who feigned surprise at George's presence, but Margaret knew every single expression that her friend possessed. And this one had traces of what she'd seen when Dottie had been around John.

He really loves her, thought Margaret. *And she might just love him back.*

The thought resurrected a mixed set of emotions. It was always supposed to be John. And now it couldn't be.

But they kind of made sense together. A glimmer of hope in all this madness. Certainly the state of the world and these particular circumstances might accelerate such a relationship to mere months. Even as Dottie and John's romance had enjoyed the luxury of many years of simmering.

And now, here he was. At Dottie's side at the most important moment of her life.

That had to mean something.

It took a half hour to drive the remaining blocks, but at last they pulled up to the imposing redbrick structure that served as the area's hospital.

"I'll go for help," Margaret said, already halfway out of the car. She pulled open the glass doors of the entrance— impossibly heavy—and then went through two other sets before finally arriving at the receiving desk.

"My friend is having a baby! Where do I take her?"

The receptionist put on the glasses attached to a cord around her neck and looked toward the entrance.

"Where is she?"

"In the car. Outside. With a . . . friend." Margaret's breaths were frenetic despite the short run and her lungs felt like she'd swallowed knives. Her racing heartbeat had gotten a head start in George's car.

"We'll send a wheelchair out for her. There's no need to worry."

How did she know there was no need to worry? Had she

seen Dottie? Did she know Dottie? Had she delivered any babies herself? The woman answered telephones. How did she know that everything would be okay?

Margaret bit her lip and inwardly chastised herself. She had to calm down. This was something that had happened billions upon billions of times since the beginning of the world. This was how nature was designed.

But that thought didn't help as she'd hoped. This was Dottie's *first* time. And that made it feel like the first time in the entire history of the human race.

The receptionist gave Margaret some paperwork, and filling it out was a welcome distraction.

Name. Dorothy Maria Troutwine.

Address. She closed her eyes. It would have to be Gladys's—312 Harrison Street.

Gladys! Gladys didn't know yet. Margaret remembered that she didn't have a shift today and had gone with Oliver into Manhattan, where he was doing some research on the up-coming Commonwealth Prime Ministers' Conference in the hopes of pitching an article to a stateside newspaper.

Gladys had an interest in all things newsworthy. And all things Oliver, as she'd reluctantly admitted to Margaret and Dottie.

She had to figure out how to alert her.

She filled in the next questions as best she could and was relieved that there was no question for "father."

But that question would come, surely, on the birth certificate. And writing John's name would bring on the bitterness of his absence once again.

"Owwwww!" Margaret jerked around to see a nurse

pushing Dottie in a wheelchair and Dottie hunched over in pain.

"Can't you do anything for her?" asked Margaret.

The nurse smiled, a model of amicability even as Margaret felt like she'd been turned inside out.

"We'll take good care of her," she promised. "There is a waiting room on the fourth floor. We'll bring you updates there. In the meantime, you can find something to eat in the cafeteria in the basement. It could be a long night."

Dottie grabbed Margaret's hand with terrifying force.

"Don't leave me!"

Margaret looked at the nurse, pleading with her eyes.

"I want to go in with her. I'm her sister," she said. A stretch of the truth to be sure, but she would have been if Dottie had married John.

The nurse shook her head. "We'll take good care of her," she said again, as if she heard this request several times a day. It both riled and comforted Margaret. But she had to admit that there was nothing else she could do.

She slouched onto a bench near the door, and as she hoped, George came in shortly after.

"Where is she?" His eyes looked as wild as Margaret felt, strained and worried, but the rest of his collected demeanor demonstrated the reliability that she'd always appreciated in him.

"They wheeled her away. They said we can wait on the fourth floor and they'll bring us news when they have some."

"Hey, doll."

Sharp needles of pain shot through Margaret's back as she untangled her limbs from a most awkward position. She rubbed her eyes and Gladys came into view.

Where was she?

The hospital! Had she slept through the baby's birth?

She stood up on wobbly legs and Gladys pulled her into her arms to steady her.

"Did I miss it?" Margaret asked.

"Nah. Dottie wouldn't dare have a baby while you were asleep. Things slowed down for her as quickly as they'd sped up."

"What time is it?"

"Just past midnight."

She remembered now. George had brought her a cold chicken dinner from the cafeteria and magazines from a nearby newsstand. She hadn't been able to read a word. Even the one with Lauren Bacall on the cover, reminding her of Gladys's time at the Stage Door Canteen. Instead, she'd watched George pace for hours and hours.

She pulled away from Gladys and looked around. George had at last retreated to the couch across the room, his long frame curled into a ball.

"How did you know to come here?" Margaret whispered.

"Sometime while you were getting your beauty rest, George called the party line at my building incessantly until someone picked up and agreed to leave a note on my door."

"Is Oliver with you?"

Gladys shook her head, and her curls, flattened from the length of the day, looked as if they, too, had endured much.

"He wanted to write his story while it's fresh in his mind. He'll join us later."

Margaret grinned. "Soooo did you have a nice day?"

Gladys shrugged. "If you call it 'nice' to spend hours and hours among dusty shelves at the NYPL and being told more than once to *shush* by a male librarian who wouldn't know his behind from a cantaloupe, then yes."

"I mean with Oliver." Margaret pursed her lips together to keep from giggling.

"Sure, then. It was a *nice* day."

"You're a sphinx."

"What do you want me to say? That we're in love and I want to get married and have his babies?"

"Don't you?"

Gladys sat down in the chair nearest her and Margaret collapsed back onto the sofa. "Marriage, maybe. *Maybe.*" She held her hand up to signal *stop*. "Which is more of a concession than you've ever gotten from me. Or ever will. But babies, no. I'll leave that to the Dotties and Margarets of the world."

"That's progress, at least."

She shrugged. "For someone who believes that's the natural course of life, then perhaps. Whatever you want to call it."

They glanced over at George, who resembled a Coney Island pretzel. Margaret recalled a conversation they'd had while they were waiting for news.

"Speaking of marriage and the natural progression of things, he told me while we were waiting that he wants to marry Dottie."

"That's nothing new."

Margaret leaned over the arm of the chair. "No, really. It's more than words. He bought a ring and everything. Spared no expense on a top-tier diamond—wait till you see it. A half-carat round, set in a gold band with beveled edges. I know he could have afforded an even more dazzling setting, but he had the discretion to know that her head isn't turned by such things."

Margaret smiled at the thought.

"He...he asked for my permission," she continued.

She wouldn't have thought anything could surprise Gladys, but her eyes widened and then narrowed. "What did you say?"

Margaret folded her arms and sat back in the chair, remembering how kind and sincere George seemed when he spoke to her. About how much he'd loved John and could never replace him. How he knew he'd always be second in Dottie's heart. But that even so, he wanted to take care of her—and the baby—for the rest of his life. "I told him that the only thing that would make me happier is hearing that mother and baby came out of the delivery good and healthy."

"What do you think Dottie will say?"

Margaret shrugged. "I don't know. She and John—there are few people who get to have what they had. But George—she would never have to work again. Or worry about her parents turning her out. It makes a certain kind of sense."

"You don't think she'd marry him just for that, though, would she? Haven't women prostituted themselves for enough centuries just for name and security?"

"Gladys! It's not like that for her and you know it."

"You're right. I'm sorry. I didn't mean it that way. Maybe deep down I have a little romantic bone that wants to see her marry for love."

"It's your stapes."

"My what?"

"Your stapes. It was one of the words in the *New York Times* and I haven't gotten to use it yet. It's your middle-ear bone. The smallest bone in the human body. That's your tiny little-engine-that-could romantic bone."

Gladys rolled her eyes and fanned her hands at Margaret.

"And what's it for? So he can whisper sweet nothings in my ear just like they do in the novels?"

"You said it, not I," teased Margaret. "But returning to Dottie, if she says yes, it will be for love. I'm certain of it. Just a different variety. A George love."

George stirred and sat up and Margaret hoped he hadn't heard them talking. He stretched his arms out and yawned. His glasses sat askew on his head and he pulled them down.

"Hey, Glads."

"Hey, George. Thanks for calling in the note. No doubt the building inhabitants will want their pound of flesh from me, waking them up as you did. I understand that you were quite persistent."

"Any time," he said, ignoring her hyperbole.

"I hear you—"

Before Gladys could finish her sentence, a nurse came out and walked over to George.

"Congratulations! You have a baby girl. And you can come and see your wife now."

Dearest William,

Things have been a whirlwind in the last few weeks. Dottie had her baby—a sweet little girl named Joanna Margaret. Isn't that just beautiful? I am moved by how they incorporated John's name into hers. It was George's idea. Dottie had considered Rebecca—Beck for short—but I think Joanna is exactly the right name.

A nurse mistook George for Dottie's husband, but he came back from seeing her a happily engaged man. I wouldn't have thought a hospital room had an ounce of romantic air in it, certainly not enough for a proposal, but it turns out that Dottie was more smitten with him than she'd let on to any of us. She just hadn't wanted to hurt me with that admission.

Oh, the secrets we keep. If only we let our feelings be known, especially to our best friends.

Dottie didn't proffer how he'd gone about it and I didn't ask. I guess if they are to be married, they are allowed some of those privacies.

The wedding is set for early July—almost a year exactly when she would have married John—and then they will baptize Joanna and give her George's last name of Preston. My parents took the news surprisingly well, considering the pall that has laid upon our house for the past few months. But I think the excitement of a grandchild quelled any shock at seeing Dottie with someone other than their son. Dottie's parents have not yet been to see them but have written that they will do so now that they have plans to "make things right with the Church." So—St. Charles Borromeo will see plenty of us in the next few weeks. As always, I'll be sure to tell you about everything that happens.

Please thank Tom for the lovely drawings at the end of the letters. Between your words and his art, I feel as if I am in the English countryside with you all. I looked up Chilton Foliat on a map. Actually, I went through three maps at the library before I found one that had it. What a small place it must be. So very different than Brooklyn.

I've never told anyone this, but I'd like to see so much more of the world than I've been able. I'm embarrassed to say that I've never been out of the city other than to visit relatives in Pennsylvania. First, there was school. Then, helping in the cobbler shop. When work was slow, we couldn't afford to travel anywhere. When work picked up, we were too busy to leave it.

My ambitions in this regard are not quite as lofty as my friend Gladys. I daresay that she would jump at the opportunity to ride a camel through Morocco or scale the Great Wall of China. As for me—and as I scour the atlas for every little village you name—I find that I would be quite content with seeing what you're seeing in England.

Although I hear that the Allies hope to liberate France soon. I think that would be next on my list. France. Paris.

All right, William. Make me a promise. If you conquer the Axis and make it to Paris on this grand tour of yours, have a croissant at an outdoor café. Dip it in sipping chocolate and think of me. But don't write to me about it. I might not be able to contain my envy.

In the meantime, I'll dedicate my next Coney Island dog to you.

(Why do I think you might be getting the better end of the deal?)

All the best,
Margaret (who now has a namesake!)

CHAPTER THIRTEEN

June 1944

*H*old on tight!"

"Gladys—slow down! My hand is slipping!"

"Stop dawdling, then. We don't want to miss it."

"We don't want to lose each other either."

"Geez, you'd think that attaching a few nuts and bolts would get you a seat."

"Us and ten thousand others?"

"That's immaterial."

"How many people do you think are here?"

"I'm guessing all of the boroughs in New York and then some."

"Seems like it."

Every inch of the Brooklyn Navy Yard was packed as throngs and throngs of people gathered to witness the commissioning of the USS *Missouri*. Four years in the making, 887 feet long, fifty-seven thousand tons in weight, Margaret took in its magnificent expanse with immeasurable, breathless pride. She would never know which flags that flapped in the breeze had been stitched by her hands, or how much ordnance she'd engraved would be used in battle. But Margaret Beck of Brooklyn, New York, had been a part of something that would surely make history.

How many people got to say that?

In the crush of people, Margaret could barely distinguish Dottie's voice from Gladys's and she gave every effort to not lose them. Gladys held her right hand and was weaving her way through the crowd, inching them closer and closer to the front. Dottie held Margaret's left hand, and between them, she felt like the middle car of the Tinker Toy Train in the window of FAO Schwarz.

That Gladys and Dottie were the engine and caboose, respectively, seemed apt.

"This is good enough!" she shouted to Gladys, who was pressing on. Margaret flushed with embarrassment as they wound their way through people who had arrived hours earlier, dismissing the fact that their tardiness was due to waiting for Dottie to finish feeding Joanna. It was her first time leaving her daughter with someone else, which would have been frightening enough. But she was leaving Joanna with her *parents*. Her parents, who had wanted their granddaughter to be raised by some other family. Dottie's hesitance was understandable, but Gladys and George had convinced her that there was no better way for them to bond with Joanna than to spend some time with her.

And, to be fair, they had at last proven themselves warm, though not enthusiastic grandparents, once George and Dottie announced their engagement.

Margaret knew that Dottie, too, was replete with excitement for seeing the *Missouri* completed and launched into the

East River. So she was glad that her friend had given the reins to the Troutwines for the afternoon.

"Would you look at that." Gladys stopped, having led them only a few rows away from the front, where speakers were already lining up at the podium and news outlets had fixed microphones in every possible spot. "She's a beauty."

"She sure is," Dottie agreed.

"Why are ships spoken of in the feminine?" Margaret wondered aloud.

"Because they're goddesses," Gladys answered without hesitation.

Dottie smiled. "Of course you would say that."

"I'm serious. It's an ancient tradition. Putting female carvings on the fronts of ships, like a mother or a goddess guiding it to safety."

"You only mentioned goddess," Margaret said. "Do you have something against mothers?"

"Not since this girl became one." Gladys nudged Dottie in the side with her elbow.

The crowd began to cheer as the navy band struck up a tune. Excitement buzzed through Margaret's veins like the many wires leading up to the lectern.

Gladys looked up, and Margaret and Dottie followed her lead. Though they'd been close to the *Missouri* many times, they had not been nearly touching distance to its hull before, as they were now. Margaret felt dwarfed by its towering metal edifice and marveled that such a thing could even float. The chains alone, looped and gathered on either side of it, looked as if they made up half the weight.

It was a city unto itself, built to carry nearly two thousand sailors across oceans.

She felt envious of the people way up on the top deck—little specks from her vantage point—and what position they held to be allowed to stand so many stories above the crowd. Oliver was somewhere up there, having secured a press pass. He'd acquired a second one and invited Gladys to join him, but she turned him down, saying that she was going to watch it with "her girls" and the rest of the hoi polloi from down below. But Oliver promised a full accounting later. Would he get to visit its many chambers? The *Missouri* was supposed to be state-of-the-art, complete with a library, dentist's office, and even a doughnut shop!

She expected a mouthful from Gladys, but for once, her friend was speechless.

"We're just in time," Dottie whispered into Margaret's ear. "Isn't that Senator Truman up there at the podium?"

Margaret shielded her eyes from the sun and squinted until she could see the main speaker. Indeed, it did seem to be the senator from the state of Missouri, his face familiar to them as a frontrunner for the vice-presidential ticket in the upcoming election. It was to be Roosevelt's fourth term if he won again, and conventional wisdom predicted that his failing health might render him unable to complete his years. So the vice-presidential selection was more important than ever, as there was a good chance that whoever filled the role could very well take over as president.

Margaret's father listened with rapt attention to *CBS World News Roundup* and, had he been a betting man, said that he'd put his money on Truman over the man who currently held the position, Henry Wallace. Conservative Democrats feared that a Wallace administration would be far too progressive, favoring labor and alienating the businessmen among the party.

She didn't have a strong opinion either way, never having thought even a year ago that politics was something that affected her. But now she had the sense that it was a responsibility of adulthood that she needed to embrace and vowed as she stood there to start listening along with her father. The decision for the nomination was a month away when the party met in Chicago, so she had time to catch up. But if that all came about as her father predicted, she might be looking at a future president of the United States.

Just one more reason for her blood to rush with anticipation today.

The spectacle was enough to send patriotic sentiments through anyone's veins. She could understand Gladys's passion just a bit better. Gladys had seen the world let her mother down—so she crusaded for improvement at every corner. Charitable outlets. Rights for women. Politics. When one had been affected so greatly, the fire to promote change was an infectious one. Bringing the realities in the country into alignment with the feelings such events produced.

Margaret would do well to learn from her example.

Senator Truman tapped the microphone and an immediate silence descended upon the crowd. Margaret missed the first of his words as they were scattered into the breeze, but once she focused, she was able to discern most of it.

"The christening and launching of this greatest warship of all time illustrates the decisive answer which the democracies of the world are making to the challenge of the aggressor nations."

His speech was interrupted by intermittent cheers.

"Missouri is the *Show Me* state," he continued. "The battleship *Missouri* will show all Americans—indeed, all the world—her innate seaworthiness, her valiant fighting spirit and the invincible power of the United States Navy. Today, Missouri joins hands with her sister states throughout the Union in asking the blessing of Divine Providence upon this magnificent battleship and upon her valiant men."

His left hand formed a fist and he pounded the podium for emphasis.

Margaret felt it like a heartbeat.

She thought of John. Of how this battleship and the others like it would avenge his tragic death. It would ensure the safety of William and Tom and the other boys like them who had risked everything and would love nothing more than to sit back at the table with their families and go about living the lives they had always dreamed of.

She would write to William of this moment. This event so spectacular that already she was struggling with the right words, even among her vast bank of them.

"May this great ship," Truman concluded, "be an avenger to the barbarians who wantonly slaughtered the heroes of Bataan and may the battleship *Missouri* and all the other ships of our Navy do their full share on behalf of the people of the United States to maintain the peace which will follow our total victory."

A cheer went up as the crowd squealed with unified delight, as if it were one breathing being and not thousands combined.

Margaret, Dottie, and Gladys contributed their own shouts, feeling the swell of pride in their very bones.

Truman's daughter, also named Margaret, was the sponsor of the event. At his word, she leaned far over the railing, raised the bottle of champagne in her hand, and, buoyed by the crowd, smashed it against the bow of the ship. Immediately, bubbles poured down its seam and the flags attached to its top flapped as if giving their approval. Glass shattered into the water like confetti. At that signal, the *Missouri* floated away from the dock with surprising speed, as if propelled by magic instead of the meticulous engineering. In just seconds, she had already cleared the confines of the Brooklyn Navy Yard and made her way into the East River, leaving whitecapped waves in her wake.

"It was simply the most magnificent thing I've ever seen," Margaret waxed to her parents at dinnertime. "Gosh, I wish you had both been there."

Her father shrugged in the humble way she'd always loved. Her mother had a summer cold and he hadn't wanted to leave her side in case she needed anything. While she laid down and listened to *Guiding Light*, he made a dinner of his own creation. A tough piece of pork cutlet and some undercooked green beans. But the love he put into them made them delicious. And besides, the food was far less important than the company.

"It's enough that you were there and can tell us all about it," her mother added. Her face looked tired, but her eyes glistened. "We're so proud of you."

Her words meant a great deal to Margaret, though they also inadvertently placed some anxiety in her heart. Without John, the burden of honoring her parents, of taking care of them, and of helping at the cobbler shop fell entirely on her shoulders.

And her father was noticeably slowing down. He didn't want to give up the business, but the pace of the city was wearing on him and he would need her help if he was going to keep it up.

How would she even do that? Would she have to give up her job at the Navy Yard? She had no particular love for the engraving section, but she liked being a part of something that mattered as much as it did.

She'd hoped that working in the Navy Yard would help her decide what she wanted her future to look like. Gladys's ambitions had opened her eyes to possibilities for women that she'd never dreamed about. And yet—when she held little Joanna in her arms, a love bloomed that lay deeper than anything she could have expected, inspiring a desire for one of her own one day.

Could a woman not find a way to have both?

Margaret would have thought the events of the day would have made her eager to nestle into the softness of her feather mattress, but she found herself unable to sleep. She got up well before the sun to pen her thoughts into a letter to William. She had been given the day off, despite it being a Monday, along with most of the women who had exhausted themselves with the festivities of the day before. Still, she found herself unable to sleep in late, as it had never been her habit.

She put on a light sweater and walked the letter out to the nearest blue mailbox. She hesitated before sending it off.

Increasingly, her thoughts turned toward writing to William. At first, she'd written to give some cheer to a soldier who was not otherwise hearing from home. Then his presence as a friend to John had warmed her heart. But as the months ticked by, penning words to him had become as cathartic as a diary and as vital as oxygen.

Especially of late. There was something about the last couple she'd received. It was almost imperceptible, the change she'd noticed. The letters had the same handwriting. The same flowers Tom sketched at the end. But the words—there was something about the words that was just a little more...fluid. A little more deep. As if he'd revealed a keyhole to his heart and she was the one being allowed to peek through.

Was that love? She didn't think so. Though her heart beat quicker when an envelope bearing his handwriting arrived at their door, and though she looked forward to embroidering the latest iteration of English flowers for him, she didn't think there was any more to it than the anticipation of a source of joy. Much like knowing that you were going to the ice cream parlor on Sunday. And then the pleasure when that day came.

In all likelihood, the familiarity that came with such continued correspondence naturally increased intimacy with each one. It was no more than that. Imagining that there was anything else was the simple product of being surrounded by Dottie and George, Gladys and Oliver—the fresh bloom of love surrounding her daily like an inescapable perfume.

But whatever it could be called, she found that the desire

to bare her soul to someone—even someone whose face she had never seen—was a new impulse that was intoxicating.

The other half of the equation—mutual attraction, the electricity of a touch—these were things to be considered another day. Ruminating on such things was a poor use of time, and her fingernails were chewed to their stubs from enough worry as it was.

She'd have to wait until the end of the war to find her answers to this and to all her questions about the future.

It seemed that all of life pivoted on five simple words—*when the war is over*—as if the world held its collective breath and could only exhale once one side or the other had become victorious.

It seemed as if people believed that things would return to normal, denying that the world was, in fact, profoundly changed.

She had finished off the previous letter with *All the Best*, as she had with nearly all the rest of them. But on this one, she'd signed *Love, Margaret* without even thinking. It was not a gesture of romanticism, as that's how she had completed her notes to John as well. But it was a symbol that however the heart wanted to label it, she'd grown to care for William and the expression was a sincere one.

She'd sealed the envelope immediately before she could second-guess that choice and how he might react to it, but found herself trembling now as she opened the door to the mailbox.

The letter made a plinking sound as it hit the bottom.

"First letter of the day. Must be an important one," said a thickly accented voice.

"Good morning, Mr. Bellavia," she answered, dodging his statement. The newspaper stand owner had just purchased this shop a few months ago from another Italian family who had never kept up with the newer products that the younger generation wanted. The store's wood green exterior had deteriorated over the years, but Mr. Bellavia had reinvigorated it with a fresh coat of paint and a new sign.

He pulled a worn scarf from around his neck as he opened his shuttered metal doors and began to arrange the bundle of the day's newspapers in front.

"What's your flavor today?" he asked. "Got a new box of Wrigley's in if you'd like some gum. Or if you'd care for some cigarettes to calm those nerves, Mild as May is made for the ladies."

"No, thank you," she replied, regretting that her pensiveness was on such display. If Margaret did smoke, she'd never choose something marketed specifically for women, lest she get a tongue-lashing from Gladys on the inequality of it. She had to give him credit, though, for pushing the two items. It seemed to her that chewing gum and cigarettes should indeed be bought in pairs. The one covering up the smell of the other. But she'd prefer to save the money on both and take it to the movies.

It was a strategy that she'd employed in her father's shop—to turn one sale into two by suggesting that the customer buy a set of spare laces to go along with their shoes. Her father had taught her that the profits were in such margins.

She was about to say goodbye and walk on when a headline caught her eye.

ARRIVING AT NORMANDY, shouted the front page of the *New York Times*.

Ernie Pyle's much-anticipated article about the reality of all that had happened just six days ago on the beaches of France. D-Day, they were calling it. The scant news about it had suggested that it was a horrific battle.

Had William and Tom been there? William's letters had suggested that they were getting ready to leave Chilton Foliat. But he could not tell her where they were going. He had a perfect record, so far, for not getting redacted.

She paid a dime to the shop owner and tucked the newspaper under her arm. She had to find somewhere to read it where she could be alone.

CHAPTER FOURTEEN

Tom's dreams were never of the fantastical nature that his friends at school experienced. He was amused by their retellings of elephants on ice skates or arriving to class stark naked. He wished his mind could wander to such entertaining places, but his dreams merely recalled events that had already happened.

Sometimes he got to relive a particularly happy birthday or the simple pleasures of catching lightning bugs as the sun descended over the river's waters. And other times—like now—they brought back memories in the vivid, painful color that he would have preferred to forget entirely.

This was one such moment, and Tom would have earned and then given away a fortune just to banish these thoughts forever.

The morphine made the dreams longer. Realer. Sadder.

And yet, the morphine dulled the present day's physical pain. So it was a toss-up.

Hurt in your sleep. Or hurt while awake.

Both were agony.

The choice was not his to make, though. The nurses made

it for him, quelling the sweats and yelling that emerged from his mouth and blended with the screams of the other men in the makeshift field hospital.

And so, he slept.

"What are you going to miss most?" William had asked Tom as they cleaned their rifles after a rigorous day on the range. Dick Winters seemed especially focused on honing their shooting skills, and an air of anticipation hovered over the men.

The battle would begin any day now.

"Mrs. Brown's Yorkshire pudding. I'm not sure even my mother can put it together quite like she does."

"Yeah. I'll miss everything about that old couple. When I get home, I want to send them something nice."

"I'll add to that," said Tom. "We're both Virginia boys. Maybe some salted ham. And some peanuts. And peach jam."

William licked his lips. "Oh, I wish I could see their faces when that package arrives."

"We should come back over and hand-deliver them."

"Nah, not me." William shook his head. "Once I set foot on American soil, I'm never leaving again. I've seen all I want to of this continent."

"You've seen Chilton Foliat and Aldbourne. Two tiny towns in England. You haven't even seen the real part of the continent yet. And neither of us made it to Oxford as we'd hoped."

William grew somber. "You know all that's about to change, right? We're rolling out as soon as we get the word."

Tom clenched his jaw and nodded as he inserted the bore down the barrel and scrubbed. "Yeah. I saw some of the planes. In fact, I got recruited to help paint them."

"Just imagine it. Two thousand Waco CG-4s." He spoke with the same awe as he did with the beauty of a sunset. William had adopted John's ability to see the best in a situation, and Tom had to admit that the sight of such a fleet had been as impressive as it had been ominous.

"Twenty-one hundred of them, I heard. That would be quite a feat if we didn't have the whole company working on it."

"They ordered the company to have it done by tomorrow. I think that means whatever is coming is imminent."

"I just hope they give us a briefing soon. The brass has been tight-lipped about their plans." The lack of information coming in only fueled his desire to remain in the military beyond the war. Being promoted to officer would not only please his father immensely, but it would also put him in the decision room. Now that he'd come to regard these men as his own blood brothers, he wanted to do everything he could to ensure their safety. And the ones to come after them.

His master's degree would give him an advantage. And if he performed with excellence when tested in the field, it would almost guarantee rapid promotion.

"Wherever we're sent, it will be a mighty vision to see them all in the air at the same time." William's eyes glossed over.

But the reality was that they were about to go to war. Not just the rehearsal for it. All their training, as difficult as it had been, was going to be nothing in comparison to flesh-and-blood battle.

The presence of such a substantial number of gliders only emphasized that.

By this time tomorrow, the planes would each bear three white stripes and two black stripes, making their bellies and wings look like zebras in order to identify them in the night. Word was that radio silence would be enforced not only because of the need to create a sneak attack, but also because the brass was afraid that the radio system wouldn't be able to handle all that traffic.

So they had to arrive quiet and stealthy, making their presence known only by the contrast of their paint colors.

It was rumored that Captain Winters would be promoted again, another sure sign of what they were about to face. More responsibility on a good man's shoulders. William had just earned his stripes as a corporal, and Tom was just below him as a technician fifth grade.

Sometimes those were meritorious. Sometimes they were given in anticipation of a great loss of men.

Their orders were to report to Aldbourne on the evening of the fifth. Saying goodbye to everything that they had known for the last few months in this charmed village. And though it rained through the day and did not look as if it would let up, word came through that they were shipping out regardless. In fact, the brass hoped that attacking during this kind of weather would be one more layer of protection for them. The element of surprise.

William and Tom trudged down the stairs after packing up all of their gear, roundly full from a meal that had seemed like the Last Supper. Tom looked back with sadness. It was unlikely that he would ever return to this place. This place where he'd built memories with John and William. In which he'd read Margaret's letters and begun to open his heart on paper.

Victoria laid her head on her paws and looked bereft, as if she could sense the shift in the house. Her shaggy fur hung over her eyes, only adding to her forlorn demeanor.

Tom expected to say goodbye to Mr. and Mrs. Brown as they read by the fireplace. But to his surprise, the old couple was already wrapped up in their raincoats and Wellies.

"We'll not have you walking to Aldbourne in this weather," said Mrs. Brown. "We're going to drive you. We borrowed an automobile from the Turnberrys."

"Don't spend the petrol on us," Tom protested, the British word for gasoline rolling off his tongue naturally.

Mr. Brown shook his head. "I'll not hear any objections. Anything to help our boys."

He took their heavy canvas bags on his shoulders, and Tom and William exchanged a look of surrender. They knew him well enough to realize that this usefulness gave him tremendous joy.

The rain poured and the simple car nearly got stuck in muddy ruts several times. Tom worried about how they would fly in such weather but figured that the higher-ups knew what was best. What was a little rain compared to saving civilization as they knew it? At least that's what he told himself.

At last, they pulled up to the gates at Aldbourne. Mr. Brown saluted them and Mrs. Brown pushed a homemade fruitcake into William's arms. Her eyes glistened with tears, and even Mr. Brown looked crumpled by their departure.

Tom pulled her into a hug, wanting to forever remember that she smelled of baked bread. He felt immeasurably grateful for the couple he would always think of as his English godparents.

"You boys be safe. Kick Hitler's arse for us." She pulled back from him and raised a fist before stepping back into the car.

Tom's eyes widened at the uncharacteristic phrase coming from Mrs. Brown's mouth, but then smiled when he saw her waving to him from behind the window.

"We will, Mrs. B. We will."

France! Though it had been rumored that this would be their destination, the fickleness of battle had not guaranteed it. But the orders had come through and Tom was at last going to see the land of his mother's family.

The flights were a go, and the troops were assigned to a C47 for what was being called Operation Neptune, part of the larger Operation Overlord. The mission of the Screaming Eagles and Easy Company particularly was to capture the town of Carentan, thereby connecting Omaha and Utah Beaches and preparing them for the Allied assault to come.

Carentan's train tracks led to both Paris and Cherbourg, making it strategically vital to Axis forces.

And therefore, vital to the Allied ones.

Tom's stomach churned as they strapped into the plane that would take them across the English Channel and drop them into France. When he'd taken the requisite literature courses as an undergrad, he imagined that when he made it to this country, he'd be reading a book, maybe Fitzgerald, while drinking coffee in Les Deux Magots. Isn't that what one was supposed to do? But this would be a harried, dangerous entrance into a land now occupied by those who wanted a world order that would eliminate anyone who didn't fit the Aryan recipe of perfection.

Tom thought of Hank, the grandson of a former slave, who picked peaches side by side with Tom in the late summer and had saved enough to buy a couple of acres of the Powell's land and build a house for his family. He thought of Dr. Weinstein in the town of Lanexa, who had treated his mother when she contracted pneumonia and traveled to and from their farm to check on her, long after his bill had been paid. He thought of the McClintock family a few farms over. Catholics with a bevy of children who were always so welcoming to Tom when he walked by and had invited him in for blueberry pancakes if he was nearby on a Saturday morning.

And William. Perhaps that was the most poignant of all. Men like William, who already lived in the shadows of what was acceptable in society, would have no place in a world dominated by Nazis.

Adolf Hitler would wipe all of them and the millions like them from the face of the earth if they didn't succeed in their mission.

Tom had not thought of it that way before. Not when reading the newspapers as the United States considered whether or not to join the war effort. Not even during training, where his focus had been on learning all he could and proving himself to his father. Earning a place on the fireplace mantel.

But now that the plane rattled away in liftoff, now that the rumble of the engine drowned out any word spoken between the men, now that lightning flashed in the distance and the fear of crashing into the frigid waters below crept in, he imagined the people who had populated his youth and was determined to fight for them. To fight for their right to exist and thrive and have the same unworried life that Tom had enjoyed up until now.

In fact, it became the only thing to hold on to. As he looked around, every other soldier had his own method of coping with the fear none of them would admit to. One clutched the wooden beads of a rosary. Another wove an unlit cigarette back and forth through his fingers. One strummed a guitar that didn't exist. And another puffed his chest in and out in an almost lionlike show of forced bravado as the man next to him sat stone-faced in terror.

All of them had black stripes painted across their faces, additional camouflage to their green army fatigues. But while their features were hidden and unrecognizable under the greasepaint, their anxieties were on display in this moment that delineated their passage from boys to men.

Boom!

The plane shook and Tom grabbed William's arm with enough force to bruise him.

"Thunder?" he mouthed.

William shook his head. "Antiaircraft fire."

Tom's hands found their way to his seat and he gripped the cold metal edges.

So much for the element of surprise.

He was seated near the front and could see through the pilot's window. Below them was a cloud cover so dense that he wouldn't have known if they were already over land or still over water, save for the flashes of light refracted in the wet sky.

The plane rattled with a terrible turbulence that was all the more terrifying because it was man-made. Someone down below—a faceless stranger—was firing into the sky hoping to shoot down other faceless strangers in a war that none of them had designed or particularly wanted. But as Tom looked around at the painted faces of his fellow soldiers, they were not anonymous. In fact, they were all sons and brothers. Some of them fathers. Which meant that the men on the ground were sons and brothers and fathers as well.

How could one greedy man cast the world into such a horror?

His heart, already clenched in fear, tightened even further at the tragedy unfolding. Humanity highjacked.

Boom! This one was more than a flash. The plane in front of them received a direct hit and turned into a fireball before their eyes.

Tom held back a cry. Who was in that plane? Anyone he knew? Projected losses that had looked so analytical on paper suddenly took on flesh and blood and form.

Boom! Another fireball.

The pilots jerked right, though they couldn't predict the aim of the ground guns any better than the ones that had just been hit. Something impacted the left window and glass shattered onto the main pilot's lap. He brushed it off and continued as if it was nothing.

Tom heard the wheeze of air as it whooshed through the plane like a scream.

"Stand up! Hook up! Let's go, Easy Company!"

Winters had a voice that could remarkably be heard above the roar of engines and gunfire and racing pulses.

Tom and William and the rest of the soldiers stood on wobbly legs that struggled to find their place as the plane was tossed to and fro. Their position was questionable, and Tom heard the pilots arguing about the need to gain altitude and the concern that if they didn't level up with the other planes, the parachuters could be hit by one of their own. Sucked into propellers.

It was a gruesome thought.

Danger in the sky. Danger in the descent. Danger on the ground.

Hank. Dr. Weinstein. The McClintocks. William.

Tom repeated their names over and over, reminding himself who he was doing this for.

Hank. Dr. Weinstein. The McClintocks. William.

Uncle Sam. Uncle Sam and the red, white, and blue.

Red, white, and blue. Panic rose in his chest and he clung to every familiar word as if it were a life preserver and he felt it clinch like a vise.

Tom looked around. The cords attaching all of them to the plane looked like overcooked spaghetti noodles, flapping back and forth as they were pitched about by the wind.

"Okay, check!" shouted Winters.

Tom took a deep breath and exhaled.

"Okay!"

"Okay!"

"Okay!"

It was repeated throughout the back of the plane as each man acknowledged their readiness.

The red light at the open door held steady until the first man was ready to jump.

It turned green, and he disappeared.

Red.

Green.

Another man jumped.

Red.

Green.

William jumped.

Red.

Green.

And then it was Tom's turn. He'd jumped so many times. Maybe hundreds. But never when the air was saturated with enemies.

He took a step and then another and felt the exhilaration of that first free fall. He closed his ears to the chaos around him and focused instead on the sea of parachutes that he knew were white but looked green as lightning and gunfire flashed and reflected off of them.

It seemed like the sky had a bad case of smallpox and Tom almost laughed at the observation.

Is this what it's like to go crazy? Thinking things that weren't fitting in the moment?

The ground got nearer and nearer as he passed through the cloud cover. He released his parachute and said a silent prayer that it operated as it meant to. Since losing John, he hadn't taken a single jump for granted. He twisted his shoulder to adjust the rifle attached to his back, one of the new M1 Garands that were coveted in the army over the older 1903 Springfields. Airborne was considered an elite unit with first pick of the artillery.

He gripped it as if it were his salvation. Because it might have to be.

He raised it to eye level, as he'd been taught, and kept

his finger far off of the safety catch. An accidental pull of the trigger could kill one of the other men falling through the area. Some motions, thankfully, had become second nature. The result of endless training that made these things instinctual.

Hello, France. I'd hoped we'd meet under different circumstances.

The gentle glide and the groans of the cows in the pastures below felt incongruous—he spared a thought there for Margaret—as the harsh sounds of warfare surrounded him. He bent his knees in preparation for the landing.

As his feet touched French soil, he curled into himself as he unlatched the parachute and removed the life vest they'd been issued in case of an unexpected landing over water. He swung the rifle around to his front and immediately set off, crouched as he ran in the direction they'd been instructed. They were supposed to meet up at Sainte-Mère-Église before heading to Carentan, but he was beginning to worry that they weren't where they were supposed to be. Had the plane been blown off course?

He looked around as he hurried forward and saw that he was alone. Or so it seemed as the tall, wild grasses rose high above his minimized stance. He could hear rustles, but certain that they'd landed far off course and possibly into enemy territory, he didn't know if they were friend or foe.

He reached into the pocket that covered his heart and pulled out the issued clicker.

Click. Click, went the thin metal plate.

Two times. That was the signal.

Click. Click. He heard in response.

He inched toward the sound and saw the white spade

painted on the green helmet of the 506th PIR. Someone from his regiment.

His heartbeat slowed just a bit, making him aware that it had been racing in the first place.

"William!" He forced a whisper when he wanted to shout. There was no one he would have wanted to see more.

"Tom!"

The men embraced. Quick. Tight. Amazed that they'd made it this far alive.

Even as they knew that they had so much farther to go.

Tom's eyes jerked open. Sweat streamed down his face as he relived those terrible moments. The pain in his right arm screamed in anguish as he remembered where he was.

And then, with all the veracity that mind and body could muster, he was reminded of several truths.

Despite the loss of blood and the near loss of his arm, he would recover.

Which meant that he would have to go back into battle.

Without William.

The despair of loneliness was perhaps the worst pain of all.

Because—like John—William was gone.

CHAPTER FIFTEEN

July 1944

*A*fter several months in the engraving yard, Margaret's fingers seemed permanently grayed from the metal shavings. Soap and water merely dulled them, and bleach had left them feeling raw.

They did not at all suit the best friend of the bride, and she was glad to have an excuse to wear lacy gloves today. They would hide the discoloration and prevent her from picking at her nails. Newly polished for the occasion.

Margaret tried to zip up the back of her dress but had some difficulty as the fabric was caught. She looked out her window to see if her mother was already outside so that she could call down for some help. Instead, she saw the mailman walk up their stoop, flipping through envelopes before slipping them through their door.

She rushed downstairs, her back exposed. But she didn't care. Her father was already outside and her mother was the only other person in the house.

She sorted through advertisements and bills and at last found the letter she'd been hoping for. She almost passed it by—it was typed rather than handwritten—but there it was, William's name on the envelope.

Her heart did a little leap. He was alive!

But then she saw the post date. June 3. And her stomach knotted with disappointment. It was written before her last letter. And worse—sent before the invasion in Normandy. The deadliest battle of the war that she'd heard of so far. This wouldn't tell her what she most wanted to know—if William and Tom had survived.

She walked back upstairs and set it facedown on her desk, eager to read it after the wedding.

But then she stopped.

On the back, he'd written: *Do not open unless I don't make it back from the war.*

Her eagerness melted into confusion. What could he have to say that he wouldn't want her to read unless he was *dead*?

What were you thinking, William?

It was almost worse than not receiving a letter at all, and her temples throbbed with the beginnings of a headache. She was tempted to read it anyway and slid her thumb under the seal. But no, she couldn't do that. William wouldn't have written that if he didn't have a serious reason to.

Disappointed, she turned the envelope back over and sighed when she looked again at the post date, hoping that she'd read it incorrectly.

Articles from Ernie Pyle and other journalists on the ground about the horrors of D-Day had sent her out of her mind with concern for William and Tom.

In a strange way, it had made her grateful that John had not lived to see it.

Pyle had described bodies and personal items and carcasses of vehicles strewn across sands that had once been the sites of frivolity but would forever be stained with the blood of heroes. Barbed wire and hidden ditches awaited the men, along with Germans embedded in concrete bunkers that were nearly impervious to naval fire. Land mines. Floating mines. Everywhere they looked, the men had been surrounded by an unprecedented campaign to kill them.

Some of the accounts had been more personal in nature. Tales of soldiers coming upon the bodies of the dead—friends and foes—and rummaging through their pockets for ammunition, canteens, grenades, food. Reduced to scavengers hunting for survival.

She shook it off. She'd read too much in the past few weeks, clinging to any new detail, especially accounts of the Airborne. Picturing William and Tom in every scenario and praying—she hoped not posthumously—for their safety.

She heard her mother calling from downstairs, urgency in her voice to hurry. Margaret looked in the mirror and adjusted the corsage attached to the right side of her chest. An orchid on a bed of baby's breath with a small fern leaf behind it. She tucked some stray wisps of hair into the braid that formed a crown over her head, smiling at the variations of color that the summer sun had created.

Would William think her hair was beautiful when at last they met?

She dismissed the thought as soon as she had it.

He had never acknowledged her many pleas to tell him which one he was in that picture that Mr. Brown had taken months ago, nor did he rise to her admonishment that it was unfair for him to know what she looked like when he didn't reciprocate. She'd receive the occasional "I'd tell you, but that's top-secret information likely to be redacted."

Or, "I'm the devilishly handsome one." Which was really no help at all, because if he was *actually* the handsome one, would he really say that about himself? But could she be sure that he wouldn't? It's not as if they had spent any time together. The kind that allowed for getting to know one's mannerisms and jests.

Not that it mattered what he looked like. He was no more than a friend to her, though one who had become quite dear.

And yet she hoped—was it a vain wish to have?—that he was, in fact, the tall one. The eyes that had depth. That looked serious and kind at the same time.

That was how she'd begun to picture him when she penned her own words on air mail stationery. Though she'd continue to care about him greatly even if she was wrong.

"Margaret Jane Beck, if you don't come down here this minute, we are leaving without you and you'll have to take the bus to the church."

She bristled. Her mother hadn't used that tone with her since she was a child, but she couldn't blame her. George's family had hired a fleet of cars to pick up the bridal party and close friends from all parts of Brooklyn, and the driver had just pulled up outside of their row house.

Margaret took the letter from her desk and slipped it into her pocket instead. Even if he didn't want her to read it, it was the most recent thing she had of his, and she wanted to feel as if he were attending the wedding with her. She ran down the stairs in her silk stockings, a gift from Dottie for standing up for her at the wedding. She was careful not to catch them on a stray splinter or to slip on the floor's glossy varnish. Her heels—specially made for her by her father for this occasion—were hanging from her fingers. She put them on before stepping outside and marveled as she looked down at them, pleased that something of such beauty had once again been crafted in their shop. Creamy leather with embroidered pink rosettes.

It was almost like old times.

Margaret didn't know if it was typical for Catholic weddings to last as long as this one was or if the Troutwines had paid the priest to make it purgatorially long to make up for their first daughter's lack of nuptials, but it was sweltering in the pew at St. Charles Borromeo and time ticked by with aching slowness. Though she'd only heard tidbits of the theology of Dottie's family in the years they'd known each other, Margaret suspected that the *offer it up* nature of the religion encouraged them to withstand it without complaints. Poor Dottie and George had to kneel through the whole thing, and Margaret imagined that her friend was drowning in sweat on this blazing July afternoon. If it were her, she would have been slumped over the velvet-lined wooden kneeler, but Dottie's back was as straight as if a rod were attached to it. George's too.

Was this a strain on his heart? If he was concerned, he didn't let on.

Hats off to them.

The brilliant sun shined through the stained-glass windows, illuminating the room with depictions of saints whose names and stories were unknown to her. The painted ceiling atop gothic arches looked like something that belonged in Europe. And the organ pipes seemed as if they could reach the sky. It was impressive for a little redbricked church in the heart of Brooklyn, and Margaret's chest swelled at the beauty of it.

At least it was a distraction from the heat.

That and the constant page-turning of the leather-bound missal that translated the Latin being spoken at the altar and the English printed on sheets as thin as an air mail letter.

Margaret looked back at the bride and groom. This was the day she and Dottie had playacted so many times as little girls. Taking turns wearing a white pillow sheet as the gown. Embellishing it with ribbons and scraps from their mothers' stashes. And later, when it was known beyond doubt that John would be the one to greet her at the end of the aisle, they would cut pictures from magazines and collect them in boxes.

They dreamed about the day when they'd officially become sisters. And now it would never be quite like what they'd imagined. Margaret tightened her lips and held a handkerchief to her eye.

This was a happy day. But it didn't look like what it was supposed to. George, dear as he was to them all, was not the one they ever thought they'd see here.

Dottie looked back, perhaps with that intuition that had been enriched through most of their lives. She caught Margaret's eye and smiled.

That was all Margaret needed. Life didn't always turn out as one expected it to. But that didn't mean it isn't wonderful.

"How are you holding up, Mom?" Margaret whispered as the bride and groom spoke their vows. She hoped her mother wasn't too uncomfortable. The sweater that went with her best dress was unseasonable, but she didn't think it seemly to show bare arms in a church.

Mrs. Beck held a handkerchief to her eyes and dabbed them.

"It's bittersweet," she said, understanding a different meaning. Then she sighed. "But Dottie looks so happy."

They squeezed each other's hands and didn't let go.

Mrs. Troutwine looked back at them and frowned, extending a finger over her mouth and shushing them.

Surely, Dottie's mother must be rejoicing, though. John had not been a Catholic. He'd mentioned the need for him and Dottie to apply for a dispensation from the bishop because of it, but he was shipped off before they could even begin the process.

Not so with George. In fact, his uncle was a deacon at St. Patrick's Cathedral in Manhattan. Practically Catholic royalty.

So Mrs. Troutwine could take her pucker-faced expression and…

No. They were in a church. Margaret needed to temper such thoughts.

But this one she allowed—*how on earth had this woman borne sweet Dottie?*

To Margaret, it had always been one of the world's greatest mysteries.

It all evaporated, though, when Dottie—resplendent in her white satin gown—exchanged her vows with George. Not a dry eye was had.

The reception was held at the Algonquin. Though the

appliance business came through George's paternal side—dating back to the first modern iterations of iceboxes and the like—his mother was a relative of a city newspaper editor and she had connections at the hotel long known for its literary round table. Writers for *Vanity Fair* had once met there daily and feasted on free celery and popcorn as they discussed news and politics and literature, eventually turning their endeavor into an entirely new publication—the *New Yorker* magazine.

All of this Margaret learned from Oliver, who had heard of the Algonquin all the way over in England. Still attached to Gladys despite all odds, he was accompanying her to the reception and regaling them all with stories of the legendary place on the drive.

"We'll have to keep an eye out for the cat, of course," he said with the enthusiasm of a young boy.

"The cat?" Gladys huffed. She had never had an affection for pets, thinking it preposterous that one would voluntarily bring an *animal* into their home.

"Hamlet," he continued. "The owner of the hotel once took in a stray cat and named it Rusty. But John Barrymore thought it needed a more refined name and suggested Hamlet instead. Ever since then, there is always a hotel cat. If it's male, it's Hamlet. A female is Matilda."

"That's the most ridiculous thing I've ever heard of," Gladys answered.

Margaret racked her brain and finally remembered why this sounded familiar. "Oh, I know what you're talking about! They hold the annual feline fashion show. I just came across an article about it in the newspaper saying that applications can be turned in to participate next month."

"A feline fashion show?" Gladys shook her head. "*Now* I've heard the most ridiculous thing ever."

Oliver grinned and caught Margaret's eye. She grinned back. Despite Gladys's protestations, they knew she couldn't resist going to something so unusual.

"Well, that's too bad," he said with exaggerated disappointment. "I was planning to do a story on it for the *London Times* and thought you would have liked to come with me."

Gladys shrugged. "With all that is happening in the world, why on earth would your readers pay two cents—or two *pence* as it may be—about that?"

Margaret answered for him. "Because we need to read good news. Silly news. And—correct me if I'm wrong, Oliver— but my guess is that you Brits enjoy the opportunity to have a laugh at our expense."

"*Ding, ding, ding!* You've won the prize, Margaret Beck. Since Gladys refused me, you can come along."

Gladys sat up straight, just as the driver hit a bump in the road. She gripped the edge of the upholstered seat and then smoothed her skirt as if nothing had happened. "I didn't say I wouldn't go."

Oliver and Margaret once again exchanged conspiratorial looks.

"Okay. If you really want to," he conceded.

And it was settled.

They arrived at the entrance on 44th, and a doorman in a tall felt hat opened the car door. Twelves stories of white stone and brown brick cast their imposing shadow onto the sidewalk, and olive-green awnings looked like half umbrellas over the gold-cased windows. Margaret felt like a princess, basking in the generosity of George's family to include her in such indulgences.

So this is how the rich live. But she surprised herself with her lack of envy. The excitement was in the novelty of it. And novelty always proved to be a short-lived siren. Though Dottie's financial status had just been elevated tremendously, she shared George's penchant for simplicity. In fact, they planned to buy a house in Brooklyn rather than purchase a Park Avenue Manhattan apartment so George could continue working at the Navy Yard while Dottie stayed home with Joanna. And any future children that would come.

The elegance continued as they entered the hotel. Marble floors sparkled and black pillars surprisingly reflected the light of the many crystal chandeliers. It was not a large room, but it had a grand coziness that she hadn't expected.

Eight at a time, the guests entered the elevators for the one-story ride up to the ballroom while others ascended the staircase. However they arrived, they were welcomed by a beautiful sight. Everything was draped in white—flowers, tablecloths, plates. Even the waiters' uniforms were white. Margaret considered the impracticality of it, imagining the bleach that would need to be used on the laundry later. But her mind was not supposed to be concerned. Tonight was to be one of no concerns.

Two hours into the festivities, satiated with unending trays of crab meat and canapes, the band started up with a Glenn Miller tune. Gladys pulled Oliver onto the dance floor and Margaret grinned as her friend wore herself to exhaustion with each passing song.

"Golly, they're good," Gladys said at last, standing over

Margaret as she turned around to applaud the band. "Do ya think they have any gin at the bar?"

"I've never known you to drink gin, Gladys."

"My darling Maaaahgret," she slurred, already with lips loosened by whatever she *had* found so far. "It is the most sincere wish of my heart that no one—not even you—know everything that I have buried inside me. I like to keep 'em guessing."

Margaret grinned. "Keep who guessing, Glads?"

"Them," she said, pointing to no one. She picked up Margaret's drink, still nearly full and diluted by the ice that had melted. Gladys took a sip and winced.

"Take a turn with Oliver, honey. My feet are spent."

Oliver helped Gladys into her seat.

"Would you like to dance, Margaret?"

"You don't have to ask just to be kind."

"I'm not being kind. I was going to ask anyway."

She took the hand he extended to her and he pulled her gently to her feet. They walked hand in hand to the parquet floor and the band switched to a slow song.

Oliver pulled her into his arms. She'd never been this close to a man before, and there was something pleasant about swaying next to his tall, rugged frame. It was something she'd like for herself one day. This feeling that someone was her partner in life, leading as she followed. Following as she led. As much as she enjoyed the horizons that women were nearing and had taken steps even closer to them by working at the Navy Yard, something in her yearned for this kind of relationship as well. She wondered again—could they both be had?

"May I ask you something, Margaret?"

She looked up.

"Of course."

"I've bought a ring for Gladys. Do you think she'll say yes? Or will she boot me back over the Atlantic?"

Goose bumps popped up on Margaret's arm. "Oliver, that's really...nice of you. And I wish I could tell you that I'm confident she'll accept it. But you know Gladys. She loves to surprise people."

"That's what I like about her, Margaret. *Love* about her, in fact."

Margaret nodded. "I know. Me too. Life with Gladys will never be dull. She's been on her own for so long and has well-earned opinions about, well, just about anything. I've never thought there would be a man who could tolerate that about her."

"I don't tolerate it. I appreciate it."

"You are one in a million, my friend."

He tipped an imaginary cap in gratitude and his voice turned somber. "It would mean moving back to England someday. I'm probably here until the war is over. And after D-Day victory, that may be sooner rather than later."

So many thoughts ran through Margaret's mind as she imagined what Gladys might say to that. It was really anybody's guess. Oddsmakers would be at a loss to lay bets on it.

"You know she's not going to be the type to settle down and have babies, right?"

He nodded. "I know. I have been approached by the *London Times* for a correspondent job that would take me all over the world. And I wouldn't consider it if it meant always leaving a wife and children at home. But with Gladys—with Gladys,

I think she would rather like joining me. There's so much to explore."

"I think Gladys *would* love to see the world. But I don't know if the world is quite ready for her. She'll see injustices that are centuries old and become a one-woman force for change."

"I rather agree with you there." He laughed. "But I want it anyway. I want to see it all through her eyes. And hear her opinions. She'll surely look at things in ways I never would have thought of myself."

Margaret was glad to hear him say that. Gladys certainly needed a man who loved her in all her totality.

"Here's what you do," she decided. "It can't be your idea. Gladys has to ask *you* to marry *her*."

Oliver grinned, the sheepish kind that had quickly endeared all of them to him. "Why was I afraid that you'd say that?"

"Because you already know it's true. She won't stand for feeling maneuvered or provoked. But if she realizes that she may lose you when you leave...I think we'll see her true feelings emerge."

"You're a wise one, Margaret Beck. How come some great guy hasn't swept you away?"

She shrugged. "I think the war has stolen just about every eligible young man from Brooklyn and beyond."

The band began another slow song, as if it was inviting her to bare her soul. Everyone had their own problems and Margaret's felt too trivial to voice.

And yet, he was asking.

"I want love," she whispered at last, admitting it as much to herself as she was to him. "I want love and marriage and babies and all that comes with it. I *also* want to take these things I've learned at the Navy Yard and...and *do* something with it. I don't know what yet. But I think women are teetering on some confusing precipice where we *don't* want to throw the old ways out but we *do* want to walk through the doors that are just beginning to crack open for us. And if it's hard enough for us to navigate that, how can we expect the men—especially the ones who come home and understandably want their jobs back—to reconcile that? I've...I've made my own money, and I don't want to give that up. How do I do that, though? Even if I miraculously find a man who supports that notion, what would that even be like? Torn between motherhood and working? I mean it, Oliver. It's not just a frivolous notion. How are women *actually* supposed to do that?"

She could see the wrinkle in Oliver's brow as he gave her words serious consideration, and she appreciated that he wasn't the sort to just placate her.

When he finally spoke, it was the exact wisdom she needed to hear. "What about your parents? That may be your father's name on the cobbler shop, but from what Gladys has told me, your mum has played a big role in it. Did you feel slighted as a daughter by the hours she spent there?"

"No. She would bring me down to the shop. And John. She'd read books to us and play games and let us watch what they were doing. That's how we began to learn to work with our hands."

"Exactly. Don't get swept up in the logistics of the thing. When you find the right man, when you know you're in love, build something together. Like your parents. Play more of a role than even your mother did. But draw on that example. It may be a new world, but love is like elastic. It can stretch to embrace it."

Margaret giggled. "I'm sorry. I'm not laughing at you. I'm just realizing what a lucky girl Gladys is to find a man who speaks prose like it's poetry. I think your writing is wasted on the newspapers."

"I saw him first, you know." The music had stopped and Gladys came over, a glass of gin in hand.

Margaret squeezed Oliver's hand and placed it over Gladys's. "Of course you did. And don't let him get away."

CHAPTER SIXTEEN

July 1944

The waves outside Tom's window lapped gently, impervious to the devastation that had occurred on the shores mere weeks ago. The military hospital had moved from battlefield tents into vacated hotels in Cherbourg, and Tom was lucky enough to have been assigned a room that looked out onto the Channel.

His hand hesitated over the paper and he struggled to grip the pen. The cast had been off for a few days, but his muscles had atrophied and the exercises the nurse showed him were strenuous and painful. But he kept at them. He had to get back to his men.

And he had to write to Margaret.

The hand was the least of his injuries.

Seven weeks had passed since that day in Normandy. And even though all he wanted to do was forget, it was the only thing he could think about.

The weather. The jump. The bodies.

When he and William realized that they'd been dropped

miles off course, they knew that each step was precarious. They crouched below the tall grasses, inching along and stopping whenever they heard the crunch of footprints.

Click. Click.

Every time they heard the signal, they responded in kind, and by the time they'd walked a mile through a field of yellow rapeseed, there were seven lost soldiers who had banded together.

Not knowing how to get to Sainte-Mère-Église from wherever they were, they decided to head toward their ultimate destination, Utah Beach. They could hear it in the distance from the amount of gunfire.

There were two suspected guns aiming at Utah Beach, and their company would have to take them out so that the armada of boats arriving would land safely.

But then, shots. Much closer than the beach.

They fell to the ground and crawled to the side of the gravel road they were traveling on. The gun was close. Close enough that Tom could feel his ears ringing.

It was ahead of them.

And as they approached, they heard commands shouted in German.

A chill shot through Tom like a Virginia winter. This was what they'd trained for. But nothing had prepared him for hearing the staccato words of the enemy's language.

William assumed leadership of their group and gave the hand signals for them to advance. Rifles up.

They'd arrived at a clearing. It was nearly impossible to see the German soldiers amid a sea of netting and sandbags. They'd certainly mastered the art of fortification. But Tom could see the flashes of their rifles, and their positions would be momentarily lit up.

He looked at William, who was gesturing for them to flank the Germans on the left.

Tom turned around and repeated the motion to the men behind him.

They crouched low as they approached a bunker.

Tom watched as William held up his hand for the rest of them to stop. William pulled something from his pocket.

A grenade.

He pulled the pin and Tom's heart seemed to stop as he watched. The Germans in the bunker were firing through the clearing at an alarming rate, and Tom assumed that the Americans on the other side of it must be advancing.

William crept forward and threw the grenade into the slim opening on the side of the bunker and started running back toward the woods.

The bunker exploded with spectacular force that could be felt even at this distance, leaves and branches and debris falling like rain. Tom didn't see any way that the men could have survived. For a second, he knew victory. And as he looked to his right, he saw that William's actions had opened a way for some of the American troops to move into the clearing.

His instinct was to run toward William, but he'd been given the order to stay. William suddenly stopped. And turned. Away from their direction.

He'd seen something. Someone. And he didn't want them to know that there were others.

Then—a shot.

Even among the many others, Tom seemed to hear this lone bullet zip through the air. He could almost see it, its gold casing creating a trail of smoke behind it.

All the sounds around were muffled to near nothingness.

He wanted to shout. To warn William. William, who was running away from them to protect their position. But he couldn't. Or wouldn't. To do so would negate the sacrifice William had made.

Because the bullet caught up with him.

Tom heard and saw the bullet over and over through the slow and agonizing days since. In reality, it had happened in a mere second.

And what seared in his memory most was watching William fall.

What made his ears ring was the silence, the terrible silence of William not getting up.

Tom bit down on his hand to keep from crying out. And if it had not been for the soldier holding his shoulders down to restrain him, he might have gone to his side.

The battlefield held no harbor for grief. One man among many had fallen, but there was no time to mourn them if you wanted to keep from losing others. Emboldened with anger, Tom assumed the leadership of their menagerie of six and sent two of them to find the sniper who had killed William while he took the others around to the right side of the clearing.

There, they spotted another bunker. Better camouflaged than the first because it was painted the color of its surroundings.

Tom put his hand up to halt his troops.

He pulled the grenade from his pocket, just as he'd seen

William do. He crept forward, holding it gingerly, inching toward the bunker.

A bullet whizzed past him. Then another. He dropped to the ground and pulled himself on his belly until he was close enough to throw the handheld bomb.

He took a breath. William just did this and he would too.

Hank. Dr. Weinstein. The McClintocks. William.

Margaret.

He repeated their names under his breath. They were why he was here. They are who he would die for if the price of his life demanded it.

It was strangely liberating to accept that an action might take your life. Energy to do things he never would have imagined doing before surged through him.

He pulled the pin and tossed it.

Bull's-eye.

A rush of adrenaline pulsed through him.

They'd been taught to have the *will to kill, the skill to kill, but not the thrill to kill.*

That's what separated man from the animals.

But in that moment, it was a terrible temptation to let himself feel such satisfaction at killing those who had murdered his friend.

He ran back to his men and motioned for them to run.

They made it past the German line and rejoiced when they found Americans on the other side.

He'd done it. A small thing in light of William's sacrifice, but in that one action, he felt like he'd earned his father's regard.

He scooped up a handful of dirt and deposited it in his

pocket. This was hallowed ground, the resting place of martyrs. It would remind him of William and bolster him through what lay ahead. And when this war was over—as it had to be someday—he would send this dirt to William's family and tell them about his sacrifice.

Hours later, they'd all made their way to Utah Beach. Muddy. Tired. But grateful to be alive.

Until it started up again.

It was only after Tom woke up in the hospital days later that he recalled the rest. His right hand had been broken when another soldier's bullet-riddled body fell and the butt of his rifle hit Tom's hand like a stone. Likewise, his femur and collarbone had snapped. He called for a medic, but there were too few of them to attend to so many.

He lay back, unable to move, and passed out.

"Bonjour, Capitane. Comment vous sentez-vous aujourd'hui?"

The French nurse who had attended him since he was first brought in gave him her usual greeting. She called everyone "Captain"; there was no time to learn names. Soldiers either recovered enough to return to battle or were sent home.

Or they died.

Only a handful had been there as long as Tom had.

"Bon," he answered to the question she asked every morning: "How are you doing today?"

It was not the only French he'd learned. He could say *balle* for bullet, *douleur* for pain, and *triste* for sad.

These were words he longed to share with Margaret, even if

they were acquired by listening to the badly wounded French soldiers around him. Maybe she would enjoy learning some French words along with the fancy English ones she collected. He'd have to find some with happier translations.

Flowers. Chocolate. Love.

And he might get his chance. William's actions and those of all the men on that battlefield in Normandy had significantly propelled the Allied cause. He'd heard that they were going to make a push into Paris soon. If they succeeded, the Allies will have won back France.

Hank. Dr. Weinstein. The McClintocks. William.

Margaret.

It was worth it.

But that was an easy thing to think, knowing that despite his injuries, he was expected to live. Would John and William have said it was worth it?

The thought of them brought tears to Tom's eyes, and he didn't even try to wipe them away. All the men here cried. There was no shame in it.

He imagined what it would have been like if they'd all made it. John would have been a wonderful father. William would have taught philosophy or psychology or some other heady subject at a university. Ten years down the road when this nightmare was over, they might have remained friends in the civilian world. Met up for holidays. Watched their children play together. And reminisced about Mrs. Brown's Yorkshire pudding.

The war had taken their lives. And it had rewritten the future that they might have enjoyed together.

His only consolation was reading and rereading the letters

Margaret had written to William all these past months, which he'd taken possession of at William's insistence before they left Chilton Foliat.

What kind of prescience did William possess that he could have known what this would mean to Tom?

Because the letters bolstered him more than anything could have.

Tom pulled her latest one out from under his pillow, which he kept next to the picture of her that was quickly wrinkling with time. A white line ran through the middle where he'd folded it into his pocket as they headed toward that helicopter.

But even with its damage, she remained perfect to him.

There was only one problem. She'd written the letters to William.

She had no way of knowing that it was Tom's handwriting that graced the letters. That Tom's words had fashioned the last few.

Because William had wanted it that way.

William had received one from her on one of their last days in Chilton Foliat, which he read and then handed to Tom as he always did.

"You know," he'd said, "this girl's perfect for you. If I were a different man..."

"When you get out of the army, maybe you need to take up matchmaking. Because you're relentless, William."

It wasn't until after the jump, after the battle, after Tom had awoken from the morphine haze that he'd actually read her letter.

She talked about the baby.

She talked about the upcoming wedding of Dottie and George.

She sounded the happiest she'd been since losing her brother.

She'd signed it *Love, Margaret*.

Love, Margaret. Tom's eyes rested on those precious words and his heart beat fast as if they had been intended for him.

He lingered over it, hoping that it might mean more than a casual footer. But he shook off the notion, supposing that it was merely the shift from pen pal to that of good friend.

He did, however, allow himself to make the observation that the word had been written after a couple of the letters had been penned by him alone.

Margaret sounded full of the kind of optimism that believes in a bright future.

How could he dash that?

Tom asked the nurse for some paper and a pen. "Papier et stylo, Capitane," she said as she handed them to him.

Dear Margaret, he began.

He wiped some sweat from his forehead with his sleeve.

This was going to be more difficult than he'd imagined.

I regret to inform you that William

He scratched the words out.

That's as far as he got. For two days. Two long days in which he wrestled with words in his mind, turning them over in every combination that attempted to break the news softly. But it was an impossible task.

Seeing it in ink made it all too real, as if he were watching William fall on that battlefield all over again. If it caused him this kind of anguish, how could he inflict that on Margaret? Just when she was rediscovering joy?

Dear Margaret, he tried again.

William was a good friend to both of us.

No. That wasn't much better.

Two more days went by. Tom thought about it, starting and stopping more letters than he could count, keeping them in his head so as to not waste his supply of *papier et stylo*.

Thinking about William brought back memories that he wasn't ready to relive.

Tom shook as he took a pen in his right hand, grateful that it hadn't been the one to sustain damage. If he'd had to write with his left, the chicken-scratch look of it would have pulled him out of the world he was absorbed into when he wrote to her.

Dearest Margaret, he started, a sense of peace descending on him. The first he'd felt in a long time.

Returning to her felt like a puzzle piece nestled with its exact match.

By the time this letter arrives, you will have heard all about Normandy. It was as bad as the reports likely stated. And even worse. Good men were lost and I saw things that will be impossible to forget. I won't belabor it because you know all that you need to know, and I don't want to fill your head with those horrors by reliving them for you.

So enough of that.

As I write, I am looking out on the English Channel. In

the distance is the Fort de l'île Pelée. I believe I am using all of the correct markings—I asked my nurse for help—but I am certain that I could not duplicate its pronunciation. It reminds me of pictures I've seen of that island prison in San Francisco—Alcatraz. Beyond it—and beyond my view— there are other fortifications of the last century—Forts de Chavagnac, de l'Ouest, Central, and de l'Est.

This simple town of Cherbourg is quite well guarded. And yet, things they couldn't have imagined back when they were built—airplanes, bombs, and the like—managed to all but destroy it until we came to liberate its rubble.

I see people venture out every day, still untrusting that the enemy has moved out for good. But they slip out of their homes and catch fish and sunshine and rebuild brick by brick.

It's an admirable thing.

I understand this town and its people, even from this little room. I have always been protected by the expectations of my parents—a life laid out and one that I have dutifully embraced. But the war has similarly dismantled that security and I find myself wanting to . . . create a new edifice on an old foundation.

Please forgive the metaphor. Too much salt air and too much time has softened a hardened soldier.

I want you to know, though, that with every step I took in my cracked leather boots, you were near me. Your friendship is that fortification that kept me safe. When I saw the beauty of the yellow rapeseed flowers blooming on landscape, I wanted to pick them and make a bouquet to give you. A real one, not simply the ones sketched for you at the end of my letters.

The thought resuscitated me when I feared I would suffo-
cate from the ugliness of the battle. I carried your picture in
my left chest pocket. Not as a talisman but as a reminder of
why we were there. What—who—we were fighting for. All
the beloved ones we left behind when we crossed the Atlantic.
I pressed on when I wanted to give up because I wanted to
believe that we will all see home again.

Dare I hope—I would like to see you in person when we
are on the other side of this.

This is more than we have shared before, but when you have
been surrounded by too many lives cut short, it makes you
think about the things you want to say and to say them now
rather than to wait. And say them without reservation.

Please write soon. You can't possibly know how your
letters give me the strength to continue on.

Tom set the pen down and looked it over.

The words were a surprise, even to himself. There was
something about the curve of handwriting—the slope up, the
slant down, over and over—that dulled inhibitions and crafted
courage where one wouldn't have thought it existed.

He meant what he'd said—seeing how swiftly death could
take a man created an indelible change.

The nurse had somehow procured two pencils at his
request—yellow and green—*jaune et verte*—and he drew out
the delicate petals of the rapeseed flower. He held it at arm's
length when he was finished and frowned. Individually, it was
an unremarkable blossom. But it had been the one beauty in
the battlefield—yellow so vibrant and abundant that it seemed
as if heaven itself had spilled paint upon the ground.

How he wished Margaret could see it in person.

He picked the pen up again and stared at it.

He still had to finish the letter.

Love, he began.

He took a breath.

William

CHAPTER SEVENTEEN

August 1944

As soon as Tom sent the letter off, he regretted it.

Not the sentiments. Actually, pouring onto paper what he'd been wanting to say for months felt like nothing he'd ever felt before. Perhaps the closest thing was the moment he jumped from an airplane. The second of hesitation and fear, toes hanging over the edge, questioning and hesitant. Choosing courage. Stepping off into nothingness. A literal leap of faith. And then—the exhilaration of a free fall as he looked around and marveled at the beauty that he would never have seen if he'd kept his feet on the ground.

Yes—it was exactly like that. He'd jumped.

Would she be his parachute? Or would his words fall flat and be extinguished?

No, he did not regret the sentiments. He'd seen life snuffed out too soon too many times to think that playing it safe was a winning strategy.

It was the name that made him wince. He'd signed it as William.

Why oh why oh why had he done that?

In the moment, he'd told himself that she couldn't bear more bad news just when she was finally sounding happy again. But had that really been the considerate thing to do? Or was it a less daunting way for him to share his feelings—hiding behind the protection of William's name? The familiarity of it?

He'd sent the nurse to retrieve it, begging her in his stilted French to rescue the letter before it was tossed into the mail sack with countless others and shipped off in a cargo plane.

She'd come back empty-handed, consoling him only with a warm glass of milk. The plane had taken off.

What had he done?

One little action—seven letters instead of the three in his name—had changed everything.

It was one thing to do so when William was alive. And even with his encouragement. William had rightly pegged that Tom would feel more freedom in his words if he wrote them in proxy.

It was a worthy exercise for a while. When the stakes were lower.

But shouldn't things be different now that he was no longer here?

If Margaret welcomed the words, she would welcome them as *William's* words. Not Tom's.

If the words were unwanted by her, she might stop writing altogether. Or she'd send a letter letting him down easy.

Oh, that would hurt worse than all of the broken bones he'd endured.

There was no way to come back from this. Even a follow-up note in which Tom confessed that he'd been the actual author of the letters had little hope of success. She knew him only by his drawings at the end of what she believed were William's longer messages. And although he had labored over each of those, trying to delight her with renderings of the countryside, it was not enough for her to reciprocate what he'd said.

The only alternative was that she would be rightfully angered by what he'd done. Intention, or no intention.

That was that. He'd go dark until he could figure out what to do. And it would be a long time before he'd know her response anyway. His bones had healed and he'd received permission to rejoin his unit.

They were heading to Holland.

Any letters from Margaret would take weeks to catch up to him.

Or may not reach him at all if they were addressed to a dead man.

Margaret's heart swelled when she read William's letter.

There was something about it that had reached a new depth. It was not merely the signature—*Love, William*. That just reflected what she herself had written and she could not infer any more than what she had intended in her own letter. Though it did signal a receptivity that pleased her.

It was his candor. As he'd put it, the loss of inhibition. Dottie had told Margaret that after having a baby, she was in awe of her own body and the remarkable things it was capable of. Perhaps it was the same with men— there was no more grueling challenge one could face than a battlefield. And when he'd done so—aware of the brevity and sacredness of life—he could find comfort in discovering his feelings.

She rather liked this new side of William and was flattered that he'd chosen to share those feelings with her.

She had hoped that he would mention his previous letter— the typed one with the odd message on the back of the envelope. The one she could only read if the unthinkable happened. No matter. There was no need for it now that she knew he'd survived Normandy.

As had Tom. Although William had made no mention of him, his friend had drawn a lovely likeness of a rapeseed flower. And she had just the right floss with which to embroider it.

She lay back on her bed, wrinkling the lace coverlet she'd placed across it, and held the envelope to her heart.

"Are you okay up there?" asked her mother from the bottom of the stairs. "I thought I heard a noise."

A grin spread across Margaret's face like butter on hot waffles and her cheeks burned with excitement.

"I'm just fine! I promise!"

She sighed and closed her eyes.

William and Tom were safe. Weeks of worry could rest at last and nothing could dampen the feeling of tremendous relief that came over her.

She pulled out a fresh piece of stationery. Heavier than air mail, but she was earning enough to afford the extra stamps and even the paper itself. It was lavender, embossed with silver flowers.

Dearest William,

I am delighted that our correspondence seems to mean as much to you as it does to me. I never suspected when I knit that first sock and wrote that first note that a friendship would bloom from it. But it has become the very best of surprises.

If it seems indulgent that I am writing to you on such lovely paper, I'm going to defend myself straight off by telling you that I have gotten another promotion and it was my little treat for myself to celebrate. Plus, it's something I get to share with you. You're worth the extra postage.

(Which in other times, might seem like such a trivial thing to say, but I think in these sparse days, even so much as a second cherry tomato on a salad seems like an extravagance!)

Anyway—on to the good news. The sewing job was child's play for me, only because of my many years working in the cobbler's shop. And the engraving work—well, it never really excited me.

But now! I am a welder. A woman welder. Can you believe that? We've had to take on so many jobs that the men left behind, but I'm not ashamed to say that it has been pure delight. Holding the torch in my hands is holding power itself. (A rare thing in the life of a woman, I must say. I see why it is an alluring concept.) Wearing the visor reminds me that it's dangerous. I never would have pegged myself for finding that exciting—I was such a ninny when I thought that engraving ordnance was akin to handling munitions! But my favorite thing by far is watching the sparks fly. It's like twinkling Christmas lights and the 4th of July all at once.

And by the end, I have made something that I can really be proud of. Why, just yesterday, I welded a significant part of the hull of our newest ship. Marvelously named the "Coral Sea."

I earn an extra dollar a week. Which months ago, I would have spent on department store cosmetics. (Rather than drug-store ones, not that I expect you to know the difference. But there is one.) Now I feel that each week, each month brings me exponentially closer to adulthood and away from girlish giggles and such. I am setting aside half to give to my parents and putting away fifty cents a week in an old Mason jar for no other reason than it seems like the wise thing to do.

The only black eye on the new assignment is the awful foreman. He missed the cut-off age for joining the military by a mere four months and he takes out his anger on the employees in his charge. Acting like the general he imagined himself to be. (He sounds a bit like your precious Sobel.) I never understood a man's impulse to be "in the action"— but now that I am enjoying my work so thoroughly, I see the appeal.

Not that I'm comparing it to what you're doing. Not in the slightest. But for a woman—this woman, at least—it has been the height of excitement.

She wrote a few more lines telling him about Joanna cutting her first tooth and her worry over her father slowing down. Previously, she'd tried to keep things like that to a minimum— William had far greater things to worry about. But him sharing his vulnerability felt like invitation to share hers.

When she was satisfied, she signed it,

Love, Margaret

She put the end of the pen in her mount and thought for a moment.

P.S., she started. *Please tell Tom how very much I am enjoying the flowers that he "adumbrates." (How's that for a new word?) Assuming you don't have a dictionary at your disposal, it means "to sketch an outline of something." If you're not careful, my friend, I may even begin to anticipate those drawings even more than I do your letters. Tell him to keep them coming.*

Margaret smiled as she set her pen down. William's survival was the cherry on top on a run of things that had been looking upward. The Sock 'Em Club had knit nearly two hundred pairs to date, and her new position in the Navy Yard reinforced how much she loved creating something with her hands. But these accomplishments were small in comparison to Dottie's new roles of wife and mother. And if Gladys indeed married Oliver, she'd be off having adventures in foreign lands.

It was all the inspiration she needed to imagine a future of her own. And even if she didn't yet know what they were, she was going to save for them. She gave half her earnings to help her parents, but as she told William, she kept the other half for herself.

She put on her favorite green dress with its lacy V-neck collar, feeling like mailing this letter was an occasion and ran down the stairs before the postman arrived.

"Well, I'll be a monkey's uncle!" Gladys responded when Margaret shared William's letter with her friends.

Dottie smiled as she stretched her legs and toes across the sandy beach, a picture of bliss at this indulgence. George had offered to watch Joanna so that Dottie, Gladys, and Margaret could spend the day together, as it was expected to be one of the first tolerable ones after a blazing hot summer. Margaret and Gladys had been picking up extra shifts at the Navy Yard because production on the USS *Coral Sea* was in full swing, and the Navy was hoping to put it in action as soon as possible. It was the first aircraft carrier that Margaret had had a chance to work on, and every time she saw it, it took her breath away.

"A monkey's uncle? That makes *you* one as well, then." Margaret laughed, nudging Gladys in the ribs with her elbow.

"It takes one to know one."

"Oh, you two," Dottie laughed. "You're both the furthest things from a monkey, even if your eyes are droopy these days."

Gladys pulled a compact from her beach bag and dabbed some powder all around her face. "I blame the *Coral Sea*. She is a demanding lady."

"I'm sure she is. Gosh, an aircraft carrier. I can only imagine what she will look like when she's done. I don't think I've ever seen George this excited over a ship."

"Don't worry, Dottie. You'll always be his best girl."

Dottie giggled. "I know that. He tells me every day."

"And bought you the house to prove it. With views of the river in the poshest part of Brooklyn. And five bedrooms! Do you plan to fill them all with babies?"

"In due time, certainly. Joanna is plenty for now. But enough of that. We were talking about Margaret and William."

Margaret smiled in appreciation of Dottie's thoughtfulness. Usually, she loved this kind of banter, but Dottie had George and Gladys had Oliver and for the first time, Margaret had someone of her own to swoon about.

"I'm sorry, Mags," said Gladys. "Please continue." She adjusted her towel, lathered some oil on her skin, and lay back.

"Well, I've read the letter to you. What do you think?"

She was not surprised by Gladys's answer, nor the fact that she had an opinion at the ready. "I think it's romantic and all. I really do. But I wouldn't cut off your options. You haven't even seen the boy. How do you know you'll, you know, *want* him like that?"

"Gladys!" Dottie admonished.

"Oh, come on, Dots. You're one to talk. You may act prim and proper, but which one of us got knocked up first?"

Margaret started choking on the sip of Coke she'd just taken, the drink fizzing down her throat and mixing with the roaring laugh that wanted to come out.

Dottie held her ground. "So you're telling me that you and Oliver never..."

Gladys sat up and pulled a cigarette and lighter from her bag. She lit it and took a long drag before exhaling the smoke. Her ruby-red lipstick left a ring on the paper. "I don't kiss and tell, *dahling*."

Margaret rolled her eyes. As much as she could believe it of Gladys, she could equally believe that Gladys was pulling their legs.

Keep 'em guessing, she'd once said. Margaret supposed that included her friends.

"Back to you, doll," continued Gladys. "I'm serious. Words

are nice. And you have a weird affinity for them that he seems to share. But talk is cheap, as they say. So, yes. I stand by what I said. How do you know you will *want* him like that? And even more importantly, if anything truly serious came of it, do you know if he would accept having a wife who works? Because despite the hours, I can tell that you enjoy making a paycheck."

"That's getting way ahead of ourselves, don't you think?" Margaret asked. William had mentioned wanting to meet her. He hadn't exactly included a diamond ring in the envelope. It was entirely natural that two friends would want to meet.

"Oh, let's be serious," Gladys continued. "You and Dottie are cut from the same cloth. You'll want the white-gown wedding in a chapel with your family and friends all around to cheer you on. You're not the type to play around. The world is on the precipice of improving for women and I'd hate to see *both* of my best friends miss the opportunities that are coming. I'm just throwing some cold water on the situation and telling you to proceed with eyes wide open."

"Says the woman who is about to be bitten by a crab."

"Shoo!" Gladys jumped and looked where Margaret was pointing, and indeed, a sand crab was crawling precariously close to her leg. She picked up the *Saturday Evening Post* she'd laid down and scooped the creature up, tossing it gently a few feet away.

Dottie propped herself up on her elbows and pulled her sunglasses down to her nose. "This might be the only time it happens as long as I live, but I have to say that I agree with

Gladys. You deserve every happiness, Margaret, and I hope and pray that William is the one who will provide you with that. If that's what you want. Looking back, it may well be a dreamy story to tell your grandchildren. How you fell in love through corresponding during the war. But don't give away your heart too quickly. It's too precious a thing."

Margaret pursed her lips and dug her hands into the sand, letting its granules slip through her fingers. This is not how she thought the conversation to go. She expected some kind of resistance from Gladys, but she assumed Dottie, at least, would be happy for her. This felt like they were ganging up on her. Even if they had her best interests at heart.

In fact, their hesitation had the opposite of the intended effect. She hadn't even come here with lofty notions of a future with William. Just excitement over receiving such sentiments in the first place. But now that they were cautioning her against it, she found herself actually considering it.

She let a sniffle escape.

"Oh! Shame on us!" said Dottie, sitting all the way up. "Margaret, I'm so sorry. We were too hard on you. Of course you know what you're doing and our worries are needless. Gosh, it is certainly something to celebrate. Margaret Beck is in love. I've been waiting years to say that."

Margaret wiped her nose with a tissue. "I'm not ancient yet. Twenty-three is not exactly an old maid. And I didn't say I'm in love."

Dottie rubbed her hand along Margaret's arm, and her lips curved in consolation, while Gladys folded her arms and let out a *hrumph*.

"Dottie had the hots for your brother before she came into

her *womanhood*, if you know what I mean. Before those nursing breasts of hers were even tiny buds, her heart was spoken for. She's just been waiting years for you to catch up."

"Don't be crass, Gladys." But Margaret smiled despite the admonishment.

"Don't be crass, Gladys? Margaret, that's like asking the sun not to shine." Dottie grinned.

"Or like asking La Guardia not to run for office again," Gladys offered.

Dottie waved her finger in the air. "Or like asking the A train not to break down all the time."

"Or like asking Oliver not to leave the trimmings of his morning shave in the sink."

Dottie and Margaret looked at each other and then burst out with laughter. Gladys had just admitted to more than she'd ever said about their relationship.

"If that's your way of making amends, you're doing a pretty good job." Margaret pulled both of them into a hug, wrapping her arms around their necks until their foreheads were all touching.

The best friends told you the truth that you most needed to hear.

Still, the idea of loving William had taken root.

What could go wrong?

Burying his regrets was proving more difficult than Tom had hoped, though the news of Paris's liberation was a welcome distraction.

For days, the BBC and Radiodiffusion Nationale had been reporting on the Allied troops encroaching on German lines, getting closer and closer to the city. And the French Forces of the Interior had seen some successes on the inside. Now their joint efforts had come to fruition and cheers rose and echoed throughout the hospital wing. It didn't matter who spoke English or how it was accented or who spoke French. Jubilation was a common language understood by all.

Despite Hitler's decree that Paris "must not fall into the enemy's hand except lying in complete debris," his orders to bomb the city and its bridges as they retreated went unheeded. It was said that Paris, though it had sustained some bruises, was intact.

Tom ached to see it. It was only two hours away by train and the Allies now controlled the tracks. It had always been his mother's dearest wish to see the City of Lights and to buy perfume from the House of Fragonard. Though his father's English side first touched American soil in the early 1600s, his mother's French family were newer arrivals, and she carried their stories in her heart like a treasure box.

Someday, he hoped she could see it. But until then, maybe he could do the next best thing.

He sent a note to the regional commander's office.

This is Technician Fifth Grade Thomas Powell. I have been cleared to rejoin my unit and have been instructed to take the next transport plane to Holland. Please advise on the schedule.

The response came: *At 14:30 on the 30th. We already have your name on the list.*

The thirtieth. That gave him two days.

"Au revoir," he said to the nurses who had tended to him so well. His eyes welled up with gratitude for them. They bathed the men, held their hands, listened to their cries—both the physical and emotional ones—gave them knitting needles with which to itch their skin under their casts, insisted on them using their muscles when the casts came off, encouraged them when their bodies took time to strengthen.

Tom felt as good as new, thanks to their exhausting work.

But he was ready to move on.

He was released from their care and in a rare circumstance, he had this little window of time where no one had their grips on him. His R&R train trip would be a stolen one, as he shouldn't go anywhere without permission, but his unit had left France while he recuperated, and their only expectation was that he make that transport plane.

So he would disappear. Imagine himself on a little vacation in Europe.

It was easy enough to locate the nearest train station, but he soon found that all of France seemed to be making their way to the city. Tickets were oversold, but patriotic conductors and ticket takers turned a blind eye and packed people into the train cars until there was only room to stand in the aisles. He learned, too, that many of the railroads had been destroyed by Allied bombs, so this line was one of the scarce ones that were still intact. Behind the passenger cars were several full of produce from Normandy and Brittany.

Paris was starving.

Yet the mood was celebratory.

Tom gave up his seat for an old woman who boarded after him.

He didn't need it. He'd been lying down for too many weeks as it was. And the surge of victory pumped through his veins.

The train grew more crowded as they passed Bayeux, Caen, and Rouen, the French people chattering too quickly for him to understand. But no doubt, they were sharing stories of occupation and excitement for what a liberated France might look like.

What would it be like to have Margaret at his side? Entering the City of Lights. The City of Love. Her blond hair pulled into a ponytail with a blue bow tied around it.

Her smile broadcasting her joy.

He put those thoughts aside. It was a dream that could never come true.

At last, it was announced that Paris was the next stop. The people in the seats stretched over other passengers to look out the windows and *ooh* and *aah* as countryside turned into city. He hadn't been in a large city for years, if you didn't count their brief stop in Brooklyn to board that ship to Liverpool. He'd looked west as they sailed away, passing the Statue of Liberty and all of the tall rectangular buildings that sprouted from the ground like weeds.

He didn't see the appeal. Give him bare feet in wild grass, peach juice dripping from his chin, stars above that revealed the majesty of the skies. Those were the wonders he preferred.

Still, there was a mythological allure to *Paris* that he was eager to see for himself.

Tom slung his backpack across his shoulders and stepped onto the platform. Everywhere he looked, throngs of people held up flags, and it was a bevy of red, white, and blue. It never occurred to him that the French, British, and American flags all boasted the same trio of colors. He knew that fact individually, but until he saw them together, adorning anything that could be festooned with banners and ribbons, he didn't realize that even their aesthetic was allied.

He expected the crowd to thin as they left the train station, but in the streets, the whole of the country seemed to be promenading in jubilation. He wished again that Margaret were here with him, as his loneliness was more pronounced than ever. He'd known no life other than one without siblings, but John and William's companionship had given him a desire to have someone to share the tales of the day with.

Even better if it was a girl like Margaret. All around him, couples were kissing in the shadows of buildings that had escaped Hitler's wrath. Celebrating with bursts of affection that squeezed his heart for want of it.

He even saw a group of women display their bare chests, draped only in cloth around their waists, an homage, he believed, to Delacroix's painting of *La Liberté*.

No one seemed to notice as the masses swirled around them, engrossed in their own versions of celebration.

A man tossed oranges from his balcony into the crowd, shouting, "Victoire! Victoire!"

Victory! Victory!

And then—there it was. Looming over everyone, appearing as if out of nowhere, the famed Eiffel Tower. He'd read that it had been a controversial structure, and a temporary one. Yet here it stood, outlasting the critics and overseeing two horrendous wars.

It was a monument of endurance, just the encouragement that Tom needed to believe he could go on.

CHAPTER EIGHTEEN

August 1944

The door to the House of Fragonard on the Rue di Rivoli was outlined in bronze that was polished to the point of sparkling. It stood in contrast to much of the Paris that Tom had seen as he had walked around all night. He'd decided to save money by sleeping outside on a park bench in the Luxembourg Gardens, and he'd woken to the cooing of pigeons. It had been charming until he sat up and discovered that they'd soiled his jacket. He wiped it off in the fountain and set off on his mission.

"Bonjour, soldat. Etes-vous venu pour acheter du parfum?"

A young woman opened the door. Her hair was coiffed to perfection and she wore pearl earrings that dangled just past her earlobes. She was so thin that he wondered how she even stood up straight. Was it in fashion here? Or was it starvation brought on by war?

"I . . . I . . ." he stammered. "It's for my mother. My mére."

"Ah, you sound American," said the shopgirl.

"Yes," he answered, relieved. He didn't know how he would have conducted the transaction otherwise.

"You are in luck. Is this how you say this?"

He nodded. "Yes. Luck. It is very lucky that you speak English."

"No, no, monsieur. This is not what I mean. I mean, you have the luck that you should come to the Maison du Fragonard. You see, these Nazis they close many of the shops. But here on the Rue di Rivoli, they keep us open. For their wives. And their *paramours*?"

At this, her eyes twinkled.

"Are you here *only* for your mére? Or"—she lowered her voice—"do you have a paramour?"

He smiled. What an elegant name for what he wished Margaret to be. Was it a word that she knew? He'd have to make a note of it and send it in the next letter.

If there was a next letter.

"My great-grandmother was from France," Tom explained. "And my mother always spoke of the perfume that she wore. I believe it was made of violets."

"Ah, oui!" she confirmed. "More luck for monsieur! It is one of our most popular fragrances. The German wives loved it, and so we have some in stock, even as we are low on the others."

She walked behind the counter and beckoned to him. "Come, come."

He followed her, and she held her arm out.

"Do like this," she said.

He did the same and before he could stop her, she'd pushed his sleeve up and spritzed his skin generously with a bottle of perfume. He smelled the violet mist as it wafted upward and tickled his nose.

But yes, this was the one. Floral with a hint of sweetness, just as his mother had described.

Would Margaret like it as well?

But he really couldn't buy the same perfume for his mother and his girl, could he?

Then again, that was hoping for something that could never come to pass.

"Only this one, monsieur?" She pouted. The woman set out delicate paper on the counter and began to wrap the box with the care one might have expected from a ship engineer. When she'd finished the sides with knifelike corners and wrapped it in twine, she slipped a sprig of lavender onto the top.

Tom had no idea how it would all survive the war packaged as it was, but he had to give it a try.

"Oui," he answered. She pulled out a receipt pad and wrote up the cost. It was more than he'd expected, but when would he ever get the chance to give his mother such an extraordinary gift? You couldn't buy Fragonard anywhere near the Chickahominy River.

"Wait." Tom pulled his wallet from his pocket and flipped through the bills he'd been holding on to since he'd left Virginia. He'd learned that the French were eager to be paid in American dollars.

"Yes, is there something more?" The shopgirl's face brightened and he wondered if she worked on commission.

"Something for my paramour." He bit down on his tongue as he said it. What a foolish thing to be doing.

"Ah, oui, monsieur! One does not forget his love. Perhaps the vanille? It is the scent of the érotique."

A blush spread across his cheeks, and he did not need a translator to understand her meaning.

She gestured for him to put out his other arm, and when she rolled up his sleeve, she spritzed him with a new bottle. The scent was warm and inviting, but also comfortable. Like home.

"I'll take it."

"Excellent choice."

She wrapped the package identically to the first and marked a corner of it with a V so tiny that he would never have known to look for it if she hadn't shown him.

"This way you know one from the other. And—for you? Perhaps a cologne for you to keep?"

Tom held up his hand to say no, offering a polite smile. Currently, he was a walking bouquet of violets and vanilla, something that would surely have made him the target of John and William's laughter if they were here with him. And anyway, he had a bottle of Old Spice at home that he used on Sundays, but there was no use for it here. Tomorrow, he would rejoin his unit in Holland. Back to the front. Where the enemy didn't spare you just because you smelled good.

He paid the bill, returning his much lighter wallet into his pocket, and took the handle of the bag that the woman had given him.

"Merci," he said.

"Au revoir."

He left the store and was once again swept up in a crowd similar to the one yesterday. Banners waved in the breeze, confetti fell from balconies, and the swarm of people inched its way westward. He joined them, or rather, he was absorbed by them, walking down the Rue di Rivoli until it connected to the Champs-Élysées. At that point, everything stopped because the Champs was already filled with people on the sidewalks.

He picked out enough British and American voices in the crowd to learn that there was to be a magnificent victory parade today.

A child cried behind him, and he looked to see a little girl, maybe three years old, wriggling in her mother's arms and trying to see above his broad shoulders.

"Let me help," he said, hoping that his intention overcame the language difference.

He held out his arms and the mother handed the child to him. He thought of little Joanna, John's daughter, and how he hoped to meet her one day and carry her, too, like the uncle he wanted to be.

Band music started up and Tom was grateful that his tall stature allowed him to see over the women standing in front of him. He looked up at the little girl, whose curled pigtails were bouncing as she looked back and forth in excitement.

He heard the roar of the tanks before he saw them. But soon enough, everything came into view. First a marching squad holding a banner that read U.S. 28TH INFANTRY DIVISION. The tanks rolled slowly enough to see every turn of their tracks. Soldiers sat atop them, some as still as statues, others taking the opportunity to wave and smile at their adorers.

Behind the tanks came the motorcycle brigade, and surprisingly, these were the vehicles that seemed to rouse the girl's attention.

"Mére! Mére!" she called. And her mother looked up in acknowledgment of where she was pointing.

Indeed, the motorcycles were exciting. Collectively, their engines formed a sound so loud that it reverberated inside Tom's heart. His chest swelled with pride. The war was by no means over, but this victory was one well worth celebrating.

Clap, snap, clap, snap. Next came the precise sounds of the soldiers' boots, marching down the Champs with impeccable precision, the type of discipline that helped them win back this city. Thousands and thousands of them marched down the boulevard and Tom counted them twenty-four across.

Among it all, flags waved as the people shouted, "Américain!" in a chorus.

The procession came to a halt and Tom looked far to his right to see that the Arc de Triomphe was their destination. The French military lined the street, their bright uniforms standing in contrast to the army green of the U.S. soldiers. The band played on, though their trumpeting had dimmed with distance. A speaker came to a podium, but Tom was too far to hear what he was saying.

But nobody needed the words. The wellspring of joy said all that was needed.

He would love to share this hope with Margaret, this signal that the war could, indeed, be over soon.

He handed the girl back to her mother and made his way back to the Rue di Rivoli, skimming the shop walls so as to keep clear of the people who were pressed against each other at the edge of the sidewalk. He'd seen something on his way over that had scarcely captured his attention, but now it was exactly what he wanted.

He passed a grocer and a bakery, his stomach growling at

him to stop, but he kept going until he found the newspaper stand that had what he'd been looking for.

A postcard showing the Arc de Triomphe.

He purchased two of them with some of the last change in his pocket and kept walking until he could find a park bench on which to sit. He pulled out a pen and began to write.

The first was to his mother.

And then the second:

Dearest Margaret,

I have seen such beauty in the city of Paris and hope that someday it will be more than a spot on your atlas. Maybe you will let me bring you here. There is a feeling of victory that I hope can soon be celebrated on our home ground as well. Take heart—the end is coming.

Just that much had taken up nearly all of the postcard. He put the pen in his mouth and considered what to do next. There was no space to tell her all he'd want to say about William, and even if there was, the news might dampen the excitement he wanted her to feel.

And she might question a postcard coming from Tom.

Next time. He would tell her next time when he had more paper to tell the story.

He penned a tiny fleur-de-lis in the corner. Almost a flower.

And finished it with:

Love, William

CHAPTER NINETEEN

September 1944

I asked Oliver to marry me."

Margaret turned off her welding torch and flipped her visor up.

Gladys's rosy blouse was the same shade of her cheeks.

"It's about time!" Margaret had to shout to be heard over the other workers. Gladys wasn't even supposed to be in this room, as she'd been promoted to foreman of the engraving department. She'd tried to insist on the title fore*woman*, but it never caught on and for the moment, she had to be satisfied with the nearly unprecedented advancement for one of her gender. She had also argued that she should receive the same pay as a man, but that, too, had been dismissed.

So it was no surprise to Margaret that Gladys had asserted herself into a different traditional role, that of the one to initiate a marriage proposal.

Just as she'd predicted.

"Is that all you have to say? I thought you'd be shocked."

"Nothing you do shocks me, Gladys. Don't you know that?

Except maybe you being in the welding room. If Mr. Drake sees you, it's going to be hell for both of us."

Gladys grinned. "Not so. I caught him necking with one of the girls in my department in a janitor's closet. Now that I have something on both of them, I'll use it as I need it."

"You are one ruthless woman, my friend."

"Life is a battle, Margaret. That's my motto. And the sooner you listen, the wiser you'll be."

Margaret shrugged. She had a passive admiration for Gladys. Somebody had to carry the mantle for the progression of women, and there was none better suited for it than her.

"Anyway, our shifts are almost over. I'll tell you more after that."

"What about Dottie? She'll want to hear about it too."

Gladys nodded. "I called ahead and told her we'd be over for dinner. Can you believe it? George bought her not one, but *two* telephones. One for each floor of the house."

"Awfully convenient for times like this, isn't it?"

"Yes. I'm going to teach her to use it for good. I've signed her up to make campaign calls in the upcoming election."

Margaret grinned and shook her head. "Of course you have."

"And I fully expect your participation as well."

"And of course you have it."

"Good." Gladys checked her wristwatch. "I'll meet you on the promenade in an hour. We can go together."

Margaret could hardly open the door of the welding room. It was always heavy, but this time, she had to push every ounce of her weight into it. As soon as she saw the first crack of light, a wind gust blew past and it was all she could do to keep the door from slamming back into her.

"I've got it!" she heard from the other side. There was Gladys, pulling as Margaret pushed, and at last they opened it enough for Margaret to slip through.

"There's a storm coming," Gladys shouted over the howl.

Margaret walked to the railing on the promenade and looked at the bay where the half-built frame of the *Coral Sea* bobbed in the water. The men working on it kept their balance, but she could tell that it was an effort. She'd never experienced anything like this.

"I can see that! It seemed to come out of nowhere."

"I read in the newspaper that mid-September is the height of the Atlantic hurricane season. But it doesn't usually hit us here."

"This is a hurricane?"

"Heck if I know, but look at that sky. It's a different shade of gray than in a regular storm."

Margaret glanced up, gripping her felt hat so that it wouldn't fly away. Indeed, there was an ominous cloud covering that sent a chill through her bones, darkening the sky well before sunset. Her parents were away in Pennsylvania visiting relatives and sourcing leather, and she was glad that they were out of this storm's path.

A metal screw flew past, skimming her cheek. Instinctively, she ducked in case there were any more.

"Do you think it's still safe to go to Dottie's? She's right on the water," Margaret shouted. She pressed her hand against her face. It was just a surface cut. Nothing that would last.

"I think so. If it hits hard enough, my little basement will flood. And your electricity is spotty in the best of circumstances. At least we can go and help her with the baby."

Margaret nodded and followed Gladys to the exit, where they'd pick up the bus that would take them to Shore Road.

"Get in, girls! The rain is going to start any minute."

They turned to see Dottie driving the new car that George had ordered for her. He'd been so excited to surprise her and had asked Margaret and Gladys for their opinions. They'd studied the many pictures he'd shown them and suggested a new Cadillac Fleetwood in her favorite color—baby blue—with tan seats and leather on the steering wheel. It was finished out in chrome details. Dottie had been excited to show it to them, but they hadn't expected to see it in person so soon.

"What are you doing here?" asked Margaret. "And where is Joanna?"

"I'm rescuing you. I heard on the radio that the buses are delayed, so I zipped over to pick you up. And as for your niece, I left her sleeping in the arms of the nanny."

Margaret smiled. Life could certainly be full circle. The former nanny now had one of her own. And no one deserved that more than her dear friend.

Gladys opened the door in the front and slid in next to Dottie. Margaret took a place in the back as the first raindrops fell on her shoulders.

"Just in time, Dots. Thank you."

She rubbed her hand along the soft interior and let out a long breath, her heartbeat slowing now that they were in the safety of the car.

There were few cars on the road, but a series of red lights halted their progress. All the while, the sky blackened.

"Nice wheels," Gladys commented. She rubbed her hand along the dashboard. "It's like she's purring."

"George told me some little birds helped him. Thank goodness, because I don't know much about cars. And really hadn't planned on getting one."

"And you're already behind the wheel?"

"Yes—he's been teaching me on his. I got my license last week."

Gladys whistled, as a man might do when walking by a beautiful woman.

"Must have set him back a bit. I'll bet it's nice being rich."

"Gladys!" Margaret tapped her on the shoulder. "That's not polite."

"You don't mind, do you, Dots? I wouldn't be me if I didn't ask."

Dottie smiled in the generous way that indicated her long-suffered tolerance for Gladys's quirks.

"I don't mind since it's *you*. And to answer your question, yes, it's nice to have some help with Joanna. And to have a house where I don't have to worry if she's keeping a neighbor up because of her crying. And to have a car so I can pick up you soggy ladies. But my riches do not lie in what George's family has in their bank account. It lies in my two cherished friends. And in having known the love of two good men. It's more than many women will ever get to have."

Gladys sat back and folded her arms. "That is such a typical Dottie answer."

"Do you want a different one? Because that's the only one I've got."

Margaret laid her head against the rear window and listened to their back-and-forth.

What would John think of Dottie's newfound domesticity? She missed him every single day, though the sting diminished bit by bit. It was a strange thing to rejoice for your friend and how her life turned out and yet remain so brokenhearted at the tragedy that had led to it.

Was there such a thing as perfect happiness? Or did it always come laced with some tragedy? Some shoe that would drop as soon as you'd captured it?

Would we even recognize perfect happiness if it existed without suffering its opposite?

Rain always put her in a philosophical mood. As did William's letters. She'd just received a postcard from him while he was in Paris. *Love, William*, it had said. Two words that made her heart leap. And yet, she didn't quite trust the feeling.

Joy and sorrow were like seats on a playground teeter-totter.

Back and forth.

Back and forth.

What would be extracted from her now that she seemed to have won William's heart?

The rain began to beat down in a deluge, so Dottie turned her headlights on as they slugged along and flipped the lever for windshield wipers that did not seem up to the task. Margaret could see that she was gripping the steering wheel tightly as they tried to avoid sliding around while they made their way toward the final blocks to her house. She must feel especially harried since she hadn't been driving for very long.

At last, they pulled up and she inched the car into the driveway.

"There's an umbrella underneath your seat, Margaret. You and Gladys can use that one. I have one near my door here. Hold on tight—I think they could blow away in this wind!"

"Did buying a brand-new car mean that you couldn't afford a third umbrella?"

Of course, Gladys would have something snappy to say. Margaret reached to the front and poked her in the rib cage. Sometimes she didn't know when to put the kidding to rest.

They slid out, the wind shutting the doors behind them with a *slam*, and scurried up the slippery steps to the white house on Shore Road.

Margaret shook the umbrella out on the covered porch, a futile effort since the rain was blowing on them anyway. The house was built on a steep hill, so when she turned around for a quick look back, she could see above the tree line and across the water. The whole sky was draped in darkness, and the waters of the bay beneath it formed agitated whitecaps.

"Hurry! I see lightning." Dottie pulled Margaret in by the arm just as a bolt hit the manhole cover on the street below and created a magnificent flash.

Dottie closed the door and took their jackets, hanging them on the coatrack in the foyer, and set the umbrellas in a stand made just for that purpose.

It was good to be inside.

Warm. Dry. Heaven.

"I knew you girls would be hungry, so everything is ready." She led them down the long Oriental rug in the hallway and into the dining room, which was lined with a wall of beveled glass windows. She closed the drapes, no doubt wanting to keep the storm from view.

The table was set for three with salads already plated.

"It's just us girls tonight," she announced. "George took a few days off and is in Albany with his dad opening up a new storefront. He wanted to come home when he heard about the storm on the radio, but I begged him to stay so he wouldn't get caught in it."

"The Refrigerator King still does work for the family business?" Margaret smiled at John's old nickname for him.

"More like the Refrigerator Prince, if we're being accurate," Gladys chimed in.

Dottie rolled her eyes. "Poke all the fun you want. It might not be as highfalutin as being a Wall Street banker, but before you know it, *every* household in America will have a dishwasher. Just wait and see."

Gladys leaned over and kissed her cheek. "If all that truly mattered to me, I wouldn't be marrying a newspaper reporter."

"Marrying!" Dottie dropped her salad fork on her plate and a small tomato rolled onto the floor. Her squeal could power any loss that New York would suffer in the storm.

"Dearly beloved, we are gathered here today to tell you that I have proposed to Oliver Barnes."

"I think I'm going to need some wine for this." Dottie stood up and opened a cabinet that was filled with every kind of liquor one could imagine, amber hues and dark browns, bottles more artistic than what they contained. She pulled out a crystal decanter and scooped up three goblets.

"Here we are, ladies. I don't know anything about vintages,

but George and I like this red one. And there's more where this came from." She poured generously for each of them.

A bolt of lightning flashed outside, bright enough to see through the closed curtains. The wind raged and they heard a tree limb crack and fall onto the roof.

Margaret jumped.

Even Dottie looked worried. "I have never seen a storm like this."

"I ordered it up. You know me, Hurricane Gladys!"

"You know about that?" asked Margaret.

"Don't worry, love. It's the perfect nickname. I'm just jealous that I didn't think of it first."

Dottie crossed her arms. "You're stalling."

Gladys took a cloth napkin from the table and dabbed the corners of her lips.

"All right. Here you go. I proposed to Oliver." She held out both hands to her friends and they took them, forming a circle.

With a squeeze, Dottie pulled away and leaned back in her chair, taking in that revelation. "Well, I don't know if I'm surprised or not. I mean, if I'd ever thought that you would be tying the knot, I supposed I would have pictured you being the one to ask."

"When does our Gladys ever do anything conventionally?" asked Margaret. This would be a good story to tell William. Or not. She'd already gushed about Dottie and George's wedding.

"I want all the details," Dottie insisted.

Crack. Another lightning bolt. But the windows seemed safe from fallen branches for the moment.

A uniformed woman came through the swinging door between the rooms and cleared their empty plates.

"You have a *cook*?" Gladys's jaw dropped.

"Let's get it all out in the open, Gladys. And then no more distractions until you have told your story. We have a nanny, a cook, and a housekeeper. Yes, I know that seems extravagant. No, I do not think it's necessary. But my husband loves to dote on me and as soon as I feel fully settled in, I'm going to follow your lead and learn how to use it all for good. Now— your turn. Go."

Margaret held a napkin to her mouth to avoid disclosing the huge grin that had spread across her face.

The cook brought out a plate of hot roasted beets with fresh parsley sprigs and Gladys made no comment as she waited for her to leave before continuing.

"Look. I misled you both at the beach."

Dottie and Margaret glanced at each other and then back at Gladys.

"I told you that Oliver leaves his shavings in the sink in the morning. And I'm sure you extrapolated—there's a word to share with your boyfriend, Margaret—something that wasn't entirely true. He has stayed over a few times when a story in Brooklyn kept him out late and he was too tired to go back to the city. But I slept in the bed. And he slept on the couch. Every time."

Dottie cocked her head. "Are you saying that you haven't—"

"I'm saying that, believe it or not, Saint Dorothy is the only sullied one among us."

"And he didn't try—"

"No! And that's the part that drives me batty. I told him

he didn't have to stay on the couch. And he told me that he's old-fashioned about those things. His words exactly."

Margaret laughed. At first, it was a snicker as she held back something far more guttural out of politeness. But keeping it in was hurting her chest, and at last, she let it out. And then she heard the same from Dottie.

"What? *What*, you two? You're finding this funny?"

"Oh my word," Margaret sputtered between breaths. "If I was a betting woman, I don't think I ever would have pegged you for dating an old-fashioned gentleman."

Gladys's cheeks grew red and they puffed out. "You can't help who you fall in love with, can you? It's like... it's like one of those lightning strikes. Completely random."

But Margaret recalled her conversation with him on the dance floor. Whether he was as sincerely reticent as he professed to be or whether this was part of a strategy to get her to make the first move, it was clearly a flawless plan, because it had worked. He knew Gladys lived life on her own terms. If *he'd* made advances of a more serious nature toward her, it would have put him in the same stead as every other man who'd tried and failed to get together with Gladys. If he held off, he'd almost guarantee that she would take things into her own hands. And not just for a fling, which would surely extinguish as soon as Gladys grew bored. He had long-term hopes that were about to come to fruition.

"So how did this end in a marriage proposal?" asked Dottie once they'd all calmed their voices.

The cook slipped in almost imperceptivity and exchanged their plates for steaming bowls of sumptuous-smelling beef and vegetable stew. Margaret's eyes closed in near ecstasy at the scent but didn't comment so as not to sidetrack Gladys again.

Gladys picked up her soup spoon and continued. "I'll tell you, but don't think that I proposed because I wanted to get him into bed. I'm not that dumb."

"I wasn't suggesting it," said Dottie.

"It was when he told me that he's going back to England at the end of the war. And then who knows where. It could be somewhere else in Europe. Or Asia. Or Africa. Wherever they want a reporter who is unencumbered enough to go wherever they send him. Or who has a wife who would travel with him."

"And this prompted the proposal?"

"It did." She shrugged. "It's as simple as that. When he told me his plans, I realized how much I would miss him." She wiped her eyes with her right hand and Margaret didn't dare make a mention of it. In all their years of friendship, she couldn't ever recall seeing Gladys get sentimental. Best to let her have this moment.

"It's not every man who will sport a suffragette sash at a commemoration event or keep his head together while serving up soup in the Bowery line. Or talk me into join- ing him at a damn feline fashion show and then actually having fun together. That's not a man you easily say good- bye to."

Margaret reached out and grasped Gladys's hand. "Of course you wouldn't want to let him go. And just think of the adventures you'll have as his wife. You'll get to see all those places, Gladys. You'll live in them for months on end. Your big heart that wants to bring justice to an unjust world will actually go out into that world and discover whole new purposes for you. Side by side with the man you love."

It almost made her weepy as well, thinking about how nice it would be to have someone to partner through life with like that. Could it be the man she'd been writing to all these months? She had never anticipated anything more than his letters, never felt as liberated as she did when her words flowed back on the paper. Even though she couldn't precisely picture him, as he still had never revealed which one he was in the photograph. She kept it pinned to the wall above her bedpost and said good night to them all before she closed her eyes. John, resting in peace. William and Tom, whichever they each were. At first, she'd imagined that William was the one with the cropped hair, the one who looked as if he could be any age. There was a teddy-bear comfort to him. But nothing that elicited a reaction any stronger than pleasantness.

Not the stirring of a heart.

The other one—the taller man—was more conventionally handsome. The type girls would swoon over during cinema outings. When she pictured this one being her pen pal, her pulse quickened like a silver screen embrace come to life.

One man's words overwhelmed her with their beauty. The other man's drawings made her dream of other places.

But only one in the photograph made her feel the things she'd read about in romance novels.

She knew enough from observing her parents' marriage and those of all the older couples of her acquaintance that the endurance of love did not lie merely in the physical attraction but in the sustainability of the friendship. In the end, which was which mattered little.

Although, as Gladys had once strong-armed her into revealing, she would choose the tall one with the dark hair if pressed.

She shook those thoughts from her head. Pondering this was a poor use of her time. William, Tom. They were thousands of miles away. Life was happening right now. Right here in Brooklyn.

Talking about Gladys's engagement.

Whoosh! The wind blew outside in a tremendous gust that sent a spray of sand across the window. Margaret had always heard people say that wind could sound like a freight train, but until this moment, she'd thought it was an exaggeration.

"Geez Louise," Gladys exclaimed.

Dottie was the epitome of calm, however, ignoring the fact that her house seemed to be getting battered from the outside. "I am so very happy for you, Gladys," she said, pulling the conversation back in like the good hostess she was. "But you have not answered one important question—*how* did you ask him?"

Gladys shrugged. "Simple. I told him he's going to marry me and take me with him. And he didn't say no."

As if the skies were rebelling against her buck to tradition, the lights flickered and the house was plunged into darkness.

CHAPTER TWENTY

September 1944

$\mathcal{T}$om burrowed into a corner under a bridge, letting the darkness of the night engulf him. He pulled his knees to his chest and wrapped his arms around them.

Holland was a disaster.

The men had been told that if Operation Market Garden was a success, the war would be over by Christmas. His mouth had tingled with anticipation of a Virginia ham in the center of the table, glistening with maple glaze, decorated with fresh orange slices and dried cloves.

His body ached with the idea that if Margaret would forgive him when he told her about William's death, she might accept his embrace and he would at last draw her into his arms and never let go.

The terrible defeat they'd suffered stole those hopes from him with such ferocity that he felt as if they were phantom limbs. He'd learned about such things from men in the French hospital. They'd lost arms and legs and though their eyes and their pain testified to their disappearance, the corners of their minds felt them as if they were still present.

They were ghosts.

Ghosts all around. Men, gone. Limbs, gone. Christmas, gone. Victory, gone.

Hopes, gone.

God, maybe he didn't want to meet Margaret. Or rather, he didn't want to burden her beautiful, cheery face with the hull of a man he was.

Maybe he would never tell her. Maybe he would continue to write her as William. To escape into the freedom he felt when he wrote pseudonymous words, to conjure the courage to write her things he would not otherwise say. Because Tom Powell... Tom Powell was destined for a career in the military. His education and his family history would catapult him as high as he wanted to go.

If, indeed, that was still where he wanted to go.

William, on the other hand, had almost become a character of their own creation. Sure, there had been a flesh and blood William. Whose loss he mourned every single day. But this whole thing had been at William's urging. His very design— to help Tom find the poetry in life where there had only been singularly focused planning.

Tom had hoped that it would be a diversion for Margaret too. John had described how devoted she was to their parents and to her work, almost to her own detriment. "She could use some loosening up," he'd once said. So the letters were a lark. A pastime between two people when they most needed it.

But it had become more. He could sense it. At least on his part.

Her letters had become like air.

And, like air, a shift could create a storm.

He'd never missed William more. He could use his friend's advice. John's too.

What would happen at the end of the war? When she expected her friend to return to the States and come to meet her?

He'd cross that bridge when he came to it.

And there was a fair chance he wouldn't live long enough to find out.

Tom knew his thoughts were addled with the acutely felt despair of watching too many friends bleed to death and the helplessness that accompanied it. And so he would save any decisions about writing Margaret for another day when his head was more clear and disaster behind them.

Besides, there was no paper with which to write. And if there were, it would serve them better as cigarette rolls. Some of the men had become desperate enough to light up blades of grass just to find relief in the smoky scent.

The letters would have to be written only in his mind—the thread by which he hung, clinging to memories of another life. But the hope that he might someday be able to send them was just about the only thing that kept him in the fight.

Dear Margaret, he imagined.

We'd hoped a victory in Holland would give purpose to the many losses we've suffered. But it was not meant to be.

Churchill and Roosevelt and Field Marshall Montgomery cooked up a plan for tens of thousands of airborne troops to descend on the Netherlands—specifically the territory between Eindhoven and Nijmegen—securing nine bridges that would cut off the Germans. The Market operation. The

*Garden operation would employ ground troops and armored
vehicles to take over and bulge into German territory.*

*The 101ˢᵗ Airborne was supposed to commandeer the
bridges at Son en Breugel, but when we arrived, the Germans
had already destroyed the Wilhelminakanaal at Son. Our
mission failed before we even touched the ground.*

Tom could still hear the reverberation of the gunfire that had
been all around them. He wanted to forget it. But to forget
it meant that it would be lost to history. And history had that
terrible habit of repeating itself if one didn't learn from it.

*Building a makeshift bridge put our operation behind by half
a day, allowing the German troops to rally and keep Allied
troops from the ultimate objective: crossing the Rhine. Other
bridges that had not been secured meant that reinforcements
arrived later than planned.*

Four days. Four whole days that the airborne had fought
off the Germans with none of the support they'd been
promised.

Cold, weary, broken.

Dead.

It had been the largest operation attempted by the new
airborne division of the army. Had the defeat jeopardized
its fledgling status? Twenty thousand men had descended by
parachute, fourteen thousand by gliders.

Early projections were reporting that seventeen thousand
men had been lost.

Seventeen thousand men. The nearest town of note near

his home was Williamsburg. Nine thousand people lived there. It was as if all of Williamsburg were wiped out. Two times over.

It was nearly impossible to fathom.

A sniffle shook him from his memories. He couldn't write these words to Margaret. They were too bleak. They lacked the poetry that William had eked out of him. She deserved more than a broken soldier's sadness.

He was grateful there was no paper.

In the darkness, he couldn't tell who had made the noise—someone from his unit? Or one of the British or Polish boys who were scattered in the area? The sniffle turned into a wail and oddly, it created a fissure in the hardness of his heart.

Like him, some unknown soldier had also found a hole in the darkness to rest in. If he had to guess, many woeful souls were hidden across the battlefield, wallowing for a few minutes before returning to their units for the night. Where they'd have to muster the façade of bravery. Where they'd have to pretend that they were grateful to not be among the dead, living to do this all over again tomorrow. And the day after. And the day after.

Tom's father had never admitted to feeling frightened in combat. Sobel had been an impenetrable fortress and the men suspected that he had no emotions built into him at all. But Winters—God bless Captain Winters—had told his men that a hero is not a man who doesn't know fear. It's a man who *does* know fear and faces it head-on.

For Captain Winters, if not for himself or anyone else, Tom would rally in the morning and be the stalwart soldier that he had to be and he would press on.

But not tonight. Tonight, he would mourn in darkness all that had been lost.

"Lord almighty, have you looked outside?"

Gladys and Margaret were sleeping in twin beds in an upstairs bedroom at Dottie's house. Gladys's words stirred her from a deep sleep, where she'd dreamed of William and Tom, their faces interchanging. They went from eating egg salad sandwiches at an Automat in Brooklyn to fighting on a stormy battlefield, the two moments sequentially seamless. She closed her eyes and one man pulled her into his arms. But she woke up before she could discover which one it was.

What lingered was the feeling he'd given her—as if resting her head on his shoulder allowed her to melt into his strength and find respite from the troubles of the world.

It felt like a brand-new definition of *home*, one that she didn't fully understand.

She rubbed her eyes as Gladys pulled back the bedroom's curtains.

"Seriously, Mags. I've never seen anything like this. Come here."

Margaret swung her legs over the side of the bed, surprised that she was wearing the pajamas that Dottie had laid out for her because she didn't even remember putting them on.

She did remember drinking copious amounts of wine with the girls after Dottie returned from nursing Joanna and putting her down for the night. Lighting a fire in the dark was a feat that had them descending into a giggle fit, but they'd managed it and sat with it until its embers had cooled.

Her mouth felt sticky and all she wanted to do was brush her teeth. But she followed Gladys's voice and trudged over.

What a disaster. Debris and rocks and shingles and branches littered the yard. Electric lines sagged and their poles were bent like broken skeletons.

It was the ideal tonic for a hangover. The clouds in her head dissipated and her blood raced. Is this what Gladys felt like when she marched for her causes? Because Margaret felt an unfamiliar urge to go out there and hoist limbs and bring her town back to life.

"It's what I imagine a battlefield to look like," she said. "And this is just what we see from Dottie's window."

"I'm sure Oliver will be traipsing through it all day. This is definitely something his editor might want to hear about."

"I don't think they get hurricanes in England, do they?" Margaret asked.

"Not that I know of. He'll be good at conveying it with words, though. Oliver's articles are chock-full of description. I can't wait to see what he thinks of this."

A gentle knock sounded on the door.

"Come in," Margaret called.

It was Dottie, holding a cooing Joanna in her arms, wrapped in the yellow blanket that Margaret had knit for her. The baby was oblivious to the devastation surrounding the house. Oh, to be a child again.

"Have you looked outside?" Dottie asked.

"Yes. There are no words."

"We have a couple of broken windows and the power is

still out, but Brooklyn didn't even get the worst of it. I'm hearing that Long Island is devastated."

Gladys rubbed her arms. "That explains the draft I'm feeling."

"The cook lit the stove with a match, so at least we can eat. She's making eggs and pancakes."

Gladys smiled. "And that explains the delicious scent I'm smelling."

"What can we help you with in the meantime?" asked Margaret.

"The three broken windows are on the other side of the house where a tree fell against it. We can get some blankets and pin them up until they can be replaced. And then we can walk around outside and see what other damage there is."

They'd only been in the house for a few weeks, so Dottie and George were not fully stocked with the domestic necessities befitting a house like this. The women scrounged for towels and sheets and blankets, finding just enough to do the trick. Locating a hammer, nails, and a ladder was another feat. The fresh air, cleaned by the storm, was refreshing and as they worked together, they nearly forgot about all that had happened in the middle of the night.

As they finished, the cook called them down to breakfast. Dottie laid Joanna in a bassinet next to the table and flew a stuffed rabbit toy above her head, delighting the baby and giving them a chance to enjoy the meal.

Margaret had never aspired to be wealthy but having someone make you breakfast was a luxury that she could easily settle into. Especially having someone who knew how to portion rations and turn them into something so delectable.

The cook's scrambled eggs were light on the tongue, as were the pancakes so that when she'd finished them, Margaret felt satisfied but not bloated.

The telephone rang in the hallway and Dottie went to answer it. "Gladys," she said, popping her head back in the room. "It's for you. It's Oliver."

Gladys left and Dottie returned to the table.

"Have you received any more letters from William?"

It had been a sensitive subject since the day on the beach when Dottie and Gladys cautioned Margaret about developing feelings for a man she'd never met.

Margaret hung her head. "Not since the postcard from Paris."

They used to write to each other weekly, but the last two letters had extended the amount of time between them by a great deal.

"The fighting has ramped up, though," she reassured herself. "If he could write, he would."

"I'm sure all is well. They're sending our boys all over Europe. It's probably difficult for letters to keep up."

"I'm sure that's it." But Margaret didn't point out the error in what Dottie said—it might be difficult for letters to find their units, but surely mail was going out regularly *from* the front. They were usually sent on cargo planes as equipment was transported and it was difficult to believe that if William was writing as diligently as he always did that the letters wouldn't be making their way to her.

She feared that he wasn't writing as much because something was wrong. But saying it out loud would make it too real, so she smiled and agreed with her friend.

Gladys returned, her face looking wan from the wear of the night, and perhaps from what she'd just heard.

"Oliver was checking in on us. I told him we're fine. He's heading to Long Island to look at the damage, but he's hearing that over twenty-five hundred homes were affected. And about a thousand businesses."

Margaret's stomach tightened and she put her elbows on the table as she shook her head in disbelief.

"That could have been us. That could have been Brooklyn. I mean, look at Dottie's—and we were just on the edge of it."

She thought of their cobbler shop. The Navy Yard. Their home. How close danger had come.

"And," Gladys added, "he confirmed that it was a hurricane. The gusts clocked in at a hundred miles an hour."

"A hundred miles an hour!" Dottie exclaimed. "That's faster than any train or car or airplane."

"Indeed. Mother Nature is a mighty woman."

"I guess our nickname for you is well-placed." Margaret smiled. "You're the mightiest woman I know."

"Yes. But I use my force for good."

"Speaking of which," said Dottie. "I told you that I want to put our house to some use. That's something George and I had already talked about. But now I know where to start." She set her napkin down and pushed her chair back. "So, Gladys. Put that force of yours to work and let's figure out a way we can help."

Margaret could see Gladys's mind racing through a catalog of possibilities.

"First, let's see what we have to work with. Let's take a look outside and get this house in order."

The nanny breezed in as if on cue and the women walked outside to see the damage up close. Debris and driftwood were floating in the bay, and much had been washed up on Shore Drive. They walked to the left, and Gladys stopped and held her arm out.

"Oh, Dottie. Your car!"

Dottie's beautiful new blue car was split down the middle by the weight of an enormous fallen tree. Margaret held her hand over her mouth to keep from shouting out as Gladys ran toward it. Dottie, however, sauntered over, and when she approached it, she held out her hand and stroked its shiny paint with delicacy.

"Well, it was nice while it lasted."

"Nice while it lasted?" Gladys retorted. "Dottie, you had it for a few *days*. It's totaled. There's no Easter Morning resurrection in its future."

Dottie maintained the serene look on her face. "It's a shame. I'm not disagreeing with you. But it's difficult to be ruffled by the loss of something I never expected to have in the first place when our Long Island neighbors have lost their homes. Their *homes*. And our boys have lost their lives."

A chill went through Margaret, one that carried humility in its wake. This is why they called her Saint Dorothy. Of course she would have the perspective of seeing a thing as a thing, even if it was a beautiful car. She had lost the love of her life. Margaret had lost her brother. It was nothing in comparison. But Dottie was the one who always brought them back to this better place.

Hurricane Gladys. Saint Dorothy. What nickname would they give her?

CHAPTER TWENTY-ONE

October 1944

*S*upplies! Word had gone out among the troops the day before that a shipment full of cigarettes and near beer and toothpaste and all the goods they'd missed had arrived.

Tom was most excited about the air mail paper.

He reread the letter he'd written to Margaret, cranking a flashlight every few minutes in order to see better. He'd woken thinking about her and couldn't go back to sleep.

There were some things he would never tell her. He would never reveal that sometimes he thought it would be better to die like William and John than to continue on Hell's Highway, as this offense was being called. He did not want her to know that cold feet and wet boots made him question everything he'd believed about himself and his future in the military. That it was not due to the discomfort of them—or of the many hardships they'd endured—but in the realization that as an officer someday, he would lose men—good men—to these evils and these elements. And the thought of it tortured him.

If despair was the language of the devil's land, he'd become fluent.

Margaret, on the other hand, was his reason for hope in the darkness. His lifeline to believe that there were better days ahead. Because when he wrote of them, it made them real.

He held the flashlight higher until its beam shone just over the page.

Dearest Margaret, he'd begun.

It felt so good after so long to see those words come to life beyond the many letters he'd started in his mind.

I have been remiss in writing and I cannot adequately express my apologies for that. We have been on the move for weeks. Exhausted by never-ending battles. Though I shared with you some details about Normandy in the past, I've determined that there are some horrors that are just too terrible to retell—or to relive. So please forgive the dual droughts of correspondence and of details.

Writing to you is a reprieve. I have spent countless bedraggled hours imagining the things I will share with you. But now that I am graced once again with paper and pen, I find that it is not the large events that I want to describe but the tiny ones. An odd thing, maybe, but those intimacies are really the things that glue life together, aren't they?

For example. Having so little elevates the importance of everything one does have. I found a paper clip the other day. A paper clip! It was submerged in the mud and only the tiniest sliver of it was poking out. If the sun had not hit the ground in precisely the right way at precisely the right moment, I would have missed it altogether.

I dug it out like it was buried treasure and stuck it in my pocket. I've learned—we all have—that such a find should not be treated as trivial. And it proved to be true. Since that time, the paper clip has helped me scrape dirt from my finger-nails, get to hard-to-reach places as I clean my rifle, scratch a game of tic-tac-toe onto a fallen tree trunk, and stir a scant pack of sugar into my canteen as a treat.

It reminds me of a time when I was a teenager and the country was hit hard by economic woes. I observed that transient men near our home would save and use anything they could find. A lost hair ribbon became a tourniquet when a man cut his arm on a branch. A collection of bottle tops found along the way could be wrapped up in a cheesecloth and rattle to scare off animals when the men slept outside at night. A discarded Band-Aid could be wadded up to fill a hole in a shoe.

So it is here. We have been reduced to scavengers at times. Forced to innovate from nothing. It is bleak. I'll not sugarcoat that.

I want to believe, Margaret, that we will make it out of this. That no matter where I am after the war, I will never again take anything for granted. Not my life. Not a paper clip.

War changes a man, they say. And it is true. But it is not all bad.

On a lighter note, I must tell you that Holland has the most beautiful flowers. Tulips as far as the eye can see. One would scarcely believe that the front lies just miles away. As the weather turns, the edges of their delicate petals brown and wilt. Much like the soldiers observing them. But they have reminded us that beauty exists even among ugliness. And that there is reason to hope.

He signed the letter *Love, William*.

As he looked it over, the pretense continued to wear thin and he found that what had once been liberating now felt like a prison. He longed to confess to the charade and to write unfettered. As Tom. No secrets between them.

It had been easy enough after William's death to convince himself that Margaret didn't need to suffer another loss so soon after John's. The postcard from Paris was forgivable as well—with no paper to write a proper letter and no space on the card to tell William's story, signing his name was expedient at the least.

He'd had enough of it.

"There comes a time in a man's life, Thomas, when he must determine right from wrong and choose right, no matter how difficult it is."

The first time he'd heard his father say those words, he was about three years old and had been caught spreading his finger across the iced cake that his mother had baked for the church bake sale. Perhaps it was premature to begin talking of manhood to one so small, but it was a theme his father had pressed on him all through his life.

And he wasn't wrong. Tom had recalled those words again that night under the bridge and every day since.

He set the flashlight down. He was shivering in his bunk, sore from curling in a fetal position through the night. The sun ascended through the clear plastic windows of the canvas barracks, though it did not bring warmth. Dawn had always been his favorite time growing up. The household was quiet, accompanied only by the sound of the geese that gathered in the river. For a blissful second, he could close his eyes and pretend he was there.

The other men were waking up, preparing for whatever lay ahead. There was a wilted look to them—just as he'd told Margaret—the excitement over the new supplies already overshadowed by fresh worries.

Tom was saddened by the loss of their youthful bloom. These were not warriors who had volunteered with patriotic enthusiasm. These were boys scarcely out of high school who'd had aspirations of college or factory work or other callings. Not near-death on a land they could barely find on a map.

They had become warriors. Baptized in blood.

Tom was a good deal older and was here by choice. But none of that mattered on the field. What was important was to remember Hank and Dr. Weinstein and the McClintocks and William. Every soldier had their own version. How could he give up? How could he not press on with everything he had?

Renewed determination coursed through him. He stood up, muscles stiff and bones freezing.

After brushing his teeth with the new tube of Pepsodent that he'd been given, he read his letter to Margaret one more time. He set it aside, next to its envelope, already addressed and stamped in his eagerness to send it. But he was not going to. Not this one. When he returned from today's jump, he'd write a different one.

With a new signature.

Love, Tom

He opened the pocket of his rucksack and pulled out the two bottles of perfume that he'd bought at the House of

Fragonard, surprised that they had both survived. He looked for the one with the little *V* written in the corner and put the other one back. He held the vanilla one to his nose, inhaling deeply, pretending that he could smell its warm scent through all of the wrapping. He closed his eyes and remembered what it had evoked when the shopgirl had sprayed it on his arm. It was a scent that he now associated with Margaret, even though it had never graced her skin. But he hoped that it would. And until then, it was one more thin tie to the woman whose letters had inadvertently kept him going.

He returned it to the pocket, resisting the temptation to open it. It was not something you could buy at your corner Walgreens. If he ever had the chance to present it to her personally, he hoped that having thought of her in Paris and purchased something so special, his delay in telling her about William might be forgiven.

Tom exhaled, feeling emboldened by the release in his lungs.

He took out a fresh piece of paper from the air mail pile and picked up a pen. This one had blue ink, a surprise for a standard-issue army pen. He smiled. Maybe it was symbolic of a new start.

Dearest Margaret,

It was beautiful. Beautiful and liberating. Just to write those two words from his heart and from his hand. As Tom.

This is Tom Powell. William and John's friend. You know me from the flowers I draw at the end of the letters.
I have to tell you about William . . .

"Powell! Jump time!" one of the sergeants called out to him.

He folded the page and put it in his pocket, to be finished later.

The jump was flawless up until the last second when an unexpected gust of air blew him sideways and he twisted his ankle as he landed. Fortunately, the army provided the Airborne with boots reinforced for this very reason. In any other situation, he might have needed help getting off the field, but after detaching himself from his parachute and gathering it into his arms, he was able to limp off.

He walked into the medic's tent and asked for some ice. He unlaced his boot, long since immune to the smell that permeated the leather. He smiled—he was wearing one of the pairs of socks that Margaret had knit. He'd worn through nearly all of them and had taken to wearing the army-issued wool ones just to make hers last. But his decision today to write the letter in his own name seemed a cause for a rare celebration and he couldn't think of a better way to mark the occasion than to put on the last pair he had.

If she'd sent any more boxes, he didn't know, as mail and packages were having a difficult time following the men from front to front.

But these, he had. All red. She'd included a note saying that she'd gotten down to the last yarn from her grandmother's sweater and had decided to make one pair entirely from that. They had arrived just before they'd left for Normandy, and William had tossed them to Tom.

"Red. Cupid's color. You should have them."

He'd brushed it off at the time, thinking it to be one of the ribbing remarks that they all made to each other, but as he thought back to all of William's nudging, he realized that it was intentional.

William the matchmaker.

If God was just, he would accept the sacrifice of William's life and grant success to this thing he had wanted for his friends.

"Powell," Tom heard. He looked up to see Captain Winters closing the flap of the medic tent behind him. Tom swung his legs around off the cot, but Captain Winters waved his hands down, indicating that he should sit.

"At ease. No need to put more strain on your ankle than you already have."

It's one of the many things he liked about Winters. He seemed to know everything that was going on with his men, even a minor injury like this.

"It's nothing, sir. Just a little tape to wrap it and it will be good as new."

Captain Winters sat across from him and pulled an envelope from the pocket inside his jacket. He handed it to Tom. "This just came through."

Tom took it and began to open it. "What is it?"

"Read it. You're getting promoted to corporal. Two stripes for you, Powell."

Tom pursed his lips to keep from smiling, as it was unseemly to show emotion over such a thing.

Of course, Captain Winters could see right through it. "Unclench your jaw. You're allowed to have good news."

"What about specialist?" He was skipping over a rank to get there.

Winters folded his hand in his lap and sighed. "I need good leaders, Tom. We've lost a lot of men, and the reinforcements we're getting will be green. I need someone to show them the ropes, and I know that you'll do a great job in the role of corporal. The sky's the limit for men like you. This is just the beginning."

Tom felt a knot form in his throat. Winters was about his age. But this past year, he'd become like a father to him. A common sentiment when rank mattered more than what year you were born. So the praise—a rare thing from his actual father—meant the world. "I don't know what to say. Thank you?"

"No need to thank me. You've earned it. Something to write your mama about." Then he winked. "And maybe a girl back home?"

Tom was glad he hadn't finished his letter to Margaret. This would be wonderful news to share.

"I hope so, Captain. I hope so."

"I'll have the patch for you by tonight. You good with a needle and thread?"

"My mother taught me how to hem my own pants. She'd buy them long, hand me a needle and thread, and have me sew them to size, letting them out as I grew."

Winters smiled. "Mine too. She would have had my head if I'd ever tried to argue that it was woman's work. Personally, I think you put some mothers in the brass's place and this war ends soon. And would have been over long ago."

It was Tom's turn to grin. "I think I agree with you, Captain."

Winters stood up and patted Tom on the knee. "Good man, Powell. You'll get through life well if you value a woman as she should be valued. Congratulations again." He walked out, leaving Tom wishing he could have stayed.

He'd wanted to ask Winters if he planned to stay in the military. If he thought that life as an officer was compatible with marriage. He'd not given it serious consideration before.

Not before Margaret. She'd upturned his certainty for what his future would look like and made him question it altogether.

A medic came over and wrapped Tom's ankle in gauze, telling him to ice it and stay off it for the rest of the day, but that he'd be ready for service again tomorrow.

Tom hobbled out, thankful that his barracks were next to the medic's tent. He sank into his bunk, grateful for a rare day that left him feeling full of warm emotions.

"Corporal Powell," said a private, surprising Tom that the news had spread quickly. "The helicopter came for the mail and said that it would be at least a week before they are able to come back. I know you'd wanted to get your letter out, so I put it in the envelope and ran it out to them before they took off."

Tom thanked him, and then put his hand over his mouth once the boy had walked away.

No. This was all wrong. He'd planned to tear the letter up as soon as he was back from the jump.

Because the one that had been sent had been the one he'd signed as William.

CHAPTER TWENTY-TWO

November 1944

$\mathcal{M}$argaret lifted her protective eye shield and wiped the sweat from her face. No matter the weather outside, her welding station was always hot. Fire on metal. She was careful to wash her face religiously at night because if she missed the routine, her forehead would break out in a red rash that took weeks to clear up.

The welding room, enormous because of the large pieces being built, was nearly empty. She'd asked for some overtime hours, wanting to buy and fill an even larger Mason jar, and the foreman reluctantly accepted. There were some areas of the *Coral Sea* to smooth out and Margaret had proven herself adept with detailed work.

She lowered the shield, stretched her arms, then ignited her blowtorch, its burst of flame instantly satisfying. Every single time.

A whiff of smoke caused her nose to wrinkle.

Something was burning.

Margaret laid the torch down and pulled the ear protection off.

A woman was screaming.

It was coming from the back.

The dark corner was unusually lit and as Margaret approached, the screams intensified.

Fire!

Panic rose in her throat, tasting of blood and metal, and she swallowed it down. She had to keep her head about her. She looked around for anything that could help, but there was nothing—how the hell did they not have a fire extinguisher on every wall?

"I'm here!" she shouted over the screams.

She saw a coat draped over a chair at another station and grabbed it, nearly tripping over a table leg. She steadied herself and ran back to the woman, who was now bent over on the floor.

Smoke was rising from the woman's hair and she was trying to cover it with her hands. Margaret threw the coat over her and started hitting all around it, trying to smother the flames.

The woman collapsed and her body stilled. Margaret checked her pulse on her wrists but found nothing. Then, her neck—ah! There it was. A faint *thump, thump, thump*. Slow but present.

She raced to the foreman's office to look for a phone. The door was locked, so she took a nearby torch and broke through the glass. She cut her arm trying to find the latch, but it was nothing. She had to call someone.

She picked up the receiver. "There's an emergency in the welding department! Send someone quickly!"

She slammed it down and hurried back to the woman,

whose listless body frightened her. Margaret fell to the floor and scooped the woman into her lap, trying not to inhale the awful smell coming from her. As she waited for aid, she smoothed the woman's hair, noticing that the ends were now crisp and crumbled to the touch. Her hands were burned, but it looked like they might be no more than superficial.

She rocked her as a mother might do.

"Help is coming," she promised. "Help is coming."

The next morning, Margaret was exhausted. She opened her eyes after too few hours of sleep. There were voices downstairs.

Her mother. Gladys.

What was Gladys doing here?

Margaret squeezed her eyes and rubbed her temples. Lord, she had an awful headache.

She remembered now. The woman had not woken up by the time the ambulance arrived, but they'd assured Margaret that she was alive and whisked her off on a stretcher.

Maybe Gladys had news.

Margaret's feet found the slippers by the bedpost and she pulled her robe from its hook and put her arms into it. She felt like she was in a dream. That someone else was doing the actions.

Gladys was having a cup of coffee at their kitchen table. She stood up and walked a circle around Margaret.

"I don't see it. It must be invisible."

"What is?" Margaret asked. Exhaustion weighed on her like the heavy wool blankets that lay across her bed. She wasn't in the mood for games.

"Your cape. Superwoman has one. I thought you might too."

Margaret rolled her eyes and slumped into a chair. Her mother put a steaming cup of coffee in front of her and it was the best thing she'd ever smelled.

"Gladys is right, dear. You saved that woman's life."

Margaret perked up. "She's alive?"

Gladys nodded. "George called, but you were still sleeping. So he called me. You're a hero, my friend. And it gets better. She's a widow with four small children. Ironically, her husband was a firefighter, but he lost his life in the line of duty. That job is all she has to support them."

"Will she still be able to work?"

"Yep. Her hands will recover. She'll have to bob her hair, but no damage beyond that."

"I can't believe there wasn't a fire extinguisher or something."

"There was. George went and checked. There are two. In a janitor's closet. The foreman never pointed them out."

Margaret sipped the coffee as she processed the new information. Absolute heaven.

"I have a proposition for you, doll." Gladys scooted a chair out and sat down next to her.

"What's that?"

"I know this isn't as exciting as a job in welding. But—hear me out—I have something that might do some good on a bigger scale."

Mrs. Beck leaned against the counter. "More good than saving a woman's life?"

Gladys nodded. "Saving *more* women's lives. Margaret, I've been pushing for the Navy Yard to start an office that is specifically for women and I've won. I'll be making sure new hires are well trained. And that they learn the ropes. After last night, I'll inspect anywhere they are working to ensure that the safety standards are every bit as good as the departments where the men are working. You brought to light a real issue, Margaret. And I could use you by my side not just in that department but all over the Navy Yard making sure that it is a safe and welcoming place for all the women who keep coming to work here."

Margaret leaned back. Wow. It did seem like important work. But she had come to enjoy what she was doing so much. At the end of the day, the results of her work were tangible in a way that desk work couldn't hold a candle to. She'd always enjoyed the satisfaction of a vigorous morning of housecleaning, the sparkling results a monument to her efforts. In the welding department, the stakes were higher. The ships she was working on would carry troops across oceans, heading for victory.

Gladys must have seen the hesitation on her face.

"How about this. Give me three days a week in the office. Two days a week welding. Would that make you happy?"

The caffeine was bringing her to life, enough to consider what Gladys was saying.

"Yes. Yes, I think I'd like that."

Gladys pulled a cigarette from her purse and lit it. She inhaled deeply and then let it out. The smoke tickled Margaret's nose.

"Good. That's what I hoped you'd say. I'll tell George. He

wants to scout for a space soon and get a budget approved for it."

"Well, it sounds like something you'll be good at."

"*We'll* be good at it." Gladys pulled the cigarette from her mouth. "Hey, watch this. I've been working on it."

She took a deep inhalation and then formed an O with her lips. She blew it out slowly, and marvelously, a ring of smoke emerged. Well, it was more of an oblong shape, but still quite impressive. Margaret smiled. Now that Gladys had gotten what she came for, she was on to the next thing.

"Damn. I almost had it."

"Looked good from here," encouraged Margaret.

Gladys grimaced. "You and Dottie don't have critical bones in your body, do you?"

"But I meant it. What do you want me to tell you? That it was a little misshapen?"

"Yes, blast it all! I want you to tell me that it still needs work. I want you to tell the welding foreman that if he gives you any more lip, from now on you'll send him where the sun don't shine. I want you to tell your precious pen pal that he'd better damn well tell you which one he is in the photograph or you're not going to write to him anymore."

Margaret flushed. She'd never heard Gladys rant quite like that. At least not to her.

"You've given this a lot of thought."

"You saved a life last night, Margaret. A flippin' *life*. I think you've earned the right to speak your mind."

Margaret looked at her sideways. She was right. What Margaret admired most about Gladys was the way she spoke her mind. But she didn't think that commenting on the shape of a smoke ring quite rose to the level of necessary confrontation.

Gladys put her arm around her. "All right. You know the kind of frustration where you just want to boil up like a teakettle and let the steam fly out?"

"Yes." Margaret knew that feeling well. She looked up at her genteel mother, whom she equally admired for her amiability. Her mom looked amused.

"Here's what I do," Gladys continued. "I yell."

"You yell?" This hardly seemed like a revelation, but she let her go on.

"Yeah. A real solid, bloodcurdling scream. Into my pillow, so my neighbors don't think I'm being murdered. What I wouldn't give to find some remote piece of land to really let it out into the sky. But that's impossible in New York City. So I use my pillow. And I'm not shy about it. It's the kind that rolls up from your belly and makes your breath hot and sends your heart racing. Try it sometime."

"And that's Dr. Gladys's advice?"

Gladys grinned. "Yeah. At no charge. As long as you promise me you'll try it."

"I promise."

"Good." Gladys looked at her wristwatch. "I have to get back to the grindstone. But I'll tell George that you're in. We hope to get this up and running soon, so be ready, doll. Shine those pretty shoes of yours. You'll be an office girl soon."

Margaret looked down at her fingers, scarred in some places from where she'd gotten too close to the fire of the torch.

The Brooklyn Navy Yard had not been kind to her hands. They'd bled in the sewing wing, gotten stained in engraving, and scalded in welding.

But she relished every imperfection.

They were her own battle scars.

CHAPTER TWENTY-THREE

November 1944

$\mathcal{T}$om had begun to believe they'd never leave Holland, as the Airborne had stayed behind and helped the British soldiers pull back from Arnhem, retreating in rubber boats across the Rhine. But none too soon, the orders came for them to head to Mourmelon-le-Grand near the city of Reims in France.

The barracks—previously used by several German infantry and cavalry units and showing significant signs of wear— nevertheless had hot showers. Tom took everything off—his fatigues, the grenades around his belt, his socks, his under- wear, and left them in a pile on the floor next to his bunk. He took the issued white towel and wrapped it around his waist, pinching its corners since it was too small. Whoever ordered these provisions either thought the army was made up of children or they were too cheap to realize what a man-size towel might mean to a soldier who had been on the front lines for months.

No matter. He could hear the shouts of his fellow soldiers coming from the communal bathroom, shrieks of excitement as hot water touched their skin. He padded along the cold tile floorboards until he arrived at the room so thick with steam he could only make out blurry shapes of his friends.

He made his way to an empty showerhead and dropped the towel, not caring that it would become wet and useless but only craving the exhilaration of the hot water pouring down over his head. His chest. His feet.

The portable showers in Holland had never been heated, and many of the men decided not to shower at all rather than risk the hypothermia that would come from a cold shower in the colder outdoors. But this... this was the very definition of heaven. Better than peach pie. Better than catching fireflies. Better, even, than going to bed with that college girl. The steam permeated the pores of his skin, making it seem as if it was being absorbed into the depths of his body. He breathed it in like a thirsty man in a dry desert.

"Powell, you dog, you've got soft hair. Who knew?" Malarky stepped over from the adjacent showerhead, as there were no walls between them. He ran his fingers through Tom's hair.

"Yeah, I thought the dirt had permanently frozen on it."

"Good thing you're showering. Word is that we're going to get passes to go to Reims. French girls, Powell. French girls. Ha!" He slapped Tom on the back and hopped around the showers like a little boy who'd just received his first bicycle at Christmas.

Tom ran some lye soap across his scalp one more time, as if he could bank the cleanliness by doing it twice. You could always rely on the army to give you the most basic of supplies, and the lye was no substitute for the store-bought kind. But he rubbed his palms around it to work up some lather. In the field, he'd shorn his hair with a knife and occasionally cut it when he could find scissors. Some guys preferred just to get a razor and shave it off, but Tom's hair had always been his one point of pride. And a bare head would only have made him colder.

So it was a welcome change to have the strands feel malleable once again. He rubbed the soap across the rest of his body, and he had the luxury of time to feel every muscle. This was not the same body that had left Virginia for Georgia. He'd always been a lanky guy—tall and skinny—but this was the form of a man. And he hadn't even noticed until now. Where he'd been thin, he'd now filled out with muscle. Especially his legs. The soldiers had gone through rigorous conditioning to make their legs strong so that they could withstand a landing. He washed down to his shins and his feet, full of wonder that a year and a half could make such a difference.

His father would be proud. His mother might not recognize him.

But . . . would Margaret find him attractive?

He'd have to survive the war if he was to find out.

"Powell! Hurry up—there's champagne!" Muck called out to him this time, he and Malarky always the dog and pony show of Easy Company.

"Champagne. Please. Don't pull my leg, Muck."

"The way you're feeling your legs, I don't have to. You like what you see, pretty boy?"

Tom picked up his wet towel by its corners and slung it around and around until it was whip-shaped. He flicked it onto Muck's bare back, and Muck yelped.

"I'm not kidding, man. We're in champagne country. Actual,

real, honest-to-God champagne. Not the cheap bubbly wine you can get at Woolworth's. And the chow! You don't hear the guys' moans from here?"

"You're for real? Here I come."

Muck tossed a fresh, dry towel to him. "Hurry up or I'm taking your share."

"Thanks, man." Tom wrapped the towel around him, no longer minding its diminutive size because he could smell what Muck was talking about. Beef. Gravy. Was his nose deceiving him?

The chow in Holland had left much to be desired.

Tom stopped by his bunk and pulled on a pair of shorts and a T-shirt that he'd kept from boot camp. Light and cotton and definitely too little for the cold day, but they were all he had until they had a chance to do laundry.

The mess hall was almost deafening as hardened soldiers became boisterous schoolboys with these newfound delights. Half of them were in towels that barely covered anything, coming straight from the showers, as Tom had. The other half had chosen food first, and they were still wearing their fatigues, stiff with sweat that might have permanently frozen into it.

Tom got in line and his jaw tingled in anticipation when he saw that they were serving up beef tips and gravy—his nose had been right—as well as mashed potatoes and chocolate cookies. Two chocolate cookies, and he hadn't even had to ask for the second. Mourmelon-le-Grand might as well have been paradise.

He found his way to Malarky and Muck. Muck set a bottle onto the table with such force that Tom wouldn't have been surprised if it had shattered.

"Told you so. Champagne. Look at the label. Compliments of the people of the region for liberating them."

Tom looked around. The soldiers on KP duty were carrying boxes and boxes of them.

"Anyone seen Winters?"

"El Capitán took a train into Paris. Said he always wanted to see it. Should be back tonight."

Paris. Tom smiled at the memory of his stolen journey to the City of Lights. How had it fared in the past few months? Had shops reopened? Had it returned to its glory days?

He'd have to ask the captain when he returned. And maybe, if they were in Mourmelon-le-Grand long enough, he'd get to go back.

Dick Winters, in fact, didn't return until the next morning. Tom heard him come in, laughing with a few of the guys. Apparently, he hadn't checked the train line and had taken the last one into the city—with no more returning for the night. So he'd found a room in a small hotel and eaten chocolate croissants and jam for breakfast.

"None for us?" Tom heard Malarky ask him.

The captain pulled out a large paper bag and tossed it to him. "Would I ever forget Easy Company?"

Tom sat up straight and instantly regretted it. His head was pounding, and he couldn't recall how much champagne he'd drunk. Only that it had been a lot. They hadn't bothered with glasses; they'd just passed the bottles from man to man, and it was impossible to tell what they'd consumed.

Dearest Margaret, he composed in his head. *Someday I want to take you to Paris and stay in a hotel overlooking the green lawn of the Eiffel Tower and eat chocolate croissants and jam for breakfast.*

"Mail call!"

The men scrambled to their feet, and indeed, it was better than getting a bicycle at Christmas because it had taken months for the mail to catch up with them. A crowd formed around the unfortunate soldier who'd made the announcement and who carried the letters in a canvas bag slung over his shoulders like Santa's sack.

"Lipton. Taylor. Guth. Malarky. Powell. Guarnere. Muck. Martin. Talbert." The soldier read off names as he pulled envelopes from the bag. Tom's heart leapt when he heard his name, wondering if it was from Margaret. And then he remembered that Margaret would have written to William. Not to him. However, four letters written by his mother had arrived, and he looked forward to reading them when he returned to his bunk.

"What the hell do we do with these?" Tom half heard the soldier's question, but he turned. The man was holding out some letters to him. "You were William's best friend, weren't you? Do you want these?"

Letters. Letters for William. They had to be from Margaret. Because his family would have been informed that he'd died.

"I'll take them," he said with nonchalance, even though all he wanted to do was look down at the handwriting.

He returned to his bunk and set the ones from his mother down.

Yes—yes! The others were from Margaret. There were only three of them, but he saw her handwriting and he held them to his chest, bending over at the joy of holding a piece of her once again. Not hearing from her had been like a drought.

He wanted to rip into them, but that wasn't how he would have treated her, and it wasn't how he would treat her letters. She deserved delicacy, and he was careful to open them by slipping his knife through the seal.

He put them in order of their dates.

> *Dearest William,*
> *Gladys and Oliver*
> *Sweet baby Joanna*
> *Dottie and George bought a house...*
> *The welding foreman is an angry little man.*
> *A hurricane. The first one I've experienced.*
> *Dottie used her house to shelter people who'd lost theirs.*
> *A fire. Saved a woman's life.*

They were full of the tidbits of her life in Brooklyn and at the Navy Yard and he rushed through them because he knew he'd have the time to savor them later, as they'd all been given passes for the day. He had thought about going to Reims, but he didn't need to go meet French girls when he had the only one he wanted here.

But there was something about the letters that pierced him sharper than a bayonet.

Winters had hinted that Tom might be up for yet another promotion—sergeant. Three stripes. More responsibility. He was earning promotions faster than any other man in his family had, as far as he knew.

It was good news. It was *terrific news*, in fact. His plan to advance in the military was going splendidly and Winters had even told him that "the sky was the limit."

And yet. And yet he had not received it with the enthusiasm he would have expected of himself.

Margaret—or at least the idea of her—had offered a different path. As she talked about the marriages of her friends as well as her little niece, his mind considered a life as settled as that and it was strangely welcome.

It had sowed just enough seeds of doubt to make him think about deviating from what had always been expected of him.

It had led him to imagine a picture. on that mantel that included a wife. Children.

A surprisingly welcome thought.

He pulled Margaret's picture from his pocket—always close by. They'd been writing for over a year. At first, he'd romanticized the whole thing—and her—encouraged, as he'd been, by John and William. It had been fun to have a girl to think about. A photograph to hold on to.

But he was beginning to realize that he'd thought of her as a good luck charm. She was disembodied words on a page. A joyful diversion from the horrors he'd seen. Any romantic notions he'd attached to her had been rooted in encouragement from John and William. And he'd willingly played that game.

This was different, though. He was soon going to have to decide to go as far as he could in the military and postpone a family until the timing was right. Or take a chance that what had been a lark might actually be . . . love.

Every one of her letters revealed something he hadn't known before. They filled out the two-dimensional air mail sheets with hopes and dreams and worries and fears and gave shape to an actual woman who was giving him so much without even realizing it.

Tom ran his hands through his newly clean hair and gripped it into a fist.

No matter what he chose, they'd grown too close for him to keep up a pretense.

She needed to know him as Tom Powell.

If she chose not to continue their friendship after that, the decision for any more wouldn't even be his to make.

He owed her another letter. But it was not something he could pen in a hurry. He'd have to ruminate on it if he had any hope of her forgiving him.

"We're rolling out, men. Have your things ready. We leave at zero five hundred."

Captain Winters had given Tom the unenviable task of rousing the soldiers, many of them hungover after several days of gambling and drinking and brawling. They had reverted to the teenaged boys that many of them still were, releasing months of the terrors of battles in immature ways.

Sometimes, being older had its perks. Tom had not felt tempted to party away their break, though he could well understand their revelry.

He'd observed that war was an unnatural intruder onto the linear path of boy to man. Most of these boys weren't even old enough to vote or buy a beer. But here they were tasked with saving the *whole damn world*.

They should be seeing movies with girls on Friday nights.

Stopping into hardware stores to pick up supplies for weekend projects. Enjoying their new driver's licenses.

Tom thought their temporary debauchery was completely understandable given the opposing expectations of their age versus their circumstance. Their baby faces told one story. The weariness etched in their faces told another.

Every day, younger recruits joined them. Fresh out of boot camp. Wide-eyed and ready for the adventure of battle that would prove their manhood and worth. Tom and Malarky and Winters and Muck could warn them that they wouldn't feel like men, let alone human beings, when they were hungry and exhausted, and they'd just seen the limbs of a fellow soldier shot off as his blood watered the desolate ground.

But they kept silent. The boys would find out soon enough.

The time for champagne was over.

Because winter had arrived.

Captain Winters was being called away from Easy Company for a regimental job.

And they were heading to Belgium.

"It's Christmas Eve."

"What even is Christmas? Birth of a savior? We need a savior now. In this icebox."

Disagreements had replaced discourse.

The truck on the war-torn Belgian road hit a divot and they all lurched forward. They were blinded by the starless dark of the sky, clouds hovering from an earlier rainstorm. Mud kicked up, slipping under the canvas cover whose ropes had loosened, exposing them to the elements. Tom barely noticed. They were dirty enough to begin with.

Malarky hummed "Silent Night" under his breath, but the man next to him slapped his face and told him to shut up.

Tom watched—weary, cold, as the men unraveled. The temperature outside was far more frigid than any Virginia winter he'd ever known. It was mitigated briefly by their sardine-like tightness—which brought its own discomfort—but soon they would step out into the bitter winter winds.

He was worried. Would they even be able to fight if they were frozen? It was difficult enough to hoist a grenade launcher onto your shoulders in the best of circumstances.

When they arrived at their camp, they rolled out into foxholes, wiping snow from their eyes as they dug in. Tom's gloves bore holes in the fingers, and he had to be careful to hold the metal barrel of his rifle with his palm, lest his skin freeze to it. They were fired upon almost immediately, two bombs hitting nearby, and the men had to take cover to avoid shrapnel. The smell of gunpowder permeated the air, its metallic tinge almost suffocating.

It was over almost as quickly as it had begun—friendly fire. Americans in P-47s who thought they were Germans. But the actual Germans advanced, and they were soon surrounded.

Death seemed certain as night arrived early and the cold almost made it welcome.

General McAulliffe sent what he likely hoped were encouraging words to the troops: "We are giving our country and our loved ones at home a worthy Christmas present, and being privileged to take part in this gallant feat of arms is truly making for ourselves a Merry Christmas."

Tom felt numb. They didn't need words. They needed reinforcements.

They lay still on Christmas morning, submerged in darkness, afraid to light much-needed fires because doing so would give away their positions. Tom roused himself from the stupor that had descended on all of them. He turned his thoughts to how, in a few hours, his mother would clip candles to the tree and light them. And Margaret. Whatever her traditions were, he hoped that she was joyful.

He clenched his hands and tightened his body and willed himself to get warmer by tensing up.

"Powell," whispered Malarky as they dug into a foxhole. "You got anything in that canteen?"

Tom opened it up, unworried about the musty smell that emanated from it. He'd had a little water, but it was ice now. He held it upside down over his mouth, but nothing came out.

"We'll have to drink snow."

"I gotta drink something," said Malarky. "My piss is yellower than a rapeseed field. What about yours?"

Tom hadn't bothered to notice. When he'd gone into the woods, he could barely open his eyes since his lashes were stuck together. Let alone look at the color below.

He shrugged and formed a snowball with a small clean patch of snow that had fallen into their hold.

"Man, don't you throw that at me. We've got enough with the bullets flying over our head."

"I'm not going to throw it. Here." Tom handed it to him and then made another for himself. "Take some bites of this. Warm it in your mouth before swallowing so your esophagus doesn't freeze."

"Where did you pick that trick up?"

"Just something I learned taking care of farm animals."

"Thanks, man," Malarky said as he took a bite. "This helps."

They jumped at gunfire in the distance. Discordant, like some jazz music he'd heard. The bullets made a high-pitched sound as they breezed by that might have been music in a different circumstance.

He tried to wiggle his fingers as a piano player might, but they were stiff and black and had no feeling. He stretched his legs, but they, too, felt as if they might crack with movement.

He heard the rumble of tanks in the distance. Someone was coming and they had to find safety.

He and Malarky grabbed some branches and covered themselves, leaving just enough space to point their rifles out when the enemy came closer.

The roar became louder and louder as it neared. Engines grinding. Brittle tree branches snapping as the treads rolled over them.

Then—an American flag. Tom wanted to yelp with relief, but his paralyzed lungs could hardly muster breath, and what little he had crystalized as soon as it hit the air. The capillaries in his face warmed with anticipation, and he thought he had never seen anything so beautiful in his life.

Forty-eight stars. Home.

The 37th Tank Battalion had broken through the German lines and were there to relieve them.

Soldiers hopped out of the tanks carrying sacks of food, clothes, cigarettes, and ammunition. Newspapers too.

Never again would there be a better Christmas present than this!

There were no mail sacks, but Tom was too starved of the basics to give that much thought. Besides, he'd had no opportunity to write the letter to Margaret that he knew he needed to write.

So it was just as well that he hadn't received anything to respond to.

He did, however, grab a few pages of air mail paper and jot notes on everything he wanted to tell her. He didn't trust that in this exhausted state, he would remember.

Dearest Margaret, he started.

The headlines are ringing with Allied victories across the continent. I'm sure you're hearing about them too. Metz and Strasbourg were liberated by French troops and Albania was freed by local partisans. Americans have driven Himmler to dismantle the gas chambers at Auschwitz and Hitler has retreated to Berlin.

We soldiers are warmed by victory in our reach even as our extremities are frozen solid.

The ball has dropped and 1945 was surely met with fanfare in Times Square but we have scarcely noticed here. Calendars only mark one more day of existence. And too many days of uncertainty ahead.

I spent all of 1944 in Europe. Away from American soil. A lot of good men have been lost—Julian, Penkana, Sawoski, Webb, and the other Webb. Names that will be forgotten to history but forever remembered by those of us who still have breath.

Tom didn't think he could ever tell her about Muck. Muck had died when his foxhole was hit by a German 88 mm flak. Just one over from where he and Malarky had been.

All they found were pieces of him in his sleeping bag.

He wouldn't tell her that the casualty list had grown so long that it was almost difficult to mourn. That the men avoided crying because the tears would turn into ice on their faces. Already, their eyebrows and hair were like rock.

Let her believe the headlines. The ones that omitted how very dire things still were in many corners of this continent.

"We're moving out!" Those had become Tom's least favorite words because it meant his enjoyment of the newly arrived bounty was short-lived. He folded his note and stuck it in his rucksack.

More weeks went by, minutes and days and hours blurring into one. One field looking like the next, one bombed town blending into another. Tom was not alone in forgetting the name of their location on any given day—they thought in coordinates and obstacles.

Tom lost Margaret's photograph somewhere in the mud when a burst of sporadic gunfire had them racing to dig more foxholes. Once all had quieted, he'd used his shovel to scour every bit of the rock-hard ground he'd treaded, desperate to find it even as he knew it would be impossible.

He'd stopped only when a medic had been called to treat him for hypothermia. He found out later that he'd been ranting with delirium—"I have to find her. I have to find her."

He was back on the field the next day, a body that couldn't be spared. The only thought he could muster about the loss of the greatly worn photo was the hope that it would disintegrate into the soil and nurture any flowers that might dare to emerge come spring.

She deserved that much.

Dearest Margaret, he jotted onto his pages.

Rumors are flying about more Allied wins, but our Airborne tastes victory and defeat with the to-and-fro of a tug-of-war game. The town of Foy has changed hands a full six times, the locals as weary of the roller coaster as we are.

I've been promoted to sergeant, which feels more like a move of desperation than merit. As one is killed, another takes his place, and I guess my number was next. Though my father would be proud, there are even more men for whom I'm responsible. It's frightening, coming earlier than I would normally merit. I'm not sure I'm ready.

I once thought it would be an honor. Now it frightens me. I have nothing to give them. We are low on ammunition, medical supplies, and food.

He would not tell her these things. In fact, his notes were filled more with things he never wanted her to know. But writing them to the idea of her was the only respite he felt.

He no longer gave thought to the fireplace mantel.

Or his mother.

Or any of the people whose memories he'd clung to like a mantra back in Normandy. He was too cold to consider anything except lasting one more minute.

And he barely wanted to do that.

The men who'd died of exposure were better off.

At the end of every battle—won or lost—there were bodies piled to be sorted later, their dog tags wrapped around their necks to identify them. Medics used the fatigues of dead men to tear into tourniquets to save the living. Chaplains prayed over them in groups rather than giving individual absolution. Snow fell white and landed pink as it mingled with the blood-stained ground.

Tom typed letters to families who would grieve upon receipt of them.

It was a terrible task.

Every day brought another battle as the Germans seemed bent on taking out as many troops as they could even as their ultimate defeat seemed inevitable. Maybe that even fueled their ire. Revenge upon all they'd ceded.

During a particularly gruesome fight, Tom ran into the supply tent to forage for any ammo that had been scavenged off of dead bodies and found one half-used belt for a machine gun. He grabbed it, hoping to find a gun to match it, and ran toward the nearest foxhole as he saw explosions of snow indicating advancing Germans. A sound zipped through the air that had the distinct mark of a grenade, and he saw it fall near some of his men reloading their rifles.

"I'll see you soon," he said to John and William.

He jumped on top of the grenade and all went black.

CHAPTER TWENTY-FOUR

January 1945

*H*appy New Year, dolls!" Gladys whirled into the women's office wearing gold tinsel as a headband. She sprinkled some onto Margaret's desk and tossed some into Dottie's hair. Dottie was helping out for a few hours with filing. Her parents—having been won over by George's devotion to their daughter and granddaughter—now took Joanna every Monday.

Margaret stood up. "Where have you been? It's January fourth. We've been worried sick."

Gladys held up her hand, on which sat a slender gold ring. "This might answer your question."

"You didn't."

"We did."

"Without us?"

Dottie sat in a chair across from Margaret, and Gladys leaned against the desk.

"Come on, ladies. When have you ever known me to do things the traditional way? I'll have none of the white dress and church organ stuff. We went to the court, signed some papers, said some things, and here we are."

"And Oliver was okay with this?" Dottie asked.

"It was Oliver's *idea*," Gladys gloated as she hung her coat and purse on the coatrack. "And if that doesn't tell you how well he knows me, I don't know what does."

Margaret folded her arms. "Then where have you been all this time?"

A red tint built on Gladys's cheeks. "Honeymooning. In the Poconos."

"Nobody goes to the Poconos in January. Isn't everything closed?" Margaret had never actually been, nor did she travel in circles of people who took regular vacations.

Gladys grinned. "You're assuming we actually wanted to *go* anywhere."

She waited for Margaret and Dottie to realize what she was saying and waved away their eye rolls once they'd figured it out. "We did get snowed in, though. And the little hotel we were staying at lost their phone lines. So I couldn't have called you anyway. Sorry, ladies. But here I am now."

Margaret stood up. It was impossible to remain frustrated with Gladys, especially in light of such joyous news. But it had been a difficult few days without her, not to mention the panic she'd felt with no word from her friend. "Well, you're the *manager* here, so I guess you can do whatever you like. But I had to step in. We've had forty women come in this week and I could have used your help."

Gladys sat on the end of Margaret's desk. Her red-and-blue tweed skirt had tiny gold strands that caught the reflection of the overhead light. "You're not cross, are you? Please don't be. Really, we didn't expect to be away more than one night and that was over the holiday, so the office wasn't even open. I didn't leave you high and dry on purpose."

Margaret shrugged. There was no use splitting hairs over something that had already happened. And besides—Hurricane Gladys had gone and done it. She'd gotten married.

Margaret felt her resentment slip away. Gladys was okay and the Brooklyn Navy Yard had somehow continued to stand in her absence.

"Well," Dottie conceded, standing up and drawing Gladys into a hug. "We couldn't be happier for you. Welcome to the club of old married couples."

"I highly recommend it, Mags," Gladys teased. "Your turn will be next."

Margaret turned her back to them and opened the filing cabinet. She fumbled through paperwork instead of replying, occupying herself with nothing. "Not likely," she finally said. "Maybe that's just not in the cards for me after all."

With every day that passed without a letter from William, her heart grew heavier. The old adage held true here—absence makes the heart grow fonder. Every day that the mailbox did not contain word from him made her anticipate it even more.

And worry more. If she was not hearing from him, something might be wrong.

It was the only thing that kept her from acknowledging the possibility that she could be falling in love with him. There was no reason to consider a future with a man who may not live to see it.

Dottie had patiently listened to her woes on the subject over a few afternoons spent at the Beck home while Margaret's parents played with Joanna.

Margaret could hear her whisper to Gladys, "She hasn't heard from William in a while."

"Still? Geez, Mags. That's rough."

Margaret shrugged.

Gladys leaned over and put her hands on Margaret's shoulders.

"This might be an unpopular opinion, but my vote is that you don't turn yourself into a nun. I'm not saying to ditch him. But if another boy crosses your path, don't pine for something that might be an illusion."

"Gladys," Dottie said in an admonishing tone.

Gladys tilted her head. "What? You're thinking it. But I'm saying it."

"Just because you have Oliver live and in the flesh doesn't mean that you know everything about love."

Margaret stood up and placed her hands on the top of her desk. She hung her head down and her hair brushed its surface, a smile emerging on her face despite her sour mood. She straightened herself and crossed her arms, looking at both of them.

"I have the two best friends in the world, you know. Can we just focus on that?"

Gladys came around the desk to pull Margaret into a hug. "I know, doll. You're right. I'm just defensive when I see my friends feeling hurt. You know I love a good cause."

"I don't want to be your cause. I just want . . ."

"What?" asked Dottie softly.

"I just want to know he's okay."

"What the hell are you doing, Powell? Take cover!"

Tom felt himself being dragged through the snow and was pulled into the foxhole. He looked down at the grenade he was still holding. The grenade! He tossed it out toward German lines, as far as he could. It landed on the ground. And did nothing.

A dud.

He'd expected to die.

Why had everything gone black?

"What kind of nut are you diving on a grenade like that?" asked the solider who'd yanked him into the foxhole.

"I didn't want it to get you guys."

"That's some guts, man. Thank you. You hit your head pretty hard when you landed. I think on a rock that was hidden in the snow."

That explained it. The ache in his head. And in his stomach. He winced as he touched that spot and opened his jacket to check it out.

Blood. He'd been cut on something that tore through the fatigues. But when he checked his skin, the wound was superficial.

He wasn't sure whether to feel relieved or disappointed. The only thing that seemed to offer certainty right now was death.

"Incoming!" someone shouted before someone could call for a medic.

The soldier grabbed Tom by the shoulders until he was fully belowground.

A bomb exploded so near them that Tom's ears went silent.

Tom woke to a blinding light and welcomed the thought that he was dead. At last.

That would mean that he'd never have to face battle again.

The light retreated and he blinked before seeing a shadowed figure hovering over him.

"How many fingers am I holding up?"

The words sounded as if they were said through a tunnel, but Tom could understand them easily enough.

Tom squeezed his eyes closed and then opened them again.

He was alive. It was not a relief.

Though at least he hadn't lost his hearing.

He could barely make it out but took a guess. "Four."

"Who is the president?"

"FDR."

"Sit up for me, son."

Tom pushed himself up on wobbly arms but immediately wrapped them around his stomach. Dizziness overtook him and he leaned over the side of the bed and vomited right on the floor.

"I'm sorry," he whispered. A nurse was immediately at his side, offering him a towel and wetting a mop.

The doctor had a squared jawline and looked as if there was nothing he hadn't seen.

"I heard you got into a brawl with a grenade. Mighty brave of you. That's the stuff medals get awarded for."

Tom started to shake his head, but his brain felt like it was rattling from side to side. He rushed his hands to his temples.

"You're concussed, son. The grenade was a dud, lucky for you. But you fell onto a rock that was hidden by the snow. Don't talk—I know what you're going to ask. Yes, you'll recover. And, yes, they're going to ask you to get back on the front lines just as soon as I clear you."

Tom lay back. He felt like a cat with nine lives that were getting checked off one by one. He didn't know how many other near misses he might have. And as much as he might want them to be over with here in the hospital, that wasn't really where his heart was. He couldn't wish that for his mother and father—or for Margaret.

If Tom died, all three of them would be lost to her. John. William. Tom.

There was a rustle of the canvas curtain and Captain Winters came in.

"What are you doing here?" Tom asked. He immediately regretted that he hadn't saluted. In his confusion, he'd forgotten protocol.

"I told the regiment I needed to come back to the unit for a bit. And what did I find? Sergeant Powell decided to be Captain America?"

Tom grinned. "Sergeant America to you."

Winters's laugh was heartier than Tom had ever heard.

"Well, I came here to find out if our sergeant is returning to us and I think we can resoundingly say yes." He sat on the corner of the bed and put his hand on Tom's arm. "I'm not going to sugarcoat it for you. We're almost there. The Germans are retreating right and left. But they're putting up a fight. This is not over yet."

Tom closed his eyes. The idea of going back was terrifying

and he could feel his blood race at the mention of it. "What a waste of life. Think of how many could be saved if they'd only surrender."

He let out a sigh and turned his head so that Winters couldn't see the tears forming in his eyes.

But he knew what Tom knew—that either of their lives could be taken just as the war was coming to an end.

"Tom, I've known you for a while now. You've kept things close to the vest, but I'd like to think that I've done a good job observing my men. You perform as well if not better than the best of them. But there is something bothering you. You don't have to tell me—I'm not your confessor. But whatever it is, I suggest you remedy it. And soon. If you've ever seen fireworks, you know that the grand finale is what they save the biggest ones for. We're about to head into that. I need you to be more focused than you've ever been. I need you to survive this. And all the men I've put in your care."

Tom raised his right hand and brought it to his forehead in a salute. There was nothing he wouldn't do for Captain Winters.

"Here you are," the nurse said. Her gentle voice was a relief to his ears. The concussion had caused him to become especially sensitive to noise. The doctor assured him that it was temporary. But he appreciated her discretion. "I've brought you that pen and paper you asked for."

Tom thanked her and sat up as she put pillows behind his back. When she walked away, he was left alone with his task.

He might live through this battle. He might not. And if the worst happened, he did not want to go to his grave without having told Margaret the truth. Winters had been right—his worry over it was a dangerous distraction. He'd been waiting for the right time. And it had just presented itself.

He took the pen and pressed it to the paper.

Dearest Margaret,

I have written this letter in my head so many times to you in the last few months that I don't need to pen draft after draft to get it right.

This is Tom Powell. Tom, who drew the flowers for you.

I hope they've made you smile.

My handwriting is surely familiar.

That is what I am writing to explain.

John, William, and I shared everything. Socks, cigarettes— though I passed on those—letters. Unless there was something of a private nature said, we considered letters to be community property. No matter whose family had sent them, they sustained us more than I could ever describe.

From the beginning, William could tell that reading your letters put a smile on my face. He said it was a particular smile that he never saw me wear any other time. He pinned your picture to my pillow and I never removed it. Not until we left Chilton Foliat. It was nice to wake up to your beautiful face.

I lost it a few weeks ago during a battle. It had survived Arctic temperatures and got scratched by shrapnel and it even got bled upon. It had faded and white lines ran down where it was folded.

But it was my most treasured possession, for all that it symbolized. "You" have been with me, Margaret. Your picture reminded me every day that there was something worth living for.

And now for the difficult part. You see, of course, that I have spoken here of William in the past tense. And this is why I have put off this letter for far, far too long. William died in Normandy. All the way back in June. He was a hero, Margaret, and I will love and remember him until my last breath. On that first day in France, he ran to a bunker full of Germans and tossed a grenade into it, killing all the men. But a sniper lurked in the trees and caught him right in the chest. I saw him fall. I think it got him instantly because he didn't even shout. Just collapsed and never moved. It is something that haunts me to this day. I often think of his parents and his sisters in Arlington. The first thing I want to do when I return—right after I see you—is go see his family. And tell them how much he was cherished.

I know you'll need some time to grieve through that. So please put this letter down if you feel like you need to. Cry on it—I chose heftier paper instead of air mail so that it can withstand your tears. Or maybe you'll want to rip it up when you read what I have to say next.

You'll be confused, of course, why you continued to receive letters from William when D-Day was already so long ago.

To that, I can only say, I'm sorry. I'm sorry. I'm sorry.

You deserve an explanation. Please do not see this as an excuse, because I don't pretend that what I did was right.

John asked you to write William because he hadn't received any letters from home. And it was so kind of you to do so. Just before William was going to write you back, he injured his right hand and couldn't grip a pen. So I played secretary to his dictation.

He liked my handwriting better anyway.

Eventually, through an administrative snafu, dozens of letters from his family arrived at the same time and it was the happiest I'd ever seen him. By then, his hand had mostly healed and it took up all of his scarce free time to write them all back.

But there was still the question of your letters. Neither of us wanted them to go unanswered. You delighted us all with your big words and your optimistic outlook and, with the gaps filled in by John's tales of his sister, I felt like I'd really gotten to know you.

I kept writing and he would occasionally contribute some thoughts, but as time went on, the letters were mostly mine.

Until they were entirely mine.

My favorite moments have been the ones in which I was writing to you.

The flowers, at least, were always my own. And I delighted in knowing that, if you liked them, it was my gift you were enjoying.

At William's behest, though, I continued to sign his name. And, thinking that he might want to take them over one day, I agreed.

As for the rest—once we'd lost him—I have no excuse other than to say that in my grief, I could not bring myself to write to you as the stranger I was and impart that news.

And, I couldn't bear the thought of telling you about another loss so soon after John's death.

You'd become a lifeline to me. Everything I was experiencing, I thought of in relation to how I would tell you about it. Every letter you sent brought me peace when there was none surrounding us.

But I don't want to go another day without telling you. It is important to me to live a life of honor.

I hope you will find room in that generous heart of yours to forgive me. I offer only explanation, not excuse.

Love, Tom

CHAPTER TWENTY-FIVE

February 1945

$\mathcal{M}$argaret marched over to the telephone booth on the corner and plunked in a nickel. She dialed the rotary until she'd entered the party line in Gladys's brownstone.

It sounded fifteen times before someone picked up the extension, to which she insisted that they knock on Gladys's basement door and tell her there was a call for her.

It was then that she realized it was Saturday morning and she'd probably woken half the building. But it was too late to take it back now.

A sleepy Gladys finally answered. "What is it, doll? Oliver was out late on a story and then we went into Manhattan for drinks. We just got back a few hours ago."

"Dottie's house. One hour. I'll see you there."

She slammed down the phone before Gladys could respond.

She dialed Dottie's number, happy, at least, that she had telephones that weren't shared with any neighbors.

"Hello?" answered the cook. "This is the Preston residence."

Margaret could hear Joanna wailing in the background.

"This is Margaret. Please tell Mrs. Preston that Gladys and I will be there in one hour. We need to talk."

She put the receiver down and huffed back to her house to get her coat and boots. She'd run out in her robe and slippers once she'd read the contents of William's—no, *Tom's*—latest letter.

She wished she told them half an hour. This couldn't wait.

Sixty minutes dragged on. Margaret managed a lopsided braid and decided against cosmetics. The girls had seen her without them before. Maybe not George, but she didn't care.

At last, ten o'clock arrived. She stepped off the bus and marched up the steep hill to Dottie's house. Gladys was already waiting. She held a cigarette between her two fingers and her eyes bore the baggy look of weariness. Last night's cosmetics had not yet been washed off, and the remnants of blurred mascara didn't help.

"You're all in a rage this morning, aren't you?" she asked. "This is a new side to Margaret Beck."

"Get used to it."

Margaret was about to rap on the front door when Dottie opened it, Joanna balanced on her hip.

"I'm sorry, sweetheart," she apologized. "She's cutting some teeth, and it's been a night. I'll hand her to the nanny as soon as I'm able to nurse her."

She welcomed them into the parlor and put a blanket around her shoulders before settling into a chair. Margaret and Gladys took the couch.

"Ouch!" Dottie yelped.

Gladys looked sharply at Margaret, frustration in her eyes. "What's so important that you woke my husband up, pulled me out of bed, and forced Dottie to hurry through getting her titties chewed up by a teething child?"

Margaret covered her gasp with her hand, the weight of her selfish behavior sinking in. Tom's blasted letter had come in yesterday's mail, but she only saw it this morning. And since then, she'd thought of nothing other than steaming about it to her friends. Yes, this was important news. But she could, in all honesty, have waited for a more proper time of day.

Although with a few more hours, she probably would have torn her pillow to bits, leaving a feathery snowfall on her floor.

Remembering Gladys's suggestion, she'd screamed into it instead.

Margaret had never felt anger like this.

She took a breath. "I'm sorry. I'm sorry. But I had to tell you—William is dead."

"Oh my darling!" Dottie's voice melted like butter and she extended her free hand out to Margaret. Joanna's busy feet were kicking from underneath the blanket, and Margaret was temporarily distracted by again feeling sorry that her innocent little niece would someday have to know the darker sides of life.

"Margaret," sighed Gladys. "We didn't know. Of course that's something we'd want to hear right away. You were right to call us."

Dottie nodded. "How did you find out? Did you get a telegram?"

Margaret's mouth wrinkled. "No. I wasn't on any kind of list since I'm not family. If I were, I would have found out that *he died in June!*"

Gladys sat straight up and cocked her head. "In June? Then how—"

"How have I still been getting letters from him?"

"Well, yeah."

"Tom. Tom Powell. William died *right in front* of him. Shot down by a sniper in Normandy. But that's not even the whole of it. The letters—nearly all of them have actually been written *by Tom*."

Dottie unlatched Joanna, and the nanny, with her keen sense of timing, swept the baby into her arms and took her away, patting her back over her shoulder. Dottie folded the blanket and then joined Margaret and Gladys on the couch.

She held Margaret's hand. "What do you mean?"

Margaret's jaw quivered rapidly like on a cold day where her teeth would chatter.

Gladys pulled a handkerchief from her pocket. "I brought along a few of these. I thought they'd come in handy. You were in a state."

"Thank you," she managed.

Dottie's voice almost cooed with velvety sympathy. "Why don't you tell us all about it? From the beginning."

Margaret had had the foresight to bring all the letters she'd received, including the new one. The one that confessed the truth. She handed the stack to Dottie and Gladys and sank into the couch while they read the letters, passing them between each other.

Hmmms and groans and oohs and aahs and various sounds emitted from each of them. Margaret closed her eyes and leaned her head back, listening to them. Her one comfort right now was knowing that they were here to support her.

They spoke at the same time.

"That's just rotten," huffed Dottie.

Just as Gladys said, "That's so romantic."

"Romantic?" Dottie turned to Gladys with surprising force, so much so that it nearly made Margaret laugh in spite of it all. She could hardly believe the role reversal. Maybe since Gladys was a newlywed, she was more susceptible to Cupid's arrow.

"Yes," Gladys defended. "Okay. He misled you. I'm not saying that isn't a concern. But did you see his explanation? I'd say it's pretty understandable."

"You are really letting him off the hook?" Dottie argued.

"You've never lied? Never *ever*?"

"I try not to."

"So you're telling me that you told your parents about your pregnancy as soon as you found out?"

Dottie's face flushed. "That's different."

"How is it different?"

"I didn't *lie*. I just—"

"I just didn't tell them the truth." Gladys's voice was a high-pitched singsong as she mimicked Dottie.

"But—"

"Look, I'm not knocking you for it. I would have done exactly the same thing. I was one of your accomplices, in fact. I took you into my home to *prolong* the deception. What I'm saying is that you had good reason. Sometimes there is a good reason to lie."

Margaret watched them as if they were a vaudevillian show, and she had to admit that Gladys had a point. Still, Margaret wanted the satisfaction of their mutual indignation. She was rankled and she wanted Gladys to be too. In fact, Gladys was almost always rankled about something. Why not now? Unless in her ire, she was seeing something that Margaret couldn't.

"But—" she began.

"Oh, Margaret," Gladys said, rolling her eyes. "I know all about you telling Oliver that he should let me propose to him. And don't worry—I'm not mad about that. This is not what it's about. But it does show that you have your secrets too.

"And," she continued, without letting anyone respond, "even more than that, do you think George should have told Dottie all these years that he was in love with her?"

"No, but I don't see—"

Gladys was on a roll. "And why is that?"

"Because of John."

"Exactly. Because of John and you and your parents and Dottie. If George had told the truth about his feelings, it would have hurt a lot of people. So he kept the secret. Until it was the right time to speak up."

"Really, Gladys, I don't think this is the same thing," Dottie interjected, but the hesitation in her voice told Margaret that she wasn't as confident as she originally had been.

"It is. The situation is different, and the players are different. But it's the same thing. He withheld the truth because telling you, Margaret, would have hurt you. I'm not excusing it. But I'm saying that we have all done it. So let she among us who has never lied cast the first stone."

Margaret laughed. Not a robust one, as she was still buried under the cloud of the morning, but it was as if a life preserver had been thrown into the pool in which she was drowning. She was grabbing on to it. Not yet out of danger but being reeled in to safety.

"Gladys, have you gone biblical on us?" she asked.

Gladys folded her arms and sank back into the couch. "No. It's just common human knowledge."

Margaret felt her heart thawing. "And you were the one who cautioned me against William. Why the change of heart? Has marriage softened you? Dottie, has our Gladys become a big old teddy bear?"

"Stop it! I haven't gone soft. But this is what I see. I see that it's not the *name* that matters. From what I can tell, William's contribution was introductory, at best. You don't know him *personally*. So what does the name even mean to you? William. Tom. Bugs Bunny. *That is not the important part.* It was Tom's words that put that smile on your face. Tom is the one who bled his feelings onto paper. Tom is the one you actually wrote to."

Her voice lowered. "He's the one asking for your forgiveness. Which is not an easy thing to do. I should know. It's never been my strong suit."

Margaret looked at her friend. The one who always told it like it was. Maybe she had, indeed, missed the whole point.

"Ladies, I have some breakfast for you." The cook peeked her head into the living room and once again Margaret marveled that Dottie's help had impeccable timing and discretion. There was nothing like breaking bread to even the playing field between warring factions.

Dottie led them into the dining room and she pulled back the curtains to reveal the light that was beaming into the space. It refracted on the bevels, casting rainbow spectrums onto every surface. Margaret smiled at the beauty of it. And even felt reassured. However this turned out, there were some things you could always count on. Sunlight. Rainbows. Friendship.

As the cook set a plate of toast and sausages on the table, George sauntered in wearing slacks and a perfectly tailored burgundy sweater that looked like one of Dottie's creations.

"Good morning, ladies," he said. Seemingly unsurprised by their presence.

"May I?" Dottie asked Margaret, and Margaret nodded. She didn't even need to finish that question to know what her dearest and oldest friend meant.

As they ate, Dottie filled George in on the news of the morning, and Gladys handed him the letters, which she had not yet let go of.

"Darling," he said to his wife when he'd been fully apprised of the details. "I never like to disagree with you, but I have to say, I'm siding with Gladys on this."

Margaret watched Dottie's expression, and her initial indignation—already disappearing—seemed to melt away in her husband's presence.

"How do you mean?" she asked.

"Well," he said, pushing his chair back. He looked at Margaret, remembering that this conversation was really about her in the first place. "All I can say is that I know what it's like to be a man in love. And to have to hold that love in until it is best for all parties to know."

Gladys let out a triumphant sound under her breath.

"Do you really think so, George?" asked Margaret. "I hadn't really thought about it from his point of view."

"And wouldn't the world's problems be mitigated by doing just that." He said it as a statement more than a question.

"Yes."

"Now—what do you want to do about it?"

CHAPTER TWENTY-SIX

April 1945

*T*he mail had arrived more steadily since the Airborne had left Bastogne. It had been a brutal few weeks of battle, but they'd triumphed. And the victories for all the Allies continued to mount.

Tom hadn't had to wait long for Margaret's response, though the few weeks between the letters had made him more nervous than any enemy he'd faced.

Tom—her missive had started. It was void of the *dears* and the *dearest*s that had become so familiar between them. Albeit those had been addressed to William. But he took it as a good sign that she'd written him at all.

> *I have had some time to reflect on your revelation, and in fairness, I brought Dottie and Gladys and George in on it. As you said that you, John, and William shared all of your correspondences, I feel that it is only fair to have done the same.*
>
> *The conclusion is that yes, I forgive you. It was terrible to learn of William's death, but I didn't initially consider how*

difficult his loss must be for you too. So, I begin with passing along my most sincere condolences. He indeed sounded like a wonderful friend and if you and John cared for him as much as you both seemed to, I'm sure his absence left a hole that has been difficult to fill.

I reread all of his letters—your letters—and imagined you sitting down to write those beautiful words. Drawing those flowers. Entertaining me with big words you'd discovered.

I also read another letter. One that you don't know about. William—the real William—sent something that I was only supposed to read upon his death. He typed the envelope, clever boy, since I wouldn't have known his handwriting. After you told me the news, I opened it.

His consideration in it made the fact that I never really knew him all the more painful. Because what he said revealed the soul of a person I would have liked to know.

He explained that he'd adopted the role of Cupid when the notion to do so came into his head. He made excuses to you about being too busy to respond to me and insisted that you sign his name because he knew you were "too much of a gentleman to steal his friend away without some help."

His regard for you, in fact, would rival the most robust advertising campaign on Madison Avenue.

And while it does not excuse your subsequent decision to continue in that vein, it does shed light on all that led to it.

So. I can think of no better way to honor him than by remaining open to what I will consider his dying wish. Even if he didn't know how very soon that date would be.

With all that we've exchanged, you and I have a long way to go to truly get to know each other. And whatever that develops into—friendship or something more—it has to be based on the foundations of truth and openness. My trust in you going forward can never be shaken again. I must have your assurance that you will always be forthright with me. And if you lay an oath to that on the memory of William, I will accept it.

Having said that, I am eager to put this behind us and resume our friendship. I have not yet told you that the letters and flowers became a lifeline to me too.

I would love to see them both continue.

All the best,
Margaret Beck

Tom's first letter to Margaret—written as himself—began as if they had just been introduced. He told her that he was, indeed, from Virginia. But far from Arlington, near the Chickahominy River. He told her about his family, their farm, his college years.

His intent to continue in the military even after the end of the war.

Even as he wrote the words, he felt his stomach knot. He was no longer as certain of that path as he had once been.

The war was almost over and mail planes were arriving with regularity. He made sure every weekly pickup included something for her. And he was delighted that every mail call since his admission had contained a response from her.

There was hope.

He'd also added to her bouquet—freesias, bluebells, and poppies.

My dearest Margaret, began his fourth such letter.

I'm sitting outside a tent on the Rhine River. It is glistening, perhaps because the sun is at its highest point and sends its beams across a wide swath of the water. In the literature courses I took in college, we were expected to detail the symbolism we found in it. All I wanted to do was read the story. But as I look at this vision, I dare to believe that it is a sign of a brighter world about to emerge.

Easy Company just returned from crossing the Bavarian Alps—spectacular, by the way—into the southern part of Germany. We came to a camp called Kaufering outside the town of Hurlach. I'd heard that these kinds of places existed, but I would not have believed that they contained such evil until I saw it with my own eyes. Kaufering had been a sick camp, victims of typhoid fever sent there to await their turn to die. We'd packed loads of medical materials ready to care for the people we found imprisoned there. But when we arrived, we found five hundred bodies instead. Stacked as if they were refuse in a rubbish pile rather than the fathers, brothers, mothers, sisters, wives they had been.

The Germans had killed them even as they knew they were losing the war.

Together with the townspeople, we buried the dead, wrapping bandages around our noses to withstand the stench.

I found the body of a man who reminded me of my father. About the same age. Similar hair and contours of the face. Gaunt, though, from starvation. I cried into my fist.

There was once a time when I would not admit to that. But inhumanity is what bred this horror. I will never again be afraid to show that I feel.

Captain Winters predicted a spectacular battle at the end of this. But it was not the Grand Finale, as he called it. That battle was an interior one—one that will last well beyond the war. In every decision I make from here on in, I am going to ask myself—is this the right thing to do? Because small decisions beget larger ones.

I've struggled with knowing what path my life should take, Margaret. But that lesson will serve me well no matter what choice I make.

Love, Tom

"There she is! The Statue of Liberty! God love it, she's a sight for sore eyes."

The troop ship—another Cunard Line beauty that had been requisitioned for war—carried the victors into New York Harbor. After Kaufering, the 101st had been sent to Zell am See and Kaprun in the Austrian Alps, training and awaiting transport to the Pacific theater. It had been disheartening, to say the least, that once one side of the world was saved, they were gearing up to travel to the other.

More time away from home.

But after several months of waiting, Japan, like Germany, had surrendered. The official ceremony had taken place on the deck of the USS *Missouri*, and Tom felt a tingle of pride on Margaret's behalf that the battleship she'd worked on had been the site of the end of what was being called World War Two.

They'd written back and forth while he was in Austria, where the 101st had retreated until the fighting was finally over. He'd noticed that each letter grew ever warmer and it was his dearest hope that they'd both put that last chapter fully behind them. On the anniversary of William's death, Tom sent her a vile of half the dirt he'd collected in Normandy. And she sent him a pair of yellow socks. A very un-soldierly color, she admitted, but one that evoked the sunshine that a new day was bringing.

He wore them proudly. Once upon a time, John and William would have razzed him for it. But now he believed that if they had all survived, his two brothers in arms would have encouraged him to cling to every sappy memento of happiness. For their sakes.

Margaret's last letter had spoken of the future.

Gladys and Oliver will soon move to England and then to wherever the London Times sends them. They've offered Gladys her own column speaking about women's issues around the globe, and though the pay is a pittance, she is excited for the opportunity. I'm going to take over Gladys's job as the manager of the women's office, which means I'll have to leave my position in the welding department. But I might not have had the job for long anyway. The men will be coming home soon and rejoining the workforce, and there are rumors that almost all of the women will be asked to leave.

Maybe it is just as well. I've had time to reflect on what I've learned at the Brooklyn Navy Yard. Especially about myself. I learned that I want to work with my hands. I've learned that coming together for a common purpose is a remarkable thing to behold. I've learned that I always want to work near a chocolate factory and smell chocolate-flavored air.

But more than all that. I've learned that the most precious parts of life are watching Joanna take her first steps. Observing the love of Dottie and George and Oliver and Gladys and discovering that I want that for myself as well. And I've realized how important it is that I take care of my parents.

I don't know the details of what my future holds. But I know "who" it holds. And that's all that matters.

She'd signed it just a bit differently:

> *Until we meet,*
> *Margaret*

Tom had not told Margaret that the Airborne was coming home. He hardly would have had time to do so anyway, as their long-anticipated departure seemingly came overnight. But as he thought about it and imagined what would be both a first meeting and a reunion, he decided that he wanted it to be a surprise.

A flock of Canadian geese soared in a V formation overhead as the ship blew its horn, its tired wail echoing into the city air. Sailboats and fishing boats cut them a broad swath as they slowed into the dock, and throngs of exuberant people waved American flags at their arrival. Margaret might even be in that crowd—cheering on the soldiers coming home but not knowing that Tom was among them.

He gathered his rucksack, thinking that it would never matter to him how much he might possess because he'd had only this bag for the last two years and had gotten by with no more. He slung it over his shoulders and disappeared into the ocean of those gathered, a brass band marking the occasion.

Tom didn't need to check the address. He'd written it on so many envelopes in the past few months that he almost knew it better than his own. The black paint on the door was peeling; if he could get ahold of some paint, he'd take care of that for the Becks. He knocked on the door, suddenly feeling every nerve in his body as they rattled his confidence.

The door opened and he thought his stomach might lurch. A beautiful woman answered, one he recognized from the photograph that John had by his bed.

"Dottie?" he asked, surprised to see her.

Her eyes narrowed as she tried to place him, but then they widened.

"Tom! Tom! Oh my goodness, you're home!"

She pulled him into an embrace that was as tight as anything he would have expected from his mother. Especially considering they had never met. He felt the roundness of her belly against him. Was she pregnant again?

He grinned. "How did you know it was me?" And then he looked at his uniform. "Oh, the name. Powell."

"No." She giggled. "It wasn't that. You're the handsome one in the picture. Margaret will be so pleased."

Despite Margaret's requests, Tom had managed to evade telling her which one he was in the photo, a nod to how William liked to keep her guessing.

"Come in, come in," she said.

He stepped inside and walked around various toys that were strewn on the floor. A doll and a teddy bear and a jack-in-the-box.

"Does Grandma's big girl want a cookie before lunch?"

A woman walked in holding the hand of a toddling girl, and he knew that they must be Margaret's mother and Joanna.

"You've caught us unprepared," Dottie apologized. "I brought Joanna over to visit her grandparents and we were just about to sit down to eat. Would you care to join us?"

"Yes, that would be nice," he said. "Thank you."

His stomach growled in agreement.

Introductions were made, and Tom felt an instant ease with Margaret's family, who apologized that she was at work. Photographs of John and Margaret and Joanna lined the walls as well as a wedding picture of George and Dottie. It was as if even the walls of the home were a welcoming hug, and it stood in contrast to the militaristic feel of his own.

He paid particular attention to the pictures of Margaret, grinning at the images of her childhood pigtails to her elegance at what must have been a school dance to the woman she was today—standing on a pier holding her hat against her head so it wouldn't blow away. Laughing into the wind.

He couldn't wait to meet her.

Her family gave him a seat at the head of the table and plied him with chicken salad and oatmeal cookies. Dottie offered to ring Margaret up at the Navy Yard, certain that she could get away since she was the boss, but Tom insisted that he wanted to surprise her. He'd taken a chance that he'd find her here. But maybe this was even better.

They had so many questions about his farm in Virginia and about his family. And though he sidestepped the questions they had about the war, he regaled them with stories of the John that he had known and loved.

Mrs. Beck kept a handkerchief to her eyes nearly the whole time. With any luck, he'd be sitting with William's mother within the next few weeks. And then his own.

At one o'clock, Mr. Beck kissed his wife on the cheek and told her that he had to get back to the shop. A shipment of velvet and threads had come in and he was going to begin working on the party shoes that he wanted to put in the display window in time for the holidays. Three short months until shopping season was barely enough time to meet what he expected to be a tremendous demand.

Brooklyn was ready to celebrate the turn of the year.

"Wait, please," Tom asked as Mr. Beck stood from the table. "Before you go, I have to ask you something."

"Anything, son," the man answered, swelling Tom's heart unexpectedly. Margaret's dad had a kindness in his eyes that Tom had never seen in his own father's.

Tom stood and placed his hands on the table. "I'd like to ask for your permission to take your daughter to dinner."

Mrs. Beck jumped up and pulled him into her arms, and Tom didn't remember ever receiving quite so many hugs in one day. Mr. Beck came over and shook his hand.

"I respect you for asking, Tom," he said. "And if it was my permission to give, you would have it. But I've learned one thing being surrounded by only women in the past two years. They have minds of their own. Better ones than mine. So I'll leave that answer to Margaret."

Joanna slapped her hand into applesauce as Dottie squealed, "I'm calling Gladys!"

CHAPTER TWENTY-SEVEN

September 1945

Gladys picked up the phone and smiled. Then she buttoned up, responding to the person on the other end in a very businesslike way. "Sure. We can do that. No problem. Send him over."

Margaret wrapped twine around the box that held the scant personal items that Gladys had decorated her office with. Margaret, on the other hand, was determined to make the place feel homey for as long as the position was hers.

It was a task that distracted her from thinking about how much she would miss Gladys when she and Oliver left for London next week.

"Well, I told you it would happen," Gladys said matter-of-factly.

"What?" asked Margaret.

"The men are coming home and they're going to requisition our office and staff for some of the interviews."

Margaret sighed. "We were expecting that."

"Starting today."

"Today? But they haven't given us any instructions on it yet."

Gladys looked at her watch. "Look. Do me a favor. That was a call saying that our first soldier is coming in at three o'clock. I need to go to the main administration building and turn in my badge. Can you be on hand to give him the standard application until they tell us what else they want to do?"

Margaret shrugged. "Sure. That's easy enough. But while you're over at admin, please tell them that we need a little more notice in the future if they want this to be smooth."

"Will do. Oh—look at the time. Nearly three now. See you in a bit, doll."

Gladys hurried out, and Margaret slid over to the large leather seat that was to be hers starting tomorrow. She'd placed on it her finished pillow and admired the color it brought to the space. Twenty-seven varieties of flowers found in western Europe as drawn for her by Tom Powell. She'd run out of room to stitch more, so she'd started a second one and hoped that he would discover many more to send to her.

She opened the closet where she kept her personal items and pulled out a canvas bag that contained the items she wanted to be surrounded with every day. Her desk had been in an open room across the hall from Gladys's office, but now this room would be hers. With enough wall space to put her touch on it.

The first was a newspaper clipping of the Japanese surrendering on the *Missouri*. She'd had it framed, and it symbolized more than Margaret could put into words. Years of hard work on the part of Brooklynites. Her own personal participation in it. And, most important, the end of the war that had taken too many lives.

She remembered standing in the crowds at its launching.

The pride that burst within all of them as they saw the magnificent vessel head into the water. Who could have known what an important role it would go on to play?

The Brooklyn Navy Yard would continue building ships—they had three aircraft carriers in various stages of construction and she hoped to see an airplane land on one of them someday. However, there was talk that the navy would start using private shipyards as well and that layoffs were inevitable, starting with the women.

To add to that, the federal government was planning to rename this place with its 144-year history the New York Naval Shipyard. It would take effect in November and already, letterhead and signs were being ordered to reflect the change. It was an unfortunate thing in the eyes of those native to Brooklyn. Yes, they were a part of New York City, but it was like saying "yellow" when "chartreuse" was more specific.

Then again, few shared her flair for the distinction of language. Except for William. And Tom. They would surely appreciate how this represented so much more than a name change.

And now she was being asked, without any preparation, to interview one of the men coming home. One by one replacing the strides the women had made. Though she could hardly deny them the solidity of a job when they had been overseas fighting for two years and more.

She hoped for a day when there might be a more equitable arrangement between the sexes, but for now, she would rise to the hand dealt to her.

A knock sounded on the door.

"Come in," she answered.

She pulled out the standard application that they gave to the women and hoped it would suffice.

A tall young man came in. He was wearing pants that were too short and a shirt that was too tight and a fisherman's cap on top of his head, pulled down low enough to cast his eyes in a shadow. A gentleman would remove his cap, but perhaps Oliver and his precise mannerisms had rubbed off on her too much. She had to cut this guy some slack. He was likely one of the ones who'd come over on the Cunard vessel today.

"Ma'am," he said with a deep voice. A shiver traveled from her head to her toes, and she tightened her sweater around herself.

"Hello, soldier." She hoped he'd see that as an invitation to give her his name, but he did not comply. "Have a seat."

He was a quiet one, and having skipped lunch, she was too hungry to encourage him if he didn't want to say more.

He sat down and she handed him a clipboard and pen along with the application.

"You can fill this out. I have some work of my own to do. We'll look it over when you're finished."

"Thank you."

Goodness, he certainly hadn't won the war with his loquaciousness. He'd likely be suited for one of the mechanical jobs that didn't require a lot of conversation.

He took the clipboard from her and his hand brushed hers as she did so. She shivered again, this time as if she'd touched an electrical socket, and pulled back quickly. He sat a little higher than she did and he looked down at her as their eyes locked. His were big and brown, even as they sat beneath his cap and what looked to be a mop of hair underneath it.

He almost looked like—but no, that was a crazy thought.

Still, something about him made her cheeks feel warm.

Hmmm. Cold and warm. How could she feel both at the same time?

She gripped the edge of her desk and decided to leave him to it. She swung her chair around, delighted by its ability to swivel, and returned to her canvas bag where she could hide whatever strange things she was feeling.

She pulled out another framed picture—John's official military photograph. How dashing he'd looked. How eager to do his part. His would sit right on her desk, just as he had in her former location.

The soldier scratched away as she continued. He seemed keenly interested in what he was putting on there, though it had asked only the most basic of things—name, address, experience, references, and so forth.

She pulled the next one out—a family portrait of George, Dottie, and Joanna. Her niece looked like a cherub in her white eyelet dress. The picture would be outdated soon enough, as Dottie was five months *in the family way*. Once again, she'd refused the rabbit test, protesting the practice by buying Joanna a bunny of her own.

Then, one of her parents. John had taken it a few months before he went to basic training. It was their twenty-fifth wedding anniversary, and he'd wanted to do something special for them as a gift.

And finally, the most precious to her of all. Because except for John, she got to see all the others on a near-daily basis. But these three had only a presence of black and white and gray shades on paper she'd kept protected in glass.

She swiveled again, her back to the soldier, and studied the picture she knew by heart. Her finger traced the outlines of her brother's face, and then the two others. William and Tom. Tom and William.

Tom—wait. She held it closer to her face and stared at the taller one, as she had so many times since it had been sent to her.

Could it be?

She turned slowly to peer at the soldier and hoped he wouldn't notice. But when she faced him, he had set the application down and was sitting up straight.

She narrowed her eyes and tried to take him in. The lines of his jaw. The set of his lips.

"That's a nice picture," he said, pointing to the one in her hands.

Margaret looked down at it and then back up at him.

Possibly. This man in front of her was more filled out than the one in the photograph. William/Tom was lanky.

Her hopes were deceiving her.

"Are you finished with the application?" she asked. She was embarrassed by the shakiness in her voice.

"All done and ready for your perusal."

Huh. *Perusal.* Most people would just say *to look at.*

The name was blank, eliminating the clue that would have confirmed her suspicions.

Address:
Mount Airy, Virginia

She couldn't breathe. Tom was from that town.

Occupation:

Farmer

Professional experience:

Sergeant in the 101ˢᵗ Airborne. Recipient of the Bronze Star for Valor in Holland.

Master's degree from the University of Virginia

Position you're applying for:

Margaret Jane Beck's dinner date tonight

Her eyes welled up and she put her hand to her mouth. She was thankful that she'd worn her hair down today—it fell over her face and he shouldn't be able to see her reaction.

After all this time. After all they'd been through—together, yet apart—here he was. Tom. Tom, the tall one. Tom, friend to John and William. Tom, the man she'd come to dream about, awake and asleep.

She cleared her throat and kept her composure.

"You didn't state your name, soldier."

"I didn't?" He smiled and leaned in. He smelled of Dove soap. Just like the kind her mother bought.

Gosh, it was hot in here. Gladys's office didn't have a window.

"You know, someone once lied to me about his name. I'm not sure that omitting it is much better."

He stood up and came closer until he was hovering over her desk.

"Then that's a mistake that I'll never make again."

His eyes—the eyes she'd longed to see. So near. They were so near. She wanted to close her own but was afraid the mirage would be gone when she opened them again.

She whispered, "And you think you have a reasonable chance of getting the job you're applying for?"

"Well, now, that's not totally up to me."

A smile spread across her face. Even though she couldn't see herself, she knew it was the crooked one she saved for what made her the happiest. But this was so much better than Coney Island or Cary Grant.

She stood up and leaned forward, over her desk. She was grateful for it. Her legs felt as solid as an ambrosia salad and if she didn't have the stability of the desk, she might collapse.

He raised his right hand and stroked the side of her cheek and she let the tears fall.

Relief. Joy. Love.

"Margaret," he breathed.

"Tom?"

He nodded as she whispered.

"You're here."

The door swung open and Gladys walked in. The desk still stood between Margaret and Tom, but they'd been too impatient to move around it. Tom had wrapped his arms around her shoulders and she felt his deep, soulful kiss all the way down to her toes. Margaret—not pulling away from him— waved Gladys away. But she should have known it was an impossibility.

"It's all arranged, doll!"

Tom turned around and put his hand out.

"Tom Powell."

"Gladys Sievers."

Of course, she'd insisted that Oliver keep his name and she keep hers.

"Nice to meet you, Gladys."

"If you hurt her, I'll put a bullet in you since the Germans missed."

"Gladys!"

"Margaret, if he's going to become a part of our little enclave, he'd better get to know me as I am right now."

"She's kidding," Margaret assured him.

Gladys folded her arms. "I'm not."

Tom turned back to Margaret. "I'm glad you have such fierce friends. But I promise, Gladys," he said over his shoulder. "You can keep your gun holstered. You won't need it."

Gladys grinned and threw her arms around him. "Welcome to the family."

She handed Margaret a box. "Dottie pulled this together for you. Your best dress, some stockings, and some shoes. I'm on hair and makeup duty. And, Tom, there are some things here for you too. Those clothes Margaret's dad lent you are all wrong, so Dottie guessed your size and bought something else."

"Those are my dad's clothes? I thought they looked strangely familiar."

Tom looked down and grinned. "Yeah. Your mom found something he hadn't worn for a while. They don't quite fit."

Gladys rubbed her hand down his arm and grinned. "You can say that again. The army put some muscles on you."

"Why the clothes?" asked Margaret.

"Why, you're going out on the town, doll. You and Tom. You're going out for a nice steak dinner at Delmonico's, courtesy of George and Dottie. And if you want to stay in the city..."

"Gladys!"

"I'm just saying. You have a lot of catching up to do."

Tom grinned and shook his head. "I just had a good start with her parents. I'll have Margaret home at a respectable hour."

Gladys rolled her eyes. "Respectability is overrated."

"Not in my book."

"Oh, geez," she huffed. "You two squares can have each other."

Margaret ushered Tom into an empty office and then she returned to Gladys's—hers, once five o'clock hit—and changed into the clothes that Dottie had so perfectly selected.

When they stepped into the hallway, Gladys whistled.

"Well, aren't you two the king and queen of the dance?"

Margaret looked down and blushed. She was wearing a pair of new shoes that her dad had made and her mother had embroidered. They had been set aside to put in the display window, but now they had a better purpose.

They walked out, hand in hand, with Gladys leading. Just outside the Navy Yard, Dottie's new car—this one a buttery yellow—glistened with newly washed sparkle. On the back, tin cans were strung along the fender and a hand-lettered sign read:

JUST MET.

EPILOGUE

June 1949

Washington, DC, was festooned with red, white, and blue banners that celebrated the fifth anniversary of D-Day. It was the perfect place to meet. George and Dottie came in from Brooklyn and Tom, Margaret, her parents, and the twins came up from Richmond. And William's family already lived across the Potomac in Arlington.

The Navy Yard had seen the decline that they'd expected at the end of the war, and Brooklyn in general had suffered. Margaret's job had been eliminated almost as soon as it began and Tom's yearning for the beauty of Virginia had started to turn her head toward that as a possibility.

They'd originally made the trip to Mount Airy within a week of his return from Europe to meet his parents, and Margaret found that, if anything, his words had not done it justice. Virginia was verdant with trees, lush canopies of them shading out the sky on one-lane back roads. And the Chickahominy River offered a serenity that Margaret didn't even know existed. It was bliss to sit barefoot by its shores and let the little waves lap over her toes.

Birds chirped instead of car horns, and she finally knew what she wanted—some time away from the city.

She said *yes* when Tom proposed a few months after he'd returned and shortly after that, they bought a little house of their own between Mount Airy and Richmond. Mr. Powell's health had declined while Tom was gone, and Tom started taking over the management of the two-hundred-acre family farm. His father would never admit it, but he was glad that Tom had left the military after the war.

Tom didn't need words, though. His father had placed their wedding picture in the very middle of the mantel.

Margaret's parents had fallen in love with the area when they came to visit and wanted nothing more than to be with their daughter and her family. They'd opened a shoe shop in the fashionable part of Broad Street, and the ladies of Richmond went crazy for them. They gave Margaret a third ownership, and she and her mother embroidered shoes during porch swing visits.

The store was called Beck & Daughter.

When they were old enough, Margaret's twins, Dorothy and Willa, would help out. Just as John and Margaret had.

"Balloons!" Willa shouted when the festivities on the mall began. Tom bought four of them. Two for his daughters and two for Joanna and little Georgie.

"Say thank you to Uncle Tom," Dottie instructed her children.

"Thank you, Uncle Tom," they said in unison.

William's mother smiled. "I can't believe how much they're all growing. It seems like every time I see them, they're each six inches taller." She fidgeted with the little glass pendant on her necklace, filled with the other half of the dirt that Tom had brought back from Normandy.

Margaret patted her girls' heads. "Willa eats peaches as if we'll run out. Just like her father. And Dorothy could win a milk-drinking contest if there was one."

"Guess who!" Margaret felt hands cover her eyes.

She turned around. "Gladys! What are you doing here? And, Oliver! I thought you were heading to Zurich soon."

Gladys shrugged. "Oliver prefers political reporting to banking stories. He's accepted an assignment here in DC. And I'm going to march into the office of the editor at the *Washington Post* and demand that he hire me too."

Nothing had changed.

"I can't believe it. How did you know where to find us?"

Gladys and Tom exchanged a look. "Oh, I know someone who knows how to keep a secret."

Dottie and Margaret hugged her, squeezing her neck tight. "I'm so happy to see you," Margaret said. "Gosh, I can't believe we'll get to do this more often."

Gladys's articles about the plights of women around the world had been a mere ripple in the *London Times*, but she'd always said that a ripple preceded a wave and the right kind of wave was a tsunami.

The parade began and the children were hoisted up on the adults' shoulders. Mr. Beck took Willa, and Oliver scooped Dorothy up.

Tom put his arm around Margaret and gave her a kiss on the cheek. "Mmmm," he said. "You smell good."

"I used the last few drops of the Fragonard perfume. Even though I've only used it on special occasions."

"You know what that means, of course."

She turned to him, struck as she always was, by how much she loved her husband.

"What's that?"

"I'm going to need to take you to Paris."

ABOUT THE AUTHOR

Camille Di Maio left an award-winning real estate career to become a bestselling author. She has a bucket list that is never ending and uses her adventures to inspire her writing. She's lived in Texas, Colorado, Pennsylvania, Virginia, and California, and has spent enough time in Hawai'i and Maine to feel like a local. She's traveled to four continents (so far), and hopes to get to all of them someday. Camille studied political science in college. She loves to spend Saturdays at farmers' markets and belts out Broadway tunes whenever the moment strikes. She lives with her husband of twenty-four years in coastal Virginia, has two kiddos grown and flown and two still at home. Rescue pets have been a long-term passion for her, the most recent addition being a German shepherd puppy.

UNTIL WE MEET

READING GROUP GUIDE

AUTHOR ESSAY

February 2020 found me in a place that profoundly changed the world eight decades ago—Pearl Harbor in Honolulu, Hawai'i. Almost to the day that I docked in that beautiful city, the world learned a new word that would once again change everything—*coronavirus*.

Where one aggressor was massive—with its kamikazes and bombs and spectacle—the other was microscopic.

I stood on the deck of the USS *Missouri* and surveyed my surroundings. I am not one to cry easily, but the gravity of where I was provoked a profound sense of awe and gratitude. And the tears followed.

Before me, encased in glass, lay the documents that signaled the end of World War II.

Little did I know that humanity was once again about to embark on a global battle of an entirely different nature.

I wrote this book about WWII during a worldwide lockdown. And though I had explored some of its themes in previous books I'd written, never did I feel as connected to the characters' experiences as I did this time. Food rationing (or toilet paper, as the case was), uncertainty, loss, worry.

We learned new skills. Businesses pivoted and updated. We all discovered how to Zoom. I deepened friendships with neighbors by having "Sidewalk Happy Hours" six feet apart—when previously, we'd all been too busy to get a common date on the calendar. I started a new hobby of canning fruit. (My peach preserves were delicious. My watermelon jelly, not so much.)

But I didn't have a notion, on that February day, that these things were about to happen. That life as we knew it was going to change. I breathed in the Honolulu air and listened to the lapping ocean waves and imagined a time when the people of that city were similarly unaware of what was just around the corner.

They say history repeats itself. Which comes in handy for a historical fiction writer.

Until We Meet takes place on the other side of the country: Brooklyn, New York. It is two years after the attack on Pearl Harbor, and the United States is in the middle of the war. Three women work at the Brooklyn Navy Yard building that very same *Missouri* that I stood on. Not knowing the significance that ship would bear just two years later. Margaret, Dottie, and Gladys are just like you and me. They have hopes and dreams, they want love and employment and happiness. They do charitable things while laughing together. They worry about their families.

Though romance is a thread throughout my books, it was the friendship of women that intrigued me most as this story developed.

Of the three, I think I am most like Margaret. Drawn equally to tradition and progress. Content and yet the carrier of dreams. However, I had great fun writing Gladys—all sass and fire, two words that do not describe me. Or at least the me that most often comes out—perhaps writing her revealed my inner rebel more than I realized.

Similar to inhabiting the life of a character in one of the many high school musicals I once performed in, writing gives me the chance to step into another's shoes and play.

I was also excited to incorporate letter writing into the story as that medium has had a profound impact on my life. At one time as a teenager, I had twenty-two pen pals world-wide. This was long before the *internet* or *E*-anything were a part of our vernacular. Long before words on a screen became poor substitutes for those in ink. It was through those letters that I discovered places beyond my own borders and made friendships that helped me through those rough young years.

Though none of them were of a romantic nature, I do believe that true and deep friendships can develop through such a format. And I believe love, too, can emerge.

Pen and paper provide an anonymity that, ironically, best allow us to reveal our truest selves.

Even now, I write close to fifty letters a year.

As much as I enjoyed writing about the characters, one of the most fascinating things to me about writing historical fiction is learning something about which I know little and correcting assumptions I'd previously made.

For example, I was excited to learn that the commissioning of the USS *Missouri* took place in June 1944, which fit very well with the storyline. Then—the horror!—I realized through research that a launch (which comes with a lot of pomp and circumstance) and a commissioning are two separate events, often months apart.

The *launching* of the battleship, during which the champagne was broken and the speech was given by Senator Harry Truman, happened in January 1944. Then—as apparently it goes with shipbuilding in general—it was sent into the open waters where months of test drives and interior work took place. A *commissioning* happens when the ship is ready to go into service. Sometimes, this includes a new round of pomp and circumstance. Sometimes it doesn't.

The commissioning of the USS *Missouri* happened on June 11, 1944.

Shipbuilding novice that I am, I didn't initially realize that they were two separate events. And my husband—a U.S. Marine—didn't know that either. So I didn't feel too bad.

For the purpose of storytelling, I needed the celebratory event to take place in June because the excitement would then be tempered with the discovery of all that happened days before on D-Day. So, as historical fiction writers have the license to do, I combined the *launching* with the *commissioning*. And with the assumption that many readers would—like me—not know the difference, I wanted to clear up this necessary inaccuracy in an author's note for the purpose of education.

So now if that's ever a *Jeopardy!* question, you'll know the difference. (That's my answer for every otherwise useless fact that I learn.)

An additional timeline I stretched was that of the wedding reception at the Algonquin Hotel. The Algonquin is a small boutique hotel in the heart of New York City. I have stayed there several times, but any trip to New York finds me having at least one overpriced, cinnamon-sprinkled cappuccino there just to soak in the literary ambience. It was renovated to what you see today in 1946, and George and Dottie's wedding happens in 1944. However, I wanted to weave a scene of this beloved and historic place into the book and hopefully inspire readers to visit it when they're in the city. To do so, I fudged the years by a hair. However, the story about the history of the cats is true and to this day, you will find a resident cat at the Algonquin. As of this printing, it is currently a Hamlet.

(In the lobby of the Algonquin, you will find a small display case of books about New York or written by New Yorkers. My third book, *The Way of Beauty*, sits face out right next to a memoir by Howard Stern. It is a rather interesting pairing.)

Of additional historical note, there was, indeed, a hurricane that hit the Long Island area in September 1944. I had not originally set out to write a scene like that, but it seemed too good a detail to pass up!

And finally, I painted the travails of the 101st Airborne with very light brushstrokes. But indeed, they endured unspeakable difficulties throughout World War II. I encourage anyone who would like to learn more to read or watch *Band of Brothers* and other books about the war. Thank you to them and to all of our men and women in uniform.

And thank you, reader, for taking this journey with me. May we all enjoy a future that is free from these worries of the past and the present. But more than that, may we all come together and be stronger as a result when, inevitably, they challenge us anew.

DISCUSSION QUESTIONS

1. In *Until We Meet*, Margaret, Gladys, and Dottie are each traversing a world that was just beginning to offer career choices for women. If this book were set today, do you think any of the characters would have made different decisions than they did in the 1940s?

2. With which of the women do you most identify and why?

3. The author has several letters written between her grandparents during WWII. Does your family have letters from the past—wartime or not—that give you a window into the past? What is something you've learned from them?

4. The military requisitioned many homes in wartime, similar to Littlecote. And families like the Browns took soldiers in. If you were ever asked to house people in such a situation, what would that look like for you? Would that affect your life for better or worse?

5. The art of letter writing is all but lost in our social media world. How do you think this has had a positive and negative effect on us?

6. Did you ever have a pen pal? What are your favorite memories of that?

7. Tom reaches a crossroads as he's in the hospital in which he must tell Margaret about William—or continue writing in his friend's name. Do you think his choice was justified given the circumstances? How would the story have played out differently if he'd told her the truth from the beginning?

8. Margaret, Gladys, and Dottie meet weekly to knit socks for the soldiers. And Margaret embroiders a pillow for William as she receives the letters. Do you have a love of crafting and if so, what is your medium?

9. You've been away from home for several years. Your ship sails past the Statue of Liberty on the way to the dock. What are you thinking? Who are you most looking forward to seeing? What are you most looking forward to doing?

10. Is the start of Tom and Margaret's romance the letters? Or once they meet in person? What do you think their first date looked like?

VISIT **GCPClubCar.com** to sign up for the **GCP Club Car** newsletter, featuring exclusive promotions, info on other **Club Car** titles, and more.

 @grandcentralpub   @grandcentralpub   @grandcentralpub